DORIS L

NOT AT HOME

Doris Elizabeth Langley Moore (*née* Levy) was born on 23 July 1902 in Liverpool. She moved with her family to South Africa when she was eight. She received no formal education, but read widely, under the influence of her father.

Moore moved to London in the early 1920s, and wrote prolifically and diversely, including Greek translation, and an etiquette manual. In 1926 she married Robert Moore, and they had one daughter, Pandora, before divorcing in 1942.

She published six romantic novels between 1932 and 1959, in addition to several books on household management and an influential biography of E. Nesbit.

Moore was passionately interested in clothes, and her own clothes formed the basis of a collection of costumes, to which she added important historical pieces. Her fashion museum was opened in 1955, eventually finding a permanent home in Bath in 1963.

In addition to books, she also wrote a ballet, *The Quest*, first performed at Sadler's Wells in 1943. Moore also worked as a costume designer for the theatre and films, and designed Katharine Hepburn's dresses for *The African Queen* (1951).

Doris Langley Moore continued to write books, with a particular emphasis on Lord Byron. Her last novel, *My Caravaggio Style* (1959), about the forgery of the lost Byron memoirs, was followed by three scholarly works on the poet.

Doris Langley Moore was appointed OBE in 1971. She died in London in 1989.

TITLES BY DORIS LANGLEY MOORE

Fiction

A Winter's Passion (1932)
The Unknown Eros (1935)
A Game of Snakes and Ladders (1938, 1955)* **
Not at Home (1948)*
All Done by Kindness (1951)*
My Caravaggio Style (1959)*

* available from Dean Street Press and Furrowed Middlebrow

Selected Non-fiction

The Technique of the Love Affair (1928, reprinted 1999)
E. Nesbit: A Biography (1933, expanded edition 1966)
The Vulgar Heart: An Enquiry into the Sentimental Tendencies of Public Opinion (1945)
The Woman in Fashion (1949)
The Child in Fashion (1953)
Pleasure: A Discursive Guide Book (1953)
The Late Lord Byron: Posthumous Dramas (1961)
Marie & the Duke of H: The Daydream Love Affair of Marie Bashkirtseff (1966)
Fashion Through Fashion Plates, 1771-1970 (1971)
Lord Byron: Accounts Rendered (1974)
Ada, Countess of Lovelace: Byron's Legitimate Daughter (1977)

** Published in 1938 under the title *They Knew Her When: A Game of Snakes and Ladders*. Revised and reprinted in 1955 as *A Game of Snakes and Ladders*. Dean Street Press has used the text of the 1955 edition for its new edition.

DORIS LANGLEY MOORE

NOT AT HOME

With an introduction by
Sir Roy Strong

DEAN STREET PRESS

A Furrowed Middlebrow Book
FM40

Published by Dean Street Press 2020

First published in 1948 by Cassell & Co.

Cover by DSP

ISBN 978 1 913054 57 1

www.deanstreetpress.co.uk

To my Sister
MAB SAYER

and my Friend
WILLIAM CHAPPELL

.

INTRODUCTION
By Sir Roy Strong

"I WAS the first writer to take the reader through the bedroom door". That announcement to me by Doris Langley Moore (1902-1989) has always stuck in my mind. I only came to know her late in her life, in the mid 1960s when I was involved in establishing The Costume Society. I already knew her work for I was early on fascinated by the history of dress and consumed her pioneer volumes *The Woman in Fashion* (1949) and *The Child in Fashion* (1953) while I was still at school. I had also travelled down to Eridge Castle in 1953 where Doris opened the first version of her Museum of Costume which was to find its resting place in Bath some ten years later in what is now called The Fashion Museum.

She later became a friend, a formidable one making me quickly grasp why she had gained a reputation for being difficult. She was. But any encounter with her tended to be memorable providing fragments of a larger mosaic of a life which had been for a period at the creative centre of things. Later encounters were remarkable like the one when she took me out to lunch at The Ivy so that I could sign her passport photograph as a true likeness when transparently it had been taken through a gauze! This was the occasion when she suddenly volunteered that she had been the handsome Director of the National Gallery Sir Philip Hendy's (1900-1980) mistress.

If the material existed Doris would be a good example of the new emancipated woman who burst on the scene in the 1920s flaunting convention. She, of course, rightly takes her place in the *New Oxford Dictionary of National Biography* but what we read there raises more questions than it answers. Here was the Liverpool born daughter of a newspaper editor who, having passed most of her childhood in South Africa, suddenly arrives on the scene with a translation from the Greek of *Anacreon: 29 Odes* (1926). Two years later came the even more startling *The Technique of the Love Affair* (1928) under a pseudonym 'a gentlewoman' of which Dorothy Parker wrote that her whole love life would have been different if she had had the good fortune to have read this first. It has apparently stood the test of time and was reprinted in 1999. Two years before Doris had married and, although she did not divorce her husband until 1942, one would conclude that that marriage rapidly went on the rocks. Indeed I recall being told that her husband had gone off with the nanny of her only child, a daughter called Pandora. She never married again.

Doris was an extraordinarily multi-talented woman who moved with ease within the creative art set of the era. She was closely involved in those who were to become the Royal Ballet and, in 1943, wrote the scenario for a patriotic ballet *The Quest* to get the future Sir Frederick Ashton out of army. The music was by William Walton and the designs by John Piper, and Margot Fonteyn and Robert Helpmann dance in it. Again I recall her telling me that the members of what were to become our Royal Ballet at the opening of the war were all up in her house in Harrogate. And, after I married the designer Julia Trevelyan Oman, she took us out to dinner with William Chappell, the designer of Ashton's *Les Patineurs*. Then there were connexions with the Redgrave family who appear dressed in Regency and Victorian costume in her books. Vivien Leigh also figures in these books, again Doris remarking disparagingly of Olivier's part in the famous break up.

Between 1932 and 1959 she wrote six romantic novels, appreciated today by a readership which scours the Net for copies. All of this sat alongside a sharp academic mind which she applied in particular to a life long obsession with Lord Byron. Again I recall her opening a lecture on him describing how she had fended off a young man trying to kiss her at her first ball by drawing back and saying "Have you read *Childe Harold*?" Her first book *The Late Lord Byron* (1961) revolutionised Byron studies and two more of equal importance followed, *Lord Byron, Accounts Rendered* (1974) and *Ada, Countess of Lovelace* (1977).

But her greatest legacy must be The Museum of Fashion in Bath. Doris was obsessed by fashion and details of dress. I remember her noticing the way that I followed in town the correct gentleman's etiquette of wearing one glove on the hand which held the other. She herself followed fashion and indeed her hats were the subject of a Sotheby's sale. Why was her contribution in this area so important? Doris was the first person who moved the study of dress out of the antiquary's study into the land of the living. When it came to wheeler dealing with historic dress she had no equal. To her dress was vivid visual evidence of the attitudes and aspirations of a whole society. In that she ranks as an original enabling others to follow in the path that she blazed. She began collecting in 1928 and was to campaign for a museum for some twenty five years until at last it came to rest in the Assembly Rooms in Bath. And, typical of Doris, it embraced the new from the outset inaugurating the annual Dress of the Year Event which took off with a Mary Quant mini-dress. But then we can still see her in action for we can go on line and watch her in the first ever BBC colour television programmes from 1957 on the madness and marvel of clothes.

Roy Strong

I

MISS MACFARREN took the carpet-sweeper and the housemaid's bucket down to the basement and came back to put the finishing touches to the sitting-room. Often and bitterly as she had begrudged the hours spent in sweeping and dusting and polishing here at the cost of the work for which she was fitted by nature and training, this morning she acknowledged that her toil had not been thankless. The room was delightful; it was unthinkable that her visitor should fail to like it.

She stood in the doorway and looked at it earnestly, trying to see it with the eyes of the prospective tenant: only of course, she thought, lightly rubbing her fingers together, the prospective tenant wouldn't know at first that on these walls and in these book-shelves was almost the finest private collection of botanical prints in London. (That exasperating 'almost' was the triumph of her nefarious rival, Dr. Wilmot.)

Miss MacFarren's glance swept over the Aubusson carpet with its soft yellows and pinks entwined in a mysterious harmony, the deep armchairs in cinnamon satin covers, the Empire desk, the Venetian chandelier, the immense glass-fronted bookcases which had been one of her brother Andrew's luckiest finds, and the two great windows in their draperies of cinnamon velvet. Andrew's extravagance in removing the unpleasant fireplace acquired with the room, and putting in a basket grate and a handsome carved wood mantelpiece decorated with sheaves of wheat and clusters of fruit, had been abundantly justified. She was catholic enough not to quibble at an early-Georgian mantelpiece in a late-Georgian room: things good of their kind were seldom ill-assorted.

Over the mantelpiece was a symmetrical arrangement of prints from Thornton's *Temple of Flora*, including the rare carnations, the tulips, and the roses, all glowing with a subdued brilliance. Wherever the walls were not covered by books, they were adorned with pictures of flowers, chiefly hand-coloured engravings presenting an effect at once delicate and vivid. But with all this elegance, which made not the least pretence of being unstudied, there was no lack of comfort. The armchairs were capacious, the sofa practical. There were built-in cupboards to hide the day's untidiness, a useful drum table, a rosewood 'Canterbury' filled with magazines and papers.

The last of the war damage, fortunately slight, had been made good. Miss MacFarren contemplated the windows with satisfaction, knowing she would be able to forget those horrible opaque panes—like patches of court plaster on an injured face—which had at last been decently replaced with glass. The ceiling was once again intact, and the pictures and furniture concealed certain scars of repaired plaster seaming the walls.

Only one scar could never be concealed, and that was invisible to any eye but Miss MacFarren's. Reluctantly her gaze travelled to the second shelf of the larger bookcase. There was apparently no gap, for the space had been filled in with other books, but Miss MacFarren knew and would always know that the pride of that library, her brother's peerless herbals, the Culpeper, the Gerard, the sumptuous John Parkinson, had been sold at Sotheby's to keep the house going. Her brother, being dead, did not know, and indeed if he had been alive he might have been forced to the same measure. Income was depleted, expenses nearly doubled, and one could not move to cheaper quarters because there were none to be had. Still, she felt the guilt of that transaction as if it had been a betrayal, and her sense of loss was poignant. The books had been left her by Andrew with the rest of the home, and she loved them for themselves and for him. It was to spare herself from further sacrifices of the same magnitude that she had resorted at last to the expedient now before her.

To share the house! At fifty years of age, with nearly all her interests centred between these four walls, it was a tremendous departure. Efforts of adaptation would be required that might prove extremely tiresome. It would have been easier, superficially, to leave these premises altogether and set up some new sort of existence elsewhere with only a selection of her possessions; but there were strong reasons against a step so irrevocable. Her younger brother, Colin, might return from Canada with his new wife; her nephew, Mory, might decide to give up his present mode of living, and then it would be calamitous to have parted with the family home. Having clung to it through the grinding discomforts of the war, to renounce it now would be ironical, after all.

And she had a horror of becoming one of those drifting gentle-women who live in bed-sitting-rooms, cook over a gas ring, and change their library books on Saturday in preparation for the lonely week-end. In the house, with her own well-stocked bookshelves, her working materials, her good radiogram, she was never lonely. Sharing it would be a nuisance, but it was better than being cast out altogether.

Moreover, this Mrs. Bankes, who was now on her way to see her, had the highest recommendation from the best possible quarter. Harriet Greenway, a woman not likely to judge by anything less than a first-rate standard, had gone so far as to say that in Mrs. Bankes she would find a tenant whose care and consideration would be worth guineas a week off the rent. And since she must take a stranger under her roof, who could suit her better them a quiet and cultivated lady whose husband, now with the Army of Occupation in Germany, would only make intermittent appearances in that feminine household? Not that Miss MacFarren disliked men; she was perfectly at ease with them, having brought up a nephew and kept house for two brothers; but she knew that in their lordliness they are more disturbing as domestic companions than women and she was longing to catch up with the work interrupted by the war. Everything had been explained to Mrs. Bankes by Harriet, and Mrs. Bankes had shown the most entire readiness to adapt herself.

It was true that, with lodgings of every kind so scarce as be literally at a premium—for this was August, 1945—Mrs. Bankes might well promise anything that would make her acceptable, but Harriet, who knew what sort of person she was, could guarantee her good faith. Harriet had said, with more than her customary emphasis: 'She's a really *congenial* woman! She *adores* fine things! For a house like yours, my dear, *ideal*!'

Harriet was selling Mrs. Bankes with the same brisk and authoritative enthusiasm she used for selling the stock of her antique shop in Wigmore Street. But the stock at Greenway's was genuine through and through and Miss MacFarren was in the habit of relying on her friend's verdicts.

A pot of maidenhair fern placed in the centre of the drum table completed her feeling that she could be certain of the room, and she went out into the hall to make certain of herself. Choicely framed in the Venetian mirror she saw a rather stout lady with nicely groomed grey hair and a pair of dark eyes that looked as highly polished as the jet buttons on her dress. Her lips were thin and firm but they smiled readily: her teeth were her own and she was proud of that.

Not by any stretch of imagination could she believe that she seemed a day less than her full age. To this she had resigned herself, but her clothes were matronly rather than spinsterish. Not for her the lank tweed skirts and shapeless cardigans, the dreary duns and bottle greens, by means of which well-bred ladies commonly make the gesture of abjuring sex appeal. Her grey and black dress flourished a little collar of snowy hand-made lace. There was a scent of lilac in the folds of her corsage; Lilas de France, a present from her dear, distinguished, unscrupulous nephew, bought in Paris amongst who knows what gifts for women with very different claims upon him.

Satisfied that neither she nor her house would cut a contemptible figure, she went to the top of the basement stairs and called down placatingly: 'Mrs. Manders, I'll answer the door. Will you make coffee as soon as you hear the bell?'

'Just as you like,' said Mrs. Manders in the tone she used when their wills were in severest conflict. She had not hidden her disapproval of the house-sharing plan. It had been impossible, positively impossible, to make her understand that the house must be shared or abandoned. Mrs. Manders could not take seriously the difficulties of people who lived in Harberton Square and whose incomes had enabled them to spend money on luxuries. In her eyes, Miss MacFarren was indulging an absurd whim, and she had no intention of adjusting herself to all those changes of routine which were bound to be required when the house was run on a new basis.

She had taken a dislike to Mrs. Bankes in advance and had made it clear that, if the project was realized, she would get her wages somewhere else. It was a pity since she was the only honest and capable woman Miss MacFarren had employed for several years; but perhaps Mrs. Bankes would want, in any case, to engage her own domestic help. . . .

Harriet had rung up to explain that the visitor was on her way in a taxi, and Miss MacFarren was surprised when one quarter of an hour succeeded another, and another succeeded that without bringing her. She had finished her sitting-room preparations some-what hurriedly, had urged Mrs. Manders to make the kitchen ready for inspection without delay, had taken what she supposed would be her last look round before the interview with her ears alert for the front-door bell. But before Mrs. Bankes appeared she had had time for a final reconnaissance of every room in the house. It was a little disconcerting because she could not help speculating after half an hour as to traffic accidents, and there was a growing rest-iveness in the kitchen about the coffee. She was dialling Harriet's number to ask whether there had been some misunderstand-ing, when the slamming of a car door and a light rapping with the knocker checked her.

Miss MacFarren went forward with a faint uneasiness. Under the knocker was a clear legend PLEASE RING. People who knocked instead of ringing annoyed her, for the sound could not be heard unless one happened to be on the ground floor. Well, here she did happen to be, and, calling to her face a look of pleased expectancy, she opened the door.

On the step was a woman laden with flowers, a wonderfully smart woman with a white cloth coat, a yellow taffeta turban draped in the newest style, and white wedge-heeled shoes as complex as a Chinese puzzle. Her hair was pale gold and her ivory-coloured face suggested rather than achieved the most extraordinary beauty. With a smile of such radiance as lies only in the consciousness of flawless teeth, she extended from amongst the flowers a lemon-col-oured suede glove.

'I'm Antonia Bankes,' she said, being drawn over the thresh-old by Miss MacFarren's light handclasp, and before she had come three paces into the hall she cried: 'Oh, how attractive! Oh, what a lovely entrance!' Her smile played like a beam of light on the mirror, the gilded console table, and the pictures.

Miss MacFarren left her for a moment to take it in and called down the stairs, since the bell had not been rung that they were ready for coffee.

Mrs. Bankes laid her flowers on the console table and was ushered into the sitting-room. Her exclamations in the hall were nothing to the raptures that the sitting-room inspired. 'Oh, but it's divine! Oh, but it's the prettiest room I've ever seen in my life! Where did you—how did you come by all these enchanting things?' She walked round with clasped hands, gazing ecstatically, then suddenly her smile seemed to become rather weary and she sat down.

'I was beginning to think there was some mistake,' said Miss MacFarren in her pleasant, firm voice, in which there was still a lingering accent of the Hebrides. 'Mrs. Greenway told me you were on your way just after eleven.'

'So I was. I stopped the taxi to buy some flowers at that ravishing shop in Cherry Street. I never can resist that window, can you? Then while I was there, I thought I'd better try the shop next door for lipsticks.'

'And your taxi wouldn't wait, I suppose?'

'Oh yes, I persuaded him to wait.' The smile flashed on again for an instant. 'Just look what I managed to get from under the counter!'

She opened her lemon-coloured felt handbag and produced, with the friendliest air in the world, several packages of cosmetics which, leaning forward, she poured into Miss MacFarren's lap. 'Dark blue mascara,' she said. 'So difficult to find now! And a Rubinstein eyebrow pencil, and two of those heavenly deep pink lipsticks—not the loathsome orange-red ones that you can buy by the hundred. Would you like one?'

'It's very kind.' Miss MacFarren's inflection was slightly bewildered. 'I don't think I need one just at present, thank you.'

She examined Mrs. Bankes's purchases with polite interest before handing them back, and took the opportunity to examine Mrs. Bankes as well. She could see now that the face which at a first glimpse had looked girlish was not that of a very young woman. Smiling it defied time, but in repose the mouth and eyelids drooped in a tell-tale way. There were no lines on the fine, creamy skin, but under the wide eyes with their heavy lids and thickly made-up lashes were faint shadows. The well-kept hair almost certainly owed all its gold to the hairdresser. It was possible, seeing Mrs. Bankes's face as it appeared now, to guess her age at something above thirty-five, but her figure was obviously invincible. She was tall and exquisitely slender: her carriage was perfect, from the poise of her small head set on a graceful neck to the light movements of feet with impeccably arched insteps. As she stood up to slip off her coat, Miss MacFarren noted the enviable compactness of her waist and diaphragm, the suggestion of a breast modelled in breathing marble beneath her summer blouse of pearly muslin. Harriet had not exaggerated the distinction of this singular woman, though she had wholly failed to prepare her friend for the peculiar alternations of vagueness and directness in her manner.

'Now how much of your beautiful house can we have, and what are you going to charge us for it?' she asked abruptly after several minutes of conversation about lipsticks. Her large grey eyes were fixed on Miss MacFarren as if to compel her to answer explicitly without an instant's delay.

'Hadn't you better look at it first?' Mrs. Bankes's assumption that she had already been accepted and that it was merely a question of terms was odd and disturbing. As a matter of fact, though she might be handsome and fashionable, she had not so far done anything to justify Harriet's adjective, congenial. Flattering the house was not enough. It must be made plain that there were certain practical requirements to be fulfilled.

'I thought we'd have a cup of coffee,' she went on, 'and talk things over before I show you round.'

'Mrs. Greenway says it's all desperately lovely. I can tell at once whether I'm going to like a place or not.'

The coffee was brought in at this moment, and Mrs. Manders was saluted with a courteous greeting and a smile so warm and brilliant that it melted her glacial surface and elicited a 'Good morning' actually coupled with the precious word 'Madam'.

'Will she stay?' Mrs. Bankes whispered as soon as the cook-general had retreated. 'Can we share her?'

'Wouldn't you prefer to engage someone independently who'd suit herself to your own routine from the start?'

'Not a bit. I'm sure you've got things organized in the most celestial way.'

'I'm afraid Mrs. Manders doesn't like the idea of working for two mistresses—only I don't suppose she'd call it "mistresses",' she added, remembering wanly that deference must now be paid to servants but not exacted from them.

'But the mistress will still be you,' Mrs. Bankes rejoined with the lightest flicker of a frown.

'No, you'll be doing your own housekeeping.'

'It'll still be your house. What a nuisance to get somebody new when, according to Mrs. Greenway, this one's a perfect treasure!'

'Shall we talk about that when we've discussed the main points? We haven't really arranged anything yet.'

'About money and all that,' said Mrs. Bankes, and her manner was more naïve than crude. 'How much do you want? We're not frantically rich, worse luck.'

'I told Mrs. Greenway I was prepared to make a considerable reduction to a very careful tenant.'

'You'll find me madly careful.'

Miss MacFarren made allowance for the strange idiom. 'The trouble is there's much more work in this house than one servant can do if the kitchen is to be properly looked after. Before the war, when my brother was alive and my nephew was at home, I used to have a cook and a maid living in and daily help as well. Of course, that's out of the question now. . . . I've been doing a lot of the housework myself, and whoever comes to share the house with me will have to share that too.'

'I like housework. I've got quite a "thing" about it,' Mrs. Bankes broke in cheerfully.

'I shouldn't have thought it to look at you. Personally, I detest it.'

'But I'm not clever at other things as you are. (Mrs. Greenway showed me your marvellous picture books.) I'm an ordinary home-loving woman with nothing to do but make the most I can out of wherever I happen to live. I promise you I'm not a bit afraid of housework.'

Despite the earnestness of the eyes focused intently upon her own, Miss MacFarren was disposed to be incredulous; but she reflected that, after all, it was rash to judge from appearances. Harriet had said that Mrs. Bankes was very domesticated.

'Well,' she resumed, 'we should have to work out a plan for running the house. The next thing I ought certainly to tell you is that I must spend a good deal of my time doing very concentrated writing and drawing. I need reasonably quiet tenants. Naturally, I don't want to be oppressive—'

'We're madly, madly quiet,' Mrs. Bankes interrupted.

'Though I love children, for instance,' Miss MacFarren continued stolidly, 'I wouldn't care to have any here at the present time.'

'My adorable sweetie-pie children are still in America. They were there all through the war with my husband's mother, and now she can't bear to let them go. Isn't it cruel of her?'

Once again Miss MacFarren's reaction was purely sceptical. It seemed necessary to indicate her conditions with particular care. 'I assume that, if your children should come back to England, you wouldn't expect them to live here?'

'Never, never, never.'

'It seems unkind to exclude children, but in any case this is hardly the house for them.'

Mrs. Bankes looked at her watch and asked with an undertone of impatience: 'How much rent do you want?'

'My proposal is that you should have half the accommodation and pay half the expenses—plus anything it might cost you for cooking and service. I don't think people who share a house can be expected to share meals.'

'You're so right. I couldn't agree with you more.'

'You'll want to do your own catering in your own way. Mine is very simple, and I shall attend to it myself. That's why, I think, the woman to replace Mrs. Manders must be entirely your affair.'

'What does that mean, exactly?'

'That you engage her and pay her wages. She would be doing a little for me too, but then'—she put down her coffee cup and braced herself to cope with the hated clarities of business—'I'm not proposing to charge you anything for the use of the furniture.'

'That's ridiculous,' said Mrs. Bankes. 'You ought to charge something.'

'No, if I can have half the expenses taken off my hands and the furniture properly looked after, I shall be quite satisfied.'

'That's terribly fair of you.'

'I've written down what I think the expenses are likely to come to rent, rates, electricity, gas, and so on.' She produced a sheet of notepaper and was beginning to analyse the items when Mrs. Bankes interposed:

'My husband always attends to the bills. I only want just a rough idea. I never could begin to understand figures.'

'You'll find what I think will be the weekly average at the end.'

Miss MacFarren handed her the paper and her eyes wandered down the column. 'How deliciously cheap!' she said. 'Less than I've been paying for one room at the Asturias! When can I move in? I should like to be here in time for my husband's next leave.'

Though she could not but be a little disarmed at this candid recognition of the bargain offered, Miss MacFarren mistrusted her headlong eagerness. 'The pig is still mostly in the Poke,' she answered. 'Wouldn't you like to see the rest of it?'

'I mustn't take too long. I've got a date at twelve o clock.'

'It's that now.'

'Yes. I'll just whisk round, shall I?'

'Well, first this room,' said Miss MacFarren, astonished. 'This would be for you, except that I should have to have access to it sometimes on account of the books. I can't move them because I've nowhere to put them.'

'We shall adore to have them in our room,' said Mrs. Bankes, running her hand gracefully along a row of gleaming leather strips. 'They're so lovely. Dare we ever look at any of them?'

Living in hotels for years didn't fit in at all with the picture of the home-making woman who loved domestic work. And it was simply silly of her to offer unacceptable concessions.

'You'll find in a few weeks that you'll be needing all the cupboard space you can get in your living-room,' she said, and led the way back into the hall.

'At the end there'—she pointed down the passage—'is the study. That's the room I shall keep for myself. It used to be the dining-room. I've bought an electric kettle and a hot-plate, so I shan't have to bother you too much in the kitchen. The present dining-room's in the basement, but it's quite a nice light room. That'll be exclusively for you, as long as you don't mind my keeping the little garden instead.'

'It'll save a lot of tray-carrying up and down the stairs to have the kitchen and dining-room together.'

'That's just why I had the old back kitchen converted,' Miss MacFarren returned with a little more warmth, for she was pleased that the advantage had been so quickly noted. 'Shall we go upstairs first and see the bedrooms?'

She marched upwards, a sturdy, brisk figure, while Mrs. Bankes followed with a springy step, exclaiming delightedly at the further examples of Thornton's *Flora* on the staircase.

'They run all the way up to the top of the house. I like series of pictures on staircases.'

'So do I. I adore them. Oh, how celestial those flowers are, shining like little white flames.'

She had singled out the Persian Cyclamen. 'That's always been rather a favourite of mine,' said Miss MacFarren.

'And this one—you'll think I'm insane!—looks like Jack's bean-stalk when it had grown right through the clouds.'

'What! The China Limodoron! It certainly doesn't resemble any of the Fabaceas.' But she acknowledged inwardly that there was a sort of poetic aptness in the comparison.

She opened a door on the half-landing. 'This will be your bath-room. I shall have the one on the next flight.'

The bathroom, though it was an exceptionally good one, did not interest Mrs. Bankes so much as a row of Chelsea china flowers on a shelf outside the door, and, forgetting the hour, she lingered over these and examined each of them separately with joyful cries.

The big front bedroom—actually Miss MacFarren's own bedroom—had been allotted in prospect to the tenant? It was somewhat austere in style, having been furnished long ago for the occupation of Andrew. There was a very fine suite in bird's-eye maple, a large bedstead of canework, a patchwork quilt of great intricacy made by the owner's grandmother, and some minutely executed water colours of floral subjects; but Miss MacFarren felt compelled to apologize for the absence of those agreeable frivolities that usually adorn a lady's room.

'Don't give it one thought,' said Mrs. Bankes, satisfied with a cursory glance. 'I can have lots of fun arranging some bits and pieces of my own in here. What are those pretty, pretty pictures?'

'Some of the originals for my *Evolution of Flowers*,' Miss MacFarren answered with modest pride.

'Too heavenly for words!' was Mrs. Bankes's comment, but she paid no further attention to the admirable paintings which had given the name of Elinor MacFarren a prestige amongst not only botanists and garden-lovers, but connoisseurs of the fine arts.

'The back room on this floor would have to be shared between us,' she proceeded, hurrying her visitor into the next apartment. 'It's the spare room. No doubt we could easily arrange for our guests not to overlap.'

'Oh, easily!'

Mrs. Bankes scarcely seemed to listen to this. 'What's that?' She pointed to another door.

'The linen closet,' said Miss MacFarren, opening it.

'How sweet! And what's upstairs?' she enquired in a preoccupied manner.

'Two bedrooms corresponding to these. The front will be mine, and the other's Mrs. Manders'.'

Mrs. Bankes looked a shade crestfallen. 'Is that all?'

'Except for the attic where the luggage is kept. You wanted more space?' The question contained some regret and much hope. On the one hand she had a vanity concerning the house which made her unwilling that it should fall short in any respect, and, of course, if the Bankes plan came to nothing, another plan would have to be started; it was not as simple as letting a self-contained flat. On the other hand, Mrs. Bankes, though eager to please, had as yet only made one clear impression—that she was unpunctual and careless. And her personality had in it some more elusive quality that inspired a nameless misgiving.

'More space?' Mrs. Bankes repeated with one of her sudden accesses of vagueness. 'No, I only thought it would have been nice to have another room for—for sewing or anything. Couldn't the maid sleep in the attic?'

'Out of the question,' said Miss MacFarren flatly. 'It's a stuffy little crowded box-room. You'd better come up and see it for yourself.'

'No, no, I haven't time. I must rush away.'

'Without seeing the kitchen?'

'Oh dear, I'd forgotten that.' Once again the quick frown ruffled her smooth forehead.

'Would you like to telephone and explain about being late for your appointment?'

'It doesn't matter. I'll just dash down and—wait, I've had an inspiration! Suppose you ask Mrs. Whatever-her-name-is to show me the kitchen? By herself, I mean. It'll give me an excuse to talk to her about staying on.'

Miss MacFarren could only maintain in a limp, nonplussed voice: 'I'm sure she doesn't want to stay on.'

'Wouldn't you like her to?'

'Yes, naturally I would, but—'

'Well then, just for your sake I positively must see what I can do with her.'

Mrs. Bankes's smile was one of purest benevolence, but that 'for your sake' merely aggravated Miss MacFarren's distrust, such nonsense it was when everyone knew that the labour of finding and initiating a decent servant was the worst misery a housewife could be called upon to face.

'Speak to her by all means if you wish,' she said. 'I'm afraid it won't be much use.'

But after ten minutes in the basement, during which Miss MacFarren thought uncomfortably of the anonymous person or persons who had been waiting since twelve o'clock, Mrs. Bankes came up with a beaming face. 'What an angelic little dining-room! And as for your Mrs. Manders, she's a perfect dear!' Her stage whisper was well calculated to carry down the stairs. 'I can't tell you how much I like her.' Then, in a low but triumphant voice as they moved farther down the hall: 'She's going to stay. Isn't that a comfort?'

'You must have charmed her,' said Miss MacFarren, but the tribute was reluctant. The smile, the flatteries, were a spell that, as far as she was concerned, had failed to work; and yet she could see how it might have worked if the first step had not been made so very much wrong foot foremost. Naïvete was engaging, but Mrs. Bankes had carried it too far. Offering a lipstick indeed, without an apology for being three-quarters of an hour late!

'When can I move in?' Mrs. Bankes diverted from the mirror and her powder-puff the placid yet searching gaze with which it was apparently her habit to put direct questions.

'Hadn't you better think it over? You've been in such a hurry this morning.'

'I'm always in a hurry, but I know what I want.'

Miss MacFarren sought vainly for a way of escape. The candidate had expressed herself as willing to fulfil all conditions. She had made no demands. There were no adequate grounds for rejecting her. Harriet, who had organized this interview with such ardent beneficence, such faith in her own good judgment, would consider her friend's objections nebulous, capricious, irrational. Perhaps they were. She could only find the strength of mind to temporize:

'I shall have to write to you in a few days, Mrs. Bankes. It will take time to get the house rearranged.'

'But why trouble? We'd like it just as it is.'

'I must make *some* preparations,' she insisted, on the verge of asperity. She took herself in hand, and added more urbanely, 'You wouldn't want to find my clothes in your wardrobe and my letters in your desk.'

'That won't bother me in the least. Joss will be back on leave in a fortnight, and he's so dreadfully tired of hotels. He'll love the house. This sort of thing'—she waved her lemon-coloured glove towards the rows of prints and the ormolu candelabra—'means more to an American than it would to most Englishmen, as a matter of fact.'

'Your husband's an American then? Mrs. Greenway didn't tell me that.' Miss MacFarren's surprise was sheerly pleasurable. For three years that race had had an exotic fascination for her—a secret fascination, for she would never have braved the raised eyebrows of those who accounted a taste for 'the Americans' as a form of wartime hysteria, and one especially ridiculous in a maiden lady of fifty. Nevertheless their high spirits, their quaint and varied modes of speech, their promiscuous bonhomie, had provided her with lively entertainment which she knew she would miss when they had gone: and the courtesy they still maintained towards women had sometimes touched her deeply, restoring her self-respect when much standing in trains and dragging of portmanteaux had severely shaken it. Though she was aware of the ingenuousness and would not have confessed it, the idea of having one of these interesting beings under her roof was an attraction. She brightened. 'I thought he was with the Army of Occupation?'

'Yes, the American Army of Occupation. He's a war correspondent—Joss Bankes of the *Washington Recorder*.' Mrs. Bankes spoke with complacency. Evidently some prestige attached to her husband's name and occupation.

'Then you may not be in England very long?'

'Just a few more months. I was wondering if, as a great favour, you'd let us come here on a month-to-month basis?'

Miss MacFarren experienced a perfect thrill of relief. Being able to give a month's notice made the whole prospect quite endurable. At the worst, the troublesome bond could be dissolved within a few weeks from now.

She consented readily, even graciously, and, after only an instant's further hesitation, promised to have the house prepared within the fortnight.

'Now I must fly, I really must,' said Mrs. Bankes, well pleased with her successes. 'I'm hideously late. Is it possible to get a taxi round here?'

But while Miss MacFarren was explaining the best position for catching a passing taxi, her visitor's eye fell on a pair of life-size china cats on either side of the front door, and she paused to pick one of them up with a little squeal of delight.

'Oh, what angels! Oh, what loves of pussies! I never in my life saw anything that was so completely my idea of heaven!' She held the ornament as if it had been a living animal, stroking it tenderly and kissing its face.

They were indeed a handsome pair of cats, so painted that they appeared to be wearing pink and blue garments trimmed with lace and ribbons. Their smiles were as radiant as Mrs. Bankes's own, their eyes were made of shining green glass, and, as if to display the fullness of their good nature, each was wearing round its neck a locket containing the miniature portrait of a dog.

'What are they? What are these dreams of bliss?'

'They're signed Gallé of Nancy.' Miss MacFarren was now too preoccupied with the thought of whomever might be waiting for her lingering guest to be capable of making an expansive reply, though the subject was one which normally appealed to her. 'I'll send you some sort of agreement in writing,' she said, holding open the front door. 'You mustn't go without your flowers.'

'Heavens, had I forgotten my flowers?'

Mrs. Bankes set down the cat, not on the floor where she had found it but on the very edge of the console table, and gathered into caressing arms the roses and lupins and carnations. 'Aren't they divine? I can't live without flowers, can you?'

'I don't,' said Miss MacFarren, glancing towards the splendours of her walls. She replaced the cat with a rather pointed gesture.

'You must have a tea-rose. You simply must!' Mrs. Bankes with some difficulty pulled one from the tightly tied-up bunch and placed it charmingly in Miss MacFarren's hand.

At last she was gone. Miss MacFarren stood in the doorway looking after her with painfully mingled feelings, but the predominating motif was that she had almost certainly never taken such a dislike to anyone in the whole course of her prudent and well-organized life.

2

THE MACFARRENS had long been, in their quiet way, a distinguished family. Old Andrew MacFarren, Elinor's grandfather, who had lived almost all his life on his own island, had written a book about the game birds of the Hebrides which, though published in 1886, was still in some demand. He was a dead shot and an ingenious ivory-carver. He had made a set of ivory and ebony chessmen for each of his children and grandchildren, all designed by himself and full of invention. His wife was reputed to have modelled wax flowers to perfection, having learned the art in London from the celebrated Mrs. Peachey.

One of their daughters, who had married an Edinburgh man, became known far and wide for her wonderful cultivation of stove-plants. Two orchids and a begonia had been named Simsia (her husband was a Mr. Sims) as a tribute to her skill. It was to this relative, Aunt Nita, that the tastes of the next generation must have owed their direction; though perhaps something was also due to Uncle James, whose travels in the Far East had resulted in the presentation of a number of rare Asiatic plants to the Royal Botanic Gardens of Edinburgh.

Andrew MacFarren, Elinor's brother, who settled in England when the family lost possession of their island, had been associated with the Royal Botanic Gardens at Kew for twenty years, and his services had been rewarded with a knighthood, which he had not, however, lived to enjoy for long. Her younger brother Colin, who was interested rather in scientific agriculture than horticulture, had recently taken an appointment at a Canadian university and was following the tradition of solid, sober achievement.

There was only one member of the clan whose career had been spectacular rather than sober, and whose distinction was more colourful than quiet. This was, strangely enough, the nephew whom Miss MacFarren herself had brought up, the son of her elder brother who had been left a widower after a very brief married life.

Mory at thirty was a film director—a most extraordinary departure, for he had started out in a junior post at the Museum of Natural History. By the merest chance, this occupation had led to his being asked to give some assistance in the production of a series of nature films. He had found the work extremely congenial, and had made such good use of his small opportunity that a bigger one had soon been opened to him, and this too he had turned to account. A private income left him by his father had given him from the first a position of advantage. The outbreak of war seemed for a while to have deprived him of all the ground so dexterously won, but a bullet through his foot in the Cretan campaign had terminated his military service at a providential moment.

Slightly crippled, he was given employment on a documentary picture sponsored by a Ministry during a period of great expansion and development in the British film industry. It was noticed that he had not only a talent for rapidly mastering techniques, but an uncommon aptitude for 'handling' people. In effect, so brilliant was this capacity that the influential persons who discovered how clever he was at handling other persons were quite unaware that they themselves were being handled. For Mory's contacts with film-promoting circles had made him what no MacFarren had ever been before, an exploiter of personality, a careerist.

The Ministry picture had resulted in an engagement on a story feature, and before the end of the war he was sufficiently established to be able to choose the subject for his next film. He had been quite at ease from the first among the excitements, the disappointments, the delays, the urgencies, the bluffs and showdowns, of that disillusioning world. Indeed, he seemed to thrive on them. Gaily but warily, his head unturned by success, unbowed by frustration, he drank with the right men, flattered the right women, used terms of endearment with a freedom unknown to all previous MacFarrens, and almost as freely scattered money on anything that took his fancy. Unlike any other member of his family, he was adaptable, a characteristic which involves a certain want of probity.

His Aunt Elinor regarded him with awe, astonishment, fond pride, and puzzled disapproval. He lived with a woman who was not married to him, who was, in fact, married to somebody else, and this was merely the culmination of a long series of wanton love affairs, each more flagrantly illicit than the last. He had deserted the society of scholars and scientific men, his father's friends, and preferred instead—well, it must be admitted, almost anybody. On being released from the Army, he had declined on various pretexts to return to his comfortable home, and had taken an expensive flat in Strangford House, where he derived unflagging pleasure from playing French music-hall songs on a radiogram, joining loudly and raffishly in the improper parts.

On one occasion when she had called on him, she had found him with a girl whose hair, dyed almost pink, was embarrassingly dishevelled, and on his face were the tell-tale marks of lipstick. Another time he had answered the door in his dressing-gown at three in the afternoon, and she had a strong suspicion that someone was concealed in his bedroom. It followed that she did not call on him often—scarcely ever, except when he had to countersign some document in connection with his father's estate, in which she had a share.

It was not that she was ignorant of young men and their ways; she had read books, she had grown up with two brothers. But Mory sowed wild oats as systematically as if he were bedding out some useful vegetable for the kitchen garden. He seemed to invite one to approve of his crop.

There was something lovable about his strange candour, and since he was making a great success of his life, it was no use taking too gloomy a view; but Miss MacFarren was grieved that their ways should lie so far apart. From her point of view, it would have been much better if he had gone on working at the Museum and she had kept house for him until he took a nice young wife for whose children she could knit woollies and draw pictures.

Though he had not lived with her for several years, she persisted in looking upon the house as his home, and therefore felt it was proper, when the prospect of sharing it materialized, to write and notify him. Her letter remained unanswered for several days, and then he telephoned to ask if he could come and see her in the afternoon. Miss MacFarren never took any pleasure in their appointments until she actually saw him on the doorstep, he was so often compelled to ring her up and tell her, with apologies of boundless charm, that he couldn't, after all, make it: there was an emergency story conference, a difficulty at the studio, an important man to see who couldn't be got hold of at any other time. She did not doubt the genuineness of his excuses because she was so sure of his affection. Like filial affection it took her for granted; its attentions were fitful, but, when a direct appeal was made, Mory could be depended upon.

Today no crisis detained him. At four o'clock his taxi turned into Harberton Square, and he limped across his aunt's threshold on the stick he had been obliged to use since the unpleasant incident in Crete. Mory's limp had already become part of his personality; by a process of integration, he turned every defect into an attractiveness. Bright red hair gave piquancy to his sensitive features. The sharpness of his retroussé nose, the breadth of his cheekbones, conveyed an impression of liveliness and youth. He could have passed for several years younger than his age.

Miss MacFarren had no difficulty in perceiving how his vitality, his generosity, and his lack of scruple, would combine to make him fascinating to women. Again, he was the only MacFarren who was demonstrative, and though she could not respond in kind, being naturally reserved, she found it hard to resist his coaxings and embraces.

As soon as he saw her, he put his hands on her shoulders and kissed her heartily on both cheeks, as she had seen him kiss a film star at the Savoy. 'Aunt Ellie, my darling!' he cried, and she was rather proud that it was the tone he used for film stars too. 'What's all this horror about your having to let the house?'

'To share it,' she corrected.

'That's worse. What are you doing it for, darling?'

'I thought I'd explained that I can't afford to keep it up. Come into the study, Mory. We can have tea in the garden.'

She led the way into her large back room, which opened upon a tiny garden, walled and secluded.

'I'm glad to see you're at work again, Aunt Ellie,' he said, going up directly to the deal table on which she had spread out her drawing and painting materials and two or three jugs of flowers. 'What is it? Still the *History of Horticulture*?'

'Floriculture: I couldn't bear the alliteration. Look, I'm drawing sweet peas. It's not a bit easy to make them convincing.'

'You can do it if anybody can, dear. You know, I've had the originals of your title pages framed for the wall of my office. I can't tell you what a kick it gives me to tell people they're by my aunt.'

Miss MacFarren smiled and sighed. Those splendid title pages for the two volumes of the *Evolution of Flowers*, with their garlands and bouquets, were favourite works of hers, and she had been delighted when Mory had asked her to give him the originals for Christmas. 'If it weren't for this dreadful hiatus in the production of books—my sort of books—I shouldn't have to have strangers here.'

'You make me feel very guilty, Aunt Ellie.'

'Why should you?'

'Because if I were living here myself, I should be paying part of the expenses.' He drew an elbow chair to the open french window and politely waited for her to take the only armchair before seating himself. 'I've simply got to hang on to that flat, dear. It's the right kind of atmosphere for the life I have to live. You'd hate it too if I were here now . . . telephones ringing at all hours, people dropping in for drinks, and my incorrigible way of getting mixed up with floozies. . . .'

'Does that mean girls?'

'Yes, light-minded girls, Auntie. Of course, there aren't so many now that I have Geraldine to keep them away, but still, you'd never really settle down happily with Geraldine.'

'I don't suppose I should,' said Miss MacFarren. 'I dare say it's much better while things are as they are for you to live at Strangford House, though it must cost a very great deal of money, Mory.'

'That's just the trouble, darling. I seem to earn a lot, but what with income tax and my appalling expenses, I'm really spending it as fast as I get it.'

'I know. I know.' She repressed a desire to give him some good advice.

'You'll be glad to hear I'm not touching the money father left me—'

'It's a great relief to know that.'

'But I mightn't be able to go on like that much longer. Geraldine's husband is divorcing her with me as correspondent—a nuisance, isn't it?—and if he claims damages, he'll probably get a whopping great sum and I'll have to draw on capital.'

'Oh dear, what a very—' Miss MacFarren was going to say 'sordid business', but, resolving not to be disagreeable, she murmured instead, 'dismal prospect.'

'Still, I can't bear to think of my beloved aunt taking lodgers. Would a hundred pounds tide you over, dear? I might manage a hundred now, and another later in the autumn.'

'Mory, I couldn't dream of accepting it from you. It's quite enough that your father should have left me everything in the house without your having to pay for upkeep when you don't live here.'

And, as he tried to press the money on her, she insisted, 'In any case, my dear boy, I'm committed too far to get out of the bargain now. In fact, some of Mrs. Bankes's luggage is actually arriving this afternoon.'

'Well, what is the bargain exactly?'

He pulled a long face when she had explained the arrangement. 'You've certainly got the worst of it, Aunt Ellie. You're letting them have much the better half of the house. I only hope they'll be tactful about it, otherwise you're going to get so mad at yourself for being such a bad business woman.'

'I don't see that I could have done less.'

'Nonsense, darling! Giving up your own bedroom! Letting them have by far the best sitting-room—'

'But this room has the garden, don't forget, and the radiogram.'

'I still think they've got very much the best of it. Remember you're giving them the dining-room!'

Miss MacFarren had to admit on reflection that she had parted with the lion's share, but she argued to reassure herself: 'It was worth making a little sacrifice to be sure of getting people who can really appreciate the house. This Mrs. Bankes—I can't say I took to her, because I didn't, but she was most enthusiastic about all our nice things.'

'Anyone would be enthusiastic about your nice things—they're yours, dear, not ours—if they were getting the use of them for nothing.'

'No, no, Harriet Greenway says her taste is wonderful, and she ought to know. Another great point is that she isn't going to clutter the house up with things of her own. As you know, we haven't much space here for a lot of extra stuff, and luckily Mr. and Mrs. Bankes have nothing but their hotel luggage. She's been living at the Asturias—'

She was interrupted by a tapping at the door, and Mrs. Manders put her face into the room with an ominous blank expression. 'Miss MacFarren, Moseley's van's here. Would you mind telling me what's to be done with all them packing-cases and things?'

'Packing-cases?'

'Yes, and great big trunks—my word, I don't envy the men having to carry them.'

'There must be some mistake. Mrs. Bankes distinctly told me—' Without waiting to complete her sentence, she hurried out to the front door, and addressed the two men who were lifting cases from the van. 'Are you quite sure those are for this house?'

'They're labelled clear enough, lady—"Mrs. Bankes, 16 Harberton Square" . . . three crates, two wardrobe trunks, and a divan bed.'

Miss MacFarren turned stricken eyes upon her nephew who had followed her. 'What am I to do? She asked me if she could send just a few odds and ends in advance.'

'You'd better bung them back. Explain that you can't have them here.'

'Oh, Mory, that's easier said than done. I don't know that I'm entitled to refuse her personal luggage.'

'Very personal luggage!' Mory laughed, pointing to the box-spring bed which was now being unloaded. 'Did she take her own bed to the Asturias?'

'Did the bed come from the Asturias?' Miss MacFarren asked the nearest vanman.

'No, lady, none of this stuff come from there. It's all out of our warehouse. We've 'ad it in store.'

'Not the bed, Bill,' the other man contradicted. 'The bed's from the Rathbone Furnishing Co. I picked it up meself there yesterday.'

'The mystery deepens, the plot thickens,' whispered Mory, who had gone out in the street and looked at the bed. 'It has a price ticket on it and a label saying "Sold. To be collected Thursday." Thursday was yesterday, Aunt Ellie.'

'You're not trying to tell me she went and bought a bed to send here? That would be senseless. I'll ring her up and find out what it's all about.'

Politely dismissing Mrs. Manders and begging the men to refrain for a few minutes from delivering their consignment, she put through a call at once to the Asturias, only to be informed, after a brief delay, that Mrs. Bankes had gone away for the weekend.

'It's no use,' she said, signalling to the men to bring the things into the house. 'I don't think I should be justified in turning them away. I ought to have stated plainly that I had no room for more than ordinary luggage.'

'But if she told you she only had a few odds and ends?'

'Unfortunately, I've been paid a cheque for thirty pounds in advance.'

'Return it to her!'

'I've cashed it. But that's not the point. She's made all the arrangements for her husband to come here for his leave, and she's arriving herself next Wednesday. No, I'm afraid it's really irrevocable. . . . Would you take those up to the landing on the next floor?' she said to the vanman, noting with dismay the two American wardrobe trunks of immense size which had now been deposited in the hall. 'The packing-cases will have to be left down here for the time being. Oh dear, oh dear, we shan't be able to turn round.'

'What about the bed?' asked Mory, who seemed unduly amused.

'Something has occurred to me about the bed.' She glanced up at the vanmen, staggering on the stairs under their burden, and though they had no ears for anything but admonitions to 'Go easy there, Bill!' and 'Try to 'oist it a bit 'igher, 'Arry!' she lowered her voice.

'You see, there's only a double bed in the room that Mr. and Mrs. Bankes are going to have. Perhaps they prefer to sleep separately—he's an American, you know—and she didn't like to tell me, so she's bought this extra bed. Of course, it'll entirely spoil the appearance of the room.'

Mory's provoking giggle had not changed since he was fifteen, and was largely inspired by the self-same themes. 'Where did you get this idea about the way Americans like to sleep, Aunt Ellie?'

'Surely twin beds were an American invention?'

'I know this much—they're an invention of the devil. I loathe the things.'

He spoke with so much feeling that she felt she had better change the subject and called down to the basement: 'Mrs. Manders, we'll have tea as soon as Moseley's men have gone.'

'That's fine, because I've got a studio car coming for me at quarter to five.'

They stayed to see the bed carried upstairs, and went into the garden, where there were deck-chairs already unfolded. Miss MacFarren brought out a light rosewood table in readiness for the tray. 'Now you must be business-like,' said Mory, 'and put down on the Bankeses' account "Gratuity to vanmen, two shillings"!'

'Oh, I couldn't, Mory! You need to be a practised landlady to carry off a thing like that.'

'You'd better be a practised landlady or you'll find yourself wishing you'd never started.'

'I've got the right to give them a month's notice, so it can't ruin me. . . . And Mrs. Bankes may be much nicer than one expects.' She had been saying this to herself every day for a week. 'Dislike at first sight is just as irrational as love at first sight.'

'And just as inescapable.'

'Oh, do you think so? No, I've often grown to like people I didn't care for at all at first.'

'"Didn't care for" is so negative. Have you ever grown to like anyone who actively got on your nerves? I haven't.'

'I can't remember. It wouldn't be right to say that Mrs. Bankes got on my nerves—not quite right. She puzzled me. There was something strange about her.'

'Have you taken up her references?'

'I've taken up her husband's references. They were excellent. She speaks of her husband with bated breath. I'm trying hard to picture him.'

Miss MacFarren visualized as she spoke a concourse of American types as she had seen them in streets and restaurants, trains and buses, shops and cinemas. Tall slender men inclined to a slouching carriage and a loping walk, with hair flaxen to mouse-coloured, and blue or grey eyes that suggested Scandinavian origin; short stocky men, large-featured and dark-eyed, some of them probably Italian-born, some Jewish of a more intense racial strain than is often found in England; a small class of pale dyspeptic-looking men with glasses and preoccupied faces; tanned men of beautiful physique whom she liked to think of as descended from Red Indians . . . this type was her favourite—with magnificent teeth set in a wide and boldly modelled jaw, high cheekbones, a rather low brow, and a small blunt nose, not like the high-bridged nose of the Indian but curiously in keeping all the same with this best of American faces. Miss MacFarren speculated as to which of these categories would hold the war correspondent, and then she said aloud: 'I always think of Americans as either Henry James men or O. Henry men.'

'He isn't by any chance,' said Mory, 'the journalist, Joss Bankes?'

'Yes, that's right.'

'I should think, in that case, your rent's quite safe. He's very popular and very highly paid. As a matter of fact, he's really a good writer of his kind.'

'Well, that's a comfort. People who are good at their jobs nearly always have something to recommend their characters.'

'What a theory, Aunt Ellie! I shall have to take you on a tour of the studios.'

Mrs. Manders now appeared with the tea-tray, but while she was setting it out for them, the front-door bell rang, and, grumbling, 'What, again?' she retreated to answer it. In a moment or two she reappeared, announcing that a car had come for Mr. MacFarren.

'Why, he's miles too early!' Mory protested. 'He'll have to wait till I've finished my tea.'

'There's a young lady in the car, sir,' Mrs. Manders pointed out almost courteously. She never called any visitor 'sir' except Mory.

'Who can that be? I'd better go and see, Aunt Ellie.'

Miss MacFarren knew that if the lady was not asked in to join them Mory would have to go without his tea, and she struggled to decide whether she could properly receive Geraldine, that most appallingly illicit of mistresses. She determined to hope for the best from Mory's own good feelings—not that she placed any great reliance on his moral perceptiveness—and, with an apology for the trouble given, requested Mrs. Manders to bring another cup 'just in case'.

Mory came back immediately saying; 'Do you mind, darling, if I bring Miss Albert in for tea?' And seeing his aunt's rigid face as she observed that the girl was close behind him, he whispered cheerfully: 'No, dear, it's not Geraldine. You may breathe again.'

Miss MacFarren and Miss Albert were then introduced more or less formally, another deck-chair was unfolded, and the tea was poured.

Miss Albert, who seemed surprised to find herself having tea with an elderly lady in a garden, said nothing except 'How'd you do?' and it was Mory who explained that, having to visit the studio on a similar errand to his own, she had availed herself of the conveyance. 'We're going to see them run a rough cut from the new Martinez picture.'

'Are you playing in that?' Miss MacFarren asked politely, convinced by the young person's beauty that she must be a film actress, but Miss Albert replied with a brief negative.

Miss MacFarren feared the newcomer was shy and addressed herself to Mory; 'Is it something you're working on?'

'No, Aunt Ellie, we're merely friends of the director, Pio Martinez. Maxine—Miss Albert has a wonderful flair for cutting and he likes to have her opinion.'

'I wouldn't call it a flair,' said Maxine, daintily poising her tea-cup. 'I just know when a thing's lousy and I say so.'

Miss MacFarren was slightly startled. She had never quite got used to the word 'lousy'; indeed she had never had occasion to. It seemed to come very strangely from Miss Albert's lips, which were so prettily formed that they ought only to have uttered the most delicate sentiments.

Her face had a babyish fullness and roundness that gave it innocence, and the unusual thickness and length of her dark lashes made it appear that her eyes were modestly veiled. When she opened them wide, one could see that they were of a violet blue. She was hatless and her hair, brushed with an upward sweep, recalled to Miss MacFarren the look of a little girl whose curls have been pinned up at bath-time. Tendrils escaped and caressed her rounded temples. Altogether a more infantine and endearing type of loveliness could not be imagined.

'You are—of course you're sure to be a film actress?' Miss MacFarren proceeded, seeking to be amiable. 'I dare say I ought to know your name.'

The visitor, looking sulky in a particularly childish way, responded: 'I don't know whether I'm a film actress or not. I've been in several pictures, but the silly—' She paused as if to swallow some unsuitable word, and Mory suggested:

'Blighters.'

She tacitly consented to the term. 'They won't photograph me properly. They make me look like a pudding.'

'Oh, but they couldn't, Miss Albert!'

'They do though. Just like a damn pudding! But Pio Martinez is having me tested properly next week—by a real ace cameraman. I'm sure I could be photographed if they'd only take the b—' She bit the word off short, breathed in, and finished, 'beastly trouble.'

'I'm sure too,' Mory murmured sympathetically. 'I can't think why they haven't found the right angles yet.'

Miss MacFarren privately considered that it might be because the young actress had no angles. From head to foot—and this entirely without excess—she was composed of charming curves.

'You have to sleep with a damn cameraman to get photographed decently in England,' Miss Albert grumbled as if she were speaking to herself.

'Maxine means it figuratively, Aunt Ellie. The cameramen are actually married without exception, and highly respectable.'

'That's all you know,' she persisted unheeding. 'I had a cameraman try to sleep with me the very first day I was ever on the set.'

'More tea?' Miss MacFarren enquired sharply.

'Thank you. I think I will, just for a change. I haven't been drinking much tea lately.'

'I think there *is* less tea-drinking, and perhaps a little more coffee-drinking,' Miss MacFarren conceded, resuming her social manner. 'People have to try and eke out the ration.'

'My tea ration goes far enough.' Maxine made an artless grimace. 'It's the gin ration that gets me down. Do you know anyone who can lay hands on a few bottles, Mory? Black market, I mean.'

'If I did I shouldn't tell you in front of my aunt,' Mory answered in jesting earnest.

Miss MacFarren endeavoured to maintain the affability due to a guest. 'I can quite believe the shortage of spirits is most annoying to people who have to entertain a great deal, as you do in your profession. I have a quota of one bottle a month—whisky, you know, because my brother used to take a little.'

'One bottle! I call it simply silly.'

'Oh, but it's more than enough for me. In fact I've accumulated about fifteen bottles.'

'Fifteen bottles—my God! Would you like to do a deal?'

'Now, now!' cried Mory. 'If my aunt does any whisky deals, it'll be with me. Drink up your tea like a good little Maxie. The boys in the projection room will hate to stay over-time.'

Maxine, who had left a brilliant semi-circle of vermilion on her tea-cup, made up her lips with meticulous care, powdered her face, ran a moistened finger along her eyelashes, and replaced a tendril or two of hair. Then she rose and shook her dress out with an undulating movement. 'I think the picture's going to stink,' she said. 'I'd rather stay in this nice little garden with your aunt. It isn't every aunt who has fifteen bottles of whisky.'

'I have four bottles of gin too,' Miss MacFarren informed her demurely.

'My God! I shall have to come and live here!'

With a lively smile that showed for the first time two captivating dimples, she waved in a childlike fashion and drifted out.

Mory handed her into the car and returned for his hat. 'I'm afraid she shocked you, Aunt Ellie,' he apologized, kissing her. 'She simply doesn't realize what she sounds like.'

'If only her language were as pretty as her face!' Miss MacFarren could not refrain from saying.

'Language or no language, she mows the men down. She'd mow them down if she were dumb. She's really only half-dumb. Good-bye, Auntie! Take care to keep your lodgers in their place!'

She wished he wouldn't call them lodgers.

3

MRS. BANKES had telephoned after the week-end to say she would arrive on Wednesday afternoon. Actually she came on Wednesday morning, accompanied by two friends and the most prodigious quantity of baggage ever bestowed in a taxi. She stood in the hall directing the friends and Mrs. Manders as to how to dispose of the baggage, some of which went down to the basement, some up to the bedrooms; but herself she carried nothing except an empty birdcage.

'Isn't this utterly ravishing?' she demanded, waving it gracefully towards Miss MacFarren. 'I bought it from your Mrs. Greenway. I do think there's nothing so pretty as an early-Victorian birdcage.'

'It's very, very pretty,' said Miss MacFarren, 'but I can't help being glad it's empty.'

'Do you hate to see dicky-birds in cages? So do I.'

'Where are you going to put it?' Miss MacFarren's tone was animated by relief.

'Here in the hall, I think.'

Miss MacFarren stiffened. The hall belonged equally to the tenants and herself, and she did not consider they could reasonably start decorating it with meaningless birdcages, yet she knew it would seem ungracious to reject the ornament, and indeed she was by no means fully certain that she was entitled to do so. To share the hall might mean to add to the decoration if one or other felt so inclined. Fortunately, her mute reaction passed unnoticed, for Mrs. Bankes was busy giving her friends further instructions about the baggage.

The friends were very smart women like Mrs. Bankes herself, but substantially younger. They seemed to regard it as great fun to run up and down the stairs at her direction. All three of them, in fact, behaved as if the whole business were an amusing game, and even Mrs. Manders, though she had loudly lamented her promise to stay on every time her eye fell on the packing-cases, the wardrobe trunks, or the new bed, was infected with the general light-heartedness, and made a joke of the disorder in the kitchen.

As she had not expected Mrs. Bankes until the afternoon she had still to finish the rearrangement of the cupboards. The new tenant, for all that she had been living in a hotel, had managed to bring with her a number of cartons of food in tins, packages, and bottles—presents, she said, from friends in America and elsewhere—and as soon as her luggage was more or less out of the way, she went into the kitchen and began unpacking her stores and placing them on the shelves which were not yet ready for them. Miss MacFarren at once came to the maid's assistance in clearing and cleaning the cupboards, but, wishing to do it methodically, she was slow; and Mrs. Bankes was in such a furore of gay impatience that she put the previous contents higgledy-piggledy on the floor, or into other cupboards intended for different purposes. The result was an extreme confusion, in the midst of which Mrs. Bankes suddenly lost interest.

'I must go and see if my female friends are being useful upstairs,' she said. 'Mrs. Manders, do be a real poppet and rig us up something to eat. We'll be madly hungry after so much hard work.'

'I'm sure you will,' Mrs. Manders said sympathetically, 'but what shall I do for rations, madam?' Miss MacFarren noted with envy how the mode of the request had pleased her. She herself could never manage that kind of jauntily confident approach.

It appeared that Mrs. Bankes had brought no rations but intended to get them later, and Miss MacFarren could hardly do less than offer her own in the meantime. A lunch was devised of tinned soup, macaroni, and salad—most of the ingredients borrowed. Mrs. Bankes went upstairs to join her friends, and soon their squeals of laughter and mock-abusive epithets could be heard descending and receding as they scurried between the ground floor and the bedrooms.

'Tiggy, you great oaf, you aren't going to leave the portable gramophone in the bathroom?'

'Tonia, you maniac, I positively refuse to carry a suitcase that's filled with lead!'

'Penny darling, those are books—books for the bedside!'

'They must be dreadfully boring ones.'

A loud gust of laughter followed. 'Penny, you are funny! Tiggy will help you.'

'I can't. I'm swooning under a mound of dresses and hats.'

Miss MacFarren had resolved to keep very strictly to her own parts of the house, and never to show the slightest curiosity as to the doings of her tenants, but she did not think it would be kind to put this determination into practice until they had settled in, seeing how much there was to be learned about a new home. So, having done what she could in the kitchen—feeling almost dazed at the muddle and ill-judged haste of Mrs. Bankes's proceedings—she went upstairs to make sure that all was plain-sailing in the bedrooms.

She found the party of three tittering like wild schoolgirls over an attempt to move the new bed from the front room to the back without taking off the pillows and covers. (She had, for appearance's sake, had it made up and completed with a quilt.)

'Tonia, you ape, it can't be done! We shall have to—positively have to tip it over.'

Tiggy and Penny turned the bed on its side, throwing the coverings in heaps on the floor.

'I wonder what made her put it in this room?' said Mrs. Bankes, not seeing that Miss MacFarren was on the landing.

This was an embarrassing moment. She did not intend to inform these giggling girls of the theory which had led her to place the bed, cumbersomely enough, in the double room, and remarked quite amiably, gazing into space: 'I had no idea what you could want done with it. I thought at first it had come here by mistake.'

Mrs. Bankes looked faintly, very faintly, perturbed, but she answered airily: 'Didn't you get a message that it was for the spare room? How naughty of them to forget! I noticed there was only one bed and I thought we might just occasionally need two. Wasn't I lucky to get it?'

Miss MacFarren was too annoyed to reply. Had they been alone together she would certainly, at that moment, have had the courage to point out that Mrs. Bankes was not justified in making such an important addition to the room without consulting her: but her good breeding forbade her to express herself freely in front of strangers, and Mrs. Bankes continued in her facetious way: 'My two lady friends, Mrs. Jermyn and Miss Hall-Brown, are going to be heavenly angels and help with my unpacking, so I've promised they can sleep here if it's all the same to you.'

The brightest beams of the powerful smile were directed straight into Miss MacFarren's jetty eyes. Unwilling to respond with the mere scowl which was all she felt capable of producing, she lowered her eyelids. 'The spare room is not occupied,' she said in an abstracted voice, and then walked away as if she had recalled some urgent task.

Once in her study, she paced up and down fuming; yet at the same time making an effort to reason with herself. It was her greatest strength and her most inveterate weakness that she desired at all times visibly and beyond dispute to have right upon her side. She could not bear a position that was, from any point of view, assailable. That was why, at a time when everyone who had rooms to let was taking full advantage of their scarcity value, she had disposed of hers on terms which could leave no conceivable doubt in the tenants' minds as to the fairness of the bargain; why she had considered their comfort before her own in the domestic plan.

Now this anxiety to remain above criticism—liable to be called self-righteousness by those who do not benefit from it—made her reflect very seriously on how far it was legitimate to object to any of Mrs. Bankes's proceedings, and she came to the conclusion, half angry, half relieved, that nothing absolutely unwarrantable had so far been done. Mrs. Bankes had been very inconsiderate in the kitchen, and yet she had not antagonized Mrs. Manders, whose goodwill in that department mattered more than her own. She now had an equal share in the spare room, and was therefore perhaps within her rights in adding an extra bed, though she had failed in tact not to have mentioned this need beforehand. Or wasn't it possible, Miss MacFarren asked herself in her eagerness to do justice, that she had imagined it more tactful to present a bed as a *fait accompli* than to express a desire which the other might feel called upon to fulfil? It was a mistaken view, but one which might be held in good faith. As for bringing two friends to stay on the very first night, that was surprising, but became less so when one saw how much help she wanted in dealing with her luggage.

Of course she had lied about the luggage, pretending that the quantity was trifling—a stupid lie indeed, destined to be found out immediately. . . . . But after all, for this very reason, to call it a lie might be wrong. Was it not rather an example of Mrs. Bankes's own fantastic idiom, which one would come to understand in time—an idiom rich in inappropriate adverbs and utterances which were not meant to be taken literally?

So did she endeavour conscientiously to persuade herself but when all was inwardly said, she still knew herself to be full of dread and distrust; she still wondered immeasurably at Mrs. Bankes's effect upon Harriet, who had recommended her with such enthusiasm. Nevertheless, she made a fresh resolution to let no prejudice get the better of her temper, to carry out her part of the bargain not merely with honesty, but with cordiality.

As the new inmate's arrival had been timed several hours earlier than the household expected, Miss MacFarren had not yet provided herself in the study with the means of making her lunch—for it was her intention to use the kitchen as little as possible now that Mrs. Manders was no longer her employee: and she decided that it would be best on this first day to go out for the meal. After waiting half an hour to be served, she lunched badly and rather expensively at the nearest local restaurant, and returned home to make her own coffee, having no patience with the nefarious beverage generally disguised under that name by public caterers.

When she came in, laughing badinage seemed to be ringing all over the house. 'It sounds cheerful,' she told herself with an attempt to be convincing, but in her heart she thought it noisy and troublesome. She remembered, however, with what a solemn air Mrs. Bankes had assured her that she and her husband were a quiet couple, and concluded that all this shouting and running about were part of the settling-in process which would presently be done with.

While her coffee was infusing aromatically in the percolator, a tiny problem arose, occasioned by the ringing of the front-door bell. To save Mrs. Manders from perpetually having to climb the basement stairs, it had always been understood that Miss MacFarren answered the door herself except when she was known to be engaged with a visitor. But from this time on, there would be at least an equal chance that the bell was for Mrs. Bankes. Which of them then should do the answering?

As it happened, Mrs. Bankes and Mrs. Manders must have asked themselves the same question, so that all three of them appeared at the front door simultaneously.

'Well, I call this service!' said Harriet Greenway, striding into the hall. 'Good afternoon, Elinor! How d'ye do, Mrs. Bankes? Very glad to see you, Mrs. Manders!' she added in a cosy parenthesis to the maid's retreating back. 'Now which sitting-room do I get invited into?—because I've come to call on you both equally. I thought that as Mrs. Bankes is a sort of protégée of mine, I ought to look in and see if everything was going according to plan.'

She glanced benevolently from one to the other. Mrs. Bankes was able to return one of her radiant smiles, and Miss MacFarren summoned as much pleasure to her face as she could manage. Harriet's sense of well-doing was so obviously delightful to her, it would be cruel to deprive her of it for an instant.

'Everything is going quite, quite marvellously,' said Mrs. Bankes. 'It couldn't be more comfortable. Joss will worship it.'

There was something disarming about praise so generous and whole-hearted. Miss MacFarren's expression of strained brightness relaxed into natural amiability, and she said to herself: 'Bad beginnings often make good endings. At any rate, she's immensely appreciative.'

'Won't you all come and have coffee with me?' she suggested cheerfully, 'I'm in the very act of making some.'

'I'm afraid I've chosen a bad moment,' said Harriet. 'You know I can only get away from the shop at slack hours. My assistants are so half-baked these days.'

'No, this is an excellent moment. Do call your friends to have some coffee, Mrs. Bankes!'

'Thanks, we've had some already, and we're frantically busy unpacking. I can't bear to see this lovely house littered up with my luggage. I honestly can't bear it!'

'Then don't let me interrupt you,' Harriet entreated earnestly. 'The house is the first consideration.'

She stayed to offer a few courtesies, then followed Miss MacFarren who had retreated to attend to the percolator.

'Elinor,' she said, sitting down and taking a pinch of snuff from a jewelled and enamelled snuff-box, kept in the pocket of her tweed Norfolk jacket, 'Elinor, I can't tell you how well I think this arrangement is going to work out. I just know it intuitively.'

'She seems very easy to please,' said Miss MacFarren selecting a compliment that could be uttered without qualification.

'Yes, she's charming, perfectly charming. And she thinks you're charming too.'

'Oh nonsense, Harriet!' (Miss MacFarren took her courage in both hands to say 'Nonsense' to a friend she had secretly always regarded as formidable.) 'I know very well that charm is not my strong suit.'

'I tell you, the moment you turned your back just now, she said, "Oh, Mrs. Greenway, I do hope she likes me as much as I like her!"'

Miss MacFarren did not know whether to feel guilty, because the attraction had been so far from reciprocal, or merely incredulous: the remark might so easily be one of Mrs. Bankes's non-literal statements. She busied herself with pouring the coffee, murmuring, 'I think it's more likely the house that has taken her fancy.'

'The house too, of course. A woman of so much taste couldn't fail to admire that. She'll take great care of your things, my dear. You should see the way she handles anything fragile in my shop.'

'I suppose you've never met her apart from your shop?' Miss MacFarren enquired, speaking nonchalantly, for she did not wish it to appear that the question was directed by her doubts.

'No, but you get to be able to sum up people pretty shrewdly after a few years in the antique business.'

For the first time in their eight years of friendship, Miss MacFarren admitted a suspicion that Harriet over-estimated her own shrewdness. It was a difficult admission because Harriet had made that shrewdness an article of faith; her friends swore by it; it was proverbial. 'My dear, you must consult Harriet Greenway,' they would advise each other as if she were a fortune-teller. 'She'll know exactly what to do.' And Harriet never refused to tackle any problem, and never shrank from proposing drastic solutions. In fact, drastic solutions were her speciality. She believed in the tonic properties of change.

It was she who had made Lady Violet Scapley sell that beautiful burden, her ancestral home, and buy instead a neat modern villa which gave no trouble—and this although such an exchange would have gone quite against the grain of her own taste. Though an agnostic, it was she who had persuaded the neurotic Mrs. Mullington to give up half-hearted Christian Science and join the Seekers of the Holy Grail; she who, though childless, had taken Lottie Warbey in hand early in her pregnancy and insisted on her leaving the dreary family doctor and going to the man with the new 'nature' methods—the most remarkable of all the natural methods introduced during the past forty years. Everyone enjoyed yielding to the guidance of Harriet, because her bold suggestions opened novel prospects and her masterful character seemed to sweep away barriers. She imparted confidence too, having made so great a success of her own career, begun late in life.

Harriet's interest in other people was inexhaustible and nearly always took a benevolent shape. Although she was not a self-effacing character, being somewhat dominating and assertive, she was at any rate the reverse of self-absorbed. She loved to confront other people's dilemmas, to fight vicariously other people's battles. She seldom spoke of her personal affairs, but devoted herself to listening, trenchantly questioning, and giving oracular counsel. In consequence, she was much sought after and had come to believe in herself sincerely as one with a special gift for beneficent intervention. Her own conviction, since she was a person of integrity, carried weight with others.

But now that doubt had entered Miss MacFarren's mind, she thought of Lady Violet Scapley and wondered whether she was actually happy shut out for ever from Scapley Park; she knew that Mrs. Mullington was still neurotic even though searching for the Holy Grail; and she had heard a rumour, discredited till now, that Lottie Warbey's pregnancy was going none too well despite the regime of the naturalist practitioner. Was Harriet's shrewdness, so widely taken for granted, a delusion? Or was Mrs. Bankes truly a gracious, cultivated lady whom she, Elinor MacFarren, had seen, through some astigmatism of her own, wholly out of focus?

She framed in her mind all sorts of questions, and in particular whether Mrs. Bankes's domesticity had been revealed to Harriet from any source other them Mrs. Bankes's self; but she could not find any way of couching the enquiry that did not imply a criticism; and if there was one flaw in Harriet's boundless philanthropy, it was that she grew rather cross when its effects were for an instant challenged.

Of this indeed, Miss MacFarren had confirmation immediately, for to change the subject she mentioned that she had met, while waiting in a cake queue, a friend of Lottie Warbey's.

Harriet made a percussive noise: 'I'm beginning to lose patience with that girl! I suppose her friend told you this ridiculous rigmarole about her fancying she's ill.'

'She said she was having a great deal of sickness.'

'It's nonsense, of course—pure imagination. I sent her to Mr. Meersch, you know, who has this wonderful natural method of living on practically nothing but grated raw vegetables and taking limbering exercises till the very last day. Her mother has been working against him, trying to uphold the utterly obsolete ideas that kind of woman clings to. Heaven knows how all her unfortunate children managed to survive! Well, she's thrown Lottie into a state of conflict, and the result is this tiresome sickness.'

'But I understand the diet doesn't agree with her. She doesn't like the carrot juice.'

'Perfectly absurd! She's simply greedy for ordinary food and drink.'

'Her friend says she finds the exercises a strain.'

Harriet made her percussive noise again, but louder. 'She's lazy—bone lazy, and that's the long and the short of it. If she persists in the exercises, she'll be able to have the baby without an anaesthetic. Mr. Meersch guarantees it.'

'Perhaps she'd prefer an anaesthetic,' Miss MacFarren ventured.

'Mr. Meersch detests anaesthetics in childbirth . . . but if she won't be sensible I shall wash my hands of her.' Harriet took another pinch of snuff, and Miss MacFarren thought remorsefully how, only a few days ago, talking to Lottie's friend, she had never dreamed of supposing that childless Harriet was hardly the person to advise an expectant mother: it had seemed so proper for her to advise everybody. Once again she changed the subject.

'Have you seen anything of my hated rival lately?' This was Miss MacFarren's not serious yet not altogether jocular way of referring to the great Dr. Wilmot, Professor of Semantics at the University of London, whose hobby it was to collect botanical works, and who, as a result of methods that she regarded as wanting in scruple, had acquired a number of rare items which she did not possess.

'Oh, yes, I knew I had something to tell you, Elinor! Did you realize who it was that bought your books at Sotheby's?'

'Don't please say it was Dr. Wilmot!' Miss MacFarren pleaded with a note of dismay. 'He certainly didn't need my 1597 Gerard because he had one in his own collection. I remember it well, a poorish specimen with an eighteenth-century binding and a damaged title page.'

'Obviously he couldn't resist the chance of a better copy. He got one of the dealers to bid for him.'

'Just like him,' said Miss MacFarren bitterly. 'He never does anything in the open.'

Harriet rather callously laughed. 'He might say the same of you. Do you think he would have let you get those French water colours for double the price if he'd known—'

But the sentence remained unfinished, because there was a tap on the door and Mrs. Bankes's head appeared, with its piled curls of beautifully groomed hair looking like an arrangement in spun sugar.

'Oh, Miss MacFarren, it's awful of me to disturb you but what would you like Mrs. Thingummy to do now? She's finished clearing up the lunch things.'

Miss MacFarren would have been glad to reply: 'You know perfectly well it has nothing to do with me! And isn't it about time you got to know Mrs. Manders' name?' But instead she responded smoothly: 'I dare say she expects you to make your own routine. Working for me she always had an hour or two off after lunch.'

'Yes, I just wondered whether there was anything you'd like her to do for you before she goes off.'

'That's very kind, but I think it will be best if Mrs. Manders does nothing for me but the things we've already discussed.'

'That does seem so desperately hard on you. I honestly wish you'd go on thinking of the house and Mrs. Manders as *yours*.'

Miss MacFarren affably but vigorously disclaimed any such view, and Mrs. Bankes, nodding to Harriet with 'Don't let her be too unselfish!', withdrew.

'Now I call that charming!' said Harriet. 'She's determined you shall feel as much at home as ever.'

'Still, it's best to begin as we mean to go on.' Miss MacFarren was surprised that Harriet could not see how fulsome and unpractical Mrs. Bankes's suggestion had been. 'One can't share the house and yet go on regarding it as one's own. It wouldn't be fair. More coffee, Harriet?'

'Thanks, one sip. I know how scrupulous you are, my dear—when you're not trying to do down a fellow-collector—but the best of an understanding with a really friendly character is that it isn't a niggling contract to be carried out *au pied de la lettre*. I assure you Antonia Bankes *is* a really friendly character. She's been in and out of my shop—oh, dozens of times in the past few weeks and I know something of her by now.'

'What does she do there?' Miss MacFarren asked with a wondering smile.

'She—well, I can only put it like this, she gloats over the stock. She handles everything, plays the musical boxes, tries on all the trinkets, goes into ecstasies about Coalbrookdale inkstands and Chelsea scent bottles, finds out the secret drawers in the old bureaux . . .'

'But does she ever buy anything?' Miss MacFarren interrupted, laughing.

'All kinds of things. That birdcage in your hall came from me, and she's bought a wonderful pair of seventeenth-century gilt grottoes—a little damaged, unfortunately—and a carved Saint Francis in a sort of shrine which would have cost a great deal of money if it had been perfect; and a superb old Bristol chandelier which I was able to let her have fairly cheaply because some of the green glass leaves are broken. . . . I suppose she'd be much more sensible only to buy one first-rate specimen occasionally, but she does so enjoy herself, one somehow can't judge by the ordinary rules.'

'Where does she keep all these things?'

'At Moseley's Repository—except the birdcage, which she picked up in her taxi this morning. That's how I knew she was on her way here.'

'No doubt she's hoping to take her antiques to America,' Miss MacFarren speculated.

'Yes. I must say she's had some marvellous bargains from me. When one sees so much enthusiasm, one can't remain quite business-like.'

'It's a good thing your customers aren't all enthusiasts.'

'Practically speaking, you're right. Do you know, she positively kissed me when I let her have a musical workbox for cost price—genuine cost price, my dear.'

'She must know a great deal about antiques to have so much love for them.' Miss MacFarren tried not to betray her unbelief, but she was afflicted with a most exact and painful recollection of her Gallé cat left balanced on the edge of the console table.

'No, she knows very little, but she's tremendously anxious to learn. I've been teaching her all manner of things—superficial things at first, of course, but she'll get more knowledge by handling the stuff.'

Harriet pulled out her watch, a garnet-set fob watch with thread-fine wheels that whirred visibly in a transparent casing. She rose, smoothing down the Harris tweed skirt that made her look as if she still lived in the country where she had once been a landed gentleman's wife.

'I must go. I only popped in to give you both my blessing.'

She faced herself squarely in the overmantel mirror, and ran a pocket comb through her short, pepper-and-salt-coloured hair, grumbling lugubriously: 'It's no use, nothing makes the slightest difference! Would you believe this hair was set by Dominique yesterday? And this face, my dear! To think what this face has had lavished on it in the way of creams and lotions! Oh, to look like Mrs. Bankes!'

Miss MacFarren never knew what to answer when her friend lamented, as she frequently did, the shortcomings of her outward aspect, for it was true that the hairdressers left her hair as unruly as ever, and the beauty parlours had never been able to whiten her rough, ruddy complexion or to fine down the shapeless contours of a face and figure that could not at any time have been graceful. One wanted to say to her: 'Harriet, you're not good-looking, but anyone can see that you're a nice, kind, intelligent person. And anyhow you've turned fifty. Why not leave it at that?'

But Harriet would never leave it at that, for she adored beauty, and though she pursued it discreetly, at a distance, wearing tweeds, and with a perfect comprehension of her hopeless ineptitude, still, she would never quite give up the quest.

Seeing her gazing ruefully in the mirror, trying to make the best of herself, Miss MacFarren was able to perceive something of Mrs. Bankes's fascination for her—Mrs. Bankes whose waist was so slender, whose step was so springy, whose skin was so fine, whose hair remained unruffled after a morning of bustling activity. At fifty-odd one admires the qualities one has longed for and missed with an envy that is nostalgic and affectionate rather than jealous. And in Mrs. Bankes, the confiding eagerness of youth was combined with the cosiness of maturity.

Moreover, Harriet loved to teach. Nothing would please her better than to explain to a responsive novice the marks on china, the differences in glazing pottery, the fashions in design, the richnesses of old craftsmanship. If Mrs. Bankes, besides looking elegant, chose to play the flattering pupil, it was not, after all, very astonishing that she got musical workboxes at cost price and had persuaded her teacher to believe that she was polished, considerate, and domesticated.

To Miss MacFarren it all sounded what Mory would call phoney. 'Even now,' she thought, in her nephew's phrase, 'she's putting on an act to impress Harriet.'

Indeed the noise and giggling had stopped and the house was strangely quiet when Miss MacFarren went through the hall to see Harriet out. There was a great deal of litter. One of the packing-cases had been partially prized open and wood shavings were pouring over the floor. Through the sitting-room door a confusion of miscellaneous objects could be seen lying on the Aubusson carpet—coats, a gramophone, a pile of records, a writing case, a shopping basket heaped with oddments. Straw and shavings had apparently overflowed into this room from the hall.

'How relieved you'll both be,' Harriet murmured sympathetically, 'when all this nuisance of unpacking is done with! It's nice that

Mrs. Bankes can get it out of the way before her husband has his leave . . . furlough I think the Americans call it.'

Miss MacFarren dropped her voice to say at the front door: 'Of course you never had a chance of meeting Mr. Bankes?'

'No, but she tells me he's brilliantly clever and extremely good-looking. Isn't it a comfort that you and I are no longer susceptible?'

'Cold comfort,' said Miss MacFarren with a wry face. But this was mere jesting, for she had long reconciled herself very contentedly to a single life.

As she turned back into the hall, Mrs. Manders came up the basement stairs, not in her outdoor clothes, as one expected to see her at this time of day, but still wearing her cap and apron and carrying various sweeping implements. She looked a little sheepish seeing her former employer, for she had always been a great stickler for regular off-duty hours. Her tone was defensive as she volunteered to explain:

'I promised Mrs. Bankes I'd just sweep the floors and tidy up a bit. A lot of them glass and china things of hers was packed in sawdust and stuff and it makes a mess.'

'Yes, I suppose it's best to stay on the job till it's done.'

'It won't be done today—not by a long chalk!' Mrs. Manders shook her head with grim relish. 'You should see the state they've left the bedrooms in.'

'Left them!'

'That's right. They've gone to the pictures.'

Miss MacFarren was so far shaken out of her resolution never to comment on her tenant's doings as to exclaim:

'Gone to the pictures! But Mrs. Bankes said she couldn't bear this untidiness.'

'No more she can.' Mrs. Manders was evidently enjoying the situation. 'She said it was getting on her nerves, and then she suddenly remembered some picture they wanted to see, and off they went, inside of ten minutes. So I told her I'd clear up what I could.'

Miss MacFarren decided to be speechless.

'She's a nice lady, a very nice lady,' Mrs. Manders continued, as if rebuking the unspoken criticism. 'Lively and good-hearted I should call her . . . seems to have a nice pleasant way with her.'

'Very pleasant,' said Miss MacFarren.

'I expect we shall have a bit of life in the house now,' Mrs. Manders went on ruthlessly. 'She's getting up a party for Mr. Bankes's homecoming. Well, Captain Bankes I should call him because he's an officer by rights. I will say the way she asks a favour, you can't refuse, if you know what I mean.'

Miss MacFarren felt she could safely reply that she knew exactly. She picked up an electric iron which had been left on the console table, placed it thoughtfully on the half open packing-case, and went back to the room which was to be her refuge.

4

JOSS BANKES'S furlough was postponed for a fortnight, and the intervening time was filled with disconcerting experiences for Miss MacFarren. She could only hope that, as Mrs. Bankes seemed to be merely marking time until her husband's arrival, her mode of living would change when he eventually appeared.

Tiggy and Penny, after retaining possession of the spare room for several days, were immediately supplanted by two other guests; while from morning till night there was a succession of visitors whom Mrs. Bankes referred to as her 'female friends', her 'lady friends', her 'girl friends', but never by any chance as her friends. They were supposed to be helping her to settle in, and it was true they sometimes turned their hands to minor tasks, but no one could doubt that their real function was to keep her company at meals, to go to the pictures, the hairdresser, and the dressmaker with her, and generally to prevent her from bearing for one hour the heavy burden of solitude.

Their visits involved innumerable telephone calls. Whenever Miss MacFarren answered the telephone, it was sure to be for Mrs. Bankes or one of her companions; and when she wanted to make a call herself, the instrument was nearly always in use. As the telephone was rented in Miss MacFarren's name, it had been arranged at Mrs. Bankes's suggestion that a small cash-box should be placed beside it labelled with a request that payment for calls should be deposited within. After four days, curiosity compelled Miss MacFarren to open the box; it contained five halfpennies and a threepenny-bit. She anticipated the day of reckoning with discomfort.

Her first impression of Mrs. Bankes's friends was that they bore as close a resemblance to one another as the chorus of a musical comedy. They were all fashionably dressed, alternately flippant and gushing in manner, and 'rushed off their feet', 'in a tearing hurry', and 'frantically busy' doing nothing, apparently, but meeting one another for purposes of amusement. But by degrees she began to distinguish one from another—to notice that this one had a louder voice and that one a shriller laugh; that this one was as young as twenty-five and that one perhaps as old as forty; that this one would give her a polite 'Good morning' and that one would pass her on the stairs with vacant eyes. Yet the resemblances remained far more striking than the differences, and she came to the conclusion that, as Mrs. Bankes made demands upon her friends which necessitated habits of leisure and certain well-defined tastes, they were bound to have a great deal in common.

The first few days of house-sharing would have been a strain even under the most ideal conditions, but the presence of such numbers of strangers, whom she saw almost whenever she emerged from her room and heard almost whenever she retired to it, gave her a sense of displacement which was poignant.

Mrs. Manders, on the other hand, was visibly enjoying the bustle and excitement of her new life. She was working far harder than she had worked in Miss MacFarren's service, with no limits to what she might be called upon to do at inappropriate hours, but she was being coaxed, cajoled, familiarly spoken to, by a bevy of ladies, whose comings and goings, whose sayings and doings were a livelier entertainment than Miss MacFarren had ever been able to provide. And she admired the extravagance of Mrs. Bankes's housekeeping, that permitted her to buy poultry and salmon and mushrooms and melons at prices which had long banished them from the MacFarren table.

Whenever she encountered her former mistress, which could not be seldom in a small house, she would tell her what a sweet lady Mrs. Bankes was, and offer titbits of information such as that this morning she had given her the prettiest little handkerchief, and that they were going to have grouse for dinner, and that nice-looking Mrs. Reece had come down to the kitchen with a gift of eggs. Miss MacFarren perceived that Mrs. Manders felt obliged to vindicate her position, being found so often doing more than her normal duties. Only by vaunting the superiority of the Bankes regime could she justify her willing enslavement.

'The new brooms are sweeping clean,' thought Miss MacFarren, and wondered which would crumble first, Mrs. Bankes's flattering attentions or Mrs. Manders' eager obligingness.

That Mrs. Bankes was insincere and unreliable she had suspected from the first and now saw proved in different ways every day. Her non-literal mode of speaking amounted to sheer prevarication. She would say anything, resort to any verbal device, however impossible to sustain, in order to avoid unpleasantness, to get her own way, to defer some piece of business it was weariful to attend to.

For instance, when she spilt a bottle of ink on the hall carpet, she first tried to conceal the accident by placing a rug over the stain, then when it was inevitably discovered, mentioned with perfect insouciance that she was sending a message to a 'little man', highly recommended by a friend, who specialized in removing inkstains from carpets. No such person having turned up, Miss MacFarren asked some days later whether he was to be expected; Mrs. Bankes looked blank for a moment, and, as unconvincingly as a child whose face is sticky with the jam it denies having touched, answered that her letter must have been lost in the post. After a further delay, Miss MacFarren enquired for the carpet-cleaner's address, so that she might save trouble by getting in touch with him herself, and the reply was so palpably evasive as to leave no room for doubt that he had been a fiction.

When one of her misrepresentations was exposed by events, she accepted the situation with little or no embarrassment. Thus the extensive luggage and the three packing-cases, containing the harvest of many shopping expeditions, quite gave the lie to her original picture of herself as a woman almost without possessions, but she made no reference to former conversations when crowding her own ornaments and books among those which belonged to the house. She had simply said what would make her sound a more desirable tenant when there had seemed a want of eagerness on the other side, and now that she was installed, the pretence could be silently dropped.

Not indeed, Miss MacFarren acknowledged, that there was likely to be any conscious pretending in a mind so full of caprices. Her various make-believe rôles probably deceived herself at least as much as anyone else. If she dusted a room, she saw herself as a woman whose work was never done; if she invited half a dozen friends to tea, she became a society hostess. After a single early night without company, she would describe herself enthusiastically as one who lived the simple life: the following evening, a theatre and a supper at the Savoy convinced her that she was caught up in a ceaseless round of pleasure. Such Miss MacFarren presumed to be the shifting kaleidoscope of her mind, judging from the snatches of conversation that pursued her about the house, the talks on the telephone which she was reluctantly obliged to overhear, and the interchanges between herself and Mrs. Bankes when they met in the hall or kitchen.

There was only one topic on which her opinions did not appear to be so fluid as to be capable of changing their shape completely at any moment, and this was the excellence of Joss Bankes, his cleverness and goodness, courage and importance. She would refer with whimsical affection to her two little daughters, to whom she frequently sent comic postcards, but she seemed well content to leave them with her mother-in-law in America. Her husband, on the other hand, was obviously missed greatly. She wrote to him every day, repeated little items of news from his letters as if they could not fail to be of first-rate interest to anyone who might be privileged to hear them, and read avidly any of his copy which came to her in papers sent from abroad. She never mentioned public affairs except to say, in the tone of one who quotes an oracle, that Joss thought this or Joss had prophesied that; and Miss MacFarren suspected that her versions of his utterances were quaintly garbled, for she seemed to have only the smallest grasp of facts and ideas beyond the bounds of her personal experience. She told numerous anecdotes of Joss's bravery as a war correspondent, his ingenuity in getting stories, his boundless popularity, his disinterested conduct in joining the army at the beginning of the war, though he had not foreseen at the time his present assignment. If anyone spoke of having a problem, she would suggest: 'Wait till Joss comes! He'll know!' and this omniscience ranged from importing hock to authenticating an Old Master.

When she finally learned by telegram that he would be with her the next night, the 'female friends' occupying the spare room were speedily uprooted, though it was Sunday, the 'lady friends' who came to call were made to dust and sweep and burnish everything, and the 'girl friends' who telephoned were laughingly warned to keep out of sight until they were summoned to the party. On Monday Mrs. Manders was kept busy buying and preparing all the delicacies available, and Miss MacFarren gladly helped to tidy the house, which until then had never had the disorder of Mrs. Bankes's arrival properly cleared away.

At last the portmanteaux were emptied and stowed in the box-room, and places were found for trifles which had threatened to become mere litter. Mrs. Bankes was determined to show to advantage the home she had so cleverly found for a husband who was tired of hotels. Miss MacFarren had considered her incorrigibly lazy and disorganized, but now it was demonstrated that, given the needful impetus, she could work with a daemonic energy and singular concentration. Cupboards into which everything had at first been thrown higgledy-piggledy were turned out and made impeccable, muslin curtains sullied by the London soot were washed, pressed, and re-hung, every vase was filled with flowers, linen was changed, and the tumbled linen closet restored to the most perfect neatness.

Miss MacFarren had volunteered her assistance with this as with other tasks, happy to seize the opportunity of checking the inventory, which until then Mrs. Bankes had never been prevailed upon to look at, but which she now confirmed in a quite elaborately business-like manner.

'Your husband must be an exceptionally tidy person,' said Miss MacFarren with her questioning smile.

'No! Why?' Mrs. Bankes looked up from a pile of towels with an expression of deliberate stupidity.

'Because you're making everything so beautifully spick-and-span for him.'

'Oh, but I always adore things to be spick-and-span. I'm madly tidy, really, but in a new house it takes time to get straightened out.'

Miss MacFarren, who knew that Mrs. Bankes was 'madly tidy' in the same sense as she was 'madly quiet', evaded comment by asking if she had been married many years.

'Just ten. Ten years full of adventure! My husband's work takes him all over the place, of course, and before the war I went nearly everywhere with him.'

'I envy you having travelled so much. I've never managed to get out of Europe.'

'Oh, we've been half round the world, I should think. That's why we know such swarms and swarms of people. Everyone who meets Joss always wants to go on seeing him.' From all that had been said about the Bankeses' married life, Miss MacFarren could easily gather that they were an uncommonly devoted couple, and she could not help speculating, with an apprehensiveness that increased as she became better acquainted with Antonia, as to the character of the man who found his satisfaction in such a companionship. She told herself firmly that men who were both intelligent and honourable were often attracted by vapid, unsteady, and artificial women, just as women of the highest merit allowed themselves to be victimized by shallow and unscrupulous men; she called to mind cases within her own recollection; but her reason was powerless against her exasperation, and she had begun to fear that the husband, instead of bringing relief, would merely prove a further imposition.

It was uncomfortable, when Mrs. Bankes was being so pleasant and well behaved, to stand beside her engaged in a calculation as to whether a month's notice could only be given on the first of the month, and how may weeks she ought decently to wait before declaring that Harriet's protégée was hopeless. She busied herself with the inventory, murmuring: 'Three green bath-towels and three pink . . . One green is in use, and one pink must be in the wash.'

Mrs. Bankes solemnly ticked off the item and initialled the page. 'Now what's left? Only the table linen . . . Oh, bother, there's the front-door bell! I didn't want any visitors this afternoon!'

'Shall I go down and say you're not at home?' Miss MacFarren was anxious, while she had her tenant in this useful mood, to keep her at work until the inventory was checked.

'That would be angelic! We could go through the cutlery and kitchen things after tea.'

Miss MacFarren hurried downstairs, but not in time to forestall Mrs. Manders. The front door had already been opened, and she could see, as dark as a profile portrait against the September sunshine, a tall broad-shouldered man in a close-fitting jacket and a service cap.

'It's Captain Bankes!' cried Mrs. Manders, as who should say, 'I see him on his golden throne, the good Haroun Alraschid!'

With a gesture learned in some phase of polite training which she had chosen to forget for many years, she dived forward and attempted to seize one of the two suitcases he had planted on either side of him on the doorstep, but he warded her off and carried them into the hall, protesting in a shocked voice: 'No—*please*! No—*thank you*, Mrs. Manders!'

At this evidence of recognition, Mrs. Manders became more than ever the old retainer. 'My word, sir, this will be a surprise for madam! She didn't think you were coming till tonight!'

'I didn't expect to, Mrs. Manders. It just happened a friend of mine came over in a plane that left a few hours earlier.'

He put the suitcases down again with an air implying that he could have swung them round his head if he had been so inclined, glanced appreciatively about the hall, and noticed the grey-haired, dark-eyed lady waiting to greet him. He hastened to her with an outstretched hand.

'This must be Miss MacFarren!' Looking at her unsmilingly yet cordially, he took her hand and held it fast. 'I'm glad to know you, Miss MacFarren. Tonia has told me a lot of very nice things about you.'

Coals of fire descended on her head. She had never said any very nice things about Mrs. Bankes. In fact, she had refrained from seeing Harriet Greenway for a fortnight so that she should not have to commit herself to expressions of approval that would have been falsehoods.

'I've heard a lot of nice things about you too,' she said. 'Mrs. Bankes will be so pleased to know you're here. Do fetch her, Mrs. Manders!'

'I'm pretty glad to be here myself, Miss MacFarren. I can't tell you how good it is to know I'm going to sleep tonight in a house—a real home with books and pictures and things that aren't sold by the gross. And from what I hear, this is just about the nicest home I could have found my way to.'

As he spoke, Miss MacFarren looked searchingly into his face, trying to determine whether his warmth was genuine or spurious, and she found it one of the most likeable faces she had ever seen. By no means as good-looking in conventional terms as his wife in her enthusiasm believed, nevertheless it had qualities of kindliness, manliness, and good sense, which made it peculiarly attractive.

His features were large, his forehead and cheekbones broad: his clear blue eyes, strikingly open in their gaze, were set far apart. The effect was altogether one of spaciousness. His nose was prominent and strongly modelled, his mouth wide and firm with that jaw-line, distinctively American, which Miss MacFarren ascribed to the Red Indians. His skin had a weather-beaten look, his cheeks and forehead were furrowed with deep lines, but a small clipped moustache, by its fairness and suggestion of urbanity, rather softened the rugged impression.

Despite the lines, it was evident that he was not more than thirty-five, probably two or three years his wife's junior, and compared with Miss MacFarren a young man.

Her admiration of young men was purely academic. She had been spared from any tendency to hanker after the unattainable, except as an artist and a botanist, and she was able to regard Joss Bankes as if he had been an interesting print or a handsome book in a category she did not herself collect.

His low-pitched voice and purring accent might grow monotonous in time, but now they had the charm of entire novelty, and his earnest geniality, though it was a shade ponderous, pleased her more than his wife's self-consciously dazzling smile and flatteries offered so carelessly that her actions were often totally at variance with her words.

Responding with a warmth of manner almost equal to his own, she drew him into the front room. 'I hope you'll be comfortable, Captain Bankes. I dare say you're looking forward to a great deal of rest after all you've seen and done in Germany. This is your sitting-room.'

'Well, what a beautiful place! I'm not surprised Tonia was glad to leave the Asturias.' He stared round him with gratifying aston-ishment. 'My, I'm going to be happy here! This is just exactly the sort of room I love.'

She had leisure to observe as he strode over to the bookshelves and stood with becoming reverence before the pictures from Thorn-ton's *Flora*, that his legs were long, and that his lumber-jacket tapered down from broad shoulders to a taut and narrow waist. Miss MacFarren had an eye for such matters. She had imagined in her youth that she was in love with the noble nature of an officer in the Argyll and Sutherland Highlanders, only to discover after many disillusionments that it was really the shape of him in evening dress that had attracted her. He had caught her once round the waist, in the days when her waist was slender, and she could still remember, as vividly yet elusively as one remembers a perfume, the unyielding hardness, strange but captivating, of his torso as she had ventured to put her arms round him.

'Where did you find all these exquisite things, Miss MacFarren?' (He pronounced it 'ex*qui*site' and her name 'MacFar'n'.) 'It's a life-work surely?'

'A life's pleasure,' she was about to say, but her reply, like herself, was brushed aside as Mrs. Bankes came running into the room.

'Joss! Darling!' She flung herself towards him with a completely spontaneous movement, and in an instant his embrace enveloped her. Miss MacFarren did not stay to see their greetings, but she had time to observe that they looked like a picture of lovers reunited as she pulled his head down in her arms and his face was pressed ardently to hers.

*   *   *

The Bankeses had such an enormous circle of acquaintance that it was quite easy for them to collect upwards of thirty people for a party at two days' notice, especially as, owing to the shortage of wine and spirits, there were few social functions taking place at the time. Mrs. Bankes sat indefatigably at the telephone. She rang up a number of hotels, several private dwellings, three or four newspaper offices, the American Embassy, and some military departments in Grosvenor Square; and she succeeded in rounding up not only her husband's favourite compatriots in London and her own principal girl friends with their boy friends, but also various donations of gin, whisky, and sherry, and a case of beer.

She was ecstatic, if somewhat repetitive, in her expressions of gratitude when one prospective guest produced a chicken, and another potted shrimps, and the generous Mrs. Reece brought a pear of ducks from the country. She had a very easy and agreeable way of procuring gifts and kindnesses, and everyone was delighted either to contribute to her house-warming or to welcome Joss to England. Miss MacFarren envied her knack of organizing so considerable an entertainment without more fuss than she apparently found enjoyable.

For herself, the party was a source of mild embarrassment. She feared Mrs. Bankes might feel compelled to invite her since she was in the house, and, unwilling to be forced upon them by proximity, made an appointment to take a friend to dinner at a restaurant. Thus she would be able to say both with tact and truth that she was otherwise engaged. But, slightly to her discomfiture, no invitation was proffered.

When, on the day, she went into the kitchen to wash up her tea things, Mrs. Manders was scraping celery, Miss Hall-Brown, otherwise Tiggy, was cutting bread, Mrs. Bankes was polishing glasses, and an American officer was opening tins.

'Did you ever see such a hive of busy bees?' said Antonia gaily, as Miss MacFarren apologized for disturbing them. 'Joss is out collecting some of the drinks so that we can mix them in advance.'

'The only thing to do now the stuff's so scarce,' said the American.

'Yes, otherwise some of the guests keep pouring themselves half-tumblers full of gin while the others have to go short. That's what Joss says.'

'You're shocking Miss MacFarren,' Tiggy put in with a little spluttering laugh. 'She probably wouldn't touch gin or whisky if you paid her.'

Miss MacFarren had in her own locked basement cupboard fifteen bottles of whisky, four of gin, some four dozen of sherry, and about half a dozen of old brandy, besides sundry bottles of wine, some remaining from her late brother's cellar, some accumulated by herself in the belief that her nephew might return to his home to live. She had been about to offer some assistance in case the drink supply should not be adequate, but Miss Hall-Brown's remark annoyed her in some nameless way, and she only rejoined: 'I like a rum toddy when I have a cold.' She regretted the words even as she uttered them, for they made her seem even more old-maidish than Mrs. Bankes's friends already thought her.

They went on talking about the party, but nothing was said implying that Miss MacFarren was expected to attend, and she took care to leave the house before the guests were due to arrive. Although she admitted that there was no reason in the world why she should be asked to her tenants' celebration other than a sort of good nature which might become troublesome to all concerned, she was nevertheless, in a faint degree, disappointed. She had believed that Captain Bankes would invite her, since at every encounter he addressed her with particular amiability.

She came home as late as she could, having taken her companion to a cinema after dinner, and, informed by the babel of voices and music in the sitting-room, that the guests had not departed, tried to slip up to her bedroom unnoticed. But before she had mounted half a dozen stairs, Captain Bankes came up from the basement carrying a soda siphon.

'Miss MacFarren, where have you been?' he cried. 'Why didn't you come to the party?'

'I've been out with a friend.'

'Well, I call that mean—not to come to our party when we live in the same house.'

'It sounds very hilarious,' she responded, not choosing to reply that she had not been invited.

'Come on in and join us! It isn't too late.' He was a little drunk, and sought in a convivial spirit to pull her down by the wrist, her hand being on the banister.

Smiling, she shook her head. 'I like to be in bed by midnight.' Releasing herself she thanked him and proceeded upstairs.

A few minutes later, Mrs. Bankes called her from the floor below. To save herself from too frequent climbing of the stairs, she had a facetious way of singing out names like a jodeller. It was practical and sensible in so steep a house, but Miss MacFarren always felt foolish when she heard herself being jodelled to. It seemed an anti-climax to reply in a normal, prosaic voice:

'Yes, Mrs. Bankes?'

'Won't you come down to the party?'

Miss MacFarren realized that Captain Bankes had prompted this approach. 'Thank you so much, but I'm just getting ready for bed.'

'You're sure you won't come and have a drink?' Her tone did not succeed in concealing her relief.

'Thank you. I've started undressing.'

'It was naughty of you to go out. Joss is quite hurt.' Miss MacFarren tacitly agreed to play this game of pretending she had been asked to the party: it was more dignified than pleading the want of an invitation, but she was irritated by the bluff. It was possible, even probable, that Captain Bankes was unaware she had been left out, but on Mrs. Bankes's part she was sure the omission had been quite deliberate.

The gramophone was played and the laughter and chatter ascended even to the second floor till about half-past twelve Miss MacFarren recognized that this was not an unreasonably late hour for a party of celebration, and though sleep was out of the question, she made no inward murmur. But as it unfortunately happened, the water cisterns were immediately above the ceiling of her room and when, as late as one o'clock, someone below took a copious hot bath the disturbance became really annoying. The tank was twenty minutes refilling, and what worried Miss MacFarren even more than the prolonged gurgling in the pipes was the dread of having to mention the matter to her tenants.

She had been so determined to let them live their independent lives in whatever fashion they pleased that she had been prepared to overlook all sorts of liberties that might be resented by ordinary landladies; but bathing late at night must obviously not be allowed to become a frequent practice. How often ought she to let it happen before explaining her difficulty? As the noise of the cistern was inaudible on the lower floors, no one could be blamed for failing to realize that it had kept her awake till half-past one.

Half-past one indeed! It must be getting on for two and, though silence now prevailed, she was still very far from sleep. The atmosphere of the house had not for weeks—not since she had been hurried into her unwilling preparations to receive Mrs. Bankes—been conducive to easy repose. The change of bedroom, the encounters with visitors so alien in their manners, the interruptions in her work, the new and very inconvenient relationship with Mrs. Manders, the restraint she had been obliged to exercise in taking any steps which might seem to encroach on Bankes territory . . . it had all proved something of an ordeal, and must have done so even if Mrs. Bankes had been the paragon that Harriet thought her. As it was, the incompatibility between them was so enormous that the mere thought of it was like wind on water, sweeping away all the accustomed serenity of her mind.

She turned on the light and looked again at her watch. At this rate she would get no rest at all, for it was her unlucky habit always to wake early in the morning. Her experience of blitz nights had taught her once and for all that she could never hope to make up lost sleep in the daytime. At the recollection of the broken nights of recent years, she called to mind that the specific she had sometimes taken to calm her shaken nerves had also been useful in producing drowsiness. Still in the medicine chest was a flask of rum, already mixed with the flavouring of lemon which alone rendered it tolerable to her. It occurred to her forcefully that a strongish dose, such as she had administered to herself in the worst air raids, might get her to sleep quite quickly.

The medicine chest had been moved on the arrival of Mrs. Bankes to the upper bathroom. With a deeply troubled conscience, since she could not even claim to be suffering from a cold in the head, far less an air raid, she put on her dressing-gown and crept down to the half-landing. Back in her bedroom, a lukewarm toddy was rapidly prepared with water from the tap. Sipping guiltily, but sensible of a rewarding drowsiness, she told herself that this sort of thing must not be allowed to happen too often.

5

THE NEXT MORNING Miss MacFarren, who took tea in her bedroom, came downstairs at her customary hour of eight and found in the hall unfestive evidences of last night's festivity . . . empty glasses and overflowing ashtrays on the gilded console table, an unfamiliar mackintosh hanging from one of the ormolu candelabra, siphons and bottles on the floor near the basement stairs, an odd glove dropped near the front door.

She was tempted to glance into the room where the party had actually been given, and, deciding a little dishonestly that, since no one was yet about, this would be a good opportunity of fetching some books required for her day's work, she quietly opened the door. On the wide, satin-covered sofa, a man lay asleep wrapped in the eiderdown from the bed upstairs, his tousled head reposing on a heap of brocaded cushions. This and an impression of dirty plates and glasses strewn everywhere and of crumbs and sandwich fillings trodden into the carpet, were all she had time to register before retreating precipitately.

She went to her study feeling extremely angry, but yet, according to her invariable custom, stemming the tide of her indignation as well as she could to weigh the rights of the matter. Could a tenant be justified in hanging a coat on a candelabrum? Never. But she conceded that it might have been done without the knowledge of Captain or Mrs. Bankes. Were the occupants of furnished rooms entitled to use a drawing-room sofa as a bed? She could not deny that, on occasions of emergency, it might be reasonable for them to do so. But was it not a sheer abuse for them to turn one's best cushions into bed-pillows? As to this, her vexation seemed entirely warrantable. They would have to be told. . . . Yes, they would have to be told, she assured herself sternly, but she flinched from the dreadful prospect of telling.

She threw open the french windows and stared into her little garden, seeing only her Aubusson carpet sullied with the remnants of sandwiches. Would it not be better, since Mrs. Bankes had been a thoroughly unsuitable housemate from the first, to refrain from singling out particular causes of complaint and simply to give a month's notice as soon as she legitimately might? It would create a certain awkwardness with Harriet, but could it be worse than the present situation—avoiding her friend day after day because she neither wanted to lie to her nor to embarrass her with the truth?

The clicking of the door handle checked her unpleasant train of thought, and she turned to find Mrs. Manders standing on the threshold with some fragments of opaque glass held in a newspaper.

'I've just found these in the dustbin,' she announced abruptly.

Miss MacFarren darted forward with a movement as near a light bound as a stout lady of mature years is ever likely to achieve. 'It's my green Bristol chalice!' she groaned. 'Oh, Mrs. Manders, how *did* it get broken?'

'I'm sure I don't know, miss, nor how it got into the dustbin. I think they ought to have told you, whoever done it.'

'Leave the pieces with me,' said Miss MacFarren, who was nearly in tears. 'I shall have to mention it if Mrs. Bankes doesn't.'

'I wouldn't be surprised if she never does—hiding it away like that.' Mrs. Manders did not seem to be in as good a temper as usual with her new employer. 'She's hoping you won't miss it most likely. She little knows you!' With a grim ghost of a smile she laid the newspaper on the work-table.

'I suppose it's not my business,' Miss MacFarren found herself saying appealingly, 'but I should be very grateful if you could brush the sitting-room carpet this morning, even if it means not giving me so much time.'

Mrs. Manders fidgeted with her apron a trifle sheepishly. 'I'm sorry, miss, I was just going to tell you, I shan't be able to give you any time at all today. You should see what a mess they've left me to clear up in the kitchen.'

'Really, Mrs. Manders . . . !' She suppressed an inclination to say something acrimonious. 'Well, I hope you can manage to fit my rooms in tomorrow. We only scamped them last week, you know.'

'I would if I could, miss, but they've got four people in to lunch tomorrow, and the spare room's full again. It'll be as much as I can do to get through *her* work.'

Miss MacFarren had been brought up in the days when there was still a general belief in social distinctions, and she had been taught that one must not criticize one's equals or superiors in the presence of those who served them; so she continued, but with much difficulty, to bite back her irate protest.

She was, after all, providing Mrs. Manders' living accommodation, or at least half of it, and her tenants were enjoying many amenities for which no charge had been made; and she had asked nothing in return but a negligible amount of kitchen work and the cleaning of her rooms once a week. The first week this had been done with *empressement* and Mrs. Bankes had begged her—fatuously, of course—to command Mrs. Manders' services to the fullest extent. The second week, owing to some entertainment in the house, the cleaning had been cursory. And now, the third week, it was not to be done at all; for the day after tomorrow was Saturday, and Mrs. Manders did not, on the strictest principle, turn out rooms on Saturdays.

Miss MacFarren's wrath at what she regarded as a breach of faith, all the worse because there was no written agreement concerning service, would have prevented her from settling down to her intricate work even if she had not had to turn to and clean the rooms herself. When she considered the injuries under which she laboured—which included, apparently, the complete annexation of the spare room by Mrs. Bankes—she could have walked straight up to the obnoxious woman and ordered her out of the house. But unfortunately it was not yet half-past eight, and Mrs. Bankes never rose till nine.

Miss MacFarren laboured furiously for the next two hours with dusters, brushes, mop, vacuum cleaner, damp cloth, and chamois leather; and the expenditure of physical energy calmed a little her feverish anger. She knew on reflection that Mrs. Bankes could not be ordered out of the house, but she was resolved to present a month's notice on the 22nd of September, the date corresponding to that of her arrival in August.

She would state, quite firmly in writing, her numerous reasons for being unwilling to go on with the arrangement, and would show a copy of the letter to Harriet. She began to compose it in her mind: 'Dear Captain and Mrs. Bankes' . . . No, it had better be to Mrs.

Bankes alone, since her husband had so far had little or no part in the offences. And yet, was it not a sort of impropriety to address only the wife if the husband were also in the house?

This and other problems in the same connection occupied her thoughts to an extent which made her fear she would not be able to concentrate on the *History of Floriculture* for the whole day, more especially as Mrs. Bankes was jodelling up and down stairs to her various guests in a manner eloquent of endless disturbances.

However, at about eleven, voices in the hall and the banging of the front door, followed by a silence which seemed profound by contrast with the previous bustle, informed her that for the time being peace might be expected in the house. She had lost so many days lately that she deemed it essential to her self-respect to take the opportunity of collecting her scattered ideas and hewing out, at any cost of toil and effort, some further paragraphs of her chapter on 'The Italianate Garden'. She laid on the desk her card-index box, her file of photographs, and her leather manuscript book, trying as she did so to fix her mind rigorously on her subject. Now the coast was clear for her to find the books she wanted, and if there was not a succession of telephone messages to take down for Mrs. Bankes, she might be able to make some progress.

But on her second entry into the sitting-room, she found Captain Bankes stretched out at full length in an armchair before an electric fire, reading. He rose immediately and greeted her with his usual grave cordiality, which conveyed so strongly the impression of benevolence.

'Miss MacFarren, come right in! What can I do for you?'

'I thought you were out,' she explained rather stiffly. It was embarrassing to be aware, while he was not, that she intended to deprive him of his haven. 'I needed two or three books, but I can come back later.'

'Now please, please, Miss MacFarren! Take what you want right this minute! Tact is all very well but you mustn't make me feel like a usurper.'

As he said this, he smiled a broad slow smile, showing the even row of healthy teeth which Miss MacFarren was persuaded he inherited from the Mohawks or the Cherokees. It had quite a melting effect on her—so much so that she was able to admit to herself how surprisingly well the room had been set to rights since she had last seen it. Either Mrs. Manders or the guests, perhaps even Mrs. Bankes herself, had been working prodigiously.

With a word of thanks in a less remote tone, she opened one of the glass-fronted bookcases.

'Your library is beautiful,' he said solemnly. 'I found a book this morning that I'm going to like tremendously.' He held up the large volume he had been reading, and she saw it was her own *Evolution of Flowers*. 'Where did you acquire so much knowledge? You make it so interesting. It never struck me that vegetation had evolved like animal life.'

'I come of a sort of botanical family.'

'The MacFarrenaceae? I'll bet there aren't many of them can draw like this!'

She leaned forward to look as dispassionately as she could at the picture of the Fritillaria and found it very pretty. 'I'm glad you like that one.' She was beginning to be quite good-humoured. 'This is my favourite.'

He held the book open for her and she turned the pages until she found the plate of Lilium Tigrinum.

'Gorgeous!' he cried. 'You've made real tigers of them. Tigers burning bright in the forest of the day.'

She smiled, glancing downwards because his earnest eyes made her a little shy, and decided that the carpet, now brushed, only needed a brisk rub with her special carpet-cleaning fluid.

'Have you written any other books?' His manner conveyed a boundless interest and eagerness.

'Only a text-book for students and one of Bexley's *Garden* Series. I'm at work now, though, on something more in this style.'

She told him quite expansively about the *History of Floriculture*.

'You're a remarkable woman, Miss MacFarren,' he said when she had made the project clear. 'That easy-going culture of yours reaches a pretty high level. And I don't mean only your books, but this house and everything about you.'

It was a very un-English kind of speech, but she could not help liking it and showing that she did.

'Have any of your books been published in the States?'

'Not yet, I'm afraid.'

'Would you like me to send some of your manuscript to the New Aldine Press? It's run by a great friend of mine.'

'Thank you so much, but I think I ought to consult my publisher over here first.' The excuse, though dishonest, was the product of honesty, since she could not accept a favour from one with whom it might not be possible to maintain friendly relations.

'Well, let me know any time you feel inclined. You ought to go to the States. They'd like you there. Yes, they would too.' He seemed to be studying the question, trying to picture exactly what her effect would be, as if it were a matter of personal concern to him.

Anyhow, he ended inconsequently, 'I know we were mighty lucky to get a home like this in London—mighty lucky! Tonia has the best nose for a good thing of any man, woman, child, or dog I ever encountered in my life.'

Miss MacFarren found spirits enough to smile at the way he pronounced dog 'dawg' even while she cringed inwardly at the thought of the disappointment she was about to inflict on him. On the 22nd, only nine days ahead and before his leave was over, the blow would fall. Perhaps after all, it would be better to wait till the 1st of October. He would be gone by then, and she could deal with his wife alone, as was fitting seeing that she had dealt with her in the first place. Yes, she mentally postponed the unpleasant operation till next month.

'I feel it's up to me to tell you, Miss MacFarren,' he resumed as she murmured some acknowledgment of his compliment, 'you could be charging a darn sight more for this place. Half the expenses—it's ridiculous when you think what we get for it!'

It was disarming to be shown how fully he appreciated the somewhat quixotic nature of the terms she had made—too disarming, for it forbade her to mention how grossly his wife was taking advantage of them. She became wily.

'My idea was that it would be worth more to me in the long run to have really careful tenants than to charge a high rent and risk having my things knocked about.'

'There's reason in that,' he rejoined without uneasiness. 'I only hope Tonia's parties and everything aren't bothering you.'

The sincerity of his manner so encouraged her that she felt she might explain at least why it was troublesome for late-night baths to be taken; but before she could pronounce half a dozen of her delicately chosen words, the door was flung open and Mrs. Bankes appeared looking radiant in cool green linen and a white leghorn hat trimmed with flowers, and carrying, as she so often carried, a sheaf of flowers on her arm.

Miss MacFarren closed the bookcase and grasped the little pile of books she had collected in a business-like style, to convey that she had not come to this room merely to chat, but Mrs. Bankes, beaming and debonair, greeted her with every evidence of being delighted to find her there.

'So you've come to our sitting-room for once? You usually shun it like a plague spot. There's really no need to be so madly tactful, is there, Joss?'

'Miss MacFarren is naturally unobtrusive,' he replied seriously.

'I've bought you these.' Tonia held out her bouquet, her face lighted up with the desire to please.

'For me!' Miss MacFarren retreated almost physically from the unwelcome gift.

'Yes, because you were so terribly, terribly nice to us about the party. Not making a tiny bit of fuss though you must have thought we were turning the house upside-down! All my friends said "What a heavenly landlady!"'

'Well, it's very kind of you.' Miss MacFarren succeeded, by a great effort, in achieving an adequate degree of suavity. 'But really I'm not entitled to them.'

Covered with confusion, she took the flowers, and edged as near the door as she could. Escape was now imperative. 'Peonies—so lovely! I'm very, *very* fond of peonies!'

'I adore them, so I felt sure you'd like them too.'

Miss MacFarren had a horror of seeming ungracious, but never had a gift come at a more inapposite moment. 'Their colours are quite beautiful,' she said. 'They'll look charming in my study. I must go and put them in water at once.'

To make room for the flowers, she had transferred her burden of books to her left arm, and now, in her attempt to get away gracefully but rapidly, she lost her grip and let them fall to the floor. Captain Bankes sprang from the chair in which he had once again settled himself, but Mrs. Bankes had picked them up before he could reach them.

'I'll take them to your room for you,' she declared, as one whose kindness was without limit.

Miss MacFarren could scarcely refuse the offer. She had momentarily forgotten the green glass fragments on the work-table, those tell-tale fragments which it would now be so inopportune to lay before Antonia.

But Antonia's eyes lighted on them as soon as she came into the room. Her quick frown darted between her brows for an instant deeper and more expressive than Miss MacFarren had yet seen it. Then her face became singularly blank, her mouth drooped with a curious slackness.

'What in the world is that?'

'It was found in the dustbin this morning—the green vase from your mantelpiece.'

'Oh dear! I wonder who put it there?'

Miss MacFarren would have been prepared to stake a run of *The Compleat Florist* that Mrs. Bankes had put it there herself, so she said nothing.

'I suppose it must have been that wicked Mrs. Manders.'

She was compelled to protest. 'Oh no, Mrs. Manders has never hidden a breakage. Absolutely never! I don't imagine Captain Bankes would have done it either without saying anything about it. Perhaps it was one of your guests?'

'How horrid! Yes, it must have been.' She accepted this explanation with relief. 'There were too many for us ever to know which one. Can it be mended or anything?'

'I'm afraid not.'

'What a nuisance! Don't tell me it was worth pounds and pounds!'

'It was a good piece of glass,' said Miss MacFarren stolidly. Of her harrowed feelings she could say nothing with the maddening bunch of peonies in her hand.

'We shall have to buy you another like it, we positively must!' Her voice and face brightened considerably. 'As a matter of fact, now that I come to think of it, I've seen one almost the image of it. Yes, I'm sure I have. It was in one of those antique shops on the

Brompton Road. Shall I just take a little piece of the glass to make certain of the colour?'

Miss MacFarren hoped that she was telling the truth, yet feared she was lying. But since it was neither polite nor expedient to declare this view, she let her discuss the question of shape and colour and wrap a portion of the chalice in her handkerchief, apparently dedicating herself to the quest for its fellow as if it had been as sacred as the Holy Grail.

* * *

The affair of the Bristol chalice turned out to be of precisely the same pattern as the affair of the inkstain on the hall carpet—a pattern destined to become hideously familiar. The chalice was not referred to again by Mrs. Bankes, and when Miss MacFarren at last enquired whether she had succeeded in finding the promised replica, she reacted at first with a dazed look, visibly seeking to recall what lie she had told, then with a new lie to cover up the old one. The next time the matter was mentioned, her excuse was both transparent and impatient, implying that it was very tiresome and niggling not to forget the breakage.

A suggestion that the approximate price of the ornament should simply be added to the account was, to begin with, well received: but when she learned that it was valued in the inventory at seven guineas, she again became certain that she would be able to find a similar one, and it was to be assumed that she intended, with her flair for bargains, to try for something cheaper. She would readily have bought Miss MacFarren an expensive gift in order to win her gratitude, but merely to pay compensation for an object she had broken was too dull and unrewarding to be considered.

The prospect of having seven thankless extra guineas added to the bill had its effect, and after two or three days she sent a message asking if Miss MacFarren would mind coming to the sitting-room. Wearing an expression of conscious well-doing, brightly reflected in the admiring faces of the two friends who were with her, she presented a pair of green Bristol bottles which were meant, she explained with the shy pride of a schoolgirl making an offering to a headmistress, as a substitute for the broken chalice. She hoped Miss MacFarren would like them; they were not quite the same, it was true, but she herself had found them irresistibly pretty.

'The little serpents twining round their darling necks!' she cried, clasping her hands together. 'Aren't they celestial?' And her friends agreed they were too celestial for words.

They were indeed pretty enough, but even in mint condition, their value would have been less than that of the piece they were meant to replace; and, as one had a damaged stopper and the other was chipped, Miss MacFarren regarded them as an entirely inadequate substitute for her flawless chalice. But in the face of such complaisance and the presence of the two young friends, whose praises for Antonia's choice were unbounded, she found it very difficult to protest that she would rather have had the money. She could only resolve to propose at a suitable moment that future breakages, which threatened to be numerous, had better be settled for in the ordinary manner.

Before she left them, Antonia insisted on showing her the rest of the afternoon's purchases, for she had been on one of her blissful shopping excursions. Miss MacFarren was mystified, not for the first time, at the satisfaction it gave her to possess bibelots which were delightful in design or workmanship, but strikingly incomplete or quite painfully in want of some repair. When she was handed a Bohemian decanter without a stopper ('I'm sure to come across a stopper somewhere,' said Mrs. Bankes), an ivory miniature frame with the corner missing, and a pearl-inlaid Georgian glove-box with both hinges broken off, she could only marvel at the taste which could admire such objects and yet not mind their shabby state.

The worst of it was, more and more of these dilapidated treasures were making their appearance among the choice embellishments of 16 Harberton Square. Harriet had been mistaken in supposing that the imperfect St. Francis, the damaged gilt grottoes, were to be kept in store until they were transported to America. They had emerged in the course of time from the last of the packing-cases: St. Francis had been placed in the dining-room and the grottoes in the sitting-room, and the crate, still containing a much dreaded chandelier, had remained, with its two fellows, an ugly obstruction in the basement passage.

The boxroom was now becoming so crowded that one could barely enter the door, and to gain access to its nethermost contents—that is, Miss MacFarren's own things—would have been the work of hours. Mrs. Bankes had filled it to what seemed capacity with her trunks and portmanteaux, had then moved there any ornaments or pieces of furniture she had no use for in the rooms she occupied, and had finally squeezed in various minor items which she had promised to take care of for one or other of her visitors. For it was part of her amiable character that she never refused to do a favour, and would find room for a friend's luggage almost as readily as for a friend.

It was when Miss MacFarren discovered that engravings of Boucher subjects, foxed specimens in frames a little knocked about, had begun to figure on the walls of the first landing among her botanical prints, that she was wrought upon to the pitch of protesting, and actually found courage to address Captain Bankes. He was preparing for his return to Germany, and, through the open bedroom door on her way upstairs, she could see him packing a valise while he sang to himself in a voice so low that he sounded like a musical cat purring. Impulsively, guiltily, because she knew his wife was out, she paused and spoke to him:

'Captain Bankes, I wonder if you could convey to Mrs. Bankes without hurting her feelings' (these words emerged from her lips unexpectedly with no volition, yet it did somehow seem desirable all of a sudden not to hurt the woman's feelings) 'that there really isn't room in the house for all these extra things she keeps bringing. I mean, I didn't understand that she'd want to have her own pictures and all that.'

She realized, as the phrases shaped themselves, that she was at a great disadvantage. She must seem like a meticulous old maid who demanded that everything should be just so, and wouldn't leave her tenants to their own devices.

But with a comprehension that forestalled any explanation she could have made, he rejoined swiftly: 'I'll certainly speak to her about it this very day, Miss MacFarren. I know just how you feel, when your scheme of decoration is all flower pictures, to see these others getting mixed up with them . . .'

'Not that they aren't charming,' she interrupted. 'It's just the crowdedness . . .'

'I know. I know.' His sympathetic voice purred back at her. 'Tonia has such a tremendous enthusiasm, such a gusto, she isn't always quite practical, Miss MacFarren.'

'I can see she immensely enjoys shopping,' was all she could think of in reply to this, but she said it as if she were paying a compliment.

'A little too immensely at times. In this case, it's particularly misguided because she knows we may have to go away almost any time.'

Although she heartily liked what little she had seen of him, she heard this announcement with immeasurable relief. It might mean that she would be spared the misery of living under the same roof for a month with a tenant to whom she had given notice.

'Do you think it will be sooner than you expected?' She tried to repress the eagerness of her tone and succeeded so much too well that he hastened to reassure her:

'Oh no, no. Miss MacFarren, don't get me wrong! We love it here.' He launched fairly out on one of his earnest speeches. 'As far as a man can be happy away from his own country, I'm as happy as a clam right here in this house. I hate like the devil to leave. And as for Tonia—why she's just like a kid with a fine new doll's house. But a journalist never can tell where he may have to go next, so I shall warn her to stop accumulating all these things you mention.'

'You won't make her feel uncomfortable about it, Captain Bankes?' She admitted to herself now that what she really meant was: 'You'll gloss over the fact that I came and complained behind her back to you?'

He understood. 'I'll simply tell her—from me, not from you— that the doll's house is full to the brim and she's got to lay off the shopping.'

He had taken it marvellously, and it had this much effect, that no new purchases had been made for two or three weeks. Then resolution had weakened, and the search for a green Bristol chalice had revived the mania. Now Captain Bankes had been gone a month, and everything was worse than before his arrival.

Female friends ran in and out of the house at all hours of the day, and slept there almost every night; accompanying males frequently had a bed made up on the sofa. The convenience of the situation, in Westminster, a few minutes from Victoria Station, Mrs. Bankes's complaisance, the desperate shortage of social amenities in London at the time—all these causes combined to swell the already considerable number of people who very frankly made use of the house. They called to leave luggage or parcels on a day up from the country, they arrived with sponge-bags for a hot bath when their own supplies of boiler fuel were running low, they dropped in for a casual meal, the restaurants being so crowded and Mrs. Bankes so happy to share out her rations or anybody else's. Mrs. Bankes loved all this coming and going. It made her feel important, it gave tangible proof of the charm and popularity which were her chief vanity.

To Miss MacFarren it was a torment that increased with the end of the summer. In the warm weather, she had been able to retreat into her little garden; though even here the busy telephone bell had haunted her. But now it was too cold to sit long in the open air, and she had nowhere to write or draw but the study, where she was conscious perpetually of the movements in the house and obliged to hear all the jodellings, the snatches of talk and laughter on the stairs, the telephone conversations in the hall. These disturbances interfered sadly with the work which had always been the source of her serenity and self-respect: and still more precious time was lost through the hopeless breakdown of the arrangement with Mrs. Manders.

The Manders situation was indeed deteriorating visibly from day to day. Against the ever-oncoming tide of entertainments, the structure of ordinary domestic routine had completely crumbled. Alternately harassed and cajoled, ill-used and petted, Mrs. Manders had become a creature of confusion, oscillating between indignation and weak surrender. She knew the kitchen was only superficially clean, the cupboards full of dust and untidiness, she knew the upper rooms were never turned out, and that Miss MacFarren was getting, as she called it, a dirty deal. She grumbled but never found strength of mind to resist the flattering familiarities, the bustle, the lively chatter that went on in the kitchen between Mrs. Bankes and her friends when they came down to help with party preparations, or in the dining-room when she served them.

Although Miss MacFarren was entitled to an equal share of the kitchen, she had always thought it tactful to appear there as little as possible. In consequence it had gradually become recognized as Mrs. Bankes's terrain, and the fact that it was constantly in use for her occasions of hospitality made Miss MacFarren feel like an intruder when she came in to wash her dishes, to take something from her store cupboard, or to cook a meal beyond the simple resources available in the study. It was largely her own fault, she realized, for having been over-courteous in the first place, but it was too late to retrace her misguided steps, and her sensitiveness drove her often to the expedient of going out to lunch or dinner rather than interrupt the gaiety of Mrs. Bankes and her visitors in the basement. This extravagance served to cancel out much of the relief she had hoped to gain from halving her domestic expenses.

Yet she had not given the intended notice on the 1st of October. She had been about to do so—had even drafted, after sleepless nights, a suitably implacable communication—when a letter had arrived for her from Captain Bankes in Germany. As if he had been a guest rather than a tenant, he had written her a bread-and-butter letter. In terms of cordial politeness he thanked her for her kindness to himself, and particularly for all that she had done to make his wife comfortable and happy in her beautiful surroundings which so many of their London friends had envied them. He felt, he assured her, that he now had a home in England. He was looking forward inexpressibly to his next visit, which might be sooner than he had foreseen.

With a heavy sigh, Miss MacFarren had resigned herself to bear her bondage in silence for another month. After all, perhaps they would have to go back to America suddenly, and then she would be glad to have ended the relationship without open unpleasantness.

6

THE DAY on which Miss MacFarren decided she could no longer conceal her injuries from Harriet was rather an eventful one. It began with disagreeableness. She had slept badly, as she so often did nowadays, and had awakened with a headache and a kind of dyspepsia that recalled an occasion when she had attended a banquet with her brother and drunk too much wine. Was it possible, she asked herself bleakly, that she had a hangover?

Although she really hated the taste of whisky, she had got into the habit lately of making herself drowsy with one or two substantial tots when the house was noisy, or when anxiety and irritation sent her thoughts racing round in her head like desperate caged squirrels. Whisky had proved as efficacious as rum in relaxing her nerves, and last night she had helped herself more liberally than usual, being kept awake by the late arrival of some unseen person who had missed his last train and come to claim a bed. There had been loud whispering and giggling on the landing below as Mrs. Bankes and Mrs. Jermyn, the guest who was already in possession of the spare room, had sought in the linen closet for the blankets to make up a bed on the couch; and in the certainty that her brocade cushions would be used as bed-pillows she had found herself angrily pouring a large extra tot.

She felt ashamed of herself in the morning, restoring the half-empty flask to the medicine cabinet, dosing herself with aspirin and bicarbonate of soda. It was in vain to assure herself that ladies of fifty who have been temperate all their lives need not be afraid of suddenly becoming drunkards; the sense of sin prevailed and was greatly strengthened by indigestion.

Then, when she came back from her bi-weekly wait in the shopping queues, she found that one of her Gallé cats was quite insanely being used as a door-stop. Seeing Mrs. Bankes in the sitting-room arranging flowers, and for once alone, she spoke to her immediately with unaccustomed sharpness.

'Mrs. Bankes, if you need a door-stop, I dare say we can find something suitable. This cat is far too fragile . . . I must ask you to be more careful with it.'

'Dear me, did *I* put it there?' Mrs. Bankes looked amiably stupid. 'I only meant it to be there for half a second, just while I'm running in and out with the flower-vases. Oh, Miss MacFarren, while I think of it, look at the lovely present that arrived from Sweden this morning! Please do have some!'

In a palpable attempt to create a diversion, she produced a box of chocolates. A child could not have been more simple, but nevertheless the ruse succeeded. In the face of so much good humour, one could not persist in reproaches about the cat. Unless one had deliberately wished to appear boorish, there was nothing to do but admire and refuse the proffered chocolates with politeness. It was always like this whenever she tried to complain about anything. The tricks for distracting her were transparent but infallible.

Pressed eagerly to help herself, she could only retreat, hugging her smiling cat. But before she had reached the door, something caught her eye which stopped her dead and, chocolates or no chocolates, drew from her lips a protesting exclamation. In the Victorian birdcage, which had been moved from the hall only a day or two ago, four brilliant jewel-like budgerigars, two green, two crimson, darted and pecked with the nervous, frustrated movements which had always made the sight of caged birds detestable to her.

'Mrs. Bankes,' she cried, 'you said you wouldn't!'

'Wouldn't what?'

'Keep birds in that cage.'

'Did I say that? Good heavens! Why shouldn't I keep some birdies if I want to?' The tone was brisk and cheerful, the smile baffling.

'I thought you agreed with me that it was—well, cruel, really.'

'Oh, it can't be cruel when they're born and brought up like this.'

'But the idea of winged creatures bred in cages is cruel in itself. Anyhow, it isn't always true. I know that before the war tens of thousands of birds were captured and imported every year.'

'Well, that's ages and ages ago.' Mrs. Bankes's smile now had a glassy quality by reason of a certain cold light in her eyes, but Miss MacFarren was sufficiently moved to persist:

'In any case, that cage looks too small for four birds, Mrs. Bankes, honestly it does!'

'I'm going to buy another in a day or two. Then I can keep the little green pets in this and put the red ones in the other.'

Though Miss MacFarren placed scant faith in this assurance, she could say no more. She knew it would seem the sheerest interference, if reported, that she had tried to prevent her tenant from keeping four budgerigars. She had put herself in the wrong as a landlady, whatever her position as a humanitarian.

But at the recollection of the woman's utter insincerity when she had first brought the cage into the house, she resolved to go and see Harriet that very afternoon—to pour her woes at last into the ear that certainly deserved to receive them. She had been able to avoid Harriet during the past weeks without any apparent coolness because her friend had celebrated the demobilization of her best assistant by going to Bath to have her rheumatism treated. Miss MacFarren had written her an affectionate letter in which she had not referred to the Bankeses, except to mention facetiously that Antonia's husband had surpassed expectations. Now she was back at Greenway's, and Miss MacFarren planned to drop in towards closing time and explain all her sufferings over a cup of tea in the cosy back room.

The October afternoon was fine, and she set out to walk until she had chilled her hot temper; for even at the moment of her leaving the house, there had been another annoyance. On the way out, she had glanced back into the hall and had been startled and dismayed to see the faience cat again in use as a stop to hold open the sitting-room door. She had hesitated a moment, with one foot on the doorstep, then, determined upon a pointed gesture of rebuke, had approached the sitting-room to remove the cat in full view of the occupants.

Standing on a ladder, taking down a picture from above the mantlepiece, was Mrs. Bankes's friend, Mrs. Jermyn, while Mrs. Bankes knotted the cord to hang an oil-painting. Mrs. Jermyn could be heard speaking in the harsh assertive voice which was her salient characteristic:

'My dear boob, surely you know that sort of woman is always goofy about animals? It's a sort of thwarted maternal complex.'

Miss MacFarren paused, wondering whether to retire while she was still unseen or to persist in her rebuking gesture, thereby inflicting a double embarrassment. They must have heard the front door open and close and thought her gone out.

'But, Penny darling,' cried Mrs. Bankes, 'I'm goofy about animals myself. Why should she think I'd be unkind to my poppets, my little love-birds?'

'The cage *is* a bit on the small side, Tonia. If I were you I shouldn't have bought four. Of course—'

She turned to hand down the picture and saw Miss MacFarren in the act of lifting the Gallé cat. As her voice came to a dead stop, Mrs. Bankes turned too, and Miss MacFarren said smoothly:

'I really should be very much obliged if you'd hold the door open with something else, Mrs. Bankes. I'm awfully fond of these cats.'

Mrs. Bankes's face slackened and drooped for an instant—her 'found out' face which Miss MacFarren was beginning to know so well. Then she exclaimed, 'Have I done it again? I must be mad!'

'What harm does it do?' Penny demanded scornfully.

'It's much too light to be a door-stop. It'll break quite easily if there's a gust of wind.'

'Yes, it might, you know, Penny,' said Mrs. Bankes in her propitiating way. 'I was just going to leave it there a single moment while we were carrying pictures to and fro. Don't you think this is a dream, Miss MacFarren? I mean, isn't it the most delicious nightmare?'

She held up the oil-painting, which was apparently about to be substituted for two of the prints from the Temple of Flora. It was a work of such comical ineptitude that, if Miss MacFarren had been in a better humour and had not seen it about to go up on her own wall, it would have given her, in some degree, the same sort of amusement that Mrs. Bankes and Penny derived from it. As it was, she stared at it with a shocked look that prompted Mrs. Jermyn to giggle.

Painted with meticulous care and yet excruciating incapacity, it represented a wedding-group in the costume of the mid-twenties standing in front of an herbaceous border and a brick wall, at the end of which a shiny motorcar waited. Colour, composition, style, and subject, all were equally outrageous. It was a masterpiece of badness, revealing a want of taste and talent so complete as to make it marvellous that the perpetrator could have deceived himself, or been deceived by anybody else, long enough to finish his appointed task.

'Good heavens!' said Miss MacFarren. 'How did you come by such a thing?'

'It's a present from Mr. and Mrs. Jermyn. Isn't it sheer heaven?'

'We found it at the back of a little furniture shop in Islington. We couldn't wait to get hold of it.'

'They paid eight pounds for it,' Mrs. Bankes put in. 'Weren't they generous and good?'

'You actually *bought* it for eight pounds?'

'Yes we couldn't have resisted it at any price, knowing how much Tonia would love it. It's signed—do you see?—Ed. Tomkins.

Do you think he painted it from the wedding photograph? I can't quite decide whether the bridegroom did it himself on their honeymoon at Bognor, or whether it was done by the bride's dear old dad to hang in the best parlour.'

'You make it sound very pathetic,' said Miss MacFarren, who knew that was not Mrs. Jermyn's intention. 'Surely you don't intend to hang it?' She was genuinely bewildered.

'Oh, we must, we must!' Mrs. Bankes set down the gilt frame so that she might stand with her hands in a praying attitude. 'It's such pure bliss! And it's quite proper, not like the Boucher pictures you didn't care for.'

Miss MacFarren intercepted a sly smile from Penny. 'I didn't think your Boucher pictures in the least improper,' she declared with affronted surprise. 'It was simply that the wall was too crowded.'

'That's why we've taken them down, these flower prints. They'll be absolutely safe in the box-room.'

'I'll find a place for them in my study,' said Miss MacFarren shortly, and picking them up, she carried them from the room at once. She was not entitled, she supposed, to object to any mural adornment Mrs. Bankes might care to introduce into her own sitting-room, and certainly, in the circumstances, she could not make a protest in front of Mrs. Jermyn. But words could not have told what she felt about the taste that could reject the exquisite roses, the noble carnations, in favour of a pitiful joke. And this Goth, who used the choicest French pottery cats as doorstops, this Vandal who could spoil the entire decoration of a wall to raise a *chi-chi* laugh—it was she whose tender care for the house had been guaranteed by Harriet!

The thing exasperated her to such an extent that she had walked quite a distance before she recollected what she had overheard about her thwarted maternal feeling for animals. 'That sort of woman' . . . naturally, it meant a woman of fifty who had never married. Stupid, grinning creature with her mocking generalizations! As a matter of fact, though she had a horror of cruelty, Miss MacFarren was not particularly emotional about animals. It had always been a secret mortification that she could not feel as ardent an affection for dogs as her younger brother and most of her friends. She had found it a strain very often to admire other people's pets, even the splendid wolf-hounds whose exercise in the park drew Harriet from her bed at seven every morning. She liked cats—she would go as far as to say she loved cats; yet she was not certain but that they were preferable in china or faience.

By a slight but pleasing coincidence, as she speculated upon this notion, she saw in a shop window a pair of bright blue-green Chinese cats, nearly life-size, with stern thoughtful faces and heads poised, haughtily alert. She gazed at them for some moments, wondering whether she should submit herself to the temptation of asking their price: there was something in the grim detachment of their bearing which she found congenial. Then, telling herself that this was no time for extravagances, she turned firmly away.

'Hullo, it's Mory's aunt, isn't it?' said a girl who had stopped beside her, and whom she found herself facing through the suddenness of her movement. She recognized at once the sweet, round face, the soft contours, of her nephew's friend who had had tea with her in the garden.

'Oh, how do you do, Miss—' Her voice hovered on the edge of some pool of memory where the name was submerged.

'Maxine Albert.'

'Of course. I'm not as good at remembering names as I used to be.'

'I never remember anything except faces,' said Maxine. 'Are you admiring the same thing as I am?'

'The Chinese cats. Aren't they enchanting?'

'They're quaint, but I wouldn't go for them in a big way. What I'd like is that dainty dish over there.'

Miss MacFarren followed the direction of her pointing finger, expecting to see something in the nature of a porcelain dish, but it seemed that the favoured object was a superb set of aquamarines in a faded blue velvet box.

'Very charming,' she said, remotely at first, since jewellery was not in her line. Then her keen eye for beauty, as well as her desire to be pleasant to an associate of Mory's, made her add: 'They'd look lovely on you, Miss Albert. They're exactly right for you, if I may say so.'

'You telling me?' said Maxine with that genial insolence which Miss MacFarren had noted at their earlier encounter. 'The question is how much wrong do I have to do to get them?' The dimples appeared in her cheeks.

'Have you asked the price?' Miss MacFarren enquired with grave interest. She could picture so clearly the pale stones glittering against that fresh white skin.

'I daren't.'

'No? And I daren't ask about those delightful cats. You see, I already have two frivolous cats that smile. Now I'm beginning to hanker after two serious cats that frown.'

'You could use them to let people know how you were feeling. These on your mantelpiece would mean you were taking a pretty lousy view of things.'

'I ought to have them now,' said Miss MacFarren.

'Is that how it is? And you with fifteen bottles of whisky!'

Miss MacFarren laughed quite heartily. She did not find Miss Albert's social manner nearly as impossible as she had deemed it on first acquaintance. She realized that she was being dealt with on the footing of an equal, and this from a person as free from any sense of inferiority as Miss Albert was flattering. Mrs. Bankes's friends hardly ever treated her as an equal because to them she was either a landlady or an elderly spinster who would be shocked by a couple of Boucher mezzotints. She had noticed that they were inclined to address her with that mixture of superficial respect and subtle impertinence which children at an awkward age will offer to a school-teacher. This afternoon she was disposed to enjoy a contrast.

'Didn't I mention,' she dared to ask provocatively, 'that I have several dozen of wine and brandy as well?'

'No, you kept that from me. Saving them up for Mory, I suppose. . . . Have you seen anything of Master Mory lately?'

'No, he's been away on location, or whatever they call it.'

'Oh yes, I forgot—in Madeira, lucky beggar!'

'Did you have any luck, Miss Albert—-with that film test you mentioned?'

'I was given a mingy little contract.' There was the infantine pout which Miss MacFarren so well remembered.

'Look where it's got me! Waiting in the street for Pio Martinez's blasted brat!'

'Oh, are you waiting for someone?' She suffered a slight twinge of disappointment. It had been rather gratifying to believe that the pause for conversation had been from choice.

'Hanging about like a dog on a chain! What do you think can have happened to the little'—she checked herself with her cherubic lips pursed, and then said mildly, 'beast?'

'Why, where is he supposed to be?' Miss MacFarren asked with concern.

'It's a she, a dear innocent wee girlie.' She pronounced the words with a gentle yet biting emphasis. 'I promised to take her into the park to see the damn ducks and things. Before she'd been with me ten minutes, she'd somehow got my coupons and half a crown out of me and rushed off to buy sweets. And here I am waiting, being tempted by blasted aquamarines.'

'Do you know which shop she went to?'

'She said "just round the corner". She's nine years old, so I told her, as long as she didn't have to cross the road—Oh, here she is, the little scourge!'

On the other side of the street, a child approached with a leisurely hopping and skipping step, waved her hand gaily on seeing Miss Albert, and called out: 'Maxie! I'm going to cross the road carefully, Maxie!'

'You'd better!' shouted Miss Albert, and watched her with baleful anxiety until she stood beside them on the pavement. Then, somewhat languidly, she scolded: 'You know perfectly well, Juanita, I told you not to cross the road at all.'

'But the shop round the corner was a nasty shop. It had no chocolates and you wanted me to have chocolates, didn't you, Maxie?' She took Maxine's hand and gazed up into her face with a smile calculated to melt the heart.

'Well, we'd better get along to the park,' said Maxine, apparently unmelted. 'You coming our way, Miss MacFarren?'

Miss MacFarren replied truthfully that she was, and they set off together, Juanita nestling her head tenderly against the sleeve of Maxine's fur coat. She was a pretty child with curly, nut-brown hair, dark lively eyes, and a smile of confiding charm. The affectionate openness of her manner was unusual in a girl of her age. Indeed, none of the gaucheries common to the nine-year-old seemed to have afflicted her, and she chattered as freely in front of the elderly stranger as if she had been alone with Maxine.

'We must keep the chocolates till we get into the park, mustn't we, Maxie?'

'How many have you had already?' Maxine demanded with what seemed an unnecessary surliness.

'I didn't have any, because we've got to keep them till we get to the park.'

'Then why have you got chocolate on your mouth, you little fibber?'

If Juanita was confused it was for the briefest instant. 'I only *tasted* one,' she said with a laughing glance which suggested that the other could take her seriously or not, just as she pleased, 'because I wanted to know which were the violet creams that you like. Then you won't have to eat the hard ones that you *don't* like.'

'Very helpful,' said Maxine.

'They're nearly all hard ones,' Juanita continued with another oblique glance. 'Wasn't it naughty of him to put in so many of the ones you don't like?'

'There are days when little Angel-face gets me down,' was Maxine's only reply. Juanita, unabashed, nuzzled her head more deeply into the lynx fur of Maxine's sleeve.

'You like violet creams and my daddy says you have violet eyes,' she remarked softly.

Maxine raised her eyebrows and was silent.

Juanita turned to Miss MacFarren. 'How many pounds of chocolates do you have to eat before you burst?'

'I never heard of anyone bursting from eating anything.' She believed in answering children's questions accurately. 'Of course, we can eat enough to be thoroughly uncomfortable.'

'How many pounds of chocolates make you uncomfortable?'

'It depends on your appetite. Some people can eat more than others.'

'I can eat more than anybody,' said Juanita with conviction. 'I bet you I can eat a hundred and ninety pounds of chocolates.'

'Oh, surely not!'

'She can if anybody can,' said Maxine. 'She cadges everyone's ration cards at the studio, don't you, little Snow-White?'

'I even got yours, didn't I, Maxie?'

Maxine looked down at her with a rather grim expression, and when she broke away from them in the park and ran towards the lake, remarked severely: 'Did you ever see such a spoiled little cuss in your life?'

'I should call her a very attractive little girl,' returned Miss MacFarren, who had been a trifle shocked by what seemed almost a hostile attitude on Maxine's part.

'And, my God! doesn't she know it? I'm going to talk to her father about her, if I never get another contract. He's so proud of the kid, he keeps bringing her to the studio and showing her off and letting everybody make a pet of her. It's the worst thing that could happen to a child of that temperament.'

'Does her mother allow it?'

'Her mother's divorced. She was the empress of all the dumb blondes, and she ran away with a coloured drummer of twenty-two—which was a lot of nonsense at her age. It gave poor Pio a hell of a jolt.'

'I'm not surprised,' said Miss MacFarren, who felt slightly jolted herself.

'Though, I must say, Pio had been asking for it. Anyone who gets mixed up with Geraldine Mace ought to know he has trouble coming to him.'

'Geraldine Mace? Isn't that—' She hesitated, trying to find discreet words for the question. 'Isn't that a friend of my nephew's?'

'A friend? Well, I suppose you could call it a friend. I wonder how soon she'll be wearing his teeth on a necklace.'

'Oh dear, you mean she's mercenary?'

'No, she's just a Queen B. I needn't tell you what the B stands for. It's her husband who's mercenary.'

'Unfortunately he's suing my nephew for damages,' Miss MacFarren ventured, seeing that Maxine was so very evidently in the know.

'Laughable, isn't it, when she's had at least three affairs, including Pio Martinez, that were everybody's business—not counting before she was married.'

'Does Mory know that?'

'If he does, he can't exactly get up and tell the judge so.'

'No, not as he's'—she brought it out boldly—'living with her.'

'She's the woman he loves,' Maxine rejoined on an ironical inflection, 'so he'll just have to take what he gets. Which is to say, Stevie Mace will take what *he* gets.'

'Oh, Miss Albert, how can he love such a woman?'

'He won't by the time this case is over.'

If the subject had not been so depressing Miss MacFarren might have smiled to think of herself feeling quite callow and unsophisticated compared with a baby-faced girl who could not be more than half her age. As it was, though she did not smile, she could appreciate the unusual experience of being able to discuss her nephew's situation with an acquaintance in his own world. It was astonishing how much, and by what natural steps, she had advanced in intimacy in a few minutes with a person whom she had considered fundamentally uncongenial.

They had been pacing, in order to keep warm, along one of the pathways near the lake, but suddenly Maxine darted forward, drawn to the lakeside by a series of frightful squawks. Juanita had succeeded in luring one of the almost tame ducks to the bank and catching it by the neck, and was endeavouring, while the unlucky bird struggled and shrieked, to put something into its mouth.

'You leave that poor duck alone!' cried Maxine. 'At once—do you hear me?'

'I'm only trying to give it a chocolate.' Juanita relinquished the victim with an injured look.

'You were trying to force chocolate down its throat, scaring it out of its wits, you little devil!'

Juanita's eyes filled with tears. 'I only did it for its own good,' she wailed. 'Just to give it a treat, horrible ungrateful duck!'

Maxine was melted now and bent down to put her arms round the child. 'All right, lovey! You didn't mean to be cruel, but another time just remember that birds don't like to be held by the neck any more than you would. You'd better go and ask it to forgive you.'

'It's flown away. Duck, duck!' she called across the lake. 'I'm sorry, duck!'

'Next time we must bring some bread and cake,' said Maxine.

'Do you live near her, Miss Albert?'

'Not far. I've got a flat in Herrick Mews. . . . Only till January, worse luck. I suppose you haven't heard of anyone with a flat to let, Miss MacFarren?'

'I'm afraid not.'

'No, I always know it's going to be hopeless, but I just ask everybody. Would you believe I've been to more than twenty house agents without being offered anything as cosy as a dog kennel?'

'I realize it's quite appalling,' said Miss MacFarren gloomily. She had been brought back to the miserable fact that, if she was ultimately forced to give Mrs. Bankes notice, the wretched woman would probably have nowhere to go.

For the moment, however, Mory's difficulties took precedence over her own, and she sought for a way of returning the conversation to its previous channel. It seemed so monstrous that he should be liable to pay for depriving a disgraceful husband of a scandalous wife. She knew that a maiden aunt, no matter how benign, who enquires too closely into the amatory affairs of her family lays her motives open to misinterpretation: yet Maxine, despite her cynical mode of speech, gave a strong impression of good-natured understanding.

But before she could frame an appropriate question, Maxine, in the middle of forcefully condemning everyone connected with the housing problem, dashed away again. Juanita was seen to be lying at full length on the ground beside the lake, dabbling her hand in the water.

'Enough of that!' Maxine commanded sternly, dragging her up by the coat collar. 'Look what you've done to your clean clothes, you little monster!'

'I dropped my hankie in the water,' said Juanita without ill feeling, 'and now it's gone. Would you like a violet cream, Maxie?'

'You must offer them to this lady first.' Maxine's baffled tone reminded Miss MacFarren of her own exasperation this morning when Mrs. Bankes likewise had produced chocolates as a red herring.

'No thank you,' she said as the paper bag was obediently tendered. 'Brush down your coat, my dear, before it gets marked.'

'O-oh yes, I must, I must! Hold these, Maxie!' Having disposed of the bag of sweets, she began to brush her coat with her hands in quite a vigorous and enthusiastic manner. 'Daddy bought me this coat, and it cost lots of coupons and money. He chose it himself.'

'It's a very nice coat,' said Miss MacFarren. 'He must be clever at choosing.'

'He's the cleverest man in the whole world,' she replied with a certain detachment, as one who states a self-evident proposition. 'When I grow up I'm going to give him a million pounds.'

'You'll have to be very, very rich to do that.'

'I shall be rich. My daddy's going to make me into a great big film star. My name will be six feet high.'

'Juanita!' Maxine protested. 'I'm sure your father never said anything of the sort. He doesn't want you to go into pictures.'

'He will when I'm grown up. I bet you a million pounds!'

'You'd better stop throwing your money about,' said Maxine, and her sulky face looked hardly older than Juanita's.

'My daddy's a Spaniard,' Juanita informed Miss MacFarren pleasantly, as if she had heard no reproach. 'Doesn't it sound funny—like spaniel? My daddy's a spaniel, a beautiful soft silky spaniel. I'm going to pull his ears.' Laughing delightedly, she seized the bag of chocolates from Maxine with an abstracted gesture and danced away down the lakeside path.

Miss MacFarren recollected that, unless she hurried, she would not reach Greenway's till after closing time and might find Harriet gone. This unlooked-for meeting had rather served to change her mood and divert her thoughts from her domestic irritations, but she had set out to unbosom herself and knew that, until she had done so, her relations with Harriet must remain a mere façade. She took leave of Miss Albert in an especially cordial manner—even going so far as to write down her address in case she should chance to hear of some suitable accommodation for her—and hastening from St. James's Park into Green Park, took a taxi in Piccadilly.

The shop was still open when she arrived in Wigmore Street, and Harriet could be seen through the glass door, spinning an astronomical globe on its axis while she talked to her assistant. But having entered, Miss MacFarren would have been glad to retreat unobserved, for Harriet was saying: 'I can't help you, Mr. Davis. I must leave by ten past five if I'm to get a seat on the five-forty.'

Of all the boring and tiresome situations! In her blind drive to relieve her feelings, it had simply never occurred to her that Harriet might not be sitting cosily waiting to give her tea in the back room. Her wish-fulfilling imagination had conjured up the whole interview under the most favourable conditions. Now, as Harriet turned and greeted her with the somewhat harassed enthusiasm of one who has a train to catch, she had to decide hastily between two unsatisfactory alternatives—either to pretend she had dropped in casually, exchange a few friendly words and go with her story untold, or else to tell it against time at an unwelcome moment.

As it happened, though she chose the former, she found herself clumsily, tactlessly, doing the latter. She had not the presence of mind to sidestep when Harriet, having taken her into the private room, proceeded to congratulate her on the success of the arrangement with Mrs. Bankes. With a heavy indignation which had been far from her intention she responded that the arrangement was, on the contrary, a total failure.

'But it can't be!' Harriet exclaimed, incredulous. 'Antonia was in here only yesterday. She said it was the most tremendous success.'

'Well, it isn't.' Miss MacFarren was startled into ungraciousness. 'At any rate, not from my point of view.' And she began, chaotically, to pour out grievances.

Harriet listened while she put on her outdoor clothes, apologizing for being in a hurry. She had to go, she explained, to see a country client who had given her the first refusal of some valuable furniture: she dared not miss the train because there would be a car waiting for her at the other end. Nevertheless she was curious to hear the story through, and begged Miss MacFarren to accompany her in the taxi to King's Cross.

In these circumstances a tale of woes emerged that sounded, even to the narrator's ears, extraordinarily confused and unconvincing. Mrs. Bankes was careless with the ornaments; she—or one of her guests—had broken a Bristol chalice and hidden the pieces in the dustbin. ('I should think that was the natural place to put them!' said Harriet tartly.) She had four budgerigars in a cage that was too small for them. ('The cage she bought from me, I presume,' Harriet interposed, as if she had been affronted.) She never gave Mrs. Manders a proper chance of doing the cleaning. Her friends overran the house, constantly occupied the spare room, and even slept on the sofa. She had hung an appalling oil-painting in the sitting-room.

'She probably has no idea,' said Harriet with a distinct coldness, 'that you like to keep the rooms "just so" even when you no longer occupy them. Very few people are as fastidious as you, Elinor.'

'I don't like the couch being used as a bed. Who would?'

'Have you said so to Antonia?'

'No, it's so difficult. She's never alone, and I hate to be the sort of landlady who keeps complaining.'

'Well, if you don't let her know, she can hardly be expected to read your thoughts.'

'It's much harder to complain than you imagine, if you're living in the same house and have to keep meeting the person afterwards. And I couldn't foresee that she was simply going to annex the spare room.'

'Isn't it possible that you didn't make your wishes clear about that?'

'I said quite definitely that we were to share it. She could have her visitors; I could have mine.'

'But have you *tried* to have any visitors?' Harriet asked with audible exasperation. 'Surely if she knew you wanted to use the room . . .'

Miss MacFarren was obliged to confess that she hadn't actually needed the room: her friends outside London lived chiefly in Scotland and the Hebrides and seldom came south under the present hardships of travelling. This admission seemed to weaken her case so much that she pressed on with another grievance and forgot till it was too late to make the important point that Mrs. Bankes, without consulting her, had extended the scope of the spare room with an extra bed.

'My dear Elinor,' said Harriet, sighing with impatience as she heard the discovery of the inkstain on the hall carpet, 'I feel for you—it's the kind of thing that's extremely annoying to a house-proud woman, as you are. But you're not suggesting that she did it on purpose? I'm afraid whenever one lets a furnished house, a certain number of accidents will happen, however careful the tenant—'

'She is *not* a careful tenant,' Miss MacFarren declared with a warmth that was almost quarrelsome. 'I don't know how she hypnotized you into believing she was careful.' She drew in her breath. Nothing could antagonize Harriet more certainly than this flat contradiction of what she had so particularly claimed for her protégée; and antagonism was the last emotion she had desired to rouse. On the contrary, she was seeking her friend's support and sympathy, and she had known quite well that these could only be won by avoiding the least hint of recrimination.

Changing her note for something softer and more conciliatory, she went on: 'Harriet my dear, if only you could see the way she handles things!'

'I've seen her time and again in my own shop.'

'She's on her best behaviour with you. You have an awe-inspiring effect on people.'

Mollified a little by this flattering suggestion, Harriet rejoined with less acerbity: 'As a matter of fact, it's you who has the awe-inspiring effect. I didn't intend to repeat this to you, but when she called on me yesterday, she told me that, though she liked you immensely, you had a way of making her feel nervous. She mentioned quite frankly that there had been breakages and that they were due to nerves. She spoke of you with so much respect, in such a really nice-natured tone, I made sure that everything had turned out beautifully.'

Miss MacFarren, for her part, was not mollified. It placed her at a hideous disadvantage to have been praised with sweet nature by the person whom she had made the subject of bitter complaint. She recognized what she had now come to know as 'Mrs. Bankes's method', the method which was always ready with a little gift, a pleasant word, to dispel any cloud of criticism which might be seen gathering.

Her anger rose in a fresh gust. 'All that's pure soft soap. She doesn't mean a word she says.'

'Elinor, aren't you being rather unfair?'

'I tell you, Harriet, she's a thoroughly untruthful woman. I could give you a dozen examples—'

'Are you sure it doesn't seem so because you're just a shade inclined to be literal-minded, my dear? She has a way of talking—I've noticed it myself—that seems wild and extravagant until you realize it's not meant to be taken seriously.'

'She said she couldn't bear to see "dicky-birds" in cages. Wasn't I meant to take that seriously?'

'Oh come, why make a mountain out of a molehill? The cage was so pretty, she probably couldn't resist using it when she saw the little love-birds for sale. One can be over-squeamish.'

Miss MacFarren could not help thinking that if Greenway's had chanced to sell an ornamental rack or thumbscrew, Harriet would manage to persuade herself that it was a harmless and appealing instrument, so great was her loyalty to her stock.

'I can see I've failed to convey the least notion of what Mrs. Bankes is really like to live with,' she announced dismally after a brief silence. 'I was foolish to try and tell you anything about it in this flurried sort of way.'

Harriet evidently realized that her doubts had been too freely shown, for she responded in an attempt to right herself; 'Well, of course, you've seen her at closer quarters than I have, and I know that people are not always the same at close quarters.' But there was no conviction in her voice.

This discussion, so nearly a dispute, had taken place on the drive to King's Cross, punctuated, as it were, by green and red signals. Now they were turning in to the station.

'Won't you come to the platform with me? There's just time to get a few more grumbles off your chest,' said Harriet, and though she spoke good-humouredly, her choice of words so clearly expressed her scepticism that Miss MacFarren positively trembled with resentment.

'No, I shall keep this taxi,' she answered brusquely.

'Right! Let's meet again next week. I'll ring you up.' The taxi drew to a standstill, and Harriet paused with her fingers on the door handle. 'Oh, I forgot to tell you, she said her husband had taken an enormous fancy to you. I *am* so sorry you don't like them.'

'I have nothing against him at all,' Miss MacFarren retorted, 'except that he can tolerate such a woman.'

She sat bolt upright, her cheeks burning, partly from resentment of Harriet's attitude, partly from the coals of fire that Captain Bankes always succeeded in heaping upon her, even from a distance.

She believed it was true that he had liked her, and the thought of his pained surprise, when he learned what a fiasco the whole experiment had been, never failed to embarrass her acutely.

Harriet alighted and drew from her handbag with her gnarled red hand a tasselled purse of blue and silver beads that might have contained the small change of a Jane Austen heroine. She paid the driver, informed him that the lady inside wished to keep the cab, and disappeared into the crowd with a cursory gesture of farewell. As she did so, a man with a portfolio ran forward waving to the taxi to wait for him, and Miss MacFarren, leaning through the open door to name her destination, recognized the bearded face and stocky figure of her great rival, Professor Wilmot.

The driver shook his head and jerked his thumb over his shoulder, indicating his passenger, and Dr. Wilmot's eyes, under their black brows, flashed into hers the hostile glance that is commonly bestowed on those who have possessed themselves of the only taxi in sight.

'I thought you were getting out,' he explained in the fluty, mandarin voice which always seemed so out of keeping with his rugged face and the raven beard streaked with grey. Then, suddenly fixing her identity, he added: 'Oh, it's Miss MacFarren! Good evening!' He touched his hat and endeavoured to look more amiable.

'Can I give you a lift?' said Miss MacFarren impulsively. The unpleasantness with Harriet had awakened a disposition to be kind to anyone else.

'Thank you. I should be much obliged. Taxis are scarce at this station. Which way are you going?'

'To Harberton Square.'

'You'd better drop me first then.' And telling the driver to go to King Charles Mansions, he jumped in beside her with considerable agility for a man who must be, as she remembered, nearer sixty than fifty.

'We haven't met for a long while,' he remarked with increasing geniality. 'Not since I came too late to bid against you for those Darien plates at Hodgson's.'

'That was a piece of luck for me,' she acknowledged.

'And for me, though I didn't know it at the time. I've just acquired the whole series in mint condition at a lower price than you paid for your rather imperfect lot.'

His eyes gleamed with triumph as he fondled his portfolio, but she was not in the mood to be browbeaten.

'I congratulate you,' she said graciously. 'Curiously enough, when my nephew was over in Paris some months ago, he bought me three of the originals.'

'What, Darien originals?'

'Yes, in pristine—absolutely pristine state.'

'Indeed!' His heavy brows could be seen beetling. 'Are you sure they're authentic? Such things are often forged in France.'

'It would hardly have been worth anyone's while to forge these at the price my nephew paid for them.'

'Cheap, were they?'

'A few pounds of coffee and five hundred cigarettes. You must come and see them. You'll find it interesting to compare them with your engravings.'

'I should very much like to see them,' said the professor with only a faint balefulness. 'We ought really to meet and compare items from time to time. I have several new little acquisitions I'd like to show you.'

'We might exchange duplicates like stamp collectors,' said Miss MacFarren.

'Since you last saw my collection,' he continued purposefully, 'I've enriched it with some herbals which I fancy even yours can't outshine. I'm prepared to say that my *Theatrum Botanicum* must be the finest copy in private hands—or perhaps anywhere.'

The wave of anger and humiliation which surged over her deepened the glow in her cheeks. Then she recollected that, in selling the herbals, she had withheld her name from Sotheby's catalogue—had carried out the whole transaction, in fact, through the agency of Harriet—and he was probably quite unaware that he was boasting of the treasures that had once been hers. Her heart contracted at his exultation, and yet she could not but be glad to see it.

Some inexplicable emotion, compounded of pride and self-pity, made her confess: 'Those herbals were mine.'

'Yours?' His dark face turned sharply towards her. 'You don't mean to say I have the copies out of your library?'

'I'm afraid so.'

'But—but why? You can't have given up? Your collection is very nearly the best in the country.'

The generosity of his tribute, the warmth of his anxiety on her behalf, revealed an aspect of him which she had never seen before. To her, he had always seemed the most ruthless of opportunists, one who would grind the last print from the widow and the orphan. That he should care about anyone else's lost possessions enough to express a spontaneous concern astonished her.

'I am one of those people to whom the war brought no profit,' she rejoined. 'My income is no longer adequate, so I had to sell some books.'

'But *those* books—my dear Miss MacFarren!' He sounded almost aggrieved.

'I had reprints or facsimile editions of those, and I don't actually collect herbals, though I love them.'

'What a wrench it must have been! I'm so sorry. If I'd known they were your copies I should hardly have been able to face you.'

'I do appreciate,' she conceded, 'that they're in a much better library than mine.'

At this Dr. Wilmot became quite expansive, and asked her if she was in too much of a hurry to come in and take a glass of sherry with him. He would like her verdict, he said, on some items that had come from Edinburgh on approval.

Miss MacFarren, having nothing to go home to but noisy disturbance and the spectacle of a declining house, and no prospect of occupation but to turn over and over in her mind how badly she had told her story and how badly Harriet had received it, readily accepted the Professor's invitation, and they left the taxi together at King Charles Mansions.

7

DR. WILMOT'S domicile was a big red-brick building of Nineties architecture where he occupied an old-fashioned, rambling flat which had once been the last word in modern luxury, and which still had many advantages over the cramped, box-like apartments that were passing for luxury flats in 1945. Here he lived in almost pre-war spaciousness and comfort, attended by an elderly, tight-lipped, admonitory, but devoted maid who had been with him since before his wife's death twenty years ago.

As he paused in the hall to take off his overcoat, she emerged from a pantry door, like a doll worked by a mechanical device, carrying a tray with a decanter and a sherry glass.

'Oh, sir, I'll fetch another glass,' she said on seeing that he was not alone.

'The other tray as well, Pearson,' he commanded. 'Miss MacFar-ren is my principal rival, so we must do what we can to impress her.'

The maid nodded a respectful but guarded recognition of the visitor, and hurried back to the pantry in a rustle of black alpaca and white starched accessories, the picture of efficiency, decency, and self-possession, a woman who must convey a sense of solidity to any household. She returned as soon as they had settled them-selves in the drawing-room with a larger tray on which were three decanters and two glasses.

'Bristol Cream, Manzanilla, or Tio Pepe?' the Professor enquired with a delicately repressed flourish.

'Why, Dr. Wilmot, what lavishness! I can hardly believe my eyes!'

'I've been eking them out for six years. I drink the quota stuff when I'm alone. It could be worse. . . . Well, which?' His hand hovered over the decanters, and she noticed that it was white, well groomed, and rather graceful; out of keeping, like his voice, with a face which reminded her ludicrously of how, in her childhood, she had imagined Jehovah.

'Which do you recommend?'

'The Bristol Cream is the best sherry I've ever had in the house. I got it from Chorton of the Natural History Museum when he sold up and went to Australia. I wish to God,' he remarked sorrowfully as he handed her the glass, 'that I'd bought the whole lot, but I didn't know how good it was going to be.'

'That's interesting! Do you know, my brother Andrew bought some of his cellar.'

'Indeed?' He leaned forward, fixing her with a penetrating gaze. 'Did he get any of the Bristol sherry?'

'Yes, three or four dozen, I think.'

'He drank them, I suppose?' Dr. Wilmot spoke severely as if this had been an unseemly thing to do with them.

'Well yes, except about a dozen which I still have.'

'Oh? You still have a dozen?' His solemn, calculating stare suggested that, while the news was not altogether agreeable to him, it yet evoked certain possibilities.

'Yes, I have some of Mr. Chorton's Oloroso too.'

'So? Chorton's Oloroso! Don't you like sherry?'

'Very much, but I hardly ever drink at home.' Her tongue faltered as she recalled last night's potations of whisky. 'I find even one glass relaxes me so that I can't do any work afterwards.'

'So much the better in the evening. I relax delightfully with sherry before dinner and port afterwards if I can manage it.'

'Ah, it's obvious that you haven't been keeping your own house, Doctor, or you'd know that the evening, nowadays, is the only time when one's free to work with any concentration.' She took a sip of the sherry. 'Delicious! So soft and smooth! It really is creamy, isn't it?'

'A dozen bottles must be a great temptation to you,' he murmured. 'They might disturb your work considerably. Why don't you sell them?'

She laughed nervously. Dr. Wilmot had the reputation, which she believed to be well-founded, of working upon the feelings of persons whose goods he wished to acquire until the effort of holding out against him became too weariful to sustain. Moreover, he liked every purchase to be unmistakably a bargain. She took a pride in keeping a little wine in the house. It was symbolic of the days when she had presided over the entertainments of her beloved brother. Indeed, it carried her back even further, to her girlhood in the Hebrides, when she had helped her father, Angus MacFarren, to check over the shipments which Uncle James, the great traveller of the family, used to send direct from Spain, France, and Germany. She knew that, if she closed her eyes, she would be able to see him clearly, standing in the coachyard, his feet lapped by the waves of straw cases and brightly coloured tissue papers, pink, blue, apple-green, in which the hock and moselle bottles were always so smartly twisted—the sugar plums of the grown-ups. The MacFarrens had always had a refined zest for the pleasures of life.

'I shall probably never be able to buy any more,' she explained apologetically.

'What does that matter if you don't want it? Why sell books when you could be selling sherry?'

'It would fetch so little comparatively. My brother certainly didn't pay more than sixty or seventy shillings a dozen for it.'

'It's worth—er—something more than that today.'

'One hears of absurd inflated prices, but I don't know where one finds the people who pay them.'

'What would you call an inflated price?' She could see that he was grappling with the problem of how to offer her sufficient inducement to sell, and yet to avoid overbidding. 'The Government-imported sherry is controlled at fifteen-and-six a bottle.'

With a face of polite interest, she remained silent.

'I dare say a pound a bottle wouldn't be out of the way for wine as good as this.'

As she still replied only with a benignant smile over her glass, he added with a sigh: 'Or even twenty-two-and-six.'

'That's quite four times the original price,' she said.

His eyes lightened.

'And yet,' she went on, 'it really wouldn't be worth my while to part with it even for that, since it has a sentimental value.' In the face of his disappointment, she continued almost appealingly, 'It seems foolish, I suppose, for me to cling to such things when I can't even afford to take up my quota.'

His eyes lightened again. 'Oh, so you have a quota, have you? Of what does it consist?'

'Two bottles of sherry a month, and whatever they can spare of wine or brandy.' She did not mention the whisky, for that had become a guilty secret.

Dr. Wilmot plunged at once into a wily plan for diverting her quota to his own cellar, and as this turned out to be practicable, he was headed off for the time being from pressing to obtain her brother's wine.

The gain he had made and the hopes he cherished, together with her undisguised envy of his latest purchase—a noble Georgian portfolio-stand—combined to raise his already cheerful spirits, and, liberally re-filling her glass, he embarked on the tale of how he had acquired this bargain:

'I saw it in a little shop in Pimlico, where fortunately I'm not known at all. I rushed in at once and enquired the price, which was modest, I'm sure you'll agree, at twelve guineas: it would have been half as much again in the West End. I was just going to offer ten— as a matter of principle—when the shop-girl informed me that it was more or less sold to another customer. He'd promised to get in touch with them the following morning and they'd undertaken not to part with it to anyone else in the meantime. Well, I managed to draw tins gentleman's name out of her, and the minute the shop was opened in the morning, I rang them up and send I was speaking for Mr. So-and-So—disguising my voice, d'you see?—and that he wouldn't be wanting the portfolio-stand after all.'

With his jubilant grin he had quite ceased to look like Jehovah: he was merely a nefarious old buccaneer whom she was most irrationally beginning to like.

'Of course, I had to nip round at once in a taxi to take the thing away before the real Mr. So-and-So turned up. Mind you'— he straightened his face, and assumed a dignified expression—'he might not have bought it in the end if I'd left it there, so I was probably doing the shop a good turn.'

'Dr. Wilmot,' she laughed, 'you're shameless. No wonder I've never been able to compete against you.'

'Ah, you've been up to some dodges in your day! Do you remember the time you tricked me out of that beautiful large-paper set of the *Botanic Garden*?'

Miss MacFarren did remember, and with lively satisfaction, though 'tricked' was hardly the word she would have chosen. She had made off with those exquisite books slyly under his very nose by arranging a bidding code with a friend who was unknown to him. He had told her she was over-eager, had twitted her with paying fancy prices; then seeing her in the sale room watching him when the lot was put up, he had tried to maintain his reputation as a man who never lost his head, and the books had been knocked down, ostensibly to the stranger. How furious he had been when, the purchaser's name being asked, that stranger had replied 'MacFarren'!

'It is a nice lot,' she said, 'but you're far and away ahead of me now. I haven't bought anything to speak of for a year.'

'You apparently have your nephew to look after your interests,' he returned somewhat acridly. 'I'd like to see those Darien originals. Which reminds me, I must show you the scrap books from Edinburgh. I don't know if they're quite in my line, but if I don't have them, I'm sure you ought to.'

It was while he was in this genial frame of mind, rummaging in a mahogany cupboard for books, telling anecdotes of his stratagems to do down fellow-collectors, that Pearson entered carrying a flat basket in which six peaches reposed on a bed of autumn leaves.

'I forgot to tell you, sir,' she said, putting it into his hands, 'this arrived today from Sir Julius Letherman. His chauffeur brought it and I unpacked it, seeing it was fruit, and put it in the fridge, sir.'

The Professor took the basket with a smile of candid greed. 'Hothouse peaches,' he said tenderly, stroking one of them with his forefinger. 'These'll be beauties, coming from Sir Julius. I don't think it was right to put them in the fridge, Pearson. Refrigeration is bad for the flavour of fruit.'

'They won't keep long without, sir. They're a bit on the ripe side now.'

'Then I must eat them soon.'

'Better have one or two tonight, sir.'

'What, alone? Peaches and wine all by myself?'

'I didn't mention wine, sir.' A look passed between them which suggested that his propensity to make excuses for taking wine was a household joke.

'It would be waste of peaches not to drink a little dessert wine with them—don't you agree, Miss MacFarren?'

'Yes, if you're lucky enough to have some.'

'I have Filhot, Coutet, and d'Yquem,' he announced calmly, but with a sidelong glance to observe the effect. 'Not that it's of much interest to you. It's quite a fiction that women like sweet wines.'

'Why, I adore them,' she protested with sincerity, 'the few I've tasted.'

'You do? Well, of course, I might have known it, considering your other tastes. But you're not an average woman. Now don't you think, Pearson,' he asked, handing back the basket, 'that Miss MacFarren ought to stay to dinner, and then it will be reasonable to open some wine?' Pearson's facial reaction was unfavourable, and Miss MacFarren hastened to assure him that she had work to do at home.

'Work! You can't work—you said so yourself! You've had two glasses of sherry. What is there to eat, Pearson?'

'Only soup and steamed hake, sir, with shrimp sauce.'

'Shrimp sauce? What could be nicer? Open a tin of something if there's not enough.'

'I really couldn't—' Miss MacFarren began, but he silenced her:

'Don't perjure yourself! You know you can and will. When we've dined, I'll show you how I'm looking after your herbals. I've had vellum cases made to protect them.'

'Your' herbals—she could hardly have refused to stay after that, even though Pearson was obviously disposed to regard her as an intruder. But she took a leaf out of Mrs. Bankes's book, and exclaimed in a clear, carrying voice while the maid was still within earshot: 'That wonderful housekeeper! How lucky you are to have her! She's such a nice-looking woman!'

She could not have done it if she had not been fortified with sherry, but it worked. While Dr. Wilmot was absent decanting the wine, leaving her to turn over the contents of portfolios, Pearson came in and whispered in a genteel and hospitable manner: 'Would you like to wash your hands, miss? Now's your chance.' It was a kindly thought, and the first of several small comfortable gestures by which she signified her friendliness.

*   *   *

Besides the dessert wine, Dr. Wilmot availed himself of the occasion to decant a half-bottle of a very pleasing Chablis, and, under its mellowing influence, she told him something of the troubles weighing on her mind. In agreeable contrast to Harriet, he was vociferously indignant on her behalf and reproached her warmly with having made so bad a bargain. If she had consulted him about her house-sharing plan, he said, forgetting how surprised he would have been at the time had she done so, he would have found her half a dozen excellent candidates among his colleagues. She ought to get rid of that hopeless woman at once (how refreshing, she thought wistfully, to confide in one who had not come within range of the insidious Bankes charm!) and he guaranteed it would not take a fortnight to replace her.

She recognized, not for the first time, how much explanation it would need to persuade anyone who had never been in such a situation that one cannot expel an inmate of one's house at a month's notice without creating an atmosphere so harrowing that it may seem almost easier to endure the present discomfort and pray for some external incident to end one's plight.

She did not dwell too long, however, on her worries, for she had no intention of spoiling the air of festivity with which the two decanters had invested the simple dinner. By the time the crumbs had been ceremoniously brushed into a tray, and the peaches placed on the table in a silver dish, she was engaged in admiring everything she could find to admire in the Professor's dining-room—namely, the books in their splendid Chippendale case, the gleaming surface of the rosewood table, and two handsome still life paintings by Van Oss. For the rest, there was little in the room to suggest the aesthetic sensibilities of the connoisseur. The mantelpiece and dado were, to Miss MacFarren's taste, quite irredeemable, the curtains a most dreary blue damask, the lights were suspended in an ugly alabaster bowl, and even the silver dish containing the peaches had a fretted border which she would have disliked intensely if she had not been in a complaisant mood towards its owner.

'That was a wedding present,' he remarked, seeing her eyes investigating it. 'It's rather a horrid dish, isn't it? But it's good solid silver, you know.'

'Oh, I don't doubt,' she returned hastily.

'I am a man of habit,' he went on, 'or perhaps a lazy man. If I start living with anything, I go on living with it, whether I like it or not. That alabaster bowl'—again he had followed the direction of her eyes—'was here when I moved in. I decided to change it as soon as I could work up energy to look for something better, so it's been with me fifteen years.'

'You have energy enough when you're making up a set of prints,' said Miss MacFarren, but such was their mutual cordiality that only the very finest ear could have detected the trace of bitterness in her tone.

'Ah, one's hobby, that's another matter. . . . The positive pleasures of life—one should always have time for those.' He rose and took the second decanter from the sideboard. 'Now you shall guess what this is, Miss MacFarren.'

The light streamed through the crystal, within which glittered the gold-topaz of Sauternes. Returning to his seat, he drew towards him with a thoughtful and grave movement, like a priest performing a ritual, two tulip-shaped glasses into which he poured a small quantity of the precious liquid. Handing one to his guest, he raised the other to his face, rapt and remote, and waved it delicately before his nostrils; then he nodded as if communing with some invisible spirit.

Miss MacFarren likewise raised her glass to her nostrils, and inhaled in one honeyed breath the scent of fruit and flowers, and the warmth of brilliant sunshine tempered by a soft shadow. 'Château d'Yquem,' she whispered.

She could see he was pleased, but he would not let her enjoy her victory too easily. 'What year?' he demanded sternly.

'Oh no, I can't! That's too much for me.'

'Taste it then!'

The taste of the wine was magical, a mysterious double taste that seemed to grow like a vapour and blossom on the palate, so rich yet so subtle, so cool yet so redolent of the summer's fullness. She felt almost as if she had taken the first sip of some enchanted potion that would restore youth and create beauty.

'Oh, it's glorious!' she cried. 'It couldn't be more lovely.'

'Tell me the year!'

'A wonderful year.'

'Well, you passed half the test. Your nose does you credit, Miss MacFarren. And if you want to know, it's 1921.'

The year meant nothing to her, for she was not familiar with the vintages, but she could guess, not only from the wine but from his inflection, that it was safe to reply: 'I feel the honour and the privilege, Doctor.'

'Let me give you a peach,' he said, selecting one.

She took another sip of wine, this time to mitigate a slight uneasiness. The accomplishment of eating fruit in a socially correct fashion was one in which she had never excelled, and it was long since she had been given any opportunity of practice. If she had had her way, she would have lifted the peach to her lips and bitten voluptuously into the luscious flesh. As it was she paused to look first at her host.

'How perfectly you do it!' she could not refrain from saying. His silver fork held the peach gently, his knife, wielded with a leisurely dexterity, made a single sweeping incision: a few fine and cunning movements and the greenish-pink velvet of the skin lay like a discarded garment.

It was really delightful to her to see the happiness with which he raised the fork to his lips, savoured the taste and texture of the fruit, and, having pronounced it admirable, drained his glass and sighed luxuriously. She peeled her own peach as best she could, cutting it into shapeless chunks, and his enjoyment was so complete that he continued to smile indulgently even when her fork slipped and sent the wet stone skidding across the polished table.

'More wine,' he insisted, replenishing her glass. 'We can be generous with ourselves, because our dinner was very light. Not that I believe in coddling one's digestion. I've always taxed mine heavily—that is to say, as heavily as the times would allow—and you couldn't find a healthier man them I am anywhere.'

'You look healthy.' It seemed possible now to turn a full, frank gaze upon him, and she noted that his eyes were bright and clear—blue eyes surprising in so dark a face, his skin ruddy but not florid, and his lips as red as berries. Though his hair was grey, it was impressively abundant, and his beard was still predominantly black. Until now, he had always struck her as an arrogant, even aggressive personality, but this evening she could perceive that his demeanour was merely firm and straightforward as became a man of authority. It was especially nice of him, she thought, to signify the improvement in their relations by telling her so unreservedly of his little ruses for gaining possession of objects which took his fancy.

'I get an extra kick out of this Yquem,' he was saying in his free and lively way, 'by remembering how I came by it. I was staying in Harrogate two or three years before the war, attending some conference or other, and I struck up a friendship with an architect named Bartlett who was taking a cure for neuritis, or arthritis, or some other "itis". It turned out in the course of conversation that he had a first-rate cellar of Sauternes, which had been part of a bequest, and he'd only recently started drinking it. Well, I'm very fond of Sauternes, as you can see, and it didn't seem to me that this fellow was exactly a connoisseur, so I fished around a little to find out if he'd sell the stuff, but he said he'd grown to like it and intended to hold on to it. I waited a day or two and then I had an inspiration. It seemed he'd heard people call me "doctor" and he'd taken me for a doctor of medicine; so I determined to live up to my reputation, and I told him that Sauternes was the very worst thing in the world for his particular "itis".'

He laughed happily, rotating his glass with another of his ritualistic gestures and lifting it again to his nose.

'I won't go into all the elaborations of it. I planted suggestions for days like an advertising copywriter. I invented scientific reasons. I even got him to put the idea into the head of one of the local practitioners and make him admit that there might be something in it. Of course, for all I know, there may have been.' He assumed his demure expression. 'It may have proved a boon and a blessing to him that I took the stuff off his hands. I must say he was rather annoyed, though, when he found that I wasn't a medical man.'

'Doctor, you're incorrigible!' She gave him the shocked applause she could see he relished, but resolved, even with the Château d'Yquem glowing, as it seemed, in her veins, to protect her sherry to the last ditch. 'I appreciate your confidence, Dr. Wilmot,' she thought—and it made her eyes sparkle, 'but you've met the one woman in London who's as possessive as you are.'

'More wine and more peaches!' Ignoring her polite remonstrance, he chose another peach for her. 'Two for you, two for me,' he said, 'and two for—no, one for Pearson, because I don't like to leave her out in the cold, and one with my breakfast in the morning. Now *I'm* going to peel this one for you. Have you ever thought that eating and drinking and collecting are the only pleasures—positively the only pleasures that get better and better as one grows older?'

'Yes, I suppose that's true.' She twisted the stem of her glass in her fingers, suddenly aware of sadness. 'I wish I weren't growing old all the same.'

'It's a nuisance in some ways even to you and me. But it must be infinitely worse for people with poor digestions who don't collect anything. You and I are much luckier than most.'

'Much luckier,' she agreed, and felt convinced as she said it. Yes, she was one of the privileged, the greatly privileged. She allowed that ravishing series of sensations to glide across her palate once more, the sweetness, the splendour, the softness, the freshness, and finding that Dr. Wilmot had now rather the air of Anacreon than Jehovah, she took courage to quote in a low voice an ode her brother had loved:

> 'When I drink wine, my spirit echoing
> Such numbers as the very Muses sing
> Reaps beauty and delight from everything. . . .'

'Charming,' said the doctor, 'charming! Go on!'

> 'When I drink wine, my brow bedecked with flowers,
> The woe-dissolving god my tongue empowers
> To chant the calm of life, the pleasant hours. . . .'

'I wonder,' he began, then broke off, hesitated as if disposing briefly of some inward objection, and resumed abruptly: 'I wonder if you have a little early nineteenth-century book called *The Juvenile Botanist*? It has about a dozen very pretty coloured plates.'

'I don't think I've ever come across it.'

'No, it's rather rare. I find I have two copies. You must let me give one to you, Miss MacFarren.'

She perceived the magnanimity of the offer. It was almost in her heart to invite his acceptance of her duplicate set of Hopson's *Flowering Grasses*, but she felt on reflection that this would be too intimate an advance at the present stage of their acquaintanceship. It could be kept for the future.

* * *

When Miss MacFarren arrived back at Harberton Square towards midnight, Mrs. Bankes was still in the sitting-room talking alternately to her guests and her love-birds. She could be heard interrupting her own conversation to say ecstatically: 'Tweet tweet, my ducky dicky-birds! Tweet tweet! Aren't you too heavenly, you

little darlings?' Miss MacFarren wandered upstairs not minding.
She was murmuring to herself:

> 'When I drink wine, my joyful thoughts become
> Sweet blossoms whirled towards Elysium
> On breezes dancing in delirium.'

8

MRS. BANKES had been installed about three months when Mrs.
Manders presented a fortnight's notice. It was made apparent to
Miss MacFarren that she was utterly exhausted with her multifar-
ious duties and had wearied at last even of the social activities of the
household, but Mrs. Bankes was only given to understand that she
was compelled for family reasons to live in another district. Miss
MacFarren was much put out by this want of moral courage, though
she herself surrendered daily to the same weakness. It would have
been a support to her if she had been able to point to an avowed
fellow-sufferer, but the Bankes technique of disarming was so effec-
tual that, not only were grievances suppressed, but Mrs. Manders,
on the verge of departure, exerted herself to the utmost preparing
for Captain Bankes's next visit.

'What's worrying me,' she grumbled, encountering Miss
MacFarren on the basement stairs one morning, 'is who's going to
look after them poor birds when I'm gone. She says "Tweet tweet",
and gives 'em a lump of sugar now and then, and that's about all she
does do for 'em.'

Mrs. Bankes had gone out shopping with the two 'female
friends' in residence, and Miss MacFarren followed the maid into
the kitchen and watched her clean out the birdcage and replenish
the porcelain feeding dishes. She had a melancholy premonition
that she would need to know how it was done.

'It worries me too, beyond words,' she said. 'What can I do about
it if she neglects them?'

'It isn't your place to look after them.'

'No, but—oh dear, how dreary they look, poor little things! The
cage is miserably small for four birds. She promised to try and get
another, but I don't think she's made the smallest effort.'

'Her promises!' Mrs. Manders snorted. 'She'd promise you the moon to keep you quiet.'

Miss MacFarren wished Harriet could hear this stricture made by one who had been, at the beginning, almost as enamoured as herself. That Harriet, though she believed herself quite free from prejudice, was really all pro-Bankes had remained a rankling thorn. Miss MacFarren had not had the strength of mind to desist from attempts to persuade her that she had mistaken Antonia's character completely; and as Harriet took even less kindly than most people to being proved wrong, their relations had now become perceptibly artificial. Each had made it a point of honour to avoid an open quarrel, and therefore they met almost as often as formerly, but the fact that the one never failed to mention any new thing that redounded to Mrs. Bankes's discredit and that the other was equally determined to represent her in the most admirable light was not conducive to genuinely cordial intercourse. Miss MacFarren would readily have forgiven Harriet's unfortunate recommendation if only she could have been induced to admit her error. Harriet for her part seemed to imagine that she was holding the scales impartially when she had weighted them visibly on the side of Antonia.

Antonia indeed! To hear her old friend so affectionately using the Christian name of one who had been a stranger to her only a few months ago, and who was still little more than a shop acquaintance—this was an irritation that she found at times hardly bearable. She was even obliged to acknowledge a twinge of jealousy in it.

And it appeared that there really were qualities to admire in that tormenting woman. She never gossiped, never took any interest in scandal, however amusing, seldom spoke unkind word about anyone. She was generous and open-hearted, a devoted wife, a most obliging friend. Her good nature was boundless, her little prevarications—which Harriet could no longer deny—were actuated not by ill feeling, desire for self-aggrandizement, or any mean motive, but only a pardonable longing to thrust aside matters that were disagreeable.

Miss MacFarren freely admitted all these mitigating features, yet somehow they did not mitigate: they only increased her exasperation by making it harder to convince an outsider that Mrs. Bankes was insupportable as a housemate. Insupportable both for tangible and intangible reasons! As at their first meeting, she still found in that apparently naïve personality some disquieting element that evaded definition.

She stared at the dejected birds. The sight of their tremulous movements, the sense of loss when she considered what her disintegrating friendship with Harriet had meant to her, the awareness of a change, undermining self-respect, in her whole mode of life—by some unpleasant kind of alchemy, these various impressions seemed to fuse into one sensation which was almost terror.

'What am I going to do when you're gone?' she cried, as if Mrs. Manders had been a strong support rather than a broken reed. She had lapsed from her original standard, the standard of a lady who would never criticize another lady in front of her servant; and now let Mrs. Manders see clearly what she felt. To do so had been her sole means of relief, since Harriet would only lend an unsympathetic ear: and, in fact, she had cherished a feeble self-despising hope that her remarks might be carried back to Mrs. Bankes, and might provoke her to make the first move towards breaking up the incompatible ménage. No ripple, however, had appeared on the serene surface of her tenant's equability.

'If you ask me—now's your chance,' said Mrs. Manders. 'You ought to give her notice by rights before she takes on another maid.'

'Yes, of course—of course! Why didn't I think of that? My brain doesn't seem to be functioning lately.'

The moment so often contemplated had come; but if the prospect of freedom inspired hope, the steps for achieving it were fraught with dismay. The idea of living for a full month with Mrs. Bankes under notice had always been a distressing one: now, when Captain Bankes was on the verge of another furlough, it loomed more dreadful than ever. Though she had condemned Mrs. Manders for inventing excuses instead of coming out boldly with the fact that Mrs. Bankes was an intolerable employer, she found herself feverishly turning over in her mind pretexts which might help her to avoid plain speaking.

Should she say her nephew desired to live at home again? No, they had one or two acquaintances not far removed from Mory's world, gossip writers, news-reel men, who might know enough about him to expose such a story. Should she tell them her brother

Colin and his wife were coming back from Canada and would need the accommodation? That was better . . . it was very good indeed: but when she came to work out the details of her announcement, she realized that it was simply not in her character to utter and maintain so gross a lie. It was useless to try and act against one's character. She would have to tell at least part of the truth.

Sitting in her study, angrily mending linen which should have been looked after by Mrs. Bankes, she sought for words in which to explain politely but with firmness that the arrangement had proved economically untenable. The disturbing atmosphere had seriously delayed the progress of her work. The heavy expense of taking meals in restaurants could not go on indefinitely, yet cooking and washing up at home were attended, thanks to Mrs. Bankes's incessant entertaining, by numberless obstacles. Then the undertaking to share the quarterly accounts had been entirely unsound since Mrs. Bankes never turned off a light, left electric fires burning constantly, and was equally lavish with all other commodities. Of course, this could be adjusted when the bills came in—she had no doubt that if Captain Bankes were only shown the inequality, he would eagerly hasten to set it right—but there was an awkwardness in making these explanations, and she had not cared to raise the point when rendering accounts for the Bankes's portion of the summer quarter, over which she had mutely remained out of pocket.

She remembered with a sigh Mory's apt warning that she would need to be up to all the devices of a practised landlady to enter into such a situation. A practised landlady would surely not suffer such agonies of embarrassment over ending it.

The slamming of the front door followed by a jodelling down the basement stairs for Mrs. Manders, brought her to her feet with the desperate briskness of one about to take her place in the tumbril. 'Now or never!' she rallied herself, laying down the tray-cloth that had been allowed to go to the laundry week after week with an ever-enlarging tear.

She went resolutely into the hall and, as soon as the shopping bags had been handed over to Mrs. Manders, said with spirit: 'Could I have a word with you, Mrs. Bankes?'

'Yes, certainly. Come in!' Mrs. Bankes's smile, though a shade nervous, was punctual in appearing, and she moved towards her sitting-room so swiftly that Miss MacFarren had to hold back, whispering:

'I mean, alone.'

'Oh, there's nothing you can't say in front of Mrs. Reece and Froggie,' she insisted without lowering her voice. 'I'm sure if I've done anything naughty they'll know about it.'

Miss MacFarren still hung back, and Mrs. Reece, who could be seen through the open doorway unwrapping a great sheaf of chrysanthemums, said tactfully: 'Froggie and I can go and do these in the kitchen, Tonia.'

'No, no, Mrs. Manders is bringing some water up.' Her tone appealed to her friend to remain with her, and perhaps her face too, for a look seemed to pass between them as she entered the sitting-room.

'Well, later,' suggested Miss MacFarren, feeling very foolish as she hovered at the door. 'Perhaps you'd find it convenient after lunch?'

'I'm busy after lunch.' In her determination to avoid being interviewed alone she spoke almost rudely. 'You don't have to mind a bit about my lady friends. I have no secrets from them.'

Miss MacFarren, in the state of bewildered resentment which had accompanied all her dealings with Mrs. Bankes from the beginning, followed her into the room, thinking:

'On your own head be it!'

'You know Mrs. Reece and of course you've met Froggie,' said Mrs. Bankes, waving towards the subdued-looking girl of about eighteen whom Miss MacFarren had seen moving somewhat furtively about the house during the past two or three days. 'Isn't it marvellous to think they're mother and daughter? They look just like sisters. I never can get used to it when I introduce them to people, especially as I knew Froggie when she really was a little frog of about ten.'

Miss MacFarren was spared from having to make any comment by the arrival of Mrs. Manders with a jug of water and a pair of kitchen scissors.

'Mrs. Reece arranges flowers like an angel,' Mrs. Bankes continued, as if by small talk she could keep at bay whatever grave subject was impending. 'Do them on this glass-topped table, Helen, then it doesn't matter if you spill the water.'

Miss MacFarren blenched. The table in question was one of her most treasured possessions. Mounted under the glass was a highly original piece of patchwork, the design of the same grand-mother who had made the counterpane in the best bedroom. Contrived of dark and light satin squares in the semblance of a chess-board, the dark squares most delightfully embroidered, it had been intended to accommodate the set of chessmen which old Andrew MacFarren had carved for his eldest son, Angus. If water were allowed to seep into the wooden frame, the heirloom might be damaged irremediably.

'It would be safer to use the drum table, as long as you put some newspaper on it first.' She was keenly aware as she heard herself speak that such injunctions for the care of her property seemed to show her up as the typical finicky old maid of jokes and stories.

'All right,' said Mrs. Bankes good-humouredly, 'what about these?' She covered the drum table at once with the expensive American and Continental magazines that filled the 'Canterbury'.

'Oh, but they'll get spoiled, Tonia! The stalks are wet,' Mrs. Reece protested. And in the little flurry of newspapers being fetched from the kitchen and the table prepared with exaggerated solici-tude, something was lost of the impetus that Miss MacFarren had counted on to carry her through her task.

She decided to revert to her earlier plan of making her communi-cation by letter, and was groping for words to convey this intention, when Mrs. Bankes, hanging her head, pulling a little kittenish face like a child who exploits its pretty coaxing ways to avert anger, murmured in an affected small voice: 'I suppose you want to talk to me about the dressing-table. I was going to tell you yesterday, but I forgot.'

'The dressing-table?' Miss MacFarren repeated with a sinking heart.

Mrs. Bankes put her fingers over her mouth as if trying too late to silence herself. 'O-oh! Oh dear! Have I said something I shouldn't? I thought Mrs. Manders must have told you.'

'I covered up the place,' Mrs. Reece put in, 'so she probably hasn't seen it.'

'Which dressing-table?' Miss MacFarren demanded. 'What's happened to it?'

Mrs. Bankes went on playing her theatrical little-girl rôle, all but lisping: 'The one in the spare room. I left the electric iron on it, and it went and made a nasty black mark. Wasn't it awful of me?'

Miss MacFarren's indignation at this new item in the train of accidents was barely tempered by relief that the dressing-table concerned was not the bird's-eye maple in the best bedroom.

'I'd better see how badly it's scorched before I say anything,' she responded with austere calm.

'You mustn't worry about it. I know exactly where I can get it put right for you.' One could almost see the mechanism of her thoughts struggling to invent some salving lie.

'That will be very difficult at the present time,' Miss MacFarren put in hastily to forestall any such inanity. The annoyance had fortified her ebbing courage and she revised her decision of a few moments before. She would make one last effort to get the infuriating woman alone, and then, whether she succeeded or not, she would speak freely.

'Would you like to come up to the spare room with me now, Mrs. Bankes? I suppose I ought to see how deep the burn has gone.'

Mrs. Bankes swiftly seized two or three chrysanthemums and began stripping their stalks. 'Froggie will show you the place. I have some people coming to lunch, and we simply must get the flowers done.'

Mrs. Reece averted her face, as if trying to detach herself from the conflict, and Miss MacFarren drew a deep breath.

'Very well. Perhaps I'd better say what I came to say first. Mrs. Manders is leaving, I understand, next Saturday. I don't know whether you've done anything about replacing her—'

'No, I haven't,' Mrs. Bankes interrupted. 'I haven't done anything at all. It's no use engaging anyone else, because Joss thinks we'll be going back to the States almost any time now.'

'Really?' Miss MacFarren wished she could give full credence to this wonderful news, but could not help feeling that it was too good to be true. 'You mean you're going so soon that you won't need any housework after next Saturday?' Scepticism and hope contended more or less equally in her voice.

'Oh, we'll give you a month's notice, of course, even if we can't stay it out.' Mrs. Bankes apparently mistook the note for a land-lady's apprehension.

'That won't be in the least necessary. I shall be quite willing to accept a week's notice. But it occurred to me that if you were going to engage a new maid—'

'No, I shall just get a charwoman to come in for a few hours every day till we leave.'

She sounded very definite, and unless one wished to be gratuit-ously uncivil in front of two listeners, it seemed there was little else one could say.

'A charwoman would certainly *not* be adequate except for a *short* period,' Miss MacFarren ventured with an emphasis worthy of Harriet. She paused with her hand on the door-knob. 'I shall be expecting to hear from you then about the date when you'll be leaving.'

'Yes, I dare say I shall know as soon as Joss arrives,' Mrs. Bankes rejoined over her shoulder, making a great play of being busy with the flowers.

Miss MacFarren took her leave, begging that nobody would trouble to accompany her on her inspection of the damage done by the iron, but Mrs. Reece insisted on sending her daughter as an escort, and since the spare room was, for the time being, their private territory, she could not persist in refusal.

The large, glossy, slightly protuberant eyes which had doubt-less earned Froggie her nickname were clouded with vicarious guilt as she raised a trinket box and a hairbrush, and drew back a linen runner from a corner of the early-Victorian toilet table. The shape of the iron was a black silhouette on the pale satinwood. Miss MacFarren could not repress a groan.

'Oh, this is worse than I thought! It must have been red-hot.'

'It was—nearly,' Froggie agreed with bated breath. 'You see, it was plugged in, and she forgot to turn it off.'

'But what a place to put it!' Miss MacFarren exclaimed, detecting a welcome sympathy in the tone.

'Mummie told her she shouldn't.' Froggie, when awestricken, was evidently inclined to whisper. 'Mummie was in a hurry, and

Tonia said she'd iron her scarf for her, and she burned a big hole in it.'

Froggie was still at an age when such deeds are met with open reproach, and not passed off with polite assurances that the harm is of no consequence. Miss MacFarren found her shocked attitude comforting.

'Did she say,' she enquired with assuaging bitterness, 'that she knew where she could find your mother another scarf exactly like it?'

'Yes, she did! How did you know?'

'I have plenty of reason to know.'

'There's another thing,' Froggie announced *sotto voce*, staying Miss MacFarren on her way to the door. 'Mummie didn't want you to think it was me who did this.' She held up the blue satin coverlet of her bed, and displayed two brown-edged cigarette burns, one of them so deep that it went through both satin and lining. 'It was like this when we came. I'm not allowed to smoke.'

Miss MacFarren made no attempt to conceal her disgust.

'Whoever did it had obviously gone to bed with the quilt on. I suppose they all do. . . . Oh, I'm sorry. I didn't mean you and your mother.'

'Mummie showed the burns to Tonia'—Froggie dropped her voice still lower, rather in consternation than in stealth—'and she didn't seem to mind a bit. She said you probably wouldn't notice, but Mummie was worried in case you might believe it was us.'

'Thank you for showing me.' She summoned a wan smile. 'I shouldn't have thought it was you, because I've always noticed your mother is very careful. It's easy to tell, you know. When people close the doors quietly, and wipe their shoes on the mat, and look for an ashtray before they begin smoking, you can be pretty sure they're not the ones who're breaking the china and burning cigarette holes in things.'

'Mummie says she doesn't think it's fair, the way Tonia's treating your house,' the indiscreet girl was emboldened to say ingratiatingly. 'Lots of people stay here because all the hotels are full. Mummie didn't feel right about it, but we have to be in London to help with my cousin's wedding. . . .'

Miss MacFarren realized that the conversation had gone too far. Consoling though she found it to have this assurance that her wrongs were commiserated, it was beneath her dignity to encourage one of Mrs. Bankes's guests to make incautious revelations. Thanking her again, she withdrew before the temptation to elicit further avowals overcame her.

*   *   *

Captain Bankes's arrival was only a little less auspicious than on the previous occasion. Mrs. Manders, by unparalleled efforts, had repaired the enforced neglect of weeks, and Mrs. Bankes, as before, had drawn upon her exceptional reserves of energy to restore order where untidiness normally prevailed. Once again her husband was able to proclaim his delight at finding himself in a beautiful house, a real home; to compare his present surroundings joyfully with the discomforts of his life in Continental cities. Once again, the warmth of his greeting made Miss MacFarren feel as if she could scarcely meet his cheerful and benevolent gaze.

But within a very few days fissures began to appear in the smooth structure of home comfort. Mrs. Manders had stayed only to see Captain Bankes installed, and was replaced by a slovenly charwoman, the best that any of Antonia's friends could find at short notice—for, most strangely, she made no serious effort to provide against the servant's departure until it actually came to pass.

Though she enlisted considerable help from her visitors, though Captain Bankes laid the sitting-room fire, looked after the boiler, and sometimes cooked the dinner—insisting that he enjoyed the change tremendously, and though Antonia herself would work for an hour or two as though her life depended on it, the standard of housekeeping necessarily declined even from the unsatisfactory level of the past few months. Breakages mounted and were assiduously but vainly concealed; kitchen cupboards overflowed with disorder; a habit of leaving the remains of meals uncleared had brought a thriving colony of mice to haunt the basement.

Sometimes Captain Bankes could be heard to utter some gentle admonition: 'Honey, don't you think it would be better to get the living-room straightened up before you have any more people in?' 'Honey, couldn't you speak to the help about the way she leaves the kitchen?'

Once Miss MacFarren, emerging from her bedroom, saw him on the landing below with the birdcage in his hand. 'Tonia,' he was saying quite sternly, 'why do you keep birds when you don't remember to feed them? Is this the way you take care of them when I'm not here?'

Four months ago Miss MacFarren would have drawn back on the first words, or made her proximity known so that she should not overhear what was not intended for her: but then, four months ago, she would not have drunk large tots of whisky in her bedroom, or made her contempt for a lady obvious to that lady's charwoman, or spent whole hours in angry idleness recapitulating injuries. So she stood quietly at the top of the stairs.

'Of course I take care of them when you're not here, sweetie,' Antonia replied with her customary serenity. 'You know when you're about, I just can't help relying on you.'

'That's all very well, but I'm not a bird expert. I hate birds in cages.'

Antonia, ignoring this, brought out one of her shamelessly undisguised red herrings: 'I made a pie this morning, all by myself. And you're going to say it's the best pie you've ever tasted.'

'That's fine, honey, that's fine!' But he was not defeated, for on the verge of descending the stairs, he turned again, dangling the cage, and enquired with sudden pertinacity: 'What possessed you to buy these damn birds, anyway? They don't look healthy to me, and they cost the earth! I won't pay for any more of these fads.'

Miss MacFarren pulled herself together and retreated into her bedroom.

But such occasioned expressions of discontent were small matters weighed against his very evident affection and pride. There could be no doubt at all that it was a wonderfully successful marriage—mysteriously successful in the eyes of an onlooker who found Antonia altogether dislikeable. Joss Bankes was an intelligent man—both his writings and his conversation proved as much; and yet he was delighted with the companionship of a woman so ill-informed and wanting in reasoning powers that at times her stupidity seemed almost artificial, a mode of concealing deep, self-seeking designs. Why did he love her, he who must have had so many opportunities of seeing through her? Miss MacFarren told herself that the problem was outside the scope of one who had lived a celibate life; nevertheless, her curiosity was driven back to it.

When, returning from some jaunt, he called out eagerly before he had closed the front door behind him, 'Tonia! Tonia!' when, in passing her on the stairs he cried, 'My! You look pretty!' catching at her fingers, when he remained silently loyal in situations where any husband less than devoted would have tried to explain, to apologize, the question What Did He See In Her? framed itself in Miss MacFarren's thoughts as forcefully as the title of a novelette.

But these were involuntary observations. With a more deliberate attention, she watched for any sign that Mrs. Bankes had told the truth when she spoke of being about to return to America. Captain Bankes had arrived on December the 6th; by the 16th they were making active preparations for Christmas, and nothing had been said to suggest that a voyage home was imminent. If this had been another invention, it revealed the strange probability that Mrs. Bankes was perfectly well aware how much her departure was longed for, and was engaged in a conscious struggle not to be dispossessed. Perhaps Mrs. Manders had not, after all, been so impeccably discreet. Perhaps Mrs. Bankes was not so insensitive to symptoms of dislike and disapproval as she chose to appear.

Miss MacFarren would have liked to make a point-blank enquiry from Captain Bankes, but chance had not favoured her with any suitable occasion. To ask him for an interview alone would be tantamount to a declaration of hostilities against his wife. There seemed nothing for it but to speak to them both together: at least it was unlikely that, in his presence, she would be fobbed off with statements of sheer mendacity.

Having made her resolution, she remained on the alert to seize a moment of good promise, a moment when they were without visitors, not engaged on the telephone, and neither getting ready to go out nor occupied with the preliminaries of a meal. Such a moment was not easy to find, but at last, at the convenient hour of four, she heard the door of a taxi slammed, and saw them from her bedroom window entering the house, laden with parcels and unaccompanied. She gave them time to take off their outdoor clothes and descended.

At the door of their sitting-room, she hesitated, troubled as she had been several times before, by a point of etiquette. She had been taught that it is as incorrect to knock on a sitting-room door as not to knock on the door of a bedroom, but such a rule must surely have been established before any social arbiter had supposed that houses might be shared. It did not seem right to walk boldly into the private domain of another family; yet knocking was rather land-lady-like than ladylike. 'Well, I am a landlady now,' thought Miss MacFarren, and she knocked.

There was a sudden scuffling within. The masculine voice was heard in a hurried muttering, the feminine one called with a sort of breathless brightness: 'Oh, do please wait one tiny second!'

'I can come back later,' cried Miss MacFarren, inclined to blush, but she had barely turned from the door when it was flung open and Mrs. Bankes, still in her fur coat, stood smiling at her with an air of peculiarly mischievous innocence.

'No no, you can come in now. It's all right,' she said, and glanced over her shoulder to where her husband was standing with the same surprising expression on his face.

The drum table was covered with fancy packages and Miss MacFarren realized, nearer to blushing than ever, that she had interrupted, not a kissing or a quarrel, but some plot about Christmas presents of which she herself was the object. Once again she felt her position to be hideously undermined. One could not take a firm line with people who had just been hiding one's Christmas present. And—oh dear!—she had not dreamed of buying anything for them!

'Come along in and sit down, Miss MacFarren,' said Captain Bankes, laying his hand on the back of an armchair. It was a long light brown hand, with strong-looking fingers, well-kept nails, and a certain elegance of movement. She looked at it approvingly, but resisted its inviting gesture.

'Thank you, I'm just going to make my tea . . . but I wanted to ask you, as it just entered my head—that is, it was in my thoughts when I saw you come in—have you any idea yet of the date when you'll be sailing?'

'Sailing?' Captain Bankes repeated interrogatively.

'Perhaps I should say flying.'

'Oh, you mean to the States. Not till late in January, I imagine. I go back to Germany for a spell directly after Christmas.'

Miss MacFarren's heart leapt up. It was evidently true they were going! Now that the end was in sight, she could even feel a little sorry for Captain Bankes's sake that the prospect was so immensely gratifying; and in her anxiety not to appear too joyful, she almost pulled a long face.

'Late in January. Of course, you'll be delighted to see your children again?'

'That's a sure bet,' said Captain Bankes vigorously. Mrs. Bankes was busy puffing up cushions.

'How long since you last saw them?'

'Eight months I guess. I've had two trips home since I was first assigned to Europe.'

'Isn't it lovely!' said Mrs. Bankes, cutting across another polite question which had formed on Miss MacFarren's lips. 'We're going to spend Christmas in the country—five whole days!'

Miss MacFarren's heart again conveyed the illusion of an unaccustomed lightness. She had feared the worst in the way of noise and disorder from Mrs. Bankes's festivities, and now she was to be free—to have the house to herself for nearly a week!

'How very nice! And where will you be going?' This time she could hardly conceal her pleasure.

'To the Jermyns, near Oxford. I worship the country, don't you?'

'Not in winter,' she replied, with her habitual accuracy.

'Oh, I worship it, winter or summer. Mrs. Jermyn keeps pigs and all sorts of delicious things.'

'We never thought to ask,' Captain Bankes put in self-accusingly, 'whether you'd mind being alone in the house. Or maybe you're going away yourself?'

'No, I like to spend Christmas quietly. And I don't mind being alone at all. I was often here alone in the blitz, and I was so frightened of the bombs that I quite stopped being frightened of burglars.'

Mrs. Bankes, who was not listening, caught her husband's eye and directed it significantly to the door of a cupboard. 'We'll have to give out our presents before we go away, shan't we, Joss?'

'Tonia, when are you going to grow up?' he reproached her fondly. 'I believe you love giving presents even more than you love getting them.'

'If we let Miss MacFarren see hers now, we'd know whether she liked it or not.'

'Maybe we should and maybe not. I can't imagine Miss MacFarren just saying in a brash way, "I don't like it".

'But we could change it if it wasn't right once she'd seen it.'

She looked really eager and excited, and Miss MacFarren guessed apprehensively that the gift was to be a substantial one. Though her mood had been much softened by the promise of deliverance, she did not feel equal to acting the grateful scene which Antonia so evidently longed for, and she was very much relieved when Captain Bankes insisted that the present should be left in a parcel to be opened on Christmas Day.

9

WHEN MISS MACFARREN promised to divert her monthly quota of wines to Dr. Wilmot, it had been arranged that he should call on her from time to time to collect the precious bottles. He had already visited her once for this purpose, but, with an impatient taxi-driver waiting at the door, he had been unable to stay more than a minute or two, and she had been glad of it, for Mrs. Bankes had a friend with her that day whose fox terrier kept up a vehement shrill barking, precluding, as far as she was concerned, all hope of conversation or even coherent thought.

As soon as she knew she was to have a few days of peaceful solitude, she wrote to the Professor inviting him to collect the wine merchant's latest delivery and ending her note with the hope that this time he would remain long enough to take a glass of the Bristol Cream with her.

Her sister-in-law in Canada had sent her nuts and raisins and the materials for a Christmas cake, which she had managed to bake one afternoon while Mrs. Bankes was at the pictures. Although it was near his dinner hour, the Professor partook with gusto of everything she offered, remarking that he would stand no nonsense from his digestion: he was master and always made his stomach understand as much. 'I say to it, "If you boggle at this simple piece of Christmas cake, what are you going to do when you come to the lobster and the steak-and-kidney pudding?"'

'Does that work?' she asked smiling.

'Certainly. It keeps it in its place. It *is* in its place, isn't it? For a man of my age, I could be in worse shape, couldn't I?'

'You are in such good shape that your age is no consideration at all,' she answered with unusual fluency, but she was conscious of a slight impropriety and did not encourage him to pursue the subject.

The Bankeses had very courteously urged her to make full use of the sitting-room in their absence, so it was there (having taken down the repulsive oil-painting and turned it with its face to the wall) that she received Dr. Wilmot and showed him such items in her collection as had been acquired since his last visit in her brother Andrew's time. He was less handsome in his appreciation today than when he had been shocked into an expression of sympathy: in fact, his general tone was somewhat belittling, and there were moments when he became once more the supercilious and arrogant character she had always taken him for. But the eagerness with which he pointed out the defects of her unique series of Dutch prints convinced her that he had not outgrown a youthful form of envy just as he had not outgrown youthful greed.

Such boyish treats were hard to recognize for what they were behind that black beard and those alarming bushy eyebrows, but, once identified, they were almost endearing, for she could couple them now with his good qualities—the qualities that made him so complaisant as he poured wine and ate peaches. She had begun by showing him the best of her possessions, but after a while, she brought out poor specimens or incomplete sets, and he cheered up immensely as he told her what splendid copies he had of the works in question and expressed his regret to see her so poorly provided.

Miss MacFarren too was well satisfied, for she had learned a great deal about managing a personality she had once thought formidable: and when they parted, she had promised to be his guest at the annual Ladies' Night of the Connoisseurs' Club.

Another visitor whom she took the opportunity of receiving at Christmas was her nephew, recently returned from abroad, and by her particular request, he brought Maxine Albert with him. Ever since their conversation in St. James's Park, Miss MacFarren had wanted to meet Maxine again, not only because she had found her unexpectedly agreeable, but because she had formed an idea that the worldly, cynical, but curiously amiable girl might have some power to help Mory in the impending divorce proceedings. Remembering Maxine's need of a flat, she had even enquired here and there in the hope that a lucky chance might give her the excuse for making an approach; no such excuse having been offered, she took the next best way of improving the acquaintance and relied on time to provide some private occasion for discussing Mory's entanglement.

Time was certainly in her favour, as Mory himself unconsciously informed her when he remarked, in his shameless way, on the unpleasantness of his position. 'Of course you know I've still got the sword of Damocles hanging over me—this dreary divorce business. Talk about shortages and queues! There's a shortage of everything connected with the law courts except red tape. You have to queue for weeks to get a girl to type an affidavit. You have to queue years for a judge.'

'Why should there be a shortage of judges?' Maxine demanded. 'They're all about ninety-two, aren't they? They couldn't have used them up in the war.'

'I suppose they're being kept for the jolly war scapegoats' trials or something. I only know that trying to get a case heard is like going back to the days of Jarndyce v. Jarndyce.'

'Why should you grumble?' said Maxine scornfully. 'Can't you wait to hand Stevie Mace the wad of banknotes?'

'You can guess what I'd like to do to Mace. What gets me down is the uncertainty. And I'd rather the case came on now, while I'm not much in the limelight, than perhaps just when my new picture's released.'

'The publicity surely won't hurt your picture,' Miss MacFarren ventured on a casual note, as if such topics were quite familiar to her.

'No, darling, but it might increase the damages for Mace. Everyone in the film business is supposed to be rich.' He frowned, flinging a cigarette end into the fire so vigorously that it ricocheted and had to be retrieved from the carpet. 'I dare say it'll drag on till Geraldine and I are tired of each other.'

Miss MacFarren was a little shocked but also a little gratified to hear him speak in this vein, and the gratification was not so much because he had hinted that he and Geraldine might part as because he admitted her so naturally into his counsels. Not that Mory had ever been inclined to secrecy, but since he had ceased to live at home, they had necessarily lost touch to some extent, and it was a comfort to find that he readily resumed his old freedom of speech with her. She believed it must be due in some measure to his seeing his young and attractive friend so much at ease with her, and she was grateful once again for the absence on Maxine's part of any artificial attitude towards her grey hair and celibate condition. In her gratitude, she replenished the glasses with a generosity which made Maxine exclaim:

'What's your aunt's idea, Mory—trying to get us stinking?' Such words came more strangely than ever from those soft rosebud lips with their babyish pout, for Maxine was wearing a velvet bonnet trimmed with white swansdown which emphasized quite touchingly her look of dewy freshness and innocence. 'I've got to go to dinner with a man in the fur trade,' she said. 'Believe it or not, his name's Wolfe, so I'd better be able to stand upright.'

'On Christmas Eve some latitude is allowed,' Miss MacFarren suggested benignly.

'To Maxie or the wolf, Aunt Ellie? . . . Oh, talking of Christmas Eve, I'd forgotten something.'

He hurried out as fast as his unequal feet would carry him and brought back a very pretty fancy basket. 'I got it in Madeira, darling,' he said. 'I thought you could put your sewing in it or something.'

'What a beauty! I haven't seen one like it for years. It'll be most useful.' She bundled rapidly out of her mind the painful thought that it would do for the extra mending imposed on her by Mrs. Bankes's neglect of the linen.

'Open it!'

She lifted the round plaited lid and recognized with astonishment and delight the proud scornful faces of two blue-green Chinese cats frowning implacably from beds of cotton-wool.

'Oh, Mory, how wonderful! These are the cats I saw in that shop near the park. . . . I adored them. Miss Albert, it must be you who told him.'

'Well, he was wondering what to get you and I knew they still had those in stock.'

'I couldn't—I simply couldn't have had a nicer present.' She threw her arms round Mory's neck and kissed him on both cheeks, an unwonted demonstration to which he heartily responded. 'I ought to kiss you too, Miss Albert. I hope you got your aquamarines.'

'They'd gone, worse luck! The wolf asked me to choose myself a Christmas present. I went to the shop, just in case, but they'd sold that set ages ago. The cats had been taken out of the window and put right at the back of everything.'

'I do hope they didn't cost a great deal,' said Miss MacFarren, placing them on the carved mantelpiece and standing back to admire the effect. 'I'm afraid they did, though. Oh dear, I have nothing to give you worthy of such a present as this. However, I must fetch what I've got.'

Her brain worked feverishly at the unforeseen problem of a gift for Maxine, who could obviously not go away empty-handed after having so cleverly guided Mory's choice. In her study a bottle of old brandy was already wrapped in holly-sprigged paper and labelled for her nephew. She went swiftly down to the little cellar and, congratulating herself on her excellent memory for conversations, extracted for Maxine a bottle of gin. There was no more Christmas wrapping paper, so, with considerable presence of mind, she stripped Mory's bottle and presented both with equal informality.

There could be no doubt at all that Maxine's reaction was most appreciative, though all she said was: 'My God, my favourite tipple! Mory, what an aunt!' She hugged the bottle to her bosom and somehow succeeded in looking like a little girl clasping a doll.

'It does seem mean,' said Miss MacFarren to her nephew, 'to give you brandy which belonged to your father and which I always feel is your own by right. But I haven't bought anything this year. Even if one has the money, the things in the shops are so awful—unless one can afford beautiful antiques like these.' She waved her hand towards the cats. 'They're splendid up there! I think I shall leave them. . . . Oh no, of course I can't. They'd never be safe with Mrs. Bankes.'

'Where are these Bankeses of yours?' Mory gazed round as if he expected to find them hidden in the room.

'Away for Christmas. I have the house entirely to myself. Rather too entirely in fact. I haven't even got a servant.'

'In that case, you seem to have a burglar,' said Mory. 'Listen!'

A door had certainly been closed quite noisily somewhere in the house, and a moment later footsteps, by no means light, sounded on the stairs. Fortified by the presence of her guests, but still decidedly nervous, Miss MacFarren strode forth to meet the intruder.

It was embarrassing all round when it turned out to be Captain Bankes. Mory, who stood protectively at her side, looked bewildered, Captain Bankes troubled, and herself guilty. Although she had been pressed to use the sitting-room, there seemed to be something scarcely decent about being caught like this freely availing herself of the privilege, bottles and decanters on the drum table, the Bankeses' own picture taken down from the wall, their ornaments thrust out of sight.

'Oh, it's you,' she said feebly. 'I thought you were away. Won't you come in?' It made her blood run cold to think how near she had been to launching into some diatribe against Mrs. Bankes which the affectionate husband might easily have overheard.

'Well, I hate to intrude on you, Miss MacFarren—you and your friends'—he ducked his head politely in the direction of Maxine, then Mory—'but I'm afraid I'll have to. Would you believe it I've come all the way back to London just to collect something Tonia forgot?'

'Good gracious! From Oxford? It must have been something very important! . . . Oh, Miss Albert, may I introduce Captain Bankes? And this is my nephew, Mory MacFarren.'

Captain Bankes shook hands and repeated the surnames with his usual sympathetic attentiveness, and Miss MacFarren, apologizing for being found in possession of the room, begged him to take something to drink.

'Definitely—most definitely, I will.' His fine Mohawk teeth appeared in one of his slow smiles. 'I don't know when I ever needed a drink more than right this minute. My, what have you got here? A public bar!'

She was glad, as she saw the pleased surprise on his face, that the spirit of Christmas cheer had inspired her to produce an impressive abundance of sherry, whisky, gin, madeira, and port: and when he had selected what he called 'Scotch' for his beverage, she poured it with a hand in whose veins the hospitable blood of MacFarren mingled with that of M'Craig, her mother's line.

'Whoa there, whoa!' he cried. 'Isn't there supposed to be a liquor shortage?'

'Not in this house,' said Maxine. 'It's flowing with gin and whisky.'

'Like Canaan,' said Captain Bankes. 'I hope the inhabitants aren't going to melt away.'

'Is that out of the Bible?' Maxine glanced at him appraisingly under the thick eyelashes that gave her eyes so charming a resemblance to shadowed violets.

For answer he declaimed solemnly, with a rather beautiful intonation: 'Then the dukes of Edom shall be amazed; the mighty men of Moab, trembling shall take hold upon them; all the inhabitants of Canaan shall melt away.'

'They took themselves pretty seriously, those old scripture boys,' said Maxine with a shade of distaste.

He sat down, extended his legs, and returned very steadily her appraising glance. His surprise was probably not less than that which he had been able to register openly at the sight of the copious refreshments, and it increased Miss MacFarren's good humour. Now he could go and tell his silly wife and that detestable Mrs. Jermyn how he had found her, not knitting bedsocks with some old spinster crony, but entertaining a lovely young film actress and an attractive nephew. That phrase about 'thwarted maternal complex' had long been rankling.

Captain Bankes lowered his eyes with a certain deliberateness, as though he feared they might betray his curiosity.

'I wanted to make a getaway without disturbing you,' he said, 'but the things I was sent back for must be in here. Tonia swore they were in the bedroom.'

'Have you got to go back to Oxford tonight?'

'Yes indeed, Miss MacFarren. It's quite a nuisance—quite a hell of a nuisance to be exact. . . . Tonia forgot to pack any of our presents for the Jermyn family in their car when they drove her down with them. She suddenly remembered this afternoon that she'd left the whole works behind.'

'But need you have come all the way to London? Couldn't you have explained?'

'Well, hardly. They're having a Christmas tree. Poor Tonia would never hold up her head again if she had to fob them off with an explanation.'

'Ah yes, it's disappointing if there are children.'

'There are children, and, believe me, Tonia's the most excited of any of them. She managed to find Penelope—Mrs. Jermyn you know—a china ornament even more horrible than that painting the Jermyns gave us. . . . Oh, you've taken it down.'

'It'll be put up again, of course, before you return,' Miss MacFarren hastened to assure him.

'That's no consolation to me, let me tell you. I don't like to see that piece of junk mixed up with your flower pictures, but it's the sort of joke that amuses Tonia—until something else comes along.' He spoke of her in that half-exasperated, half-indulgent tone that fathers use when referring to the faults of their children. 'Which reminds me, Miss MacFarren, she tells me you very kindly promised to look after the birds for her. Thanks a lot.'

She was shaken by a tremor of anger and contempt. The fact was that Mrs. Bankes had gone away without mentioning the unfortunate pets or even leaving any stock of food for them; and she had been obliged to spend valuable hours the day before wandering from shop to shop in search of bird seed. Moreover, she felt a grim certitude that if she had not been staying in the house and able to attend to the birds, and if Captain Bankes had not been there to make humane enquiries, Mrs. Bankes would have left them to starve with precisely the same insouciance. So all she was able to reply was:

'I've taken the cage to my study, so that I can't forget. . . . They don't look very healthy.'

'No. One died,' he said awkwardly.

There was a silence which threatened to be oppressive, until Maxine remarked: 'I suppose there wouldn't be any room in the cage for me? I shall be out in the street next month.'

'Why, you were looking for a flat before I left England,' said Mory. 'Haven't you found one yet?'

'Not so much as a nice wide shelf to sleep on.'

'You people certainly do have a housing problem,' said Captain Bankes. 'Everyone I meet over here seems to be looking for somewhere to live.'

'No one's looking harder than me,' Maxine rejoined, pouting. (Miss MacFarren asked herself earnestly why babyishness should be so much more attractive in Maxine than in Mrs. Bankes, and reminded herself with a suppressed sigh that this was purely a subjective impression.)

'We're in a parlous state if Maxie can't get what she wants,' Mory laughed.

'I imagine so.' Captain Bankes raised his eyes once more to Maxine's face, and there they rested. 'It helps me realize how darned lucky Tonia was to find this place. Your aunt has made us mighty comfortable here, Mr. MacFarren.'

'She's a mighty comfortable aunt,' said Mory with friendly impertinence, and he leaned towards Maxine with some suggestion for bribing a house agent.

'It's a great relief to my mind,' Captain Bankes continued, addressing Miss MacFarren in his speech-making vein, 'to be able to work on the Continent or go back to the States for a trip knowing Tonia's so nicely fixed up in London. It was quite a worry to me having her at the Asturias. To be sordid, all that entertaining used to mount up to something pretty considerable.'

Miss MacFarren hardly heard the last words of this utterance; her attention had been riveted by one phrase.

'Did you say you were going back to America *for a trip*?' She began vigorously poking the fire to conceal the anxiety with which she awaited his answer.

'Why yes, in about four weeks. Didn't I tell you?'

'I understood that you and Mrs. Bankes were going together—for good.'

'No, no! What in the world did I say to give you that impression?'

'Mrs. Bankes told me so.'

'You must have got her wrong, Miss MacFarren.' He sounded sheerly puzzled. 'I mean, about going for good. It's quite right that I was hoping to take her with me this trip, but that's only a flying visit—literally—and we certainly don't want to lose our London headquarters. . . . Say, let me do that for you!'

She was heaping lumps of precious coal on the fire with absolute recklessness. Now she put the tongs back into the scuttle and held her anger in check sufficiently to throw out with apparent nonchalance: 'So Mrs. Bankes won't be going? She'll be greatly disappointed when you tell her.'

'Oh, but I told her a couple of weeks ago. She has a new fur jacket for a consolation prize.'

Miss MacFarren needed no further information: her suspicion was altogether confirmed. That day when Captain Bankes had answered, in all good faith, her questions about the impending American journey, Mrs. Bankes had deliberately allowed her to be misled. Moreover, she had never at any time expected to relinquish her share of the house. Such a deception could only mean that she knew she was virtually under notice and yet was determined by hook or crook to retain possession, using all those tactics of delay and surprise which, in smaller matters, were already familiar.

On Christmas Eve, and in the presence of two guests, there was nothing to do but drown indignation in whisky and ginger ale. She refilled the glasses all round.

'Thank you! Thank you!' Captain Bankes stared with renewed wonder at the measure accorded him. 'This is quite a celebration! I wish I didn't have to make that next train to Oxford.'

'And I wish I didn't have to go to dinner with a man in the fur trade,' said Maxine. 'It's much nicer to sit by this cosy fire soaking gin.'

'You never said a truer word, Miss Albert—though I happen to be soaking Scotch. Isn't it the devil to get up and search for Christmas presents!' He raised himself reluctantly from the deep armchair and moved out of the fireside circle to kneel before the cupboards which his wife had said she would not need, but which were nevertheless always kept so full that they could not be opened without some of the contents spilling upon the floor.

'Aren't you going to Stella Hawthorne's party?' Mory enquired of Maxine.

'I shall turn up later. It'll give me a good excuse for getting away from the wolf. Are you going?'

'I must. Stella's earmarked for my next picture.'

'Oh God!' Maxine pulled what was intended, quite unsuccessfully, to be an ugly face. 'I do think you're mean Mory. You could get me into that if you wanted.'

'You won't be finished with *Cranford* in time.'

'Of course I shall. My sequences in *Cranford* will be through in a month.'

'Nonsense, you're running weeks behind schedule.'

'*Cranford!*' exclaimed Miss MacFarren. 'Is that the name of the film you're acting in, Miss Albert?'

'Yes, it is. But look here, Mory's aunt, you go on calling me "Miss Albert" and I'll give back your bottle of gin!'

Miss MacFarren smilingly undertook not to repeat the offence. 'Is it Mrs. Gaskell's *Cranford*?' she persisted eagerly. 'That's such a favourite of mine.'

'Then you'd better keep away from the picture,' said Maxine.

Mory explained: 'It was somebody's intention that it should be Mrs. Gaskell's *Cranford*, Aunt Ellie, but by the time four writers had treated each other's treatments, it departed a little from the original idea.'

'Oh dear, why do they bother with doing books when they make them so unrecognizable?'

'Well, in this case, Pio Martinez wanted a story with a thoroughly English atmosphere.'

'But he's a Spaniard, isn't he?'

'Yes, that's why he has this hankering to portray the English scene. And Swanziger—the head of our unit, you know—thought it would be a good propaganda picture for our American and foreign markets. Of course, the story itself doesn't give nearly enough scope for lavish production, so there've been some rather drastic changes.'

Miss MacFarren hardly knew how to comment, since her nephew seemed to accept such vandalism with amused tolerance, and his friend was playing in the film, so she only said: 'What part are you taking, Maxine?'

'The village tart,' said Maxine with another grimace.

'The village—good heavens!' Miss MacFarren was so amazed that she positively started. 'But there isn't any character of that sort in the book.'

'No, it's been written in. Pio or somebody thought it needed the contrast. They always like to get a tarty character in if they can.'

'How can they possibly fit her into the story?'

'She tries to take Squire Holcroft away from Miss Matty.'

'Squire Holcroft!' Miss MacFarren racked her memory. 'Is that the old farmer person who would never be called Squire?'

'He's called Squire in this all right. And he's a *young* farmer. He's being played by Mark Harrowby.'

'Good heavens!' Miss MacFarren repeated faintly.

'Miss Matty is being played by Stella Hawthorne,' Mory put in, evidently taking a mischievous pleasure in her discomfiture.

'You can't be serious! Stella Hawthorne is surely in her twenties, and Miss Matty is supposed to be older than I am.'

'Not in this film, she isn't!' Maxine too seemed to enjoy her reaction. 'For the first three-quarters anyhow she's a glamorous beauty. I believe she's going to end up wearing a white wig when she marries him.'

'Does she marry him? I'm almost certain that he dies.'

'No, they've changed that. In the book there's a long-lost brother who arrives from India. In the film the brother is turned into her old sweetheart. He gave up the farm and went out to India, you see, when she refused him!'

'But what's the point of that?'

'So that dear old boy can get dear old girl after a lifetime's devotion. The wedding scene's going to be a real tear-jerker.'

'Oh dear, oh dear! What a travesty!'

'If I may venture a remark,' said Captain Bankes, looking up from a pyramid of miscellaneous objects which he had turned out upon the floor, 'you seem very innocent about this film business, Miss MacFarren, considering you have a director in the family.'

'I've never been in a studio in my life.'

'Aunt Ellie! Darling! Are you reproaching me! You know you could have come any time.'

While Mory was still making his way, Miss MacFarren had not liked to intrude upon his working life, and since he had succeeded, they had seen little of each other: but now it occurred to her that she could repair something of this recent strangeness by getting him to invite her to the studio, and at the same time the occasion might serve for another meeting with Maxine. So she at once availed herself of this opening to express a strong desire to see the process of film-making, and it was arranged that she should go out to Cornfields in January on a day when Maxine as well as Mory should be 'on the set'.

'Not that I have anything to do with *Cranford*, Aunt Ellie,' Mory reassured her in the tone of one who has his pride. 'That wouldn't be up my street at all. I'm cashing in on the boom in little children. At least, I hope there's going to be a boom in little children.'

'There is in the States,' said Captain Bankes.

'Yes, but my style's realistic, you know, not whimsical—'

Miss MacFarren interrupted to ask suddenly: 'Maxine, how is that curious little girl? What was her name—Juanita!'

'Still the studio pet, practising winning ways till you yearn to lay her across your knee, poor brat!'

'I wish Pio would keep her out of the studio,' Mory declared with what was for him a considerable degree of irritation. 'She spoiled two takes for me last week by starting to talk when we were shooting.'

'I dare say she's naughty,' said Miss MacFarren, 'but she's a very pretty appealing child. She'll probably grow up to be a fascinating woman.'

Maxine shook her head. 'She won't grow up to be a woman at all unless her father learns some sense. She'll be a horrible little Peter Pan case.'

The words struck some chord in the depths of Miss MacFarren's consciousness which vibrated there in a disturbing way, and Mory had answered several courteous questions about his work before she brought her full attention back to what was going on about her.

'I can't find a damn thing,' Captain Bankes was saying. 'Do you suppose there's anywhere else to look?'

'What about the linen closet? Mrs. Bankes has been keeping quite a lot of odd things in there lately.'

This new encroachment had been a sore point, as a woman might at once have concluded, but Captain Bankes's face was entirely unclouded as he jumped to his feet exclaiming: 'The linen closet! That's quite an idea!'

'Your lodger's a nice creature,' said Mory when the door had closed on him. 'Exactly like his writings.'

'And what are *they* like?' asked Maxine.

'What do you think?'

'Solemn! Solemn, good-natured, and'—she paused and added thoughtfully—'nicely shaped.'

At this moment the telephone rang. Miss MacFarren did not stir, having little reason to doubt that it would be a Bankes call, and in a moment or two, Captain Bankes could be heard insisting to some distant correspondent that he and no other was in waiting. As soon as he began to speak, she plunged into a conversation with the others to prevent herself from listening. Nevertheless, groaning protests, expletives mild in themselves but uttered with force, made themselves audible, and no one was surprised, though all endeavoured to be, when he came back into the room lamenting that his journey had been for nothing.

'She had everything with her the whole time—every darn thing except this!' He held up a cardboard shoe-box.

Miss MacFarren and her nephew expressed their commiserations as heartily as they could without speaking rudely of his wife, but Maxine, less tactful, demanded scornfully: 'Does she often do this kind of thing?'

Captain Bankes was sufficiently annoyed to reply without his customary inhibition of loyalty: 'Just about as often as I can stand it.'

'No wonder they say Americans are such long-suffering husbands!'

'How did Mrs. Bankes come to think she'd left the presents behind?' Miss MacFarren interposed sympathetically. 'They were rather bulky parcels to overlook, weren't they?'

'She'd packed them all in cartons, it seems, and Tom Jermyn stowed them away at the back of the car with his wife's Christmas things, and they were all taken out by the maid and put away together. I went down by train, so I didn't realize . . .' He opened the shoe-box. 'This was right by the telephone. She left it out because she hadn't finished wrapping it. . . . Isn't it a hell-begotten thing?'

He lifted from protecting layers of tissue paper a naked doll with a head of fuzzy crêpe hair.

'This is what she's going to give Penelope.'

The figure, representing a little girl, held its arms in a graceful attitude and its features were coyly demure, but to its facetiously rotund stomach there clung in permanent attachment the life-size and convincing semblance of a house-fly.

'It's wax,' was all Miss MacFarren could bring herself to say. 'Not china.'

'It's hideous, whatever it is!'

'I think it's wrong to buy a thing like that,' said Maxine languidly but with a certain distinguishable undercurrent of vehemence. 'People ought not to be encouraged to make anything so disgusting, even for a joke.'

Captain Bankes stood holding the figure gingerly and staring at it with a reproachful look that brought new furrows to his face. 'It's worse than the oil-painting,' he said at last. 'Tonia wins hands down. It's much worse. The only thing that can be said in its favour, it must have been cheaper.'

'Those sort of horrors cost an awful lot of money,' Maxine went on ruthlessly. 'I'll bet I could buy a new hat—at any rate, a new pair of shoes with the money that thing cost.'

As if he were weighing these words, Captain Bankes looked sadly at her small beautifully shod feet, and then her legs, and then the rounded knees visible in the black frou-frou of silk pleats that terminated her skirt. As he did so he lowered the hand grasping the doll.

'Careful!' Mory cried. 'It'll melt if you hold it so near the fire.'

'That's what I'd like to do with it. It'd be a real pleasure to throw it in. But Tonia would be miserable if it didn't go on the Christmas tree.'

'Well, if that's Tonia's idea of a merry Christmas,' said Maxine more insolently than ever, 'give me this!' She laid an affectionate hand on her bottle of gin.

'Don't take it seriously, Miss Albert!' he implored, apologetically recalling his loyalty. 'It's only a game she plays with this friend of hers. . . . Hell! Shall I melt the dam' thing or shan't I?'

For an instant the doll hovered near the flames. Then with a heavy sigh, he laid it in its tissue paper. 'Better not. To think I came all the way back to London for this! Finding you and your friends here, Miss MacFarren, and enjoying this little celebration has just about saved my reason.'

'And I've just about lost mine,' said Maxine, 'filling myself up with gin when I ought to have my wits about me.' She rose, shook out her frilled skirt, and hugged her grey lynx coat luxuriously round her. 'What do you think you I have to do to get a man in the fur trade to give you a new fur coat—or even to let you have one at cost price?'

'You've asked two quite different questions, but I dare say you know the answers to both,' said Mory.

'After all, I didn't get the aquamarines. And I don't ask much. Not a mink or anything like that. Just a broadtail, or something quite simple.'

'Then you should try some quite simple method,' Mory returned dryly. 'You could probably work out something if you thought about it long enough.'

'I wish poor Mr. Wolfe didn't bore me. I never like to take presents from people who bore me. You feel you've got to go on seeing them. . . . Oh, well, out into the night! You coming, Mory?'

'I'm going to try and pick up a taxi,' said Captain Bankes. 'Can I give you both a lift—Paddington way?'

'I've got my car,' said Mory. 'If you wait a few minutes till I've made my aunt sign one or two papers, I'll run you to the station.'

'I can't wait, I'm afraid.'

'I'll go with you,' said Maxine, taking her bottle under her arm. 'The fur merchant lives in Park Lane. That's on your way.'

She bade goodbye prettily to her hostess, showing her dimples and making her repeat her promise to come to the studio; and Captain Bankes, assuring them all again that they had saved the situation for him, escorted her from the house.

'You'd better take care of your lodger, Aunt Ellie,' said Mory.

'Oh, my dear boy, how can you talk like that? What can be more natural than his giving her a lift since he's going her way?'

'I'm sure he hadn't an ulterior thought in his head. But if Maxine has any ulterior thoughts—well, take care of your lodger, that's all! There's something about that baby face that men have never been known to resist.'

'I can see she's a most attractive girl in spite of her odd way of talking. It's because she's so completely herself.'

'Yes, there isn't an atom of affectation in her . . . unless it's that she affects to be a little worse than she is.'

'That's exactly what I've felt about her.'

'People who can't bear shams have a tendency to sham, quite unconsciously, in reverse. She seems to have taken a fancy to you, dear. She says you're "real" and "good quality".'

'I find that I like her too. There's just one thing that troubles me a little—for her own sake. Do you think she drinks too much for a young girl?'

'That's nice, coming from you, when you've been doing your best to make us cock-eyed! As a matter of fact, I should be rather worried myself about her drinking if she weren't so desperately ambitious. She never lets anything interfere with work. She's determined to be a star, and I think she'll make the grade.'

'Is she a good actress?'

'Not very, but she can take direction. Her face is difficult to photograph, but it's worth the trouble. And of course, her sex appeal is terrific.'

'I wonder you haven't fallen in love with her yourself, Mory.'

'I was otherwise engaged when I met her, else I might have done.'

Miss MacFarren decided that, from more points of view than one, Maxine might be a useful acquaintance to cultivate.

10

IT WAS NOT without reason that Miss MacFarren had dreaded the elaborately wrapped parcel, labelled 'To be opened on Christmas Day', which Mrs. Bankes had deposited in the study. On removing the silver ribbon, the paper decorated with cupids and garlands, the layers of cotton-wool, she found an inkstand of the Regency period with two charming bottles, a sand-box, and a candlestick, all exquisitely contrived in glass and ormolu. It was a first-rate specimen and obviously a costly purchase. Moreover, it revealed a delicate attention to what might have been supposed to be her wishes, for she could remember that, in making some half-apology for the untidiness of her desk one day when Captain Bankes had come to borrow sealing-wax, she had told him how her china inkstand had been shivered in the blast which had blown out the windows.

There might be women, she acknowledged, who would have the strength of mind to refuse the unwelcome gift, and others who, having accepted it, would still be capable of informing the donors that they must expect to be homeless at the end of four weeks: herself she had not the courage or the detachment or the insensitiveness-—whatever quality or defect was requisite—to take either of these steps. She could merely resolve to try and hold her own against Mrs. Bankes in their future relations, and to remain alert for the opportunity of freeing herself which, this month, she was clearly denied.

Her endeavour to square accounts by giving the Bankeses several bottles of fine wine turned out to be an error of judgment, since its principal effect was to make her seem more friendly and familiar with them.

It was in January, a week or two after Captain Bankes's return to Germany, that she found herself involved in an unpleasantness of so open and prolonged a nature that it might, if Mrs. Bankes had taken the incident less casually, have been called a row. In her husband's absence she entertained more noisily and inconsiderately than during the brief periods of his companionship, and Miss MacFarren's nerves were already on edge from days of accumulating irritations when she was aware of a reiterated falsetto whine closely resembling the ear-torturing note of a rough slate pencil being dragged up and down on a smooth slate.

'It's that fox terrier again,' she thought with dismay. 'I do hope it isn't going to be here long.' And her relief was great when, after only a few minutes, the front door closed on the dog and its owner.

The day was cold, wet, and windy, and she flinched from putting on her outdoor clothes and seeking a place for lunch in one of the crowded local cafés. Though her attempts to prepare meals in her study were fraught with so many inconveniences that they had become rare, today she decided to use up her cheese ration in a welsh rarebit, and at the same time to luxuriate in an egg which had come into her possession.

But, going downstairs to fetch her provisions, she discovered that the cheese, the precious egg, and her week's portion of margarine were missing. She was exasperated but not surprised. Since Mrs. Manders' departure, Mrs. Bankes had formed a habit—always supposed to be inadvertent—of helping herself to Miss MacFarren's rations, her own being insufficient for so much entertaining. The study with its daily fire was not a place where food could be kept, and Miss MacFarren was obliged to continue using her share of the larder though she found these depredations most troublesome. It was true that, when she drew attention to them, Mrs. Bankes urged her eagerly to help herself in return to anything she fancied or needed from her own store; but such happy-go-lucky proceedings would have been so far out of her character that they were practically out of her power.

One part of her recent resolution, however, had been that, when she believed herself the victim of some Bankes imposition, she would not sit in her study brooding over the pros and cons of the matter and weighing her right to object until the moment for raising objection had passed, but would boldly strike while the iron of the grievance was hot. She therefore opened the door of the kitchen where Mrs. Bankes was engaged in some cooking operation, and explained that the materials for her lunch had disappeared.

'Oh, have I sneaked them? How shocking of me! Never mind! Have one of my meat patties instead!'

She offered a Minton dish on which she had arranged the patties in an ornamental manner, and Miss MacFarren's state of mind was not improved by noticing how badly it had been chipped since leaving her own service. 'Can't I have my egg?' she asked plaintively. 'It doesn't matter much about the cheese.'

'I'm afraid I must have used them both by mistake in the salad last night. But I'll be able to let you have lots of eggs next week. I'm getting some from the country.'

Miss MacFarren was half-inclined to express her disbelief in blunt terms, but decided that it would be undignified to quarrel about an egg. 'My margarine has gone too,' she said stolidly.

'Honestly, you ought to give me a good slap! Wait a minute! I think I can let you have some back. I didn't use it all.'

Miss MacFarren coldly said 'Thank you', and also accepted with reluctance one of the meat patties, feeling she was well entitled to it.

Immediately Mrs. Bankes began to talk as if she had conferred a bounty. 'They're delicious. From Brabant's, you know, the Belgian shop, the one place where they still sell meat things that are nearly pre-war. I'm so glad you're not going to have that solitary boiled egg. Too boring it would have been! Do take some of my salad too!'

But Miss MacFarren declined the salad.

During this interchange she had noticed that Mrs. Bankes was peeling potatoes, for her an unlikely piece of drudgery, and to change the subject—for she had no intention of pretending gratitude for the loss of her egg—she enquired whether the charwoman had already gone.

'I should just think she has—gone once and for all. She was a horrid dirty thing, and she grumbled all the time about the work. I was only too delighted when she took her beastly money and left.'

'I noticed she was dirty,' said Miss MacFarren pointedly. 'The work, of course, is really beyond a charwoman's powers. . . .'

She was about to make it clear, while she felt in the mood, that she did not consider the terms of their domestic agreement were being fulfilled, when the fox terrier's passionate shrill bark, which she recalled unforgettably from its previous visits, rent the air in the hall above, and she realized that the owner must have let herself in with a latch-key. The awful thought crossed her mind that visitors who are given latchkeys have usually come to stay, but she was reassured when, a moment later, dog and owner made their way down the basement stairs—the dog contending every step with a bark—and the key was laid on the kitchen table together with a loaf of bread and a paper bag.

'I couldn't get any cake,' said the woman, when the terrier allowed her to be heard, 'but I spent some of your points on a pound of biscuits. Here's your ration book.' She put it on the table beside the key.

'Didn't you bring the kippers?' Antonia asked with a shade of fretfulness.

'My dear, the queue was a mile long, and I daren't miss my train.'

Miss MacFarren withdrew to her study with the question of domestic service still to be pursued, and ate her meat patty in dudgeon. She wondered why the 'lady friend' who had said she was to catch a train lingered so long for the dog was still giving voice to intense agitation in the basement, and, undemonstrative as she was, she almost prayed aloud for the moment when she might go on with her writing in comparative peace.

Heavier than all the other discomforts to which Mrs. Bankes had reduced her was the moral discomfort of having ceased to make any visible progress with her work. Her books were more than merely a source from which, at distant intervals, she added two or three hundred pounds to her income, though that was much; they were her satisfaction, her pride, her solace, her business in life, the reason why she was at ease in spinsterhood, and why she could face the solitudes of old age without distress. Writing her calm resumés of floral history, painting her delicate representations of vegetable life, thus she had always pictured herself occupied until her hands were too feeble to wield brush or pen. But now she was accomplishing next to nothing, and in the gloom of her daily frustration, she felt that she would never accomplish anything

So when the dog began scratching and whimpering at her own door fully an hour after its mistress had spoken of train-catching, she rushed hotly out and called in a peremptory tone for Mrs. Bankes.

A playfully meek voice jodelled down to her from the first floor.

'It's this dog!' cried Miss MacFarren. 'I simply can't work.'

'What? Is he bothering you? Naughty Jimjams! Just push him away and tell him not to be silly!'

Miss MacFarren smothered the retort that sprang to her lips and demanded: 'But how long is he staying? I thought your friend was in a hurry to leave.'

'Mrs. Netley? Oh, she left ages ago. She's gone to Scotland.'

'You mean—without the dog?' Miss MacFarren's voice quite lost its well-bred restraint, and as Mrs. Bankes remained provokingly out of sight on the first landing, she herself mounted grimly to the half-landing, her heart beating in anticipation of the now inevitable horror—the scene.

Mrs. Bankes, whose arms were laden with sheets and towels from the linen closet, smiled blithely down, leaning on the banisters. 'I shall be taking care of him for a little while. He's really a sweet doggums when you get to know him.'

'Are you seriously trying to tell me that you've undertaken to have an extremely noisy dog in the house without consulting me?'

By a dramatic change of countenance, Mrs. Bankes produced her look of bland idiocy. Her eyes opened very wide, her mouth slackened. 'Oh dear, what have I done now?' she said. 'You never breathed a word about hating doggies.'

'I do *not* hate dogs—though I must say fox terriers with that piercing way of barking are not my favourite breed—but I made it quite clear at our first interview that I could only share this house with quiet tenants.'

'Well, Jimjams will be a quiet tenant when he's settled down. He's still missing his Mamma.'

'His Mamma?'

'Mrs. Netley. I always call her his Mamma,' she explained placidly.

'But he barks incessantly even when she's here.'

'I'll have to teach him to keep quiet then,' said Mrs. Bankes without a trace of sincerity, disappearing into the spare room.

Miss MacFarren resolutely ascended the second half of the flight, and stood on the landing by the open door, asking: 'How long do you intend to have the dog here?'

'Only about a week.' The reply was instantaneous, but recollecting how glibly she would lie to avoid the smallest shadow of a conflict, Miss MacFarren resolved not to be softened.

'A week will be the limit of my endurance. After that I must absolutely draw the line. There's quite enough disturbance as it is.'

Mrs. Bankes took no notice of this, but went on laying out linen for the guest beds, her face expressing complete absorption in her task.

'Since it *is* here,' Miss MacFarren continued with emphasis, 'I only hope you'll feed it and look after it.'

'Of course I shall. I dote on dogs.'

'You said you doted on birds, but you're always forgetting to feed them, and you never clean out the cage.'

She remained imperturbable. 'You've all spoiled me about the birds. I've got it into my head that somebody else'll remember them. But if there's no one but me to do it, I shall have to attend to Jimjams myself, shan't I. Besides, dogs are more noticeable about the house than birds.'

'I'm afraid they are,' said Miss MacFarren, and she went back to her own room, half-relieved, half-disappointed that the scene had not, after all, achieved full development. An out-and-out row could scarcely have failed to lead to the point when she would pronounce the decree of banishment so hard at any time to utter in cold blood, and doubly so with the Regency inkstand newly adorning her desk. But Mrs. Bankes, by refusing to lose her temper—rude though she had been in subtle ways—had dexterously spiked her guns, had succeeded once again in making her seem a cantankerous, crotchety old woman whose interferences she tolerated with uncomplaining good nature.

The episode of the dog, which was destined to surpass all other miseries suffered at Mrs. Bankes's hands, began with modified torments, consisting merely of its howling, whining, and barking at untoward hours of the night and morning. As it happened, the young girl known as Froggie had come to stay again with her mother, and, owing to their kindly attentions, the dog was fed and exercised and even to some degree conciliated. But after a week they left, and the circumstances of their departure gave rise to apprehensions which were quickly realized.

Miss MacFarren was out one morning buying drawing materials when she ran into Froggie, laden with three shopping bags and struggling to restrain the fox terrier from winding its lead round her ankles.

'Hullo, you're in difficulties!' she said, and paused to extricate her. 'Gracious! What a weight these bags are! You'd better let me carry one. I'm on my way home.'

'There's six tins of soup in that one, and two jars of jam,' said Froggy. 'They're awfully heavy.'

'Wouldn't it be easier to make two journeys?'

'I can't, because we're leaving this morning. Tonia wants me to do as much shopping as I can for her before we go.'

'Oh I'm sorry,' said Miss MacFarren with genuine regret, for Froggie and Mrs. Reece were by far the most congenial of Mrs. Bankes's many guests. 'You've both been so very good about helping in the house.'

'That's just why we're going away.' Froggie's voice dropped happily to its confidential level. 'Mummie says she only invited us because she hasn't got a charwoman.'

Miss MacFarren, who thought that Mrs. Reece's guess was probably correct, made a sympathetic murmur intended to encourage, but not to solicit, further communication.

'She rang Mummie up and said she was lonely and not well and all sorts of things, and that we absolutely *must* come and stay. And Mummie's very kind-hearted, you know, and of course it's nice for us to get up to London sometimes; so we came. And we found Tonia was as well as anything and not a bit lonely—going out or having visitors all the time while we do the housework.'

'I've noticed you've been kept busy,' said Miss MacFarren with a slight smile. 'But why has your mother consented to do so much?'

'Tonia sort of wheedles us, and it's awfully difficult to refuse when you're a guest. And Mummie couldn't bear seeing your house so neglected and all those horrid mice in the dining-room and everything.'

'Mice!' Miss MacFarren's voice if not her person shuddered. 'The house is beginning to smell of mice.'

'Tonia says they were always there in swarms from the beginning. . . .'

'That's entirely untrue.'

'Yes, we never used to see any at first. Now they come out even in the daytime and run across the floor in front of your eyes. Mummie felt she just had to try and straighten things up, but Tonia goes on having people into meals all the time, so the work piles up faster than anyone can do it.'

'I wonder she doesn't at least *try* to get a maid.' Miss MacFarren groaned.

'Mummie thinks'—Froggie's voice dropped still lower to the whisper of an awed conspirator—'Mummie thinks it's to save money, so that she'll have more for herself.'

'Oh, but she isn't a bit interested in saving money. She's very careless with it.'

'That's because Captain Bankes pays the bills. When she can put things on the account, like food and flowers and clothes, she doesn't mind how much they cost. But you see, a maid has to be paid every week in cash—this is what Mummie says—and Tonia'd rather have the money to spend.'

A sharp outbreak of barking on the part of the terrier, which had conceived a frenzied desire to attack a motorcyclist, prevented Miss MacFarren from making an audible reply, and she had time before speaking again, to recognize that Mrs. Reece's conclusion might have its basis of truth. Mrs. Bankes, who frittered away more on hair-dressings and manicures, scents and fashion papers, taxis and idle shopping excursions, than any woman she had ever known, was quite silly enough to begrudge money spent on so prosaic a matter as scrubbing and dish-washing, and quite selfish enough to try and save it at the expense of obliging friends. And her disinclination to pay for an uninteresting service would be strongly supported by her distaste for the dull business of visiting registry offices and conducting interviews.

'I don't suppose Mrs. Bankes's friends have any idea of the promises she made me when she first came.' Miss MacFarren had now frankly become a fellow-conspirator.

'I know this much,' Froggie responded, proud of her capacity to take part in this womanly gossip. 'Mummie told her she wasn't being fair to you.'

Miss MacFarren felt ashamed, but she could not refrain from asking: 'What did she say?'

'Oh, she just smiled. Mummie says you can't quarrel with Tonia. She always laughs, no matter how cross you get. Of course, she's frightfully good-tempered.'

'Frightfully!'

'Mummie's known her since she was the same age as me. She was the youngest of three sisters, and the other two were ever so much older than she was. And Tonia was her father's pet because she was much the prettiest. And her father didn't get on with her mother, and they used to quarrel about her, but Tonia always got her own way on account of being able to wind her father round her little finger. And—what do you think?'

Miss MacFarren made a suitable interrogative noise though, nursing her immediate wrongs, she was only vaguely interested in this somewhat breathless précis of Mrs. Bankes's youth.

'Well, we were talking the other day about who we liked best in the world, and I said "My mother", and Tonia said she absolutely hated her mother. Don't you think that was dreadful?'

'At least it sounds like a moment of truth.'

'She said her favourite people were her father and her husband. So I asked Mummie afterwards why she didn't seem to remember her children, and Mummie said Tonia had always refused to grow up in her mind, so she didn't really have ordinary feelings about her children.'

Refusing to grow up! 'A horrible little Peter Pan case!' Miss MacFarren recognized again the peculiar stirring of uneasiness that had first been awakened by Maxine's phrase. She had often heard people refer to one or other of their acquaintances as 'utterly childish' or 'an overgrown baby', but it had always seemed a figure of speech, no nearer to literal significance than if they had said 'utterly asinine', or called someone 'a perfect savage' or 'a man with a heart of gold'. But lately, since that seed had been planted by Maxine, she had asked herself whether it might be true that there were some people who literally—yes, quite literally—remained children in their minds. Not child-like. That was another thing: that conveyed the idea of the simplicity, the innocence of childhood. But if a person had refused to grow up, that would be because he (or, more particularly, she) had perceived, not with a child's simplicity, but with its cunning, that advantages were to be reaped from the state of irresponsibility.

Suppose that Mrs. Bankes actually had the mentality of the spoiled little girl she so often seemed, that it was no well-sustained pose but a reality, then to deal with her by rational adult standards was positively impossible. One must learn, in the most practical sense, the technique of dealing with spoiled little girls. And this was a complicated matter at the best of times, and, when they happened to wear hats by Aage Thaarup, dresses by Matilda Etches, and a hair style by Steiner, most confusing.

The dog, by a determined endeavour to trip up an old gentleman, had provided her with a few moments of silent though not peaceful reflection. After the interruption she remarked with a certain *arriére-pensée*:

'It's to be hoped that Captain Bankes makes up as a father what his wife lacks as a mother.'

'Oh, but he does!' cried Froggie. 'He's the most wonderful father. Even I can remember that. They were in England for a bit, you know, before the war. The children were tiny then, but he used to play with them and teach them so beautifully, you just can't imagine. Mummie always said he was a born father.'

She had answered Miss MacFarren's question more completely then she knew. She had solved that insistent problem, What Did He See In Her? Captain Bankes, a born father, liked Peter Pan cases; he was attracted by a woman who had refused to grow up. The childishness which made her unbearable to Miss MacFarren and perhaps tiresome eventually to everyone who knew her at close quarters, was to him an enduring charm. He was a patriarch, he accepted responsibility, he enjoyed the relationship of teacher to affectionate pupil. Separated for years from his children, it might even be that he found in his wife a kind of substitute for them.

It was quite a psychological sort of thing really, Miss MacFarren considered, surprised at her own perspicuity: there might be something like it in Freud—only, now that she came to think of it, in what little she had read of Freud, parents were not so much yearning for their children's lifelong companionship as repressing secret desires to kill them. Captain Bankes must belong to some other psychoanalytical system.

She had read somewhere years ago—was it a maxim of Da Vinci's?—a phrase that said: 'If the loved one is base, then the lover becomes base,' and, believing it to be true, she had contemplated with misgivings that were almost sorrowful this generous and honest man's allegiance to a selfish and dishonest character. But now his weakness could be interpreted as a kind of misapplied strength. It did not carry the corollary of baseness any more than a father's indulgent love towards his young family.

Interesting though it was to have produced this explanation, which she would have liked to pursue at leisure, there were the difficulties of the moment to be coped with; and when the terrier had been quieted after a struggle to fling itself upon a pair of exasperated borzois, she enquired gloomily: 'How soon do you think this dog is to be taken away?'

'Mrs. Netley has gone to Scotland for a month,' Froggie replied promptly.

'A month! Good heavens! When did you hear that?'

'Last time we were in London, when Tonia first arranged to look after him. Mummie told her then that you mightn't like it.'

Well, so much for Mrs. Bankes's 'only a week'. It was strange, no matter how little credence one placed in any of her statements, the proof that she had lied always came as a slight shock. Miss MacFarren had never since schooldays met anyone with whom it was so habitual to avoid trouble by lying. She saw it now as the symptom of an ill-guided childhood never outgrown, but that didn't make it less objectionable. 'Any more,' she thought dismally, 'than it takes the edge off the dog's bark to know it's the nature of the poor little beast.'

After the Reeces had gone she was given plentiful opportunity of becoming acquainted with the unfortunate animal's nature, for within a few days it became dependent upon her for all the comforts, beyond an occasional romp, or a bout of petting, that it was ever permitted to enjoy at 16 Harberton Square. She had spoken again to Mrs. Bankes on the subject, expressing an assumed surprise at finding the dog still in the house, had listened with embarrassment to the rapidly contrived excuses, and since there was nowhere else for it to go, had renewed her plea that it might be properly looked after. Mrs. Bankes had instantly given a demonstration of the care she proposed to lavish on the dog by handing it (on one of the Wedgwood dinner plates) a lamb chop that must have been half her week's ration.

The following day its diet appeared to consist of two dog biscuits thrown upon the kitchen floor. When Miss MacFarren, by a process of espionage which was very troublesome, had made certain that it was hungry, she crept down after Mrs. Bankes was in bed and secretly fed it. Remembering that Mrs. Bankes had seized upon her humane attentions to the birds as a warrant for neglecting them, she was resolved to do nothing for it openly.

The noise and disorder next morning were such that she decided to escape by spending the day in the greenhouses of Kew Gardens. On the hall table, she left a note for Mrs. Bankes, impressing upon her the necessity of getting another servant without delay and warning her that, although she had tended the boiler herself on the two preceding days, she had no intention of continuing to do so. She had preferred this formal method of communication, partly because she thought it might have more effect, partly because she did not choose to compete for a hearing with the dog, which was announcing its presence in the sitting-room with loud staccato yelps, timed as regularly as if they had been produced by a mechanical device.

When she returned that evening, having stayed at Kew after public hours to take tea with one of the staff, she was astonished to see her envelope lying unopened exactly as she had placed it. The dog was still vehement behind the closed door of the sitting-room, but now the percussive notes were no longer regular, but hoarse and urgent, mingled with helpless whimperings like human cries. Without pausing to make any conjecture, she at once entered the room, throwing the dog into an hysteria of relief. It leapt at her again and again, wagging its tail dementedly, its breaking voice more pitiful in gratitude than it had been in despair.

'Jimjams!' She spoke the distasteful name quite tenderly, bending down to reassure the animal with caresses. 'You don't mean to say you've been shut up here since this morning?'

A single glance round the room gave her all too emphatically her answer. The paintwork of the door jambs and the lower panels was covered with marks of tooth and claw, the floor was scattered with a variety of untoward objects, from a gnawed bone to a capsized vase lying in a heap of flowers, and oh!—she could have wailed aloud to see it!—oh! how the Aubusson carpet had been sullied!

Of course, one could not blame the dog; it had been imprisoned the whole day and had succumbed to nature; but as she set herself angrily to work with cleaning utensils, she prepared for Mrs. Bankes's home-coming in a spirit that flung Regency inkstands to the winds. Her temper was not improved by the necessity of heating kettles of water because the boiler had been allowed to go out, nor did it cool down during the three further hours that elapsed before the culprit's return.

The scene that took place was the pattern for many that succeeded it. Mrs. Bankes maintained a sort of impertinent blandness which Miss MacFarren could now recognize as the easy detachment of a child who is profoundly unaffected by the reproaches levelled at it and only says what will help to get the lecture over quickly. She had left the dog shut up, she explained, because she had been sure Miss MacFarren would disapprove if it were wandering all over the house: she had meant to come back early and feed it, but an irresistible opportunity had arisen of seeing a film with one of her girl friends, and she had not realized there would be no one at home to give ear to Jimjams's distress.

'But I told you that you mustn't expect me to look after it!' Miss MacFarren protested, with a sense of pushing her way against a great wall of cotton-wool.

'I thought you'd at least give it a drink of water and let it out if it cried. Even a person who hates dogs could do that much.'

To the last she persisted in believing that Miss Macfarren's objection to Jimjams as a guest was due to her hatred of dogs and the severity of her disposition. For instance, returning a day or two later from an afternoon outing, she found that Mrs. Bankes too had preferred to leave the neglected house, and that she had disposed of the dog by putting it out into the tiny garden. The late January weather was bitter, and it was trembling with deep-seated cold when Miss MacFarren brought it in and wrapped it in a rug before her newly lighted fire, asking herself poignantly if these annoyances would never cease. The garden was private— its privacy had been stipulated in exchange for her giving up the dining-room—and here it was invaded with the sufferings of a particularly unattractive animal.

She was waiting for Antonia again when she came in, and she addressed her with a frankness that was growing daily more uncurbed. Very overtly Antonia stifled a sigh, raising her eyebrows in a way that nearly amounted to 'pulling a face'.

'What *am* I supposed to do? You got awfully cross because I shut him *in*, and now you say I mustn't shut him *out*. I only did it because I was afraid he'd be naughty again, on the carpet.'

'You shouldn't have taken him, Mrs. Bankes, unless you were prepared to give him reasonable care.'

'But lots of dogs stay out in freezing weather. What about sheep-dogs and St. Bernards? And the ones that pull sleighs? They practically live in the Snow.'

'This is a pet dog.'

'Yes, it is!' cried Mrs. Bankes irrelevantly, bending down to stroke it. 'You're a little pet and we love you don't we, Jimjams, even though some people do think you're just a nuisance!'

That evening Miss MacFarren received a note addressed to herself by her next-door neighbours complaining of the perpetual noise of barking. Humiliating as it was, after her long years as an impeccable tenant, to have seemed to have deserved this rebuke, she was not sorry to show the letter as confirmation of her own grievance. But Antonia could only see it as the grumbling of a dog-hater. 'I never never realized,' she said in a lightly disdainful tone which yet, however, avoided being directly insolent, 'that there were so many people who couldn't bear doggies.'

After that it came about that Miss MacFarren was obliged to devote a substantial portion of every day to the unhappy terrier's service. Sometimes humanity compelled her to feed it, for she knew that its meals, though abundant when there were suitable leavings from the table, were on other occasions meagre in the extreme. Sometimes she took it for a walk, a hazardous duty which Mrs. Bankes generally evaded, and sometimes she was forced, for her own sake, to clean up after it, Mrs. Bankes having forgotten to let it out. These tasks were the more irksome to perform because they involved a great deal of stealthy vigilance. Mrs. Bankes would lie shamelessly to forestall reproach pretending the dog had just consumed an enormous meal, or that she had given it a long walk at some unspecified hour of the morning. Miss MacFarren, hitherto the most self-contained of women, was condemned to a life of watching and listening, and the fact that all this sacrifice was made for a poor little creature who had utterly failed to arouse her affection gave an additionally painful quality to the situation.

Mrs. Bankes was passing more time than usual away from home. The hordes of 'female friends' had thinned out, less eager to come to the house now that they were aware they could not set foot over the doorstep without being handed a broom, or asked to wash yesterday's pots and pans, or to get the boiler going. Moreover, at this season of the year there were fewer visitors from country districts wanting the use of the spare room, and Mrs. Bankes's friendships, being largely based on mutual usefulness, tended to wane where there was an inability or an unwillingness to be useful.

The relief from the incessant bustle of the foregoing months would have been welcome, but it was cancelled out by the fact that, when Mrs. Bankes was not entertaining and not playing the rôle of home-maker for her husband, her domestic pride crumbled to pieces, and nothing was done that could conceivably be left undone.

Miss MacFarren could inure herself to the idea that the beautifully groomed Antonia retired for the night to an unswept room and an unmade bed, but the struggle to get the boiler tended concerned her closely, and on the nights when she washed in a niggardly quantity of water heated by the electric kettle, she felt obliged to resort to unusually large tots of whisky. She was tempted to remove the most pressing difficulties by engaging a servant on her own initiative, but there were several objections to this course, above all the certainty that ministering, however grudgingly, to Mrs. Bankes's comfort would in no sense be conducive to bringing about her departure.

They had now entered upon a phase of such open disapproval on the one side and such reckless disregard for the terms of contract on the other, that it would have been comparatively easy for Miss MacFarren to utter the sentence of dismissal, but Captain Bankes had once again taken her, all unwittingly as she quite believed, at a disadvantage. Shortly after his arrival in America from Germany she had received, by air mail, a letter from the director of the New Aldine Press, offering to negotiate for an American edition of her *Evolution of Flowers*. Although Captain Bankes's name was not mentioned, and perhaps he had even forgotten the conversation of months before in which he had described this publisher as a close friend of his, it was evident that the approach must be due to his recommendation. Probably he had sent or given his friend the second-hand copy of the book which she knew he had bought on his last visit to England, and had followed it up with what he would call 'a sales talk'.

Her dilemma was heart-rending. She could not but desire American publication for her books, and here was the opportunity hitherto always denied. To reject it out-of-hand would be quixotic; to accept it in the present circumstances undignified. She could only hope that the present circumstances would spontaneously change, and that in the meantime she would be allowed to temporize. After two or three days of troubled reflection, she wrote to the New Aldine Press informing them with ingenious truth that there was 'a little complication' to be cleared up before she was free to negotiate, and that she would do her best to communicate with them at an early date.

That could not be, she sadly recognized, until she had safely parted with the Bankeses, and not even then unless the parting wore the semblance of friendliness all round. To advance herself by their agency while there was any risk of an unpleasant dénouement was out of the question. And until this problem had somehow or other solved itself she must put up with Mrs. Bankes, not so that she might obtain an American contract, important though that was to her, but because she could not reward the husband's thoughtful kindness by evicting his wife in his absence.

What with the dog, the mice, the dirt, and the daily effort to maintain some standards of decency without becoming a charwoman for Mrs. Bankes, she had now reached what she felt must surely be the nadir of her domestic fortunes. Only a solitary ray had gleamed in the first relentless weeks of 1946. Mrs. Bankes had lost the support of Harriet. Not that Harriet had brought herself as yet to admit a total error of judgement, but it was clear that her confidence in the charming, the admired Antonia, was wavering.

She had called one Monday morning, on returning from a week-end in the country, to bring some eggs to each of the two ladies of the house, dividing her attentions between them equally as she had been doing—much to the annoyance of her older friend—ever since the house-sharing plan had been carried out. On this occasion, Antonia was out keeping a hairdresser's appointment, and when the doorbell rang there was no one but Miss MacFarren to answer it. She was in the act of fetching coke from the cellar in the front area, a task the tenant always omitted to perform, so that she had the choice of either performing it herself or doing without bathwater and central heating; and as Harriet, looking over the area railings, could not miss seeing her, she had no time to slip off the ashy apron in which she had been cleaning out the boiler.

'I'll come up to the front door,' said Miss MacFarren.

'No, no, my dear, I'll come down. I've brought something for the kitchen, so I might as well.'

Miss MacFarren was not displeased that she should see the basement as it was on a Monday morning after a week when Mrs. Bankes had hardly been able to get any of her visitors to give it even a superficial look of cleanliness, and, while expressing her gratitude for the eggs, she slyly opened one or two cupboard doors so as to bring to notice evidences of neglect which might otherwise have remained unseen.

'But why haven't you got a maid—or at any rate, a daily?' Harriet asked her with a bewilderment that brought a note of querulousness to her voice. 'Dailies are quite easy to get now, at a price.'

'Mrs. Bankes is too lazy to go through the boring preliminaries.' Miss MacFarren kept her tone smooth and matter-of-fact so as to avoid provoking Harriet by any sign of resentment. 'Also I believe she thinks it's a saving to do without one. It leaves her pounds more to spend every week.'

Instead of taking up cudgels on Antonia's behalf as she had done at every previous hint of disparagement, Harriet merely looked round gloomily and said: 'What a very mistaken idea!'

'I see—I mean, I hear that you've taken to keeping a dog,' she remarked a moment later, glancing up at the ceiling whence muffled barks, timed as if by a metronome, descended from the room above.

'Mrs. Bankes has taken to keeping a dog—for someone else,' Miss MacFarren corrected her mildly. 'His name's Jimjams. He's been here three weeks.'

'I hope he's well behaved,' Harriet murmured in a subdued manner.

'I'm afraid he hasn't been properly trained. I'd better go and stop that barking, Harriet, or I shall have the neighbours complaining again.'

She led the way up the basement stairs and paused at the top to point out, with an air of non-attachment, how Jimjams had torn the green baize on the lower part of the door to shreds on various occasions when impatient to reach the basement.

'I wish Mrs. Bankes would pay a little more attention to him,' she said, still studiously preserving the calm which had been so lacking on the day when she had first revealed her woes. 'I find it very trying to have to look after him myself, on top of all the extra housework.'

'Why do you do it?'

'I only do what's strictly necessary to prevent the dog from being utterly miserable and the house from becoming simply unfit to live in.'

Harriet could make no answer, for her presence had sent the terrier into an angry paroxysm, and it was some time before he could be silenced. When at last he had been induced to sit on the hearth-rug in the study, Harriet was taking a pinch of snuff with a frowning face. Her skin looked ruddier than ever and her eyes were fixed on the farthest corner of the carpet.

'Is she all right about money?' she enquired, affecting, perhaps less successfully than her companion, the same sort of remote style. She too had tacitly agreed to banish the high feelings which had seethed beneath all their former discussions of her favourite, and to speak as if the subject was one in which she took a dispassionate interest.

'Her husband pays the bills,' said Miss MacFarren, 'so I've not had any trouble about money.'

Harriet's finger delicately traced over the pattern on the lid of her snuff-box. 'I've had a little embarrassment,' she said slowly. 'I really don't know quite what to do about it.'

It was so unusual for Harriet to be in the slightest doubt as to what to do that her finger retraced the pattern two or three times before she could bring herself to continue.

'You remember all those things she bought from me when she first began coming to the shop? They were either paid for with money she had in her purse or else I sent the bill to Captain Bankes, so *that* was all right. But a week or so after she moved in here, she took a great fancy to a bon-bon box—early Empire it was, of the prettiest workmanship I've ever seen—and she said she'd like to buy it for her husband as a birthday present or an anniversary present . . . I forget which.'

'What would Captain Bankes be doing with a bon-bon box?' Miss MacFarren enquired, smiling at the incongruity.

'She thought it would be nice for his cigarettes. I tried to dissuade her because it was so much too fine for practical use. . . . There was a bevelled crystal lid and underneath an exquisite design in little pearls and gold wires—a basket of the most intricate flowers seen through the glass.'

'Just the sort of toy-like thing that always appeals to her,' Miss MacFarren commented.

'I suppose you haven't noticed it about the house?'

'It may be in their bedroom. I never go in there.'

'Well, as she was so insistent, I let her have it for ten guineas—I should have charged fifteen to an ordinary customer—and she asked me not to send the bill to her husband, since it was a present.'

'And she hasn't paid you?'

'No, it's getting on for six months. She's had the account several times in the ordinary course.'

'What about writing her a personal letter? Though I know that's difficult between friends.' Miss MacFarren had the unworthy satisfaction of suspecting that Harriet winced.

'Oh, I couldn't, Elinor! I'd rather lose the ten guineas. But I do get annoyed when I think that I was doing her a favour to let her have the box.'

'Why not—now this is a really good idea, Harriet!—why not write a few perfectly cordial lines to say that, if she doesn't want to keep it, you'd like to take it back into stock? That's quite different from demanding the money.'

'Yes, it is.' Harriet expressed her appreciation in a series of vigorous nods. 'That would give her a chance of getting out of it without the smallest inconvenience. As a matter of fact, I should be glad to have the box back. Thank you, Elinor, for an excellent suggestion.'

Round her gnarled rheumaticky finger, she twisted a diamond fleur-de-lys, her eyes, which had been lowered, now fixed keenly on Miss MacFarren, while she said with a slightly challenging inflection: 'I dare say you've heard about Lady Violet?'

'Lady Violet?' Miss MacFarren, lost in amazement that the arch-adviser had sought and meekly accepted her advice, repeated the name with a perfect blankness of mind.

'Scapley. You must remember when she sold Scapley Park.'

'Oh yes, you thought she'd be happier in a villa at Maidenhead or somewhere.'

'Scapley Park was terribly difficult to run. Of course, it's one of the most beautiful houses in England—nobody denies that—but all the same, it was a dreadful responsibility.' She gazed at her friend as if inviting her to contradict this statement. 'Anyhow, she's going back there now. She's going to marry the man who bought it.'

'Is that good or bad?' Miss MacFarren asked submissively.

'Judge for yourself. He's a semi-illiterate ex-grocer of sixty who's made a fortune out of running football pools.'

'Why is she marrying him?' Miss MacFarren put the question uneasily, for she guessed that what Harriet was telling her amounted to a confession of total failure.

'To get back to Scapley Park, I imagine.' The tone was irritable rather than self-accusing, but self-accusation was implicit in the words, and the link in her thoughts was evident when she went on, scarcely pausing: 'I saw Mrs. Bankes go past the shop the other day. She seldom comes in now.'

'She's uncomfortable about the ten guineas, perhaps.'

'Possibly. I must say, she's a very handsome woman. Most elegant she looked in her little fur jacket.'

'She got that for not going to America,' said Miss MacFarren.

'I wish for your sake she'd gone, Elinor.'

The admission was gratifying, but it was better still to hear the familiar 'Antonia' dropped in favour of the distant 'Mrs. Bankes'. Miss MacFarren recognized with pleasure that the *status quo* between herself and Harriet was about to be restored.

11

IT WAS mid-February before there was any opportunity of going out to Cornfields to see Mory and Maxine at work. Tentative arrangements had been made on two occasions before, but Mory had rung up each time to announce, with apparently infinite regret, some difficulty, and Miss MacFarren had quite lost hope of ever finding her way into a film studio or pursuing her tantalizing acquaintance with Maxine when one evening he telephoned and offered to call for her the following morning at eight. She had the alternative of either going with him in his car at that untoward hour, or making her way to the studio alone later in the day, and the weather being cold and the place somewhat inaccessible, she had preferred the car journey.

'But, Mory,' she pleaded, 'if I'm to be sitting waiting in my hat and gloves at eight in the morning, you won't ring up at the last minute to put me off?'

Mory swore he would not, but it was with some misgivings that she made her overnight preparations for an early start. The film business appeared to possess the lives of those who lived by it to an extent that made their actions quite unpredictable and, by ordinary standards, rather unmannerly.

The next morning she was glad to be kept waiting a little while, however, because it gave her a chance to rake the ashes out of the boiler and provide a secret snack for the dog before leaving; and she decided, when these tasks were done, to steal a glance at the budgerigars, as she made a point of doing whenever she was sure her tenant was out of the way. It was fortunate that she did so, for their water-dish was empty and she had no reason to suppose that Mrs. Bankes would be punctual in filling it.

Two of the birds had now solved the problem of their small cage and uncertain care by dying; and the sight of the remaining pair always lowered her spirits. The idea of their dismal and unnatural existence oppressed her, and she stood staring at the cage, wondering whether they most disliked the room when it was empty and lifeless or when it was filled with cigarette smoke, radio music, and all the uncongenialities of human behaviour. On the whole, she was inclined to think the room must be worse for them when it was deserted, when their little quick, glittering eyes saw nothing wherever they turned but motionless objects, nothing animated by wind or rain or the shadow of any flying or scurrying creature, everything unresponsive and unchanging. Transmuted in the light of those alien eyes through which she was now seeing, her own treasures became stony, implacable, devoid of comprehensible meaning. The birds had reduced the room even as the cage had reduced the birds. She thought of them as part of Antonia's evil spell.

Then she reproached herself for her superstition. It was due, she assured herself, to having drunk too much whisky last night, but that reflection only deepened the frown on her brow. The bottle of whisky in her bedroom cupboard really undermined her self-respect, and yet each night she went to bed with nerves so frayed by the exasperations of the day that some means of relaxation seemed strictly necessary: and the whisky was a great comfort while she was actually drinking it. But the tendency to overstep the mark, to make the tots larger on occasions of greater annoyance, was always a worry the next morning.

Last night Antonia had informed her that Joss's return had been postponed for two weeks—disagreeable news, for, until he was expected, everything was sure to remain at sixes and sevens in the house. And it was followed by the disquieting announcement that he would, for a year or more, be making his home in London; the *Washington Recorder* had appointed him, at his own request, to the post of London correspondent. His days as a war reporter were over, and he had asked for a position which would enable him to settle down for a time.

Miss MacFarren had needed two decidedly large whisky toddies to help her to compose herself for sleep after hours of silent argument as to what this might portend. On the one hand it might mean that an earnest effort would be made by the Bankeses to find a self-contained domicile; on the other, it was possible that, for Captain Bankes, the pleasures of 'settling down' would specifically include living in Harberton Square. Of one thing she was sure, he was quite unaware of the failure of their double ménage. Mrs. Bankes, who loved above all things to bask in his approbation, had certainly concealed from him as much of the seamy side of her domestic life as could be kept out of view. He had said several things which showed that he believed the whole arrangement to be a striking success.

Well, it was of little use asking Mrs. Bankes what their plans were since no reliance could be placed on her answer, and she had firmly resolved to defer any serious consideration of the course to be pursued until she had enjoyed her day at the film studio, and could survey her problem from the new perspective which even the briefest change of environment may give. Of course it was easier said than done to free her enslaved mind for the whole day, but, as Mory's car drew up at the door only half an hour late, she renewed her determination with a sigh in which she intended to exhale all her worries.

'My arrival here at this hour,' said Mory when they were *en route*, 'is probably the greatest proof of devotion that a nephew has ever given to an aunt. I'm not working this morning after all.'

'Oh, Mory, does that mean you needn't have gone to the studio?'

'It does. But after that pathetic picture of you sitting waiting in your hat and gloves, I hadn't the heart to ring up and put you off. The gloves were the operative touch.'

'Don't you know beforehand whether you're going to be working or not?'

'Not always, darling. Films depend on so many things and people. This time it's a little dispute about whether am assistant art director is allowed to knock tin-tacks into things.'

'Oh dear, has something been broken?'

Mory laughed. 'Only a couple of trade union rules. We have a new assistant art director and he has very strong feelings about the way draperies should hang, so he began tacking them into position himself, using a hammer and everything, so they tell me.'

'Is that wrong?'

'They're very particular in a film studio as to who may use hammers. I gather that in his enthusiasm he went on fixing the draperies with his own hands even when they'd got two men from the right trades to deal with them—one to drape and one to hammer, you know. I'm not clear about what happened, not having been there, but it's been referred to all their various union representatives.'

'Is there some sort of strike then?' Miss MacFarren had been prepared by recent public events for any extremity.

'Oh no, it's quite an academic argument, but it appears the draperies aren't done yet, so the set isn't finished. And I shan't be able to start shooting.'

'It sounds very selfish of the art director to insist on interfering,' she suggested, rather to get her bearings than because she had formed any real opinion.

'Well, it happens that he designed these elaborate draperies and he wanted to arrange them himself. He had his point of view, I suppose.'

Mory was always sympathetic, always disposed to give everyone credit for having a point of view, even to the degree at which tolerance, according to his aunt's notions, revealed an imperfect grasp of moral values. She knew that this tolerance had a quality of eagerness which went far beyond mere passive acceptance, and that, combined with his very considerable organizing ability, it was the main-spring of the gift for 'handling' people which had stood him in such good stead. But as he entertained her, all the way to Cornfields, with tales of the film business, tales of pointless profusion and of vulgarity sometimes artless but more often deliberately contrived, as it seemed, to insult the public intelligence, she would have been glad if he had shown less cynical benevolence and more of the spirit of proper condemnation.

'But it isn't all as silly as that, Aunt Ellie,' he tried too late to reassure her. 'Good pictures do in some miraculous way get made. I'm hoping to make a few myself. And even in bad pictures, you'll find technically very good things. The film business up to now should be compared with Grub Street in the eighteenth century.'

Miss MacFarren, who was dividing her attention as dexterously as she could between the conversation and the road, which they were covering at a rather distracting speed, made only a responsive murmur.

'There was this vast new market for fiction that was being exploited by the circulating libraries. Fiction wasn't quite respectable as a profession and yet it was attracting an enormous amount of talent. The libraries thought they knew what the public wanted, and the publishers tried to give the libraries what *they* wanted, and the authors had to try and give the publishers what *they* wanted. So novels were written according to conventions which only the first-rate people dared to break, and even their work was influenced adversely.'

Miss MacFarren said 'I see' as if she were pondering deeply, while she wondered why he found it so necessary to overtake a very wide lorry which seemed to her to be going at quite an adequate pace.

'In time fiction became respectable,' he went on, falling back at the approach of a Green Line bus. 'Nobody was ashamed of reading novels any more, and it wasn't considered frivolous to go to the library. Then books could be written about things the novelist really wanted to get off his chest.'

'Is it still considered frivolous to go to the pictures?' she asked, in the vain hope of diverting him from his purpose of overtaking the lorry.

'The exhibitors seem to think so.' He nosed his car forward again. 'Films are a knottier problem than novels because they cost so much to make, and the distribution is a hell of a business. That's what's kept the film industry from becoming adult-minded.'

'I suppose so.' She tried not to notice that they were now travelling abreast with the lorry while another car headed implacably towards them.

'The whole solution lies in finding some more flexible way of getting pictures shown.' In a sudden burst of acceleration they shot forward and left the lorry behind them, without sustaining the head-on collision she expected.

'All this stereotyped glamour, this false grandeur, these corney situations, this hammy dialogue, that intelligent people complain about—you'll find their equivalent in hundreds of eighteenth-century novels. It's a stage of adolescence. Come now, darling, you're a cultivated woman—can't you see the parallel?'

She saw the parallel and also saw with relief that he was turning the car into a large gateway with a light wrought-iron arch above it formed chiefly of the legend in gilded characters: *Cornfields Studio*. A commissionaire saluted him and he drove at once into a vista which, although her reading had fully prepared her for it, nevertheless came near to startling her.

Behind the façade of a Georgian cottage standing in a neat garden towered the smoke-stacks of a liner. A few yards away stood the frowning entrance of a medieval castle with the draw-bridge raised, in the shadow of which nestled a news-vendor's kiosk apparently imported from Paris. As they rounded a bend beyond the cottage, portions of a dissected ship came into view mingled with bow-fronted shop windows, several hoardings advertising modern French products, and half a lighthouse.

'Surrealist, isn't it?' said Mory.

'Yes. Almost frightening somehow.'

'Some of it's Cranford, some of it's the French sequence in my picture, and some belongs to a sea voyage affair we finished months ago.'

He swung the car into a park divided up in sections, each distin-guished by a name painted on a board.

'Mr. MacFarren!' she said. 'How strange to find our name in a film studio!'

'Yes, I should have been pretty surprised, when I worked in the Natural History Museum, if I could have foreseen the future.'

'Are you still happy about it?' she enquired diffidently.

'I can't deny that I am, Aunt Ellie. I live a very harassing life, but everyone who makes good in the film business goes about feeling in his heart as if he'd won a sweepstake. The chances against him are so tremendous, you see.'

They had walked into a building where, among many other effects, a superb large-scale model of a village green surrounded by houses, a church, and an inn, was displayed on a raised plateau. Two men were spraying it with a faintly acrid foam produced by a machine.

'Snow,' Mory explained. 'Cranford is to be seen by moonlight in the snow, I suppose.'

'Is this Cranford? I must say it looks wonderfully right,' she remarked in surprise, for Maxine's description of the film had made her anticipate nothing but ineptitude.

'Yes, our model department does beautiful work, and the exter-iors were designed by Rafferty, who couldn't be bettered. I think you'll like all the exteriors very much.' His tone pointedly limited his praise. 'Of course, this production's nothing to do with me, but you must make do with it for the present while I go and see how my set's getting on. I'm taking you on to Stage Three where they're shooting.'

'Oh, Mory, aren't you going to stay with me?'

'Darling, now that I'm here I've a pile of things to see to, but Maxine will look after you. She knows you're coming.'

Taking her arm, he led her rapidly through a maze of passages containing dressing-rooms, make-up rooms, hairdressers' rooms, and rooms whose functions she could only guess at. Behind one door voices could be heard singing a fuddled song, and behind another tender declarations of love, but the first were so tinny and the second so ear-splittingly loud that she knew they were parts of a sound-track.

'Cutting-rooms,' said Mory. 'I'm getting so sick of that drunken sequence from *Cranford*. They seem to have been cutting it for weeks.'

'From *Cranford*!' She stopped dead.

'Yes, it's a scene in the village pub. Don't ask me the why and wherefore of it! Ask Pio Martinez! And remember, you've stepped into the eighteenth century, and this is Grub Street.'

At that moment, from the adjoining corridor a woman emerged carrying an immense pile of bonnets. Beside her walked and talked an amiable-looking man holding a tape-measure. The woman's unwieldy load so obscured her vision that she had difficulty in making progress, and the man, pleasantly chatting, took her by the arm and steered her forward until they disappeared from view through a door some yards ahead.

Mory, whose quickness at observing reactions was an essential ingredient in his recipe for success, remarked soothingly: 'He can't help her to carry anything, Aunt Ellie. He's a focus-puller, a cameraman's assistant; she's from the wardrobe.'

'Good gracious! What a strange snobbery!'

'It isn't snobbery, dear, it's a trade union rule. A cameraman isn't allowed to carry props or things from the wardrobe. Hardly anyone except a property man is allowed to carry anything.'

They had now reached the door, but as they came up to it, the words *Silence* and *Shooting*, glowing above them in red lights, brought Mory to a standstill, and they remained outside, joined by a lean and seemingly careworn man with a camera case slung over his shoulder, who was introduced to Miss MacFarren by a name she did not catch.

'Still on the prowl,' said Mory with his sympathetic smile.

'Like a blessed panther,' the lean man returned gloomily. 'Two whole days I've been trying to take Stella with Maxie and Anne in that drawing-room, but there's always someone or something missing.'

'Oh, for the time and the place and the loved one all together!' said Mory.

'They're just going to finish with the drawing-room sequence,' sighed the lean man, 'so it's now or never.'

By this time the red lights were extinguished, and they had entered what appeared at a first glance to be a vast shadowy warehouse filled with mechanical contrivances and divided irregularly by partition walls. As they walked on it was possible to make out that the partitions enclosed rooms or portions of rooms which were evidently scenes from the film in production. One, a charming drawing-room, solid-looking but for the absence of a wall, was lighted up in an inviting manner, and it was to this that they made their way. A group of people almost large enough to be called a crowd was gathered about this oasis of brightness, or rather, was beginning to disperse as Miss MacFarren and her nephew approached. Some were rising from canvas chairs, others were straggling away in conversational twos and threes, and others again were wheeling back from the scene trolleys of complicated and intimidating apparatus.

An exuberantly handsome young man in Regency costume, whom Miss MacFarren identified with satisfaction as Mark Harrowby, was minutely examining a china figurine which belonged to the scene. A pretty but somewhat commonplace type of girl, in whom she was disappointed to recognize the celebrated Stella Hawthorne, was sitting yawning on a Trafalgar chair. At the far end of the drawing-room, Maxine, wearing a tall bonnet bedecked with a startling number of feathers and flowers, was engaged in some kind of languid banter with a man poised several feet above her; for, as Miss MacFarren perceived on looking up, the apparently solid apartment lacked a ceiling as well as a wall and was surrounded above with immense lamps shedding their beams downwards.

These things she noted in wandering glances, half her attention being employed in acknowledging an introduction which Mory was performing between herself and a pale, dark, thick-set man whose manner suggested that he was accustomed to have people presented to him in an unending succession and could only by an effort distinguish one from another—an effort which, however, he willingly if wearily made. Her eyes having been so busily employed, her ears had scarcely succeeded in hearing his name, and she was glad to see it plainly written on the back of the chair he had just vacated—PIO MARTINEZ.

'My aunt,' said Mory genially, 'is a great admirer of your work'— she flinched at the unscrupulous lie—'and I know you're a great admirer of hers.' Again she flinched, seeing the pained incomprehension that flickered in the limpid Spanish eyes. But Mory continued: 'You know how much you've always like those framed title pages in my office?'

Martinez uttered a long-drawn 'Ah' of recognition and, with an enthusiasm that might have owed something to relief, exclaimed: 'The aunt who makes the beautiful pictures—this is she!' nodding several times to confirm both to himself and to them that the pictures were clear in his remembrance. 'So now you have come to see how we make pictures here? I am so sorry,' he added, speaking fluently but in a strong foreign accent, 'we have finished shooting on this set. We had to begin first thing to take just the little end of a scene we couldn't manage yesterday.'

'Of course it was early night yesterday,' said Mory, 'I had to speed up a very awkward shot too.' He turned to his aunt. 'On Wednesdays no one does any overtime. We have an agreement to let the men go by six though the heavens fall.'

'So I stop after two takes and finish the shot this morning very, very early. . . . You see how they are sleepy.' Martinez waved his hand towards a buxom Georgian housemaid, yawning prodigiously, who had just walked into the drawing-room in the most natural manner, as if she had come from the servants' hall to perform some monotonous domestic task.

'How convincing she looks!' send Miss MacFarren. But the director had turned away to speak to someone else.

At the same moment Maxine cried 'Mory's aunt!' in a voice that produced a veiled stir of interest from several bystanders, and hurried forward to welcome her.

They had scarcely exchanged greetings, however, when another and even more arresting voice, belonging to a tall, energetic man who gave the impression of being here, there, and everywhere, shouted appealingly like one calling for a rescue: 'Stills! Please— *please*! We've got to get these stills! Back on the set, Maxie, *please*!'

Maxine excused herself obediently but with a murmured execration against 'lousy old stills', and presently the set was cleared of everyone but the lean and careworn photographer and the three women in costume who grouped themselves dramatically, Maxine confronting Stella Hawthorne in a brazen attitude, while the maid hovered at the door in consternation. But when the picture was thus posed, the photographer required a certain screen to reflect or to diffuse the light, and though he had it with him, it seemed that by a trade union rule no one might touch it but one of the electrical staff. The electricians, contemptuous of still pictures, were engrossed in moving some delicate apparatus and there was a tedious delay until one of them disengaged himself, during which Mory, presenting his aunt with rapid virtuosity to the few people who still remained, assured her that she would be looked after and vanished.

At the invitation of the energetic man, whom she now knew as Roy, the assistant director, she seated herself in a chair with someone else's name on it. Next to her, doing *The Times* crossword puzzle with little appearance of interest in what was going forward, was a neatly bearded and spectacled gentleman whom Mory had introduced as Sir William Waterbond, a name she vaguely recalled as having literary associations.

Trying not to feel bored, she watched and admired the ease and unselfconsciousness with which the three actresses threw themselves, even in these moments without context, into the spirit of their rôles, a feat she would not have attempted for any bribe that could have been offered.

'How do you like the set?' asked the assistant director by way of a polite attention.

'Extremely pretty. What does it represent—in the story, I mean?'

'It represents,' Sir William Waterbond struck in without raising his head, 'the drawing-room of Miss Jenkyns and Miss Matilda Jenkyns, ladies of modest income, in a small country town named Cranford.'

'Isn't it rather luxurious?' she ventured.

The assistant director had already darted away, and it was Sir William Waterbond who again rejoined fatalistically:

'It is more luxurious than any drawing-room you or I have ever seen.'

'They seem to be dressed in Regency clothes.'

'Yes, the art director and the costume designer both prefer it. *Pride and Prejudice*,' he reminded her with a touch of triumph, 'was played in a period at least ten years after the author's death, let alone the date of the book.'

Photography on the drawing-room set now came to an end, and Maxine interrupted the conversation by remarking:

'Hullo, Willie! I'll bet you're bitching to Mory's aunt about all the things that are wrong with the picture.'

'I have long ceased to bitch, as you call it, about anything. I fulfil my contract, I am here if anyone wants me, I draw my salary, which is far more than my services are allowed to be worth, and I defy you to assert that I'm ever heard to utter a criticism.'

'Willie, you've brought griping without criticizing to a fine art.'

'My dear girl, where did you acquire your collection of unseemly American slang?'

'Straight from the horses' mouths,' said Maxine, 'when I was doing my beautiful benevolent war work at the Red Cross.'

'To think of the dangers those poor Americans had to undergo!' Sir William peered over his glasses at a face which marvellously succeeded in looking childlike under a heavy layer of make-up.

'Tea wagon's on Stage Two,' called the assistant director, darting past them; and instantly there was a final exodus; from the environs of the drawing-room, which had now been reduced to mere scenery by the dimming of its brilliant lights.

Stage Two was another vast warehouse, similar in construction to its neighbour but immensely different in the effect it presented, about half of it being turned into the High Street of Cranford, and with a fidelity of detail and a general air of reality that brought exclamations of wonder to Miss MacFarren's lips.

About this set were assembled several of the people she had already seen and a whole host of others, not only technicians but a number of dressed-up men, women, and children whom she could classify at once as extras, so obviously were they intended to make an anonymous appearance in the street. At the corner where the shop façades came to an abrupt end stood a mobile buffet such as one might see on a railway station, and beside it waited a queue which, to her surprise, Maxine immediately joined, falling into place behind Roy and the still photographer. Almost everyone in sight was either taking refreshments or queueing up for them, and it astonished her to see that, though the principals had canvas chairs to sit on, they were drinking from coarse cups without saucers, like the humble extras. Stella Hawthorne, with a man's handkerchief spread out on her lap to protect her dress, was eating a large bun, and Mark Harrowby, standing near her, had a thick slice of bread in his hand. Only Pio Martinez sat with a little tray on his lap, a tea-pot and a plate of thin bread and butter.

Miss MacFarren, having been furnished by Maxine with a chipped white cup of tea and a bun, followed her to another part of the stage where there was a handsome couch on which Maxine indicated they might sit. But sinking down upon what she imagined would be sumptuous upholstery, Miss MacFarren found that she had come into contact with the unyieldingness of a wooden bench.

'Oh, you poor soul, I should have warned you!' Maxine sympathized with a grimace. 'It's just a prop—a piece of furniture from one of the scenes. The brocade is put straight over the hard wood.'

'So I notice,' said Miss MacFarren, smiling wanly.

'How's the tea?'

'Most welcome, thank you, and the bun is uncommonly good.'

'We're all ramping for tea by this time of the morning. Most of us have been here since seven.'

'Good heavens! Why so early?'

'Hair and make-up and getting dressed take hours—much longer than for theatrical work. Pio was on the floor before nine this morning.'

'But it's a long way from London. You must have got up in the middle of the night.'

'Nearly, but I've been living out here at Cornfields for the last few weeks. The Harrowbys took pity on me when I lost my flat, and I'm staying with them till the end of my part in the picture. What I'm going to do then I can't begin to think. I don't even get time for flat-hunting any more.'

'You must come and stay with me,' Miss MacFarren heard herself saying fantastically. The idea was so startling that she felt a flutter of alarm, but mixed with the sensation there was a glow of pleasure which warmed her into adding, before alarm could quench it: 'At least it would give you a chance to look round.'

'Have you really got room for me?' Maxine's level tone held all comment in suspense.

'There is a spare room.' At the prospect of asserting her right to use this common territory, alarm was again mingled with pleasure.

'What about that wonderful rugged American you keep on the premises?'

'He's quite a nice person, though he has a most tiresome wife. He's very unobtrusive.'

Maxine's eyes, their long lashes stiffened with thick mascara, reflected a subdued light, like pools fringed with rushes, as she turned on Miss MacFarren a slow, speculative gaze.

'Wouldn't you find me tiresome as well?'

'Oh, but you're nothing like Mrs. Bankes!' Miss MacFarren's protest was vehement. 'She's simply detestable—unbearable!'

With that word, the full unpracticality of what she had proposed opened before her in a dread vista. Alarm rose and extinguished all pleasure as she recalled the dirty kitchen—in which there were cockroaches now as well as mice—the difficulties of catering, the loud penetrating voices of Mrs. Bankes's friends, her all-pervasive atmosphere. It seemed madness to have imagined for one moment that she could bring a guest into that dismal house.

And Maxine too! She was not a young woman of congenial habits, though there was something perversely captivating in her personality. She swore, she showed a marked liking for gin, she had no shame about her endeavours—her doubtless successful endeavours—to secure fur coats by means of blandishments. It was futile to pretend to oneself that she was a virtuous girl. And yet, looking at that rounded, dimpled face, so ineffectually painted to resemble the face she perhaps ought to have had, it was impossible not to feel a twinge of regret at withdrawing the rash invitation.

Withdrawing it, of course, silently. She was able to divert the conversation by enumerating some of her reasons for disliking Mrs. Bankes; and while she was still trying to explain why she had endured such a situation, a girl from the wardrobe summoned Maxine away to change her costume. Miss MacFarren was escorted back to the street scene and left to find what interest she could there.

It was being prepared for two or three shots and a mere half-dozen lines of dialogue to be spoken by an actor whose theatre commitments made it imperative for him to finish with the film immediately: and for this purpose, the assistant director informed her on one of his flying visits of politeness, it had been necessary to summon a crowd of extras and throw the schedule out for days.

'It's always the way when we use legitimate actors,' he grumbled. 'What with their tours and their rehearsals and their late hours, they cost far more than film actors in the long run.'

'But if it's just a few lines he's got to say, must you have all these people? And—good gracious!—horses too!' she exclaimed, seeing two or three authentic-looking vehicles being led on to the set.

'Scene's got to be the same as it was last time we took it. Same sequence!' He flung this reply from a distance, for he was already half-way across the set handing some typescript to the man with the tape measure.

The girl who had been carrying the bonnets was now making a display of them in one of the shop windows, where cards in a beautiful style of copperplate announced that they were the *Newest Modes from Paris* and *As Worn by the Nobility.*

'You didn't oughter be doing that, Poppy!' said a short, stocky man in an admonitory and yet not unfriendly voice as she emerged from the shop door to compare her arrangement with a photograph from which she was working.

'Who's to stop me?' Poppy demanded. 'These are from the wardrobe.'

'When they come on the set they're props, and it's only props as should 'andle them.'

'We're not going to have props touch these bonnets, not after what happened to them last time.'

'All right, yer blood be on yer own 'ead if there's any trouble over it,' said the man with an air of deep sorrow. 'I don't mind wot yer do, but I've seen this sort o' thing land the 'ole studio in a mess.'

'There's your T.U. for you!' muttered the still photographer, who was standing at the back of Miss MacFarren's chair.

'There do seem to be a great many rules.'

'Rules! If you ask me they sit up nights inventing them. Did you see the way I was held up on that drawing-room set while they flapped round looking for the man to deal with the screen? When I was a free-lance, before all this T.U. business became an epidemic, I used to carry that screen round myself and put it where I wanted it in two jiffies. Look what a fandango they make of it now!'

'Have you got to obey the rules even if you're not a member?'

'You've *got* to be a member. The company isn't allowed to employ anyone who stays out. Oh, I could tell you things!'

He wandered off, and Miss MacFarren was left for a long while looking at the preparations which were slowly, and in what seemed to her a curiously disjointed fashion, going forward. People drifted on to the set making enquiries or giving directions in terms so technical that she did not even attempt to comprehend them, and then drifted away as if they had suddenly lost interest. Huge lamps were moved trailing serpentine lengths of heavy cable. Sound-track apparatus of baffling complexity was shifted into new positions, likewise dragging thick ropes of electric wire which crisscrossed over the others and made it necessary for those who walked about the floor to pick their way gingerly. Carpenters appeared and hammered ferociously at a swinging sign which someone had thought to be in danger of falling. Extras roamed about with vacant or disconsolate faces, or made seats for themselves out of any items of studio equipment which could, even at the most uncomfortable angles be sat upon; and from time to time were apologetically chivvied from these places by technicians. An extremely pretty girl, whom Miss MacFarren had taken for an actress off duty, walked about checking details by photographs and typewritten notes with the quiet pertinacious air of a detective.

At last a girl and two men dressed in shabby finery began to take up stations which were evidently of some significance for the cameramen, and Miss MacFarren was informed that they were stand-ins representing Maxine, Mark Harrowby, and the actor for whose convenience the schedule of the day had been altered. A camera of portentous size had been wheeled on a track to a point from which the man with the tape measure made sorties towards the stand-in for Maxine who gazed with resignation at the bonnets in the window.' Artificial daylight poured over the scene—no longer credible surveyed through a forest of strange contraptions and animated by a number of straggling extras who were being instructed to walk in certain directions at certain moments. All this while, Pio Martinez had been completely detached from the proceedings, either absent altogether or listening to a stooping and drooping man in glasses with a lank moustache, who conversed with his back to the set as if it were not merely unentertaining but positively distasteful to him. But now the drooping man lounged away, and Martinez came forward and started to give numerous directions, all of which were received with ready obedience, except by the chief cameraman, who was disposed to be recalcitrant.

'Try it just this once, Johnny!' Miss MacFarren heard Martinez pleading in a low voice. 'If it is bad I take the blame.'

But the cameraman was evidently stubborn, for Martinez retreated muttering with a shrug: 'All right, let us be safe—and dull.'

Mark Harrowby now arrived resplendent in the guise of an ultra-fashionable country gentleman, and accompanied by an actor in military dress with a raffish make-up and a curled wig, who was repeating to himself some lines from a script and at the same time practising a gesture with a square eyeglass. Maxine soon followed dressed in clothes that were perhaps meant to be tawdry but had been carried out so lavishly that they created an impression of richness.

'What do I look like—a May horse?' she asked, placing herself in front of Miss MacFarren. 'A horse is not what I'm supposed to be.'

'You look very pretty,' said Miss MacFarren truthfully, 'but I think you might come as a great surprise to Mrs. Gaskell.'

'This little get-up is Pio's cosy Spanish idea of a girl who was not quite nice in the good old days—the days when there was money in it. The first costume they made for me was sent back because he said it was *bourgeois*; so you see, they've got me all tarted up with ermine tails.'

'Is it a winter or a summer scene?' Miss MacFarren enquired, glancing doubtfully at the other costumes.

'Oh, any time's ermine time in Cranford.'

'Maxie, stop talking! We are going to rehearse!' Martinez called mildly. (His mildness indeed was a disappointment to Miss MacFarren, who had been encouraged by the books she had read to expect fireworks.) 'Mark! Kenny! Come, please, we are rehearsing!'

Instantly the assistant director took up the cry in his imploring voice with its poignant inflection: 'Quiet, everybody! Quiet, *please*! Rehearsing!'

A hush fell on every chattering group, technicians went about their business noiselessly, the stand-ins retired, and Maxine took up her position gazing in the shop window, while the extras who had been selected to give naturalness to the scene made their carefully timed appearances, a child bowling a hoop, a farmer's cart, two or three women with market baskets. Mark Harrowby and his military companion came in sight and Maxine turned her head to register that she had a predatory eye on them.

'We cut there! And now, before we shoot anything, we run through that little dialogue!' said Martinez, when these movements had been worked out to a nicety. 'Kenny, you are looking at her through your glass. Maxie, you have all the time your attention on Mark.'

The actor named Kenny picked up his eyeglass with the flourish he had been practising, and said in a groping and uncertain tone: 'Egad, if it isn't the pretty little minx who makes mincemeat of our hearts at the Golden Lion.'

There was a sound between a cough and a groan which caused several heads to turn in the direction of Sir William Waterbond, who was seated on the outer fringe of a watching semi-circle, but he was seen to be intent upon his crossword puzzle.

Maxine repeated her line in this spirit, and it was eminently more effective them her former pertness.

Kenny, again groping for words and stumbling, replied: 'Faith, we must be prudent. You either charm the guineas out of our pockets or the wits out of our heads.'

'*You* don't stand to lose much either way,' Maxine retorted—somewhat brutally, as Miss MacFarren thought.

'Those lovely lips have a cruel sting.' The major sighed these words with so much feeling that Martinez asked him to try again in a lighter style.

'That's just too bad. Come round some evening and bring your friend along with you'—Maxine threw a siren's glance towards Harrowby—'and you may find me a little kinder.'

The door of the bonnet shop opened and a middle-aged woman emerged carrying a flowered cardboard box tied up with ribbon. Turning scandalized eyes from Maxine, she wheeled round and walked up the street.

'That's where we cut!' cried Martinez. 'Now go through again please!'

'My lines feel awfully phoney,' said Maxine. 'I don't think they're in period.'

'Mine are simply reeking of period,' said Kenny.

'Maxine is always making people unsatisfied with their lines,' Martinez reproved her with a kind of placid petulance. 'They have been worked on by everyone in the studio. Fritz is every day changing the dialogue. If you do it properly, it will sound better. Come, we try again.'

The passage was repeated with greater fluency, and Martinez was firmly assuring them that he could see no flaw in the lines when he checked himself to roar, apparently in the most urgent distress of mind: 'Willie! Where is Sir William Waterbond?'

'Here!' Sir William lifted his eyes calmly from his puzzle.

'Look, Willie! Look at the hat-box!' Martinez pointed accusingly at the cardboard box on the arm of the woman who had come out of the milliner's.

'Yes,' rejoined Sir William. 'I am looking at it.'

'It is square. Hat-boxes of this period are always round—no?'

'I don't know,' said Sir William, rising reluctantly.

'You don't know?' Martinez seemed to be controlling an impulse to express his sense of injury more forcibly. 'An expert—a famous authority—not to know whether hat-boxes are round or square! That is not possible, Willie!'

'I am an expert on Mrs. Gaskell, and I'm not prepared to say dogmatically that all Regency hat-boxes were round and none square,' Sir William answered stolidly.

'We must get it right. We must find out. There are people who would notice.'

'Is it really of importance after such a dialogue? If you feel nervous about it, use a round one and be on the safe side.'

There was now a substantial delay while the question of the bandbox was disputed and property men were sent to examine the studio's resources as to boxes of other shapes. The rehearsal continued but became perfunctory, and by the time it was proved that no such thing as a round box existed at Cornfields, the shooting was postponed till after lunch.

Maxine took Miss MacFarren to the canteen, and on the way they were joined by Mory, who had seen them from his office window. They took a table in a room reserved for the higher grades of artistes and staff, where Maxine exchanged so many greetings and entered into so much persiflage with neighbours, and Mory listened to so many communications made in low voices, or even in whispers, by colleagues who paused in going to their own tables, that at first there were only fits and starts of conversation. But presently the room was full, people became engrossed in their meal, and the effervescence subsided.

Sir William Waterbond was now seen searching for a place, and they invited him to occupy their fourth chair. Maxine had begun to tell them of a tiny and laughable contretemps in putting on her second costume. The elaborate hat was one she had not worn before, and an assistant from the wardrobe had been placing it on her head when someone had raised the point that this, by a trade union ruling, was hairdresser's work. The hairdresser had then taken charge of the hat and, being unfamiliar with Regency fashions, had arranged it back to front, bringing the wrath and ridicule of the wardrobe upon the hairdressing staff.

'Surely all these rules must be a tyranny to everyone,' said Miss MacFarren, 'the employees just as much as anyone else?'

'They are the new religion,' said Sir William, 'the substitute for church ritualism which has lost its grip. Most human beings desire some kind of rites and formalities that can be enforced and argued about. There must be heresies to hunt and details of belief to niggle over. One belongs to the trade union now just as one was once baptized into the true faith.'

'But from my very scanty observation,' Miss MacFarren suggested, 'there must be a number of people here who find so many restrictions troublesome.'

'Yet who nevertheless regard the authority as sacrosanct. Oh yes, quite so! Popular religions always have multitudes of those supporters. Here in the studio you'll find all the types—from the heretics who're forced to perform the rites or become martyrs to the really pious who regulate their whole lives by the strictest union principles!'

'I've already met with a heretic,' said Miss MacFarren, thinking of the still photographer.

'And a cynic. Your nephew's a superb specimen. And didn't I observe you devouring some backchat between Poppy of the wardrobe and Harry Props? Poppy is irreverent, like many women, but Harry Props is a deeply religious man. To him the rules are above question—a divine mystery. He upholds them without knowing why or wherefore.'

'Oh God, here's little Laughing Eyes!' Maxine interrupted, *sotto voce.*

Miss MacFarren glanced round and saw Juanita Martinez, charmingly dressed, beautifully tidy, like a child in a fashion plate, standing near the door, unconsciously obstructing the path of a waitress with a tray.

'When will her father learn to keep her out of the studio?' Maxine demanded with a sigh of exasperation.

'Not as long as she gets this kind of reception.' Mory, by a slight movement of the hand, called their attention to the welcome which was being accorded to the captivating child as she began to sidle daintily between the tables. Arms were stretched out to embrace her, voices cooed little teasing; or affectionate epithets, to all of which she made the response of an accustomed graciousness.

'It's only the new people who fuss over her,' said Maxine, 'and the ones who want something out of Pio. The poor little brat gets dirty looks from the rest of us.'

Miss MacFarren glanced round once again, and perceived that Maxine's remark was not without foundation. For everyone who proffered endearments there was some other whose face conveyed the idea of subtle or overt antagonism.

In passing their own table, Juanita stopped with a slight hint of challenge, as if she sensed the unfavourable atmosphere, and saluted each of them in turn: 'Hullo, Maxie! Hullo, Willie! Hullo, Mory!' She stared blankly at Miss MacFarren for an instant, then murmured in a hesitant manner, 'Hullo!'

'So you remember me?' said Miss MacFarren.

'Yes, you were there the day I gave the chocolate to the duck,' she replied simply. 'Maxie was cross, wasn't she?' Her confidential smile would have been engaging if it had not reminded Miss MacFarren forcefully of another smile which, for six months, had been significant of nothing but unpleasantness.

'What have you been up to today?' Maxine enquired, as one who expects that the answer will be mischief.

'I've been working the Moviola.'

'You were told to keep out of the cutting-rooms,' said Mory with unwonted severity.

'There's a new man, Jimmy, and he likes to have me there.' The retort was smiling but emphatic.

'He'll stop liking it the minute he stops being new.'

Juanita turned away, suddenly unheeding, and made for her father's table, where she was at once an object of fond and pressing solicitude from all except the drooping man with the limp moustache, who immersed himself promptly in reading over some letters taken from his pocket.

'Hanson has never been one for the patter of little feet,' said Maxine.

'Who is he?'

'Our production manager. He takes a pretty lousy view of human nature at the best of times; but ever since Juanita tried to win his heart by putting flowers on his desk, he's been practically a broken man. The vase leaked and deluged a pile of cheques with water.'

It was strange how the child succeeded in monopolizing the attention of everyone, even those who scarcely veiled their distaste or irritation. Her thin, high voice piped comments on things and personalities which sounded with mysterious clarity above the din of general conversation and were hailed with laughter from neighbouring tables. Facetious questions were flung at her from across the room and were answered with risible gravity or entertaining impudence. When she caressed her father and lovingly pulled down his head by the hair so that she might kiss him, there were audible whispers of admiration at the tender scene; while those who were not disposed to admire seemed to feel equally strongly in the opposite direction, so that whether by applause, muttered criticism, or the pointed silence of disapprobation, she could not fail to know that she was the centre of observation.

Before the meal was over, an incident occurred which might have shaken the complacency of a less securely poised being. The waitress, who had been paying special regard to Juanita's appetite and had promised to bring her a piece of her favourite chocolate cake, was obliged to report that nothing remained but prunes and custard. Juanita began to coax in her prettiest manner, and the waitress went back to the kitchen to make sure that no morsel of the cake was available.

'Don't you ever get tired of chocolate?' Mark Harrowby asked from an adjacent seat, with perhaps a trace of malice under his appearance of jocose benevolence. 'Every time I see you, you seem to be popping something into your mouth.'

'I haven't had chocolate cake for days and days and days, have I, Daddy?' The clear, carrying treble, pitched on a note of injured rectitude, excited a widespread murmur of humorous commiseration which was still echoing when the waitress came back and announced:

'I'm sorry, dear. Chef says you had the very last piece this morning when you came to the kitchen door.'

Juanita's blank gaze, followed by a swift slackening of all her features, gave Miss MacFarren quite a disagreeable turn, and this was intensified when she said airily: 'I only got that cake to give to someone else.' There was a snort of sardonic laughter from the man with the drooping moustache, and with no sign of discomposure other than a slight frown, she added: 'I suppose I'd better have horrible old prunes and custard then.'

The party at Miss MacFarren's table had already taken coffee and were only awaiting their reckonings, which now being presented, they rose to go, and Miss MacFarren resumed her study of film-making. But her mind was curiously perturbed, and nothing she was shown by Mory as he hurried her through cutting-rooms, wardrobes, projection theatres, immense elaborate plasterers' and carpenters' shops, or amazing conglomerations of objects called props, could long distract her from the irresistible temptation to compare the spoiled child with Mrs. Bankes.

No shooting being possible on Mory's picture during the afternoon, he had undertaken to attend a script conference, and, after her brisk tour of the studio, she was left again to watch the progress of *Cranford*. That progress, unfortunately for her hope of being diverted, was barely perceptible to an outsider's eye, for it consisted merely of taking over all over again the two shots which had already been rehearsed. Kenny was, it seemed, notoriously liable to 'fluff' his lines, and those allotted to him in the rôle of Major Gordon (for such, Miss MacFarren learned with astonishment, was the character he portrayed) were evidently particularly difficult for him to master. The first shot, in which there was no dialogue, was disposed of within an hour, but the next threatened to be interminable.

Over and over again, with the huge arc lights blazing, the camera crew in action, the sound apparatus recording, the whole stage hushed and motionless except for the actors taking part, there would be a hesitation, a fumbling, or a speech completely muddled, and Martinez, with patient resignation, would give the command to begin again. Once Kenny spoke of 'the pretty little minx who makes meat balls of our hearts', which caused an explosion of almost hysterical laughter, for it was the fifteenth take. At the next attempt, as if possessed by a fiend, he substituted the words 'mince pies'.

By the twentieth take, Miss MacFarren's mind lost its last vestige of interest in what was happening on the set and was wholly engrossed in contemplating her now settled and defined belief in the arrested mentality of Mrs. Bankes. What had formerly seemed an academic sort of theorizing became, in the light of her new observation of Juanita, a matter of urgent practical concern. To all intents and purposes, she was sharing her house with a little girl of nine—a badly brought up little girl who had the privileges and the freedom of a woman.

If one realized that Antonia was merely another Juanita with an adult's stature and a sagacious but not always sustained pose of being a woman, all the peculiarities of her behaviour, her feckless-ness, her promises so lightly made and broken, her foolish habit of telling lies that were certain to be found out, were at once intelligibly accounted for. A spoiled child, translated to an adult sphere, would have precisely this character. Even her virtues sprang from pure childishness. Her discouragement of gossip, her ready uncritical acceptance of every acquaintance, her generosity—these required no suppression of inclinations. She was indifferent to gossip as she was indifferent to world affairs, to public events, to anything outside the orbit of an entirely childish life; she was uncritical because she had no standards but those of immediate personal convenience; she was generous—as indeed Captain Bankes himself recognized—because she had a child's love of the ritual of giving. It was really not possible to picture her, even by a charitable stretch of the imagination, doing any kindness without the expectation of being thanked and basking in praise.

Everything in the bewildering jigsaw puzzle of her personality fitted harmoniously into place if the simple premise were granted that she had chosen to remain at the Juanita stage of her existence and had no intention in the world of growing up. The influences in her childhood which had taught her to take advantage of the state of being irresponsible had somehow been prolonged into the years that should have brought maturity. She had been able to replace her adoring father with a paternal husband, and had probably always lived a life of willing dependence. Doubtless, Miss MacFar-ren acknowledged, considering the matter dispassionately, she had been generally attractive to men. For some perplexing reason, they often liked women to be immature.

There was Maxine, for instance, who, according to Mory, had superlative sex appeal. He had spoken explicitly of the charm of her baby face. She was actually shrewd, sophisticated, *rusée*, but the mere appearance of childishness was evidently enough. Captain Bankes had said, after taking her to Park Lane in his taxi, that she was 'a very sweet kid', and he had added, bringing a smile to Miss MacFarren's lips, that her manner was 'completely natural'. Captain Bankes must be extremely susceptible to the idea of youthfulness to condone Maxine's unseemly mode of expressing herself on the grounds that it was natural, for Antonia never said anything stronger than 'Bother!' and Antonia, she knew, set his pattern for feminine social conduct.

The thought of Maxine reminded her with a guilty qualm of her impulsive invitation. She could only hope it had not been taken too seriously, and it was rather a relief, in the uneasy state of her conscience, that Mory came to fetch her away while Maxine was still on the set and could do no more than wave goodbye. A more formal leave-taking might have occasioned some further reference, on Maxine's part, to the proffered hospitality.

12

THE FOX TERRIER'S month had now run out and its owner was expected to fetch it within a day or two. Miss MacFarren looked forward to its removal with satisfaction, but she was worried by its want of condition, which she attributed to the fact that it had rarely of late been out of doors. She had never had time to give it all the exercise its strikingly energetic disposition seemed to crave, and in the last week, what with her visit to the film studio and her preparations for Ladies' Night at the Connoisseurs' Club, she had done little for the unlucky animal beyond secretly augmenting its diet and occasionally letting it out into her garden.

The dinner of the Connoisseurs' Club was to be their first full-dress affair since the early days of the war, and she had been persuaded by Dr. Wilmot to say a few words on botanical painting—-for it was the practice of the Connoisseurs to refrain from lengthy toasts, and instead to invite brief speeches on subjects of special interest. Miss MacFarren had not made a speech since retiring from the treasurership of the Phytology Society six years ago, and it was nearly as long since she had worn evening dress, so she was obliged to devote much labour to her preparations. Her speech was written and rewritten, pruned and polished, until it contained all that could be said upon the theme in eight and a half minutes; while her amethyst velvet dress, bought for a grand function to which she had accompanied her brother Andrew, was resurrected from its tissue paper, skilfully let out in the places where it was no longer adequate in size, steamed, and refreshed with a beautiful piece of guipure lace, a long-hoarded treasure. She hoped by these means to do credit to her host and at the same time to support her dignity becomingly as his nearest rival in the botanical field: and if the thought of Jimjams's confinement sometimes disturbed her, she reminded herself that she had done very much more for him than could reasonably have been expected, and that he would soon be restored to the home where he was much indulged and presumably happy.

On the day after her trip to Cornfields, however, his whinings, scratchings, spasms of pointless barking, and other signs of frustrated energy, were so pronounced that, at the risk of seeming a busybody, she pounced on Mrs. Bankes as she was going out with her shopping bag and suggested she should take the dog with her. Mrs. Bankes looked fretful but replied politely ('She is the little girl who has been praised for politeness,' thought Miss MacFarren):

'I'd *like* to take him, but I'm in a hurry this morning. Do you mind terribly if I leave him behind?'

'I wasn't thinking of myself. The dog badly needs exercise. That's why he's making all this noise.'

'I gave him an enormous long walk yesterday.'

Miss MacFarren burned to say, 'You did nothing of the sort, Mrs. Bankes,' but she had not as yet reached this degree of unrestraint, and confined herself to looking frankly incredulous. 'Even a short walk would do him good. He gets more out of condition every day.'

'Oh, come along then, you little nuisance!' Mrs. Bankes turned petulantly to the dog.

'Wait! I'll get you his lead!' Miss MacFarren darted into the lobby where it was kept on a hook. 'He's quite unsafe without it.'

'No, I can't manage him on a lead and my shopping bag too.' Mrs. Bankes was growing more and more fractious—for, as Miss MacFarren had known for a long while, her politeness was liable to break down when it had served or failed to serve its purpose. 'He twists himself round my ankles.'

'I certainly shouldn't take him without a lead,' Miss MacFarren reiterated with emphasis. 'It's far too risky.'

'He can't get lost. He's got his name and address round his neck.' She pointed with pride to a little disk she had had engraved at a pet shop where, in one of her enthusiastic moments before his novelty had worn off, she had taken him to be shampooed.

'That's very nice'—Miss MacFarren found herself speaking as if Mrs. Bankes were really a child—'but I'm afraid it could hardly save him from being run over.' And feeling a strong inclination to wash her hands of Mrs. Bankes and the dog, both of whom had intruded beyond all decency upon her peace and comfort, she retired abruptly to her own room.

One of the inconveniences she had been subjected to since Mrs. Manders' departure was the compulsion to answer the doorbells whenever Mrs. Bankes was out—an inconvenience the more resented because nearly all visitors, parcels, and tradesmen's deliveries were for her tenant, and the interruptions, taken in conjunction with telephone calls, made it impossible to concentrate on any occupation even when the house was otherwise quiet. But lately the decided slackening of social activities had brought a measure of relief. Morning callers had grown rare, the circle of 'lady friends' having exhausted all desire to participate in tasks which were becoming less and less ladylike and more and more like dull and dirty housework. So Miss MacFarren bore it with resignation when she was summoned to the front door in the midst of a programme on orchid-hunting in Brazil.

On the doorstep stood a broad man with pleasant, ruddy features, lightly greying hair, a checked overcoat, and a powerful brindled bulldog held on a lead.

'I've come about the fox terrier named Jimjams,' he said at once in a serious yet friendly manner. 'I dare say you'll have heard—'

'Has he been run over?' She had so fully expected him to meet this fate that her reaction was a simple hope that he had died swiftly.

'No. No, he hasn't been run over.' The broad vowels of the north country gave a lingering tone to phrases which were in any case uttered at a measured and thoughtful pace. 'I take it that the lady who was out with him isn't back yet?'

'No.'

'She hurried off so fast, I made sure she'd be coming straight home.'

'Why, what's happened?'

'I'm afraid what's happened is that your Jimjams made an unprovoked attack on my Butterfly.'

'Your Butterfly!' Miss MacFarren stared incredulously at the hideous though certainly stalwart and faithful-looking creature.

'Ay, Butterfly Bingo!' The dog, hearing its name, gazed fondly up at him and wagged its ludicrous kinked tail, 'A name that would have been famous if it hadn't been for the war stopping the dog shows. Still, this is hardly the time to tell you that, I quite realize, Mrs.—er—?'

'Miss MacFarren. Won't you come in out of the cold?' She took him to her study and indicated a chair.

'Thank you, Miss MacFadden—though perhaps you'll not wish me to sit when you've heard what I've come to say. . . . Don't be afraid of Butterfly! You can't breed a gentler dog than a well-trained bulldog.'

'I know.' She patted it on the head to show that she was not afraid. 'I like bulldogs. They snuffle but they don't yap.' A month of suffering inspired the compliment.

'Ay, I'd rather have snufflers than yappers any day. If you don't like yapping, Miss MacFadden, I'm surprised at you keeping a terrier, if I may say so.'

'It isn't mine.'

'O-oh? It belongs to t'other lady, does it? I thought it was yours because I've seen you with it once or twice coming past my place, The Yorkshire Rose.'

Miss MacFarren signified her courteous recognition of the well-reputed local public house he had named.

'You had some sense—you took it out on a lead,' he said. 'T'other lady had it gallivanting all over the street. And I came round to give you my word'—he now lengthened out his syllables to an absolutely portentous slowness—'Butterfly offered it no provocation of any kind whatsoever.'

'I quite believe you. I know Jimjams can be very troublesome.'

'Most bulldogs will go out of their way to avoid a fight, but this one especially.' He bent over to stroke the ungainly animal, which had rested its head tenderly against his leg. 'Not that you can properly call it a fight when a fox terrier grabs a dog from the Bingo kennels by the hind leg.'

'He doesn't seem any the worse for it,' said Miss MacFarren, 'though I'm sorry, of course, that you've had the annoyance.'

'Oh, bless you, it's no annoyance to *us*! This lad could polish off half a dozen fox terriers while you were saying your prayers.'

'Polish off! Do you mean he's killed Jimjams?'

'What am I telling you? Didn't I say he'd grabbed Butterfly by the hind leg?'

'You didn't say Butterfly had killed him.'

'Did I need to say it?' His tone was full of pained surprise. 'I only ask you to look at my dog!'

Miss MacFarren obediently cast her eyes over the enormous undershot jaw, the receding head with its wrinkled brow, the muscular expanse of chest, the sturdy bow legs.

'It was foolish of Jimjams to attack him,' she admitted. She had an impression that the dog was smiling benevolently as if it had done some kindly deed but asked no credit for it.

'It was suicide, Miss MacFadden. That dog, for some reason known only to himself, committed suicide.'

'I hope—I do hope he wasn't badly hurt before he died.'

'Hurt!' The owner of the bulldog laughed. 'He didn't have to be hurt. One bite, one good shake, and the deed was done.' He must have become aware that he had betrayed an undue appreciation of Butterfly's biting and shaking prowess, for he cleared his throat, assumed a grave expression, and added: 'But all I want to say is I can assure you ladies, this dog is no more to blame for what took place than a babe unborn.'

'What did take place?' Miss MacFarren demanded with reluctant curiosity.

He fixed her with his candid and convincing blue eyes. 'We were just going home from our stroll, the stroll we always have before opening time, morning and evening. Butterfly was on the lead, as he is now, happy as a king.' As if to illustrate his master's story, the bulldog sat up attentively with an expression amounting to beatitude. 'Along the street, in the opposite direction, comes this little suicide dog; prancing about in the middle of the road, and her, the lady, yelling at him to come to heel; and him paying no more heed than if she was the man in the moon. Then he sees Butterfly and begins barking and snarling. Butterfly takes no notice, just walks on peaceful and pleasant.' Butterfly in an endeavour, it seemed, to live up to this reputation, succeeded in looking positively demure.

'Then Master Jimjams comes closer and starts making runs at him—squaring up, as you might say, and Butterfly just gives a little growl—more of a yawn, it was—telling him to go along and not make a fool of himself. And the lady was laughing, because I suppose she thought, my dog being on a lead, there was nothing to worry about. But when this Jimjams went on yapping and snapping and dancing all round him, I called out to her to pick him up and get him out of the way, which she would have done if she'd had a grain of sense. Not that I want to give offence,' he put in earnestly, 'but I'm bound to say she didn't show much gumption. I didn't either if it comes to that, but I couldn't have believed the little blighter would grab Butterfly by the leg.'

'And what happened then?'

'What do you think? Before you could say "knife", he'd jerked the lead out of my hand and Master Jimjams's neck was broken. It was a matter of a second or two.'

'What did Mrs. Bankes do?'

'Mrs. Bankes?' He paused to register the name. 'I must admit her behaviour had me flummoxed. She simply stands there and asks in a gormless sort of way: "Is he killed? Is he dead? Oh, my goodness, whatever am I going to say?"' Wringing his hands and assuming a flute-like voice he succeeded in giving a fantastic caricature of Mrs. Bankes. 'Then all of a sudden she turns on her heels and disappears. I thought she was so upset she wanted to get home in case she might faint or something. So when I saw the address hanging on the dog's collar I came straight here to make sure she was all right and explain our side of the story.'

Miss MacFarren nodded judicially.

'I'm sorry for what he's done, but I ask you to believe it isn't in his nature to seek a quarrel. Miss MacFadden, there isn't an ill-natured bone in his body.'

The sagacious dog, panting slightly, thus giving itself a pathetic air of eagerness, approached Miss MacFarren, and, as it were, smiled up into her face, at the same time winningly raising a paw. Miss MacFarren hardly knew where to look, so deep was her sense of treachery to the ill-fated Jimjams, but the fact was she had taken a fancy to Butterfly.

'I dare say he acted according to his instincts,' she said, not exactly patting his head but touching it with the tips of her fingers. 'He seems a very fine specimen of his breed.'

'He's the son of Dragonfly Bingo. I can't say fairer than that.'

Her fingers had rested lightly on the dog's head, and guiltily she withdrew them, troubled by a painful question.

'What are we going to do about disposing of him—of Jimjams, I mean?'

'If you like to leave that to me, I know what to do.' It might be guessed that he had coped with this difficulty before.

Accompanying him to the door, she suggested that he should defer the obsequies until she had consulted Mrs. Bankes on behalf of the owner. 'Perhaps she might want him to go to the Dogs' Cemetery. Poor Jimjams!'

'Well, Miss MacFadden, you've been very reasonable—very reasonable indeed. I'm much obliged to you.'

'It's easier to be reasonable when it isn't one's own dog, Mr. Penroyd.'

She had known it would surprise him to be thus addressed, and she watched his reaction with frank amusement as he stopped in the act of buttoning up his coat collar to demand: 'Now how did you come to know my name?'

'It's written over the door of The Yorkshire Rose.'

'You're very observant.'

'No, but I've passed your—er—house dozens of times, and I've a good memory.'

'I don't suppose you often go into a pub for a drink, Miss MacFadden?'

'Not so far.' Her smile bordered almost on raillery.

'Nay, but you're not one to turn up your nose at us. If you'd care to come along some evening and have a drink on the house, I'm sure both Butterfly and I will be glad to meet you again.'

'I may take you at your word about that.'

The response was dictated by a fear of appearing priggish, but he evidently thought her in earnest for he rejoined quickly:

'I'll be very pleased if you do. What do you like? Whisky?'

She felt almost as if she were blushing as she answered with a semblance of deliberation, 'Yes, perhaps I do prefer whisky on the whole.'

'Good! I'll keep a little on the side for you. It's known as ginger ale among my specials. Why not pop in and have a drink this evening when you let me know what I'm to do about Jimjams?'

'I don't think I could this evening.'

'Just as you like, but I've a private room if you're shy.'

They parted shaking hands, and the jaunty swing of Butterfly's haunches, as he moved with a nautical rolling gait down the street, had something in it so endearing that she found it hard to remember he was a killer.

It was a pity about Jimjams. To have survived the whole month, at least nominally in Mrs. Bankes's care, and then to perish on the eve of release was a sad business, upsetting even to one who had always thought the dog's disposition unfortunate. She should have felt sorry for Mrs. Netley too, but she was not inclined to extend much sympathy to a woman who had been silly enough to entrust her pet to Mrs. Bankes and inconsiderate enough to have done so without consulting the view of the other occupant of the house. As for Mrs. Bankes herself, it was all she could do to refrain from saying, 'Serve her right!' In vain she told herself that the woman was mentally a child. The reply was ready: if a child behaved in so infuriating a fashion, no one less than a saint would have been able to subdue a desire to see it well chastised.

Mrs. Bankes, though she had left the house for the purpose of doing her morning shopping and had professed to be in a hurry, was still absent when Miss MacFarren returned from her café luncheon. On the doorstep stood Harriet, waiting patiently for an answer to the bell. She started when her friend touched her on the shoulder.

'Goodness me, Elinor! I thought it was Mrs. Bankes.' The idea seemed to have been a distasteful one.

'Have you been ringing long?'

'Ages. I was just giving up.'

'Good, it means we've got the house to ourselves.'

She opened the door and led the way to her study, and began to prepare the coffee percolator while Harriet talked to her without a shadow of the restraint under which they had formerly laboured.

'I'm lucky to have found you by yourself, Elinor. I was definitely *not* in the mood for Mrs. Bankes. If she'd answered the door, I was just going to ask for you and say "Good morning", and walk straight past her. I'm so angry, I can hardly contain myself. . . . Do you remember ten days ago or so, when I told you about an Empire bon-bon box she'd bought at my shop?'

'And hadn't paid for. Yes, what happened? I'm longing to hear the sequel.'

'Well, I followed your advice and wrote offering to take the box back if she didn't want it. And it turned up by post this morning with a little scrawled note saying she was so glad I needed it back because her husband thought it was too effeminate for a cigarette box.'

'Ah, that's the true Bankes touch—pretending you *needed* it back!'

'Yes, as if she were doing me a favour. And it was I who told her six months ago the thing was unsuitable for cigarettes. But that's not the worst! My dear, you should see how she's sent it back. When she took it away it was in mint condition—simply flawless. Now the gilt edges are all chipped and a lot of the little pearls are loose inside the glass as if it had been dropped. It was packed quite shockingly too. I must send it away to be repaired before I can possibly put it back into stock.'

'My dear, how appalling! But how typical! Surely you won't lie down under it?'

'My dear, what else is one to do? As she obviously had no intention of paying for it, I suppose I'm lucky to get back anything at all.'

It was so delightful to find Harriet nursing a substantial grievance that Miss MacFarren lost the last trace of the bitterness she had felt when she could gain no credence for her own sufferings, and was free at last to speak with absolute naturalness of all that had been happening. So the two friends sat together from coffee-time till tea-time in the most cosy intimacy, discussing the single subject of Mrs. Bankes in every aspect; and each was now wonderfully tactful with the other. Miss MacFarren stated again and again that Mrs. Bankes's superficial charm would deceive anybody, and

Harriet, thus exonerated from the blame of having recommended her, lavished boundlessly the sympathy so long denied.

In this propitious atmosphere, Miss MacFarren was able to explain her theory of Mrs. Bankes's self-arrested development and Harriet agreed that it was a valid deduction on the evidence presented. But where Miss MacFarren believed that this childishness was genuine, incorrigible, and unconscious, Harriet was of the opinion that it was a sustained pose, a deliberate exploitation of such as would be exploited.

'She'd grow up quickly enough if you faced her with some situation where childishness didn't pay.'

'But childishness always seems to pay since she doesn't mind losing people's respect and trust. Look, even in this matter of the box . . . She buys it though it's more than she can afford, because it's an irresistible little toy. When it turns out to be no good for the purpose she wanted it for—probably Captain Bankes really did say it was too effeminate for him—she tries to get out of paying for it. You know how children trade on the indulgence of adults to let them off their bargains? And sure enough, the one thing we rack our brains for is a way of letting her off! It's always so. Everyone finds it easier to give in.'

'But as you say, she loses people's respect.'

'That doesn't matter to her. She only cares about first impressions. Children are like that: they make marvellous beginnings but they don't keep things up. And they're used to being scolded and told when they've done wrong, so it doesn't hurt their self-esteem very much.'

'All the same, Elinor, I maintain that Antonia Bankes can grow up whenever it suits her. You may think I've been a bad judge of her character so far, but of one thing I'm certain—she knows what's good for her. Children generally don't.'

Miss MacFarren nodded thoughtfully. 'Yes, there's something in that.'

'Could she have kept that figure and that complexion if she hadn't been extremely sensible where her own interests are concerned?'

'I put her figure down to a naturally well-balanced constitution, and as for her face—do you know I believe she looks young because she's irresponsible. That smoothness and freshness—it's due to not worrying, not putting herself out. She never even seems to think very hard.'

'It's *hideously* unfair,' said Harriet, 'that being silly and lazy should be a recipe for keeping young, but I dare say you're right.' She smiled wryly at herself in the mirror. 'I at least have the satisfaction of knowing my face is covered with signs of hard thinking. If I were you, my dear Elinor, I shouldn't scruple to introduce some hard thinking into Antonia's head.'

'Oh, that 'twere possible!' Miss MacFarren sighed.

'It would do her the world of good even if it did bring a line or two to her face. She has a doting husband so it wouldn't hurt her to grow a little older.'

'I don't know. He seems to love her to be childish. He gets a bit cross when it makes her tiresome, but on the whole I'm sure he prefers her the way she is. He's a very fatherly sort of man.' She laughed. 'He's fatherly even with me.'

Harriet spluttered over her pinch of snuff. 'What a pity you aren't a little blonde of about twenty-five! He'd be more fatherly still, and you probably wouldn't have any difficulty at all in getting Antonia to look for another home.'

The idea seemed to amuse Harriet inordinately, but Miss MacFarren found it rather too near to a notion she had stealthily turned over in her own mind—turned over and looked at with shocked but fascinated eyes, and bundled away among her most unthinkable thoughts. Indeed, in her anxiety not to encounter this dark fancy in broad daylight, she headed the conversation off at a tangent, and it became merely a general complaint of the housing shortage, and a speculation as to how and where the Bankeses would find other quarters.

After tea Harriet left, and a few minutes later Mrs. Bankes returned, her arrival announced by a high-pitched giggle and a shrill rallying note which could be recognized as the peculiar properties of Miss Hall-Brown. Mrs. Bankes's own voice was uncommonly subdued, and there was a suggestion of furtiveness about her movements which recalled vividly to Miss MacFarren certain occasions about forty years ago when she had come home from forbidden expeditions wondering if she had been found out, timorously reconnoitring, and protecting herself with the presence of some school companion in front of whom she hoped to be spared from rebuke till the storm had blown over.

Feeling for once that she had the advantage, she remained in her study until the hour when it was necessary to stoke the boiler, that loathly job to which she was now, in the bitter February weather, more than ever committed. The sitting-room door was open, and as her footsteps sounded on the strip of parquet leading to the basement stairs, she could hear Mrs. Bankes's normal conversational voice suddenly drop to a sort of listening murmur. Really, it would be kind to clear the air by going in and telling her she knew what had happened to the dog. She resolved that, when she came up from the basement, she would do so.

But the discovery that, owing to Harriet's visit, she had forgotten to bring in coke while daylight lasted, incensed her, by a roundabout process, against Mrs. Bankes, and, groping with shovel and bucket in a nearly dark cellar, she quite lost any desire to make the wretched culprit's situation easier by letting her off the ordeal of confession. The sight of her roughened and reddened hands as she washed them at the kitchen sink engendered indeed an absolutely unprecedented yearning to use them to some violent purpose. She would have liked to shake Mrs. Bankes, to slap her, to push her bodily out of the house. As it was, she merely went straight back to her study and shut herself in without doing anything to end the atmosphere of suspense, though it would soon be desirable to get into touch with Mr. Penroyd regarding the disposal of Jimjams' remains.

At seven o'clock she decided to go out to dinner and take in Mr. Penroyd on the way, speaking to Mrs. Bankes when she had got into her outdoor clothes. The grime of the cellar still clung about her, and she went upstairs to wash and to change her blouse. Mrs. Bankes had now moved with her friend to the bedroom, and as Miss MacFarren paused in her upward climb to get a clean towel from the linen closet, she heard their voices plainly, for the door was ajar and on the thickly carpeted stairs and landing, her footfalls had been soundless.

'My goodness!' Miss Hall-Brown was saying on the crest of a giggle. 'You are a holy terror, Tonia! I honestly feel quite sorry for the poor old girl. I don't know why she puts up with you.'

Miss MacFarren was not quite sure whether she could or could not help hearing Antonia's reply:

'Darling, she hates the sight of me. It's only because of Joss that she lets me stay here a minute.'

She wanted earnestly now to cough or make a noise with the door of the linen closet, but then they would have known their remarks had been overheard—would have suspected perhaps that she had been listening for a much longer time than was actually the case—and the awkwardness would have been acute all round, so she stood rigid, fairly dreading the next words.

'Does she like Joss?'

'My dear, she's got a "thing" about him. You know the way old girls are liable to go when they haven't got any men, or any children, or any anything. She hasn't even got a cat. . . . Pass me that hand mirror off the bed ducky!'

'Is she all sentimental about him? Doesn't it make him laugh?'

'He doesn't know,' said Antonia, laughing herself.

'But how do *you* know?'

'Feminine something-or-other.'

'Oh.' The tone was disappointed. 'Then she doesn't say or do anything?'

'No. But I know. Only don't breathe a syllable to Joss! He'd feel silly, and then he'd stop paying compliments and buttering her up, and let me tell you, that's the only reason she hasn't tried to throw me out. . . . Do you like me with these curls high up at the back?'

'Heavenly, darling! *Does* he pay her compliments?' This time the tone was astonished.

'Only because he really does admire her work.' Antonia's voice repelled any suggestion of a more personal esteem. 'She's madly clever, you know.'

At this moment, the bedroom door was closed as if one of the speakers had realized a want of precaution—Miss Hall-Brown, no doubt, since Antonia was evidently at the dressing-table; nor was she, in a general way, much given to cautiousness. Anyone naturally inclined to eavesdropping could have been in possession long ago of all her private affairs.

Miss MacFarren found that, between guilt and anger, she was trembling, and she sat down where she was in the linen closet on a little pair of steps intended for reaching the higher shelves. Of all absurd, disgusting, unwarrantable ideas, the idea that she had ever felt anything more than a normal friendly regard for Captain Bankes was the most offensive. It was utterly gratuitous, the senseless innuendo of a dirty-minded child. If there was one thing not to be borne about being elderly and unmarried, it was this fatuous assumption by half-baked sniggerers that there was some extra significance to all one's most ordinary emotions!

In the indignation of the moment, she so far lost her sense of proportion as to forget how unusual in her experience was such a dialogue as she had just heard, and to feel herself the victim of countless humiliations. Flicking tears from the side of her nose with the consciousness that she would look extremely foolish if discovered, she sat and waited till Mrs. Bankes and her giggling companion had emerged from the bedroom ('Now you're not to leave me alone for a second!' an urgent whisper implored as they descended the stairs): then she took her towel, went up to her own bathroom, and washed away tears and the grime of coke together.

She came down in her coat and hat, and stood in the hall drawing on her gloves and steadying a temper that was still deeply disturbed before encountering Mrs. Bankes, who could now be heard in the basement directing her friend where to find the tin-opener. Her glance fell upon the Gallé cats on each side of the front door, smiling their spacious smiles directly, it seemed, at her; staring brightly with their green glass eyes in which shone dark expanded pupils. Mrs. Bankes had said, 'She hasn't even got a cat,' and here were these two handsome specimens in their flowered jackets, mocking that stupid woman's mockery. She picked up the one nearest her as if she could establish some contact with it that would give her comfort.

An instant later, a new gust of fury shook her from head to foot. The cat, free from the least blemish when she had last looked at it, now showed an unseemly diagonal scar just below its shoulder. One of its legs had been broken off at the thickest part, and set together inexpertly with glue. Taking it under her arm, she went straight down to the basement dining-room.

Mrs. Bankes, who was setting the table, was startled into a moment of visible consternation. 'Tiggy!' she called swiftly, as she nodded her flurried greeting. 'Bring the—the salad bowl, ducky!'

Tiggy hastened from the kitchen.

Miss MacFarren was surprised to find that she had suddenly grown calm and taken full command of herself. 'This cat has been broken,' she said in the coolest of voices.

Mrs. Bankes's expression wavered. Her blank look appeared but dissolved into a little apologetic smile as she recognized the futility of denial. 'Please, it was an accident,' she said with an infantine air of contrition.

'It was not mended by accident. The least you can do when you've damaged a thing so as to destroy half its value, is to mention the matter at once and not leave the owner to find out by chance. I'm sorry to speak like this in front of Miss Hall-Brown but you won't be seen alone.'

She turned abruptly and went out of the room, forgetful of Jimjams. But the shadow of a gesticulating hand on the door acted as a reminder. The hand was Tiggy's, and its movement said as plainly as words: 'Go on! Get it over!' Miss MacFarren wheeled round again and was in time to see Antonia shaking her head. 'Have you anything to say to me?' she demanded.

'I? No.' She caught her friend's admonitory frown, and went on in little gasps as one who has taken an icy plunge. 'Oh well, yes, really . . . about Jimjams. Something awful has happened! I've lost him. I let him off the lead for just a minute or two in the park and he ran right off before I could do anything.'

So deplorable was Miss MacFarren's frame of mind that it gave her a sense of triumph to hear the woman lie. She would spare her nothing, and it was with implacable eyes that she watched that vainly dissembling face. 'He has his address on his collar.'

'Yes. Oh yes, of course.' Mrs. Bankes's eyelids drooped and were lifted again in a distracted flicker: her husband would have called it a double take.

'But in that case, Tonia, you're almost certain to get him back,' said Miss Hall-Brown in evident surprise and relief.

'Perhaps. But he's probably got himself killed somehow or other by this time,' she countered uneasily.

'By a bulldog, for instance.' Miss MacFarren savoured her malice without a qualm.

Antonia, suddenly becoming very busy with knives and forks, made a feeble attempt at defiance: 'I don't know what you mean. What bulldog?'

'You know perfectly. The owner called here this morning.'

'That horrible man in the check clothes?' Antonia's naïve astonishment showed she had completely overlooked this possibility. 'Well, I call that pure cheek after his beastly dog killed Jimjams.'

'You thought he was like you, Mrs. Bankes, and that he'd run away and hide when something unpleasant happened. And then tell lies about it.' The sensation of her own coldness was almost exhilarating.

'If you knew all along the dog was dead'—Antonia covered some shadowy trace of shame with insolence—'why didn't you say so before? Just trying to trap me!'

'Tonia!' Miss Hall-Brown protested gently. It was the first time Miss MacFarren had ever heard her soften the sharp edge of her voice; and she observed, not without sympathy, that a desperate blush mantled her cheek and neck. She was a callow and strident personality, but one to whom falsehood was apparently painful.

'It was your fault, anyway,' Antonia went on, not heeding the interruption, 'making me take him out when I didn't want to! And now I shall never be able to look Mrs. Netley in the face again.'

'I warned you not to take him unless he was on a lead.'

'Oh, you and your warnings! You're always warning me . . .'

The sound of the telephone bell ringing in the hall above had the effect of a call to order from a firm, business-like voice. She checked herself with an undignified, 'Oh, drat!'

'I'll answer if you like,' said Miss Hall-Brown, eagerly escaping.

Miss MacFarren remained to speak her mind while the occasion served. 'It doesn't seem to occur to you that you had absolutely no right to bring the dog here in the first place, especially as you paid so little attention to the poor creature. As soon as your husband comes back, I shall ask him to find other accommodation. Without delay.'

It was a momentous speech and a costly one to utter, involving as it did the final surrender of her hopes for American publication by the New Aldine Press, but she made it resolutely and felt relieved to have done so.

And Antonia was sufficiently shaken to begin pulling herself together at once. 'You really and truly never told me we weren't to keep a dog,' she said with a mild and reasonable reproachfulness.

'I told you I had to live quietly. In any case, the house has been so appallingly neglected that there can be no question of your remaining here. No question.'

'There isn't anywhere else for us to go.'

'You can probably go back to the Asturias if you book at once.'

'But Joss couldn't bear to live at the Asturias—not all the time.'

'You surely didn't imagine you could go on here indefinitely? You've known for months I was dissatisfied.'

Mrs. Bankes evaded this as she always evaded disagreeableness when she could. 'Joss likes it here,' she said in a maddening small voice that was intended to be conciliatory. 'He likes the house and he likes you—honestly.'

'That's no reason why my life should be made a misery.' Miss MacFarren repudiated her supposed partiality for Captain Bankes with zest.

She had thought that even Antonia's pride, hard as it was to sting to self-defence, would have been roused by such blunt speaking, but her only answer was to say pathetically: 'It's awfully cruel to send us away just when Joss thinks he's going to settle down and be happy.'

'If you were so unwilling to leave, you should have made an effort to run your share of the house properly.'

'I don't see what's wrong with it,' Antonia sighed on a note of sincere bewilderment.

'Mrs. Bankes, really! You can say a thing like that when you know I shall find dirt wherever I turn! Look!

She ran her fingers along the top of a mirror, and held up the dust-blackened tips. 'Look at the floor! It's covered with yesterday's crumbs—what the mice and the cockroaches have left of them! Go and look in the kitchen! It's disgraceful!'

'But everything will be cleaned before Joss comes home.' Antonia seemed amazed that anything more should be expected of her. 'If I get it all done up now, it'll only be dirty again before he arrives.'

It was futile to argue with such inveterate irresponsibility, but she made one more endeavour. 'Do you think it fair that I should spend so much of my time fetching coke, raking the boiler, emptying cinders?'

'You mind much more than I do about hot water and the radiators.'

'I made a condition at the beginning which you've flatly disregarded. I asked exceptionally low terms—you quite compel me to mention this, Mrs. Bankes—because you were to provide for a certain amount of housework.'

'Then you must charge more money,' Mrs. Bankes cried triumphantly, as if she had found the solution of every difficulty. 'Joss has said lots of times that we were paying you too little.'

'No amount of money would make you a satisfactory tenant.' Miss MacFarren spoke quietly but with vehemence. 'You will receive a month's notice on the first of March, and you must be out by the first of April.'

As she turned to go, with a sense of having wonderfully disburdened herself, Miss Hall-Brown hurried down the stairs and appeared precipitately in the doorway. 'It's Joss's London office,' she said, 'passing on a message out of one of his cables. He wants them to tell you he's managed to get places for the children in the Clipper, and they're leaving on the 27th.'

She spoke with the air of bringing news that was certain to be delightful and could not, in so uncomfortable a situation, be told too quickly, and it was out before she had noticed Antonia's agonized face exhorting silence. But Miss MacFarren had noticed it, and in a trice had solved the mystery of that preposterous meekness which made Antonia bear every rebuke and plead to stay where she was not wanted. She had known all along of her husband's plan to bring their two children from America and had hoped to keep Miss MacFarren in ignorance until the very moment of their arrival, when it would be absolutely too late to refuse them house-room. They were typical Bankes tactics, the same that she had always used when doing anything to which objection might be raised— the tactics of presenting the *fait accompli*. But being under notice and openly in disfavour when the children came would make it much harder to trade on those factors she must have been counting upon; principally, of course, the 'old girl's' yearning to please Captain Bankes.

Once again Miss MacFarren yielded her emotions to a glacial coldness that seemed to brace her mind and crystallize her thoughts. 'Are you expecting your children to come here?' she enquired evenly.

'Not for long. Only a few days,' Antonia answered pat though with manifest discomposure.

'In our first interview, I explained to you that this house was unsuitable for children, that my work called for peace and quiet. You assured me they would never, under any circumstances, come here.'

'Their father is bringing them,' said Antonia helplessly. 'It was his idea, not mine.'

'Does he know that I object?'

'Oh, you *couldn't* object. When I haven't seen my poor little babes for centuries!' Antonia wailed, clasping her hands as if appealing to some heartless goddess. 'You couldn't—you couldn't object when you think how Joss dotes on them!'

Miss MacFarren drew a deep and pensive breath. She saw beyond all vestige of uncertainty that if she permitted those children to set foot over the threshold, she was lost. The 'few days' would stretch on to a few weeks, the few weeks to a few months, and they would not be able to leave, even when they desired to, because it would be so much more difficult for Captain Bankes to find other quarters for a family than for a childless couple. And she would be wronging the unfortunate children by letting them come to a house where they must perforce be so repressed, and wronging him by letting him bring them.

Presumably he had not realized they would be unwelcome. Most men were inclined to be obtuse in domestic matters, and she had remarked more than once that he was particularly so: it was natural in one whose glimpses of home life had been scanty and whose wife was too insensitive herself to have awakened any perceptions not already alert in him. If he had not been told of her stipulation in regard to the children, he would feel profoundly humiliated when he discovered that he had brought them to the house against the express wishes of the owner and in contravention of his wife's explicit undertaking: while Miss MacFarren's own rôle, trying to protect her few working hours against the noisy comings and goings, the games, the tears and laughter, of two uninhibited young people brought up on the American system, would be more than commonly unsympathetic. It was bad enough to have to set her face against the children now, without ever having seen them, but it would be infinitely worse when her rejection might seem to spring from personal animosity.

All these considerations rushed through her head as if they had been blown there by a piercing wind, and she knew that, however drastic her measures, the predicament must not be allowed to arise.

'Can't you see,' she asked rather to gain time than because she supposed Mrs. Bankes would ever see anything but her own object-ive, 'this house would be hopeless for children! They couldn't be happy here. It isn't properly furnished for them.'

'If you're thinking about your ornaments and things, Joss has got it all worked out. He's going to have them packed up and stored. . . .'

'For a few days,' she interrupted with a faint but significant smile, 'that would be too much trouble. Besides'—that keen wind had blown a spark into her mind and was fanning it to a glow—'I can't imagine where they'd sleep. You've had the use of the spare room for several months, and now I've invited a friend of my own to come and stay.'

Antonia could not have looked more astounded if she had been told that Miss MacFarren expected a visitant from some other world. For a substantial instant she was literally open-mouthed; then, taking herself in hand with little of her customary buoyancy, she faltered:

'There's the other bedroom—the one Mrs. Manders had. We were going to ask you to let them use it as a playroom, but I dare say they could sleep there.'

The fiction of the 'few days' had been dropped, like so many of Mrs. Bankes's fictions, without her giving herself the trouble of inventing an excuse. Miss MacFarren scarcely hesitated. She felt excited, invigorated. This was the extreme of provocation she had needed to make her act decisively.

'I'm afraid that room will be occupied too,' she said almost affably. 'I shall have a maid sleeping there.'

The effect of this announcement was electrifying. Even Miss Hall-Brown who, mindful of her promise to remain with Antonia, had been polishing glasses with a discreet pretence of being deaf or supernaturally detached, stood transfixed, her eyes full of wonder. But no one was more electrified than Miss MacFarren.

She continued rapidly, however, before any question could be put which might call for point-blank lying: 'As you seem to have let the servant problem slide altogether, Mrs. Bankes, I've taken it in hand myself. Where neglect has gone so far, I feel I'm entitled to make what arrangements I can.'

Whatever the effort, whatever the cost, she would have to get a maid now, and already in her icily glowing brain, the names of registry offices flashed like neon signs.

'My plans can't possibly affect you much,' she ended relentlessly, 'since you'll be leaving within six weeks.'

She had intended this to be her parting shot, but she had not counted on a sudden fusillade from her adversary. Antonia, finding that meekness had not served, reverted with the utmost agility to insolence.

'We'll go just exactly when it suits us,' she said with an audacity the more startling because of her now unmistakable childishness of manner. One might have expected the words to be accompanied by some silly grimace or schoolroom gesture. 'You can't put us out! You re not allowed to! Do you think I don't know that.'

'You have no legal right to stay here when your month's notice is up.'

'That's what you think! You can't push people out nowadays. We can go before the Tribunal, so there!'

Miss MacFarren had a very distinct impression—the most convincing of its kind she had yet experienced—that she was having a scene with an impertinent little girl. The threat was absurd, for it was inconceivable that Captain Bankes would seek such a remedy even if it were open to him; but the effect was none the less disquieting, revealing so clear a glimpse of a character destitute of ethical standards grindingly bent upon its own satisfactions, and unhampered by the restraints of normal adult dignity.

'I wonder,' she said, 'if your husband has any idea how you behave when he's not here. I fancy it might come as a considerable surprise to him.'

'If you'd ever managed to get a husband of your own,' Antonia retorted in an intoxication of rudeness, 'you might stop wondering about other people's.'

Miss MacFarren walked out of the room without feelings of any kind. She heard Miss Hall-Brown utter some despairing remonstrance and Mrs. Bankes reply in a deliberately raised voice: 'Serve her right, smug old bitch! I'm going to leave this house when I please and not a minute sooner.'

It was not until she had marched up the stairs as calmly as she had come down them that a sensation of cramp in her elbow brought to her notice the faience cat which had been sitting on her arm throughout the whole conversation, smiling ineffably. She put it back in its place, and the pain in her muscles as she stretched her arm seemed to extinguish a little of her glorious lucidity. But she set out for The Yorkshire Rose with a determined step. The landlord had exactly what she needed to fortify her for the letter she intended to write to Maxine, and she had a hankering to meet Butterfly again, a dog whose temperament seemed, in the light of this evening's swift decisions, to have ingredients worthy of emulation.

13

It was not after all to Maxine she sent her letter but to Mory, and she postponed the writing of it till next afternoon, when her head was clear with a matter-of-fact clarity different from the galvanic illumination of the night before. After much reflection, it had become apparent that she had not known Maxine long enough either to press the invitation upon her in irresistible terms or to appeal to her frankly as a potential rescuer. But these things could be done for her by a third party intimate with both, and Mory would be disposed to represent the situation as interesting, entertaining, whereas she could only put her heart into painting its vexations. Moreover, he could convey, with a candour which in her would be indelicate, that no sacrifice of personal liberty would be required of the guest, nothing, indeed but that she should firmly take possession of the spare room.

Mory was quick in apprehension, and it had amused him to see his aunt getting on so well with the most unlikely of his friends, so he went out of his way to assist the plot. Nor did Maxine require much persuasion: her work at Cornfields would be finished in a week or two. and she was glad to be offered a room in London from which to renew her search for a flat.

Meanwhile Miss MacFarren, who knew it would be easier to find a hundred willing occupants for the spare room than one for the maids' room, was resolved that she would acquire a maid even if she had to sacrifice what little she had saved through the Bankeses' tenancy to pay for the luxury. Visits to four registry offices proved severely discouraging. Her requirements were noted only, it seemed, in order that they might be disregarded: her fees were taken but no applicant was offered who had ever had the remotest intention of filling such a post as hers. After interviewing a cook who did not desire a living-in position, an old lady who wanted light duties in the country, and a woman who could go nowhere without her little boy of ten, she came as near as she had ever done in her life to writing a letter to *The Times*.

It had formerly been her custom when in need of a servant to put a card in the window of the local newsagent's, but this measure was now precluded because of its lack of privacy; Mrs. Bankes must believe her arrangements already irrevocably made. Advertising under a box number in the press was equally out of the question, for the London papers were taking several weeks to insert an announcement. She wrote to friends and acquaintances, she consulted Harriet, and was almost in a panic at the blankness of her prospects when succour came from the most unexpected quarter.

Dr. Wilmot had called for her in a taxi to take her to the Connoisseurs' Club dinner, and his first enquiry, made with more solicitude than she had thought him capable of, was whether she had got rid of 'that tiresome woman'. She replied with feeling that she hoped and planned to be rid of her in a very short time.

'And what will you do with your house then?' he demanded, turning his bushy beard and exuberant eyebrows towards her in a manner which she still found rather alarming.

'I haven't decided. I can't think so far ahead. My whole energy seems to be used up at the moment in simply trying to find a maid.'

She did not expect him to be interested; she had mentioned her difficulty only because, after a weariful day, it was uppermost in her thoughts, and she was instantly ashamed of herself for alluding to so boring a topic. But to her surprise he asked as if he really wished to be answered:

'Temporary or permanent?'

'Whichever I can get. My one ambition is to be able to brandish a maid in my tenant's face by the week after next.'

And as he still seemed curious, she explained to him how Mrs. Bankes had sought to annex both spare room and maid's bedroom and how she had said they would be occupied.

'So it would help you to be able to produce a maid even if she doesn't stay?'

'Yes, before Captain Bankes arrives from America.'

'Take Pearson then!' the high reed-pipe voice said abruptly.

'Pearson! Your wonderful, devoted old retainer! You're joking, Dr. Wilmot!'

'No, provided you hand her over to me as soon as I return from Las Palmas, I shall be delighted.'

'I didn't know you were going to Las Palmas.'

'Then, my friend, you don't read the right newspaper. I'm going as the English delegate to the World Conference on Semantics. I shall be away from the last week in February till the first in April.'

'Just when I must have a maid.'

'I was intending to leave Pearson at King Charles Mansions but it would be an economy for me to close up the flat and save her wages. And she always dislikes being there alone.'

'But she mightn't want to come to me.'

'We will tactfully prevail upon her.' The gleam of teeth through his slightly dishevelled beard gave his face a look of gentle wickedness. 'I know she liked you—yes, I remember distinctly that you made an excellent impression—and perhaps if you held out some little extra inducement . . .'

'Oh, I should gladly pay her something additional—'

'Oh no! I was really thinking—if she could imagine she was doing me a good turn by it! For instance suppose the result of going to your house, she were to bring me back half a dozen of the Bristol Cream? I say nothing of any brandy or port because, unless you had a bottle or so that you could positively spare, I shouldn't dream of letting her accept it. But something of that sort, you know, received on my behalf, would give her far more pleasure than mere money. And it wouldn't *demoralize* her.'

Miss MacFarren bowed gracefully to the inevitable. She had hoped as a matter of principle to keep her Bristol sherry out of the Doctor's hands, but if that were his price for solving the problem that otherwise threatened to be insoluble, she would pay it and rejoice that it was no worse: he might have remembered that she had a number of Dutch prints not in his own collection.

As for Pearson herself, if she had been able to take her pick of all the few domestics left in England, she could not have selected one so likely to keep Mrs. Bankes in her place as that paragon of starch and alpaca whom she had made it her business to placate when dining with the doctor. The idea crossed her mind that so much neatness and decorum might intimidate not only Mrs. Bankes but Maxine, but she dismissed it at once. Nobody could intimidate Maxine. On the other hand, it was true—and it did take some of the gilt off her splendid slice of gingerbread to remember it—that Maxine might scandalize Pearson. Nor could she check a sigh at the thought of the cleaning she would have to do with her own hands before she could submit her house to the fastidious eyes of a well-trained servant.

But as the car drew up at the hotel where the Connoisseurs were to hold their celebration, she had no difficulty in casting off these minor cares, and the sight of herself in her amethyst velvet dress, when she studied her reflection in the numerous and spacious mirrors of the ladies' room, was extremely heartening. The alterations had been a thorough success, and her new corset, a well-justified extravagance, took inches off her waist and hips without discomfort—or at least none that need prevent her from making the most of the Connoisseurs' dinner. It was a little nerve-racking to anticipate delivering a speech, but at the same time, it gave her a pleasantly keyed-up feeling which seemed to be good for her appearance. In evening dress she permitted herself a judicious use of carmine, and what with this and her well-dressed hair, sculptured in flat whorls like a pattern in hoar-frost, and the lace on her bosom and her grandmother's pink topaz necklace, she believed she could hold her own with any lady of fifty-one in the building.

It turned out to be a really delightful evening. Dr. Wilmot, to whom fell the duty of introducing her as a speaker, did so in the most handsome terms, going so far as to prophesy that, like Marianne North, she would live to see a gallery devoted to her own works in Kew Gardens; and if for a moment he seemed inclined to refer patronizingly to her activities as a collector, he quickly righted himself by paying a lavish compliment to her altruism. She was, he said, one who had acquired objects of beauty for the enjoyment of her fellow-man: thus she had that most perfect principle of the truly great collector, that if she found in her own possession any item which would be of more value in some other collector's hands, no selfish consideration would induce her to retain it. The laughter that greeted this tribute was presumably a sardonic comment on the doctor's motives—for he was among friends—rather than an expression of scepticism as to her generosity, though she hastened on rising to disclaim any intention of giving away anything.

Her speech was a decided success and she found it gratifying to be present again at the kind of function she had so often attended with her brothers, and to be known for a distinguished woman and able to pretend during a whole evening that the uncreative drudgery and squalid dangers of the past six years had left no mark.

The next day when she called on Harriet to tell her of the boon conferred by Dr. Wilmot—for he had rung her up to assure her that Pearson would 'oblige'—another small circumstance strengthened her sense of having Providence on her side. She had just explained that she was going to set the *History of Floriculture* altogether aside while she cleaned all the accessible parts of the house, when Harriet cried rapturously: 'My dear, why not try the Spikspan Service? They're the very people you want!'

And straightaway, she led her friend to the glass door of her shop and pointed a triumphant hand to a brand-new window opposite on which appeared, in vigorous yellow and green letters, the exhortation: 'Let Spikspan Clean Your Home!'

'It's a firm that's just been started by some ex-service men,' said Harriet with all her old relish for taking a situation in hand.

'Most intelligent and honest I thought them. They send men to your house in a little motor-van with all sorts of implements, and then they scour the carpets, and wash the paintwork, and polish the floors, and move all the furniture and get behind everything with vacuum cleaners. And you simply sit back and let them manage the whole business.'

'But they'll be booked up for months!' said Miss MacFarren, dazzled by this brilliant vista of cleanliness.

'No, I don't think so. They only opened on Monday and anyhow, I'm sure a friend of mine will have priority because they quite expect me to be a valuable trade connection.'

'It'll be frightfully expensive, won't it?'

'Yes, it is expensive. But look, Elinor, there's not the slightest reason why the Bankeses shouldn't pay half. You could put the idea to Mrs. Bankes so that it would look like helping *her* out of a dilemma.'

Miss MacFarren nodded in eager comprehension. 'After all, she did say she was going to get it done before her husband arrived, and I don't see how she can manage single-handed.'

'I suppose you're on speaking terms with her?' Harriet enquired with a twinge of doubt in her voice. She had heard the story of the row the morning after its occurrence.

'Oh yes. The very next day—the next time I ran into her, she behaved almost as if nothing had happened. Her childishness is quite consistent, you see. An adult, a real one, would hardly be able to look one in the face after saying such things.'

Harriet's head made a slight movement of dissent. 'It seems simply brazen to me—like the way she returned my bon-bon box.' It was evident that she regarded the affair of the bon-bon box as the summit of all derelictions.

'Brazen, but in a childish way. Children don't mind much about being in the wrong. It's pretty well expected of them that they often will be. And they can quarrel and then suddenly stop quarrelling without any of the self-consciousness that makes adults feel so awkward. . . .'

'I still think, Elinor, that you could and should help that woman to grow up.'

'I intend to try,' said Miss MacFarren, but she could not bring herself to tell her friend the experiment she had in mind. That was scarcely fit even for solitary contemplation.

'Well, let's go straight across and talk to the manager, Mr. Deacon.' Harriet indicated the Spikspan shop as if there were not a moment to be lost. 'He's become quite a crony of mine in the last few days. I stopped him from having all the woodwork painted grey like a mausoleum, and he has to admit now the yellow is infinitely better.'

As two or three swallows cannot make a summer, so two or three failures, even of the most spectacular description, cannot turn a born leader into a spiritless doubter afraid to take the initiative. Harriet had recovered from the perverseness of Lottie Warbey in giving birth to a healthy baby though she had renounced carrot juice and the Meersch Method of exercising; from the blind obstinacy of Lady Violet who had refused to be happy away from her ancestral encumbrances; and from the utterly unaccommodating behaviour of Elinor and Antonia. Naturally resilient, she had comfortably resumed, without even noticing that she did so, the mantle of the counsellor, the director. And in this instance her enthusiasm proved so well founded that she gained back much of the prestige she had lost through her former blunder.

Mrs. Bankes welcomed the opportunity of getting the laborious spring-cleaning disposed of without any more effort than was involved in keeping out of the way, and as her share of the cost would be paid by her husband its magnitude, which nearly daunted Miss MacFarren, did not dismay her. The Spikspan Service, under Mr. Deacon's personal supervision, was all that Harriet claimed for it, so that when Pearson took up her duties at the end of February, she did so under conditions that, except for the presence in the house of Mrs. Bankes, were very nearly ideal.

And Mrs. Bankes was by no means at her worst. The imminently expected arrival of her husband had, as on previous occasions, inspired an outburst of cheerful energy. She kept her part of the house in order after the Spikspan men had left, busied herself with numerous preparations, and concealed any resentment she might have felt at the frustration of the plan concerning her children. That frustration was not, in fact, so complete as might have been expected, as Miss MacFarren learned with a considerable degree of relief on the day when she had put forward Harriet's suggestion.

She had wanted to make sure that Captain Bankes had been told of her inability to receive the children, for she felt that, until Maxine and Pearson were actually in residence, Antonia was quite capable of treasuring some harum-scarum hope that all the difficulties could be overcome. So when the cleaning question had been settled, she asked with the very distant civility she had maintained since the evening of their quarrel, whether a cable had been sent to prevent the children from travelling.

'They're coming just the same,' said Mrs. Bankes serenely. 'Mrs. Jermyn's going to have them, and we'll go and spend the weekends with them in the country.'

Miss MacFarren signified in restrained but sincere terms that she was glad to hear of this happy solution, which really took a weight from her mind. The heat, or rather the exhilarating cold, of the angry scene being dispelled, she had had time to feel pity for the affectionate father whose project for a family reunion had been shattered, and to remember how poor a reward her conduct would seem for his kindness in trying to find an American publisher for her books. Her whole position in regard to Captain Bankes, who had always been so friendly and good-natured, was acutely embarrassing, but she would, at any rate, feel somewhat less uncomfortable if he were not altogether thwarted in his design of bringing his children from America.

'They'll be travelling straight to Mrs. Jermyn's place—near Oxford, you know—the minute they arrive. The children will love it there. They've got a pony and a big garden with a swing, and a cat that's just had kittens.'

She seemed genuinely pleased, and so free from rancour that Miss MacFarren's tone became almost apologetic. 'It isn't that I dislike children—quite the reverse. But they do make an upheaval in a small house. I shall explain to Captain Bankes—'

'There isn't a bit of need to explain anything,' Tonia interrupted benevolently. 'All I'll say to Joss is that you couldn't manage to let us have the rooms because of your friend coming, and the new maid. We don't have to bother him with our squabbles, do we?' she added with one of her bright smiles.

'Well, not the moment he comes back, certainly.' She had recognized a skilfully veiled appeal.

'I don't see why we should bother him at all. Poor Joss, he'll have so much to think of with his new job and everything.'

Miss MacFarren guessed that Antonia, uneasy lest her husband should find out how much he had been misled as to the children's probable reception at 16 Harberton Square, was preparing to attribute the failure of his plan entirely to fortuitous circumstances. There must be no explanation leading to the disclosure of the pledge she had given not to bring the children to the house: and characteristically she was manoeuvering to turn their angry conflict into a feminine tiff, a moment of domestic friction which it would be unworthy of either of them to report to a harassed man.

For once as it happened, Miss MacFarren's interests coincided with hers. To avoid unpleasantness with Captain Bankes, who had deserved so well of her, she would gladly refrain from telling tales on his wife—provided always it was understood that in a month they would move to other quarters. And she made this clear.

'I have no wish to discuss grievances with Captain Bankes.' She was not quite sure whether it was generosity or moral cowardice that spoke. 'If you like, I shall simply say, in the letter I'm writing you—'

'Letter! Good gracious, what letter?' cried Mrs. Bankes with a kind of playful dismay.

'I must put the month's notice in writing, but I can quite easily say it's because I want the use of the rooms . . .'

Mrs. Bankes interrupted again with a mock groan and a comically woeful grimace. 'Oh, dear, do we have to have official notices and things like the House of Commons! How dreary!'

'It's usually done. In fact, I believe it's legally necessary.'

'But it's horrid, don't you think? I mean, Joss is going to feel miserable, and what's the good of it anyway? We shall have to look for somewhere else even without getting notice, shan't we?'

'Yes, if you want to be with your children.'

'Well, why give us notice then? Joss is sure to know you're cross with me.'

'I'm afraid," said Miss MacFarren deliberately, but without sharpness, 'I must be absolutely certain you intend to leave. You mustn't forget you told me you'd go when you felt inclined and not before.'

Mrs. Bankes frowned, yet managed at the same time to keep a little smile on her lips. 'Did I say that? How silly of me! People say ah sorts of things when they're in a temper.'

'I must be business-like with you, Mrs. Bankes, because I know you to be very unreliable.'

'Only in little things,' Antonia rejoined swiftly. 'In a big thing like getting a home for Joss and my darling babas I'm madly reliable. You honestly don't have to write frightful formal letters.'

It was evident that she feared being given notice as a little girl might fear being expelled from school. Getting in and out of scrapes was all very well; scoldings and minor punishments could be endured stoically; but when it came to the awful ritual of expulsion, the situation had to be taken seriously. One coaxed, cajoled, pleaded, said or did anything to avoid exposure to the Olympian being who, in this case, was not a father but a husband.

Miss MacFarren had no wish to provoke further self-abasement. Her speeches had been slow because her mind had been wholly engaged in strategy, and she decided it would suit her very well to be gracious. She had always been a practical woman, and six months with Mrs. Bankes had taught her to add to common sense a certain suppleness. If she could achieve the miracle of parting from Captain Bankes without four weeks of tensely strained relations it was decidedly worth while to try and do so. The possibility of negotiating after all with the American publisher was not her foremost consideration, but it had its place. There was no point in throwing it away for the mere sake of making the gesture. So she said dispassionately:

'If I could believe you wouldn't try to remain here after the time is up . . .'

'Oh, but we wouldn't! We couldn't! You don't know how we're longing to have a home with the children.'

'I'm so worried about your chances of finding one in time.'

'You needn't be. I shall rush round like a whirlwind when I really start, and Joss has such crowds of friends who'll try to help. We usually get what we want,' she added convincingly.

Miss MacFarren felt that, holding such a trump card as Maxine, she could afford to take a risk with Mrs. Bankes.

'Well,' she agreed, 'if you sincerely assure me you'll be gone by April the first, I shall waive the formality of notice in writing.'

'And we shan't say anything about our quarrel in front of Joss?' Antonia's anxiety on this score was now straightforward. 'You won't mention Jimjams, will you?'

'I hope I shan't have occasion to mention Jimjams,' Miss MacFarren replied with some severity, for the thought of the ill-fated terrier was still a painful one.

'I shall never do anyone a kindness again,' said Antonia, suddenly downcast. 'It just seems to make everyone furious.'

'Your husband may hear of Jimjams from Mrs. Netley.'

'He won't see her. She's never going to speak to me again.'

Miss MacFarren could not make a pretence of commiseration so she turned the conversation back to the best method of organizing the spring-cleaning. She had had the pleasure of yielding as a favour what it was to her own advantage to concede, and she treasured a cheering belief that this time she had a trick worth two of anything Mrs. Bankes might play, so the discussion ended in quite a comfortable and harmonious fashion.

Maxine arrived two or three days after Pearson, and had time to make herself at home before she encountered the other inmates of the house. Captain Bankes had reached England on the same day, and had been taken with his family straight from the airport to the Jermyns's home where he remained for a week-end, so that she was able to establish herself in a household temporarily free from complexity.

Miss MacFarren had made the spare room extremely inviting, with cigarettes, biscuits, carefully chosen books, and two little Bohemian decanters on a glass tray. Beside them were a pair of beakers embossed with gilt, and a small lustre bowl filled with such fruit as was obtainable. A vase of mimosa—rather an expensive purchase which she had justified on the grounds that it would be useful for a botanical drawing—shed an exquisite perfume, tender and intricate as the flowers themselves. The room was warm and the light glowed richly on the Nattier blue of the curtains and the quilted satin bed-cover. The second bed still obtruded in unwanted presence; but by placing it against a wall and banking it up with cushions, she had very nearly succeeded in making it look like a sofa.

'I call this distinctly high-class,' said Maxine, making a little tour of exploration. 'Mory's aunt, I see where Master Mory gets his taste.'

'Oh, do you think he has good taste?' she enquired, pleased but surprised.

'My God, yes! Don't you?'

Miss MacFarren looked round to make quite sure that Pearson, who had been helping with the luggage, had retired. 'I'm prejudiced,' she answered, 'by his taste in women.'

'I've got an idea that might improve with practice,' said Maxine, laughing.

'Dear me, hasn't he had enough practice?'

'Not since bitchy old Geraldine took possession of him. Or is that the wrong way to put it?'

'Not at all. I've always felt she was very—well, very much as you say.'

'Mind you, I think it'll soon be a case of "Dearest our day is over" in that quarter.'

'Do you? I can't help hoping you're right. Even Mory doesn't imply that she's nice, if you know what I mean.'

'I can work it out.'

'And it seems so shocking that that man—her husband—could try and get damages for losing such a worthless wife. Of course, I fully realize that Mory has done wrong, and properly speaking, he should be punished. . . .'

'And improperly speaking, you hope he gets away with it,' said Maxine amiably. 'But even if he and Geraldine break up, Stevie Mace will still want his heartbalm.'

'How stupid of me! For a moment I thought that, if the affair ended, all that other business would fall through—'

'No, that's not how it goes.' Maxine, who was picking up one by one the various objects on the bedside table, gently shook her head. 'Not while Stevie has a legal leg to stand on . . . though he probably hasn't if the truth were known.'

'I wish it were known,' Miss MacFarren ventured to say quite earnestly.

Maxine stared in a very concentrated manner at the beaker in her hand. 'It's no use trying to rescue people,' she said, 'until you're certain that they really want to be rescued.' She turned with a particularly charming though somewhat incomprehensible smile. 'You've arranged the table like a beautiful still life. What's this?' She held up one of the twin decanters, indicating its green contents.

'Lime-juice, and the other's gin.'

'Gin!' Maxine all but shrieked the word. 'I thought it was an innocent jug of water for the night. Don't you ever stop plying people with gin?'

'I know you don't take it while you're working, but you've finished the picture now.'

'We'll drink it together,' said Maxine cosily. 'I can see I'm going to be very comfortable here, Mory's aunt. What sort of books have you chosen for me?' She ran her hand along the unequal row of volumes in the little hanging bookshelf.

'Mory brought some of them.'

'What, specially for me? How did *he* know what I'd like,' she asked rather scornfully, as if it were absurd for him to claim any intimate knowledge of her.

'He notices a great deal about people, don't you think?'

Maxine looked at her with a glance that seemed to offer some comment she might read if she pleased, and said: 'let's see what he's noticed about me! *Film and Theatre*—useful and business-like. *Prater Violet*—yes, that's about the film biz too. I wanted that. Now why *Sins of New York*? Can you imagine?'

'Oh, that's not Mory's choice,' she hastened to acknowledge. 'That's mine. I found it in a second-hand shop. It's full of extracts from old Police Gazettes. I thought the pictures might make you laugh.'

'They do.' Maxine raised her eyebrows at the lurid pink pages with their engravings of voluptuously curved women and bravos with huge moustaches. 'It's not exactly the bedside book I should have expected from a lady botanist with a clean record, but it'll suit me. What about *The Razor's Edge*? Mory or you?'

'That's Mory. He says you'll be interested because they re going to make a film out of it.'

'*Don Juan* and *Moll Flanders*—there's the Mory touch!'

'No, no, that's me again. I always think they're both such wonderful books for dipping into if one's lying awake, don't you agree?'

'I hadn't looked at them in that light,' said Maxine dryly. '*Film-Acting* by Pud-something . . . *A Voyage to Purilia*—what may that be?'

'A very good satire on early film conventions, so Mory says.'

'He certainly does expect me to be wedded to my art,' she complained with a mixture of amusement and exasperation.

'He does, because he thinks you'll go far in it.'

'Then why doesn't he put me into one of his damn pictures?' Her directness verged on impudence, but by contrast with Antonia's insincerity, Miss MacFarren found it quite endearing. '*Tom Jones*—that'll be another of *your* dainty touches, I suppose?'

'Yes, I hope you don't mind my choosing favourites of my own. I can't help preferring the classics at my age. I was brought up on them.'

'Brought Mory up on them too, didn't you?' Maxine remarked sardonically, but with an undercurrent of some warm quality that was disarming. '*Tom Jones! Don Juan!* What an aunt!'

'They never seemed to do me any harm,' said Miss MacFarren diffidently. Maxine with her cynicism always made her feel young and pleasantly silly, just as Antonia with her naïvete always made her feel old and unpleasantly sensible.

A double rap, discreet but firm, heralded the appearance of Pearson in her black afternoon dress, lace-edged apron, and starched cap—a figure of almost awe-inspiring dignity and, to Miss MacFarren, after the years of domestic makeshifts, a soothing and beautiful sight. This evening, however, she viewed that uncompromising correctness with certain quiverings of apprehension. Pearson was the sort of servant who had to be lived up to, and what the effect would be if Maxine swore in front of her, or talked in insolent slang, she shrank from discovering.

'Would you like to give me your keys, miss?' Pearson's question was couched in the perfectly non-committal tone she used for those about whom her verdict was held in suspense.

'I'd love to.' Maxine promptly produced a neat keychain. 'I loathe unpacking.'

'Well let's go down and have a glass of sherry in my study while it's being done for you,' said Miss MacFarren, inwardly worried lest Pearson should resent the casual acceptance of a service which was perhaps offered in no casual spirit.

But fortunately she turned out to be mistaken. Pearson was a member of that rare species which is always described in every epoch as 'a servant of the old school', which is to say she led a largely vicarious existence, having formed the habit of projecting her own personality into the imagined lives of those she waited upon; and therefore she was very candidly a snob. She was willing to fill the traditional rôle with artistic fidelity, but only if those she served filled their traditional rôles as masters and mistresses: and she conceived of these characters as helpless, flatteringly dependent, and incorrigibly addicted to luxury. Miss MacFarren was soon able to gather that Maxine's practised readiness in handing over her keys had given Pearson a favourable bias, while the fine quality of her luggage and the expensiveness of all that it contained was taken as an evidence of marked superiority. Maxine, as an incipient film star, cast her bread upon the waters in the shape of a film star's trappings, and from the time when Pearson put away the hand-made underwear and night-dresses of pure silk, the dresses bearing impressive labels, and the shoes that seemed scarcely to have been worn, she felt a respect for her which, though far from admirable in itself, was productive of admirable results. Miss MacFarren she recognized by her background as a lady, though she had forfeited something through her reduced style of living, but Maxine was glamorous and since so much of Pearson's life was lived at second-hand, she had a weakness for the young, the carefree, the prodigal.

So at any rate Miss MacFarren accounted for the indulgence she invariably lavished on the guest, from the first day onward. All Pearson herself ever volunteered on the subject was that Miss Albert 'made a change' after Dr. Wilmot—not that the doctor wasn't a very nice gentleman, and full of fun when he was in the mood, but it was natural that he was more set in his ways than a lively young lady like Miss Albert.

Miss Albert's liveliness was dexterously tempered to Pearson's staidness. Though she teased and made jokes, she was not, like Mrs. Bankes, noisy. The languor of her voice seemed to Pear-

son's ears eminently lady-like, and her conversation, heard in brief
bowdlerized snatches, had the same astringent and novel attraction for the maid as for the mistress. Maxine for her part looked
upon Pearson as a sort of stage character, a wonderful representa-
tion of an old-fashioned servant; and she accorded her such
whimsical appreciation as she might have offered a fellow-art-
ist giving a well-sustained performance. In short, as those whom
we bring together with the express purpose of launching a friendship may turn out, for reasons superficially trivial, to feel nothing
but antipathy, so those who seem strikingly ill-assorted may find
obscure motives for heartily liking one another, and such was the
case between those two strong personalities whose contact Miss
MacFarren had for days been dreading.

Maxine's first meeting with Mrs. Bankes, on the other hand,
produced effects that deviated little from her expectations.

Miss MacFarren was alone when her tenants arrived from their
week-end in the country, and she was able to appear quite free from
guile—so far had her morals been unhinged—as she and Captain
Bankes exchanged a greeting lacking nothing of cordiality.

'I suppose you still *are* Captain Bankes,' she said, staring at his
civilian clothes.

'You're within your legal rights to call me that if you insist—if
you absolutely insist, mind you.'

'Oh, I could never get used to calling you *Mr.* Bankes after all
these months.'

'I answer to my first name, you know,' he suggested, taking one
of those steps forward in intimacy which a reunion after absence
will sometimes bring about. 'Do you have to look so shocked at the
sight of me in these clothes, Miss MacFarren?'

'I must get used to it. I'd forgotten you were going to be a civilian.'

She could not but regret the lumber-jacket and the beige-
pink trousers that had shown his figure to such advantage, but
his face was as allusive as ever, evoking the fabulous Red Indians,
the canyons, the prairies, a whole romantic panorama which was
perhaps scarcely more familiar to him than to her. She was aware
that Mrs. Bankes was watching her, reading all sorts of infatuated
meanings into her eyes, but she was unconcerned at that. Her new

policy was to let her gape indeed, to give her something to gape at. So she said as affably as possible:

'I shall miss your uniform, but I think you come very well out of it.'

'Did your friend turn up?' Mrs. Bankes enquired with a not very well-concealed implication that Miss MacFarren's friends might avoid turning up if they could.

'Oh yes, thank you. She's been here since Saturday. I'm so sorry, Captain Bankes, that, as the house is full, I couldn't have your children here.'

'Please don't feel badly about it!' he said, but with a magnanimity which conveyed that she might in the normal course be expected to feel badly. 'In many ways it's better that they should be right where they are now, with other kids to play with and all that—though I admit they were pretty sore when they found they weren't coming to London with us. It was quite a surprise all round being whizzed off to the Jermyns', he added, ruefully smiling.

Miss MacFarren turned baleful eyes upon Antonia. 'Surely you cabled Captain Bankes before he left Washington?'

'There really wasn't time,' Antonia murmured vaguely. 'Joss, have you noticed how lovely and clean everything is? We've had it all done up by the most celestial little men.'

'There was nearly a fortnight,' Miss MacFarren said with firmness. She had tacitly agreed to conceal from Captain Bankes how he had been allowed to make his plans under a misapprehension, but she was not obliged to let him believe that she had imposed a drastic change on his movements at the last minute.

'You see these, Joss!' Antonia eagerly held a pot of hyacinths up to his face. 'I went everywhere for them because they're your favourites, aren't they?'

He looked at her reproachfully over the flowers, but his only remark was 'Very lovely, dear!'

Miss MacFarren had reached that stage of antagonism when evidences of Antonia's want of honesty were almost gratifying because she could draw from them the strength of mind to be ruthless. It was clear that, having misled her husband in a manner of vital importance, she had been either too feckless or too cowardly to give him even a falsified explanation in advance, and had resorted as usual to the *fait accompli*: in the children's presence and on the way to the Jermyns', he could doubtless be relied upon to accept his disappointment with a good grace.

But his docility was liable, as Miss MacFarren had noticed before, to break down unexpectedly. And now, with an impulsive gesture, he brusquely took the flowerpot and set it on the console table. 'I don't get the idea, honey!' he exclaimed, suddenly truculent. 'Springing this Jermyn business on me at the airport! Why didn't you cable if you had all that time?'

'What difference would it have made?' Antonia assumed an air of mild astonishment.

'The difference that I might have left the children in the States instead of working my head off to get them over with me.'

'It would have been an awful shame to leave them,' said Antonia lightly.

'But mother's coming over in May—you know that, Tonia!—and she would have been glad to bring them with her.' He turned appealingly to Miss MacFarren. 'You'll probably be ready to have them by then?'

She strangled a sound that might have been a gasp. This, the moment as it were of his homecoming, was hardly appropriate for pointing out that substantially before May he must find another domicile; but the look she flung Antonia was an eloquent warning. Luckily, as she turned the protest into a cough, casting about in vain for a change of subject, there was a succession of brisk rings at the front-door bell. Antonia, being the nearest and probably the most eager to end the conversation, succeeded in reaching the door a moment before her.

'Terribly sorry,' said Maxine, who was on the doorstep. 'I've mislaid my latchkey.'

Antonia stood in confusion, apparently unable to connect this dazzling young person with the sort of houseguest she had been expecting. Instead of moving aside to let Maxine pass into the hall, she addressed her in a manner tinged with asperity: 'Is there anyone you want to see?'

'This is Miss Albert,' Miss MacFarren intervened pleasantly. 'Maxine, this is Mrs. Bankes. And you'll find Captain Bankes here, whom you know.'

She was able to speak with suavity because the moment was peculiarly gratifying. Maxine was looking delightful in a sealskin coat, her face framed in a hood lined with white ermine (a contribution from the fur merchant named Wolfe). A spray of lilies of the valley was pinned to her lapel, and matching them a few large flakes of snow clung, by a happy accident, to her shoulders and the sealskin muff she was carrying. The cold, which might have pinched another face, had made her skin rosy and her eyes bright.

Miss MacFarren surveyed this picture of winter prettiness with an enjoyment that was partly maternal and partly quite nefarious, while Antonia acknowledged the introduction in so dazed a voice that it might be assumed her husband had failed to give any description of the encounter on Christmas Eve. Her eyes, as he warmly shook Maxine's hand could be seen following his movement with an expression almost of stupefaction.

By this time Pearson had come down from her work on the top floor, and, finding the bell already answered, would have retreated, when she noticed the snow on Maxine's coat and made it a pretext for lingering, perhaps so that she might take a sidelong glance at Captain Bankes, whom she had not yet seen.

'Now, miss, what have you been up to?' she cried, in the respectfully familiar style she used with those she liked. 'Walking about in this weather! I should think your feet must be frozen in shoes like those.'

All eyes descended to Maxine's feet, which were indeed lightly and elegantly shod.

'I can't seem to feel them,' she answered, lifting first one, then the other with a little questioning shake. 'When are the blasted taxis coming back on the road? I wouldn't mind the snow only it turns to slush the minute it touches the ground.'

'Come and warm up in front of my fire,' said Miss MacFarren.

'It's not much of a fire, miss,' Pearson put in apologetically. 'I banked it up with slack. Your coal's getting so low.'

'Someone's very kindly made a nice fire for us, Miss Albert,' said Captain Bankes, who was by the open door of the sitting-room. 'Why not come and thaw right here?'

'Thanks.' She spoke as nonchalantly as if she were unaware of Antonia's hostile stare. 'I've got to go out again in a few minutes so I'd better get warm while I can.'

'That goes for me too.' He pulled an armchair to the hearth for her.

'Do you mind if I do this?' Slipping off one shoe, she held out a charming foot.

Captain Bankes began to stir the fire with a poker. 'Come in and sit down, Miss MacFarren!' he entreated hospitably.

'Aren't you going to take your things upstairs, Joss?' Antonia had suddenly become feverishly busy, though she was still in her outdoor clothes, sorting out the magazines in the 'Canterbury'.

'Not this minute, dear.' He was still out of humour from the discussion before Maxine's arrival.

'But we don't want our lovely spick-and-span hall cluttered up with luggage and overcoats,' she persisted foolishly.

'I'll take them up later.' This time no endearment softened his irritation.

Miss MacFarren had not accepted the invitation to sit down but had compromised by taking up an easy position with her hands resting on the back of Maxine's chair. Now feeling the need of some self-respecting excuse for her presence in the room where Antonia hardly pretended to welcome her, she said:

'I mustn't lose any time in telling you, Captain Bankes, that I was very grateful to you for trying to find me a publisher in America.'

'Who? Me?' He pointed to himself with a look of comical surprise.

'Yes, I heard from the New Aldine Press. I knew at once it was your doing.'

'My doing!' His laugh absolutely repudiated the notion.

'The director is a friend of yours.'

'Certainly he is, but I haven't seen him for a couple of years. He's in New York, and I only spent a few hours there this trip.'

'Didn't you give him—or send him perhaps—your copy of my last book?'

'No, ma'am. If you want to know what I did with that, my mother has it—and she's very keen to meet the author.'

The realization that he was telling the truth plunged her into a turmoil of irreconcilable feelings. She was appalled to remember that, but for this imaginary kindness, she might by now have won her battle and put the enemy to rout. On the other hand, it was a wonderful relief to see before her the prospect of American negotiations quite unhampered by any obligation to Mrs. Bankes's husband.

'Now I come to think of it,' Captain Bankes continued, 'I'm not sure my friend hasn't quit the publishing business. The last thing I heard of him, he had an idea he was going to sell out his interest. Who signed your letter? Was it John Holman?'

'I can't recall. Wait, I'll go and get it. I'd like you to see it.'

She hurried from the room as Maxine kicked off her second shoe.

The letter took rather a long time to find, being not, as she thought, in her study but in her bedroom; and while she was putting away the papers she had disturbed in searching for it, Maxine tapped on the door and came in, carrying a leather attaché-case.

'Step on it, Mory's aunt!' she commanded genially. 'I've got to keep a date in the city and your boy friend's taking me there in the office car. It's at the door.'

'Good gracious! You make my head whirl! What has been happening?'

Maxine went to the dressing-table mirror and began to touch her face here and there with a powder-puff. 'I asked the Bankeses if they knew any local car hire service I could ring up, because I'm tired of roaming the streets for taxis. So your Mr. Bankes said he had a car from the office calling for him at any moment, and could he give me a lift? So I said—if you want every detail—that I was going a long way off, to Chancery Lane. It's the accountant who does my income-tax puzzles,' she explained, indicating the attaché-case. 'And he said that couldn't be better because he was going to Fleet Street. I wish you could have seen Mrs. B's eyes! Glazed with horror!'

She smiled the benevolent smile that brought her dimples into play, and went on in sentences broken by pauses as she smoothed a light rouge over her lips with her finger: 'I couldn't resist tormenting her a little . . . for your sake, Mory's darling auntie. . . . Do you think I don't know what I'm here for? . . . So I said to Mr. B., "Whenever I meet you, you seem to be giving me a lift!" I swear—honestly—she turned pale.'

'Unprincipled girl!' said Miss MacFarren comfortably.

She followed Maxine back to the sitting-room, where Captain Bankes was buttoning up his short, un-English-looking belted overcoat.

He glanced at her letter and handed it back to her with a shake of his head. 'No, Johnnie Holman seems to have quit all right. But this fellow, Brunskill, who's probably taken over, has a good reputation. We can talk about it later if you're going to be in, Miss MacFarren.'

'Thank you. I'm sure your advice would be most valuable.' She was happy that she was not to be indebted for anything more substantial.

'I have to look in at the office this afternoon. I didn't realize how late it was. Shall we be on our way, Miss Albert?'

'Joss,' said Antonia, with an importunity that tried in vain to disguise itself, 'I think I may as well come with you. I've got things to do too.'

'Now, Tonia, don't say you've anything to do in the city!' he pleaded, as one remonstrates wearily with a child who is becoming tiresome.

'Yes, I have. Really and truly. There's a little shop up there where I want to get something—something special.'

'The office car won't wait while you do your shopping.'

'It doesn't matter. You can drop me in Fleet Street. I'll come back by bus or tube if I can't get a taxi.'

To forestall further argument, she ran out with a complete lack of dignity to the car. Captain Bankes's face was full of embarrassment as he held open the front door for Maxine, who was heard to say softly and kindly:

'We'll be able to sit three at the back. That's much cosier on a day like this.'

The remark sounded so naïve that he smiled indulgently but Miss MacFarren was left feeling a curious and not altogether painful sensation of guilt.

14

'WELL, HOW'S Auntie's wicked plot working out?' Mory enquired, dropping in unexpectedly one evening a few days later.

'What plot?'

Miss MacFarren poured two glasses of sherry from a tray that happened to be in readiness. She had been taking sherry with Maxine almost every evening.

'Let's call it Operation Maxie.' He seated himself by the fire.

'If you mean, how is Maxine getting on—'

'I mean, how's Maxine getting off. That's what you intended, isn't it?'

'I intended nothing but to make this house less comfortable for Mrs. Bankes.'

'Darling, I'll bet you've succeeded! Come on, don't be cagey! Dish up the dirt!'

Though the terms of the request were not inviting, she did not withhold a measure of her confidence, remembering he had been of service to her.

'They simply detest each other,' she said cheerfully. 'Mrs. Bankes is like a cat or a dog that suddenly finds another cat or dog sharing its hearthrug. She bristles all over. One really gets the impression that her back arches and her hair stands on end. Maxine hates Mrs. Bankes because—well, as far as I can see, because she bought that doll with the fly on its stomach.'

'And because she's been a hell of a nuisance to you, Aunt Ellie,' Mory interposed rather severely. 'Give the girl credit for some decent motives!'

'I do. Surely you know I like her tremendously. But she doesn't seem to need motives for hating Mrs. Bankes. There's a sort of instinctive animal aversion.'

'And Bankes? Any animal aversion in that quarter?'

'I don't know what she feels about him . . . whether she flirts with him to oblige me, or to annoy Mrs. Bankes, or because she really finds him attractive.'

'She flirts with him, does she?' he asked, with an eager yet detached interest which his aunt found a little unseemly.

'You knew she would.' She spoke defensively, for she was not free from some qualms of conscience in this matter. 'Don't you remember telling me to take care of my lodger?'

He answered after a hesitation. 'Yes, I suppose I did know. How does Bankes react?'

'I imagine he's fascinated. Yes, I'm sure of it.'

A lot seems to have been going on here lately,' he said with a shade of something like wistfulness. 'A lot has been going on in my life too. You'll be glad to hear Geraldine and I have parted.'

'Yes, I am glad,' she agreed. 'But I hope you haven't been very unhappy, Mory.'

'Ending a love affair is always liable to be painful, even when both parties are out of love. Geraldine was a terror but I shall miss her for a while.'

'What about the divorce?' she asked, her practical Hebridean mind intent on damages.

'That's coming up in about a fortnight, coinciding neatly with the publicity for my picture. Ironical, isn't it, after all the delays? Mace has got it speeded up somehow.'

'How does your solicitor feel about the prospects?'

'Not very happy. Couched in divorce court language, my affair with Geraldine sounds like the worst seduction since Steerforth ran away with Little Em'ly. And Mace has got Vernon Bradley, who's a demon king at handling these cases. I shall be slaughtered by the costs, let alone the damages. Mace is asking ten thousand pounds!'

'Ten thousand pounds!' Her face and voice were eloquent of horror.

'Geraldine has always been an expensive girl,' he admitted with a wan smile, 'but no one's paid so much for her as I'm going to do.'

'She's had other lovers then?'

'Innocent Auntie! Don't pretend Maxie hasn't given you the low-down!'

She deemed it proper to ignore this. 'If she's had other lovers since her marriage, can't you discredit her husband's ridiculous claim for damages?'

'Only by washing a horrid bundle of the Maces' dirty linen in public, dear, and that wouldn't look very pretty on my part, do you think? It's all going to be quite scandalous enough without my adopting that line of defence. All I can do is to dispute the amount on the ground that I simply can't pay it. The publicity will be as damaging as the damages.'

Gloomily she replenished the glasses, resisting with fortitude the temptation that beset her to point out—superfluous as it was—the various evils of loose morals.

'Besides,' he went on, 'it's one thing to know something and another to produce legal evidence of it. When I first met Geraldine she was consoling Pio Martinez because his wife—not without provocation, mind you!—had exchanged him for a young coloured gentleman. Pio manoeuvred Mace into a contract, and Mace manoeuvred Geraldine into Pio's arms. Everybody knew it, but who can prove it now?'

'Pio Martinez, I should think,' said Miss MacFarren. 'Isn't he a friend of yours?'

'Well, not to that extent!' Mory looked amused at her simplicity. 'Pio always bore a slight grudge against me for making off with Geraldine.'

'I thought in your circle no one bore grudges for anything like that.'

'We're not so sublime as you think, darling,' he countered with gravity. 'Pio took it well on the surface because he had one eye on Maxie at the time and I suppose he cherished an idea that, as he was a big director and she was a small-part actress, he only had to beckon . . . I don't believe he ever made her, though.'

'Made her what?' she demanded with some impatience.

'Made her gratify his vile designs, Auntie. Odd considering how much power he has to put an actress on the map.'

'You must have a certain amount of power in your own hands these days,' she reminded him thoughtfully.

'Not as much as Pio. It's a strange thing about Maxine,' he went on with an abstracted frown: 'She exploits her sex appeal for everything except her career. She's immensely ambitious, and yet she doesn't seem to have encouraged Pio, and she's never made the shadow of a pass at me.'

'It's probably *because* she's ambitious—' She broke off unable, without sententiousness, to find words for her idea that a young woman who was earnestly bent on a career might think to serve it better in the long run by avoiding such amours as helped Mory to pass so much of his spare time.

'Could be.' He grew vague. 'Where is she, by the way, this evening?'

'I don't know. She comes and goes as she pleases.' It occurred to her that he had perhaps been rather more anxious to impart his news to her guest than to herself. 'I'm sorry you missed her.'

'She's out all the time, I dare say?'

'Not as much as I expected. I see a good deal of her really.' She was surprised and not a little flattered in retrospect to consider how much she and Maxine had been together. 'So far we've met every day either for tea or sherry. In the evening she generally goes out, but if she doesn't come in too late, we have a little gossip and a hot drink together before going to bed.'

She had omitted to mention that the hot drink consisted of whisky toddy made with a Dickensian lavishness, and Mory said admiringly: 'Darling, you seem to be having a marvellous influence on Maxie.'

Miss MacFarren smiled a slightly evasive smile. 'Maxine is more likely to change my character than I am to change hers.'

But Mory's mind, as practical in its way as her own, had already passed on to a more literal topic. 'When and where does she pursue this flirtation with Bankes?'

'Two people who live in the same house are always finding little opportunities.'

'Maxine can be guaranteed to make the most of them.' His enthusiasm slightly jarred on her.

'They are very little opportunities at the moment. Maxine has never been five minutes in his company without some interruption from Mrs. Bankes.'

'How do you know then that he's attracted to her?'

'I'm not an idiot, Mory, though I am an old maid,' she returned with an unwonted touch of acerbity.

'Sweetheart, I should have asked the same thing of anyone.'

'And no one could give you a cut-and-dried answer. . . . I simply know he's attracted to her, and she knows too. Moreover, I have a quite disturbing feeling that, if he gets the chance, he's going to fall in love with her—seriously, I mean.'

'Isn't that what you expected? Wasn't it to be your beautiful revenge on Mrs. Bankes?'

'No, no, Mory.' Her disclaimer was emphatic and nearly sincere. 'I only wanted to frighten her away. I didn't even suspect he'd be so vulnerable. Though heaven knows, Mrs. Bankes, behaving like a jealous child with the tantrums, has done everything to show Maxine up to advantage.'

'Then let's hope you do frighten her away,' he said, 'before it turns into what's called an ugly situation.'

Miss MacFarren sighed, for her impression was that, while Antonia was able to keep her husband under perpetual surveillance, Maxine would have—to use her own phrase—a nuisance value and no more. Antonia might be vexed, exasperated, but she was not, apparently, alarmed. There was no sign that she had taken any steps towards the promised removal at the end of the month, nor that she had given Captain Bankes the slightest inkling of the real position. She was behaving for all the world like a little girl who had been sentenced to a severe punishment which she inwardly believes no one will have the heart to carry out.

She had doubtless learned early in childhood, thought Miss MacFarren, that when one of the grown-ups was goaded into declaring: 'Now you shall not go to the party!' all she had to do, however vehement the threat, was to lie low until the hour for putting on the party dress, when the stern front was sure to crumble or some other grown-up pleaded on her behalf.

With the sanguine hopes that belong to an immature mind, she probably fancied that, before the month was out, some lucky chance would put them in the way of a house or flat, and failing this, that they would be permitted, on whatever sufferance, to remain where they were.

Her children, whose companionship she had professed to be longing for, had now, the reunion over, resumed their place of less than secondary importance. They had been deposited with the Jermyns and, so far as she was concerned, were disposed of till she should be forced to take them away. The very first of the weekends she had promised to spend with them was cancelled without compunction when it turned out that her husband's office duties would prevent him from accompanying her. It was not to be hoped that she would devote herself to the weary labour of househunting on their account.

'I must put a turn on the screw,' Miss MacFarren said to herself, lying awake that night. And then, changing her metaphor as she was almost inclined to change her mind. 'Oh, what deep waters I seem to be wading in!'

But it was Mrs. Bankes who put the turn on the screw—a very small turn, a mere nothing in comparison with what she had already inflicted, but enough to stiffen her victim's resistance and harden her heart.

The morning after Mory's call, a Saturday, Pearson approached her, beckoning with a hand that spoke of woeful revelations to come, and, being followed apprehensively to the study, extracted from her apron pocket a small fringed and monogrammed linen towel.

'Do you recognize this, miss?' she enquired with the air of a counsel in court producing some painful object for identification.

Miss MacFarren's start of horror must have given her questioner full dramatic satisfaction. 'Why, it's one of my best guest towels,' she cried despairingly. 'What has she been doing with it?'

'Using it to dry half-washed dishes, miss . . . yes, and others like it too. A pair went off to the laundry this week just as bad as this one. She's worn out all your tea towels, I suppose, and won't use any of her coupons to replace them.'

'But my embroidered guest towels . . . It's—it's unscrupulous!'

'It's unladylike,' said Pearson with the consciousness of a surer touch.

Pearson had now had full time to make up her mind about Mrs. Bankes, and had conceived an almost obsessing animosity against her. Mrs. Bankes, after a few days of immaculate domestic behaviour—the 'little housewife' make-believe that she never could keep up for long—had gradually relapsed into habits more normal to her. It was a daily complaint that she messed up the kitchen, tried to wheedle services she had no right to expect, and couldn't keep her hands off other people's rations. Worse, she was hostile to Pearson's favourite, Maxine. The winning smile, the well-practised charm of manner, which had for a while quite subjugated Mrs. Manders, had no effect on one who had long grown used to the candour and the brusquerie of Dr. Wilmot. She knew something from the doctor of

Miss MacFarren's anxiety to be rid of her uncongenial tenant, had thrown in her lot zealously on the side of her present employer, and never lost an opportunity of producing any morsel of evidence to strengthen the anti-Bankes case.

The frankness of her malice was a little disconcerting to one who believed herself free from the tendency to take pleasure in ill feeling. In her quiet and decorous way, Pearson enjoyed being at war, even in a cause that was not her own. Her narrow smile gleamed with a light of triumph, subdued but sinister, as Miss MacFarren took the guest towel from her, saying: 'I'm afraid I must speak to Mrs. Bankes about this.'

'Then you'll have to wait till tonight, miss. She's away for the day.' She paused, awaiting questions, but was obliged to go on unencouraged: 'Yes, she's had to go down to Oxford all the same. He wouldn't let her get out of it.' She pronounced the 'he' with a jerk of the head that infallibly indicated Captain Bankes, a party towards whom her disposition was benevolently neutral. 'He told her that he wouldn't have the children disappointed, and it was downright unfair to the people they're staying with; she'd promised to go every week-end and she'd have to go. She sulked a bit, but she's gone all right, and coming back this evening. She won't stay away, not while someone we needn't mention is about.'

Miss MacFarren retreated to the garden door, holding the squalid guest towel by one corner. She turned a furrowed face to the grey stone flags and the earthy borders where already, in her depressed fancy, the weeds of spring were lying in wait to overwhelm the flowers. Men had always been praised, she thought, for defending their homes, even by the most ferocious means, and when the evils that threatened them were perhaps imaginary. What blame then could attach to a woman whose household gods were daily desecrated, whose household peace was banished, if she should resolve to use without compunction the direst weapons within reach of her hand?

*　　*　　*

Mrs. Bankes had not managed to return from her unwilling visit to Oxford when her husband came home and presently knocked at the study door to ask whether Miss MacFarren still had her copy of that morning's *Times*. It was the hour of the evening when she regaled Maxine with sherry—Maxine regaling her in turn with the scandals of the studios and many other strange and unprecedented topics—and she had an idea that he was aware of this, and that the newspaper was a pretext. On her producing it, he lingered, searching then and there through the columns, and instead of begging him to take it away and read it at leisure, she artfully invited him to sit down by the fire with it, and placed a glass of sherry in his hand.

By the time he had found and digested the paragraph he had been looking for, over which he took as long as he convincingly could, a news item had caught Maxine's eye which led to a conversation about dogs, and soon Miss MacFarren was telling them about her new favourite, the ugly but engaging Butterfly.

'Surely, ma'am, you don't mean the bulldog at The Yorkshire Rose?' he startled her by asking.

'How do you come to know him?' she faltered.

'I might ask how *you* come to know him! It isn't remarkable if I do because I sometimes stop in there for beer and other beverages.'

'Perhaps I do too,' she said feebly, constrained by her promise not to tell him about Jimjams.

'Miss MacFarren, I'll bet a pound to a dollar you've never been in a public bar in your life.'

'Don't be too sure!' said Maxine. 'Mory's aunt doesn't always act in character. Not by any means. I wish you could see the bedside books she chose for me.'

'I'd like to,' he said with solemn courtesy.

Maxine rested her cheek on her palm and looked lazily at him. 'There's one fetching little item called *Sins of New York*.'

'I'm a Washington man, Miss Albert.'

Miss MacFarren was rapidly turning over in her mind a plan somewhat lacking in scruple but rich in potentialities for speeding Antonia's departure. Until this evening, as she had told Mory, Captain Bankes had never spent as many as five consecutive minutes in Maxine's presence without some pettish interruption from his wife. So long as she was able to exercise this vigilance, she would feel in command of the situation, and even perhaps exultant, like one who vigorously meets a challenge. But if once or twice, design or accident should provide them with a meeting-ground in other surroundings—surroundings inaccessible to her—surely she might at last take fright, and realize that her only security lay in removing him from the scene of danger.

If anyone had told Miss MacFarren in the summer that, before the winter was over, she would be inviting an extremely attractive girl in her twenties and a personable American who was married to go with her to a public house, she would have thought the prophecy as fantastic as it was vulgar, but, slowly reaching the pitch of desperation, she had become capable of acts without parallel in her career. So, with sensations closely resembling what she had once felt when taking her seat for a ride on a switchback railway called The Great Racer, she braced herself and said gaily:

'I don't know which of us wins your bet, Captain Bankes. I haven't been into a public bar, but I've been to a private one!'

'You don't say!' He used the tone of an adult towards an amusingly vainglorious child.

'The owner of The Yorkshire Rose is quite a friend of mine.'

'No, honestly?' This time his surprise was genuine.

'I take Butterfly our scraps—such as they are in these days. And then Mr. Penroyd and I have a chat, if he's not too busy mostly about dogs and dog shows, but sometimes about flowers and flower shows, because he likes those too. Have you ever been to the private bar there, Captain Bankes?'

'It didn't look very private when I was in it.'

'I don't mean the *public* private bar. Perhaps I shouldn't call it a bar at all. It's Mr. Penroyd's little sanctuary, with a fire and all the silver cups his various bulldogs have won. That's where I always go. Butterfly has a friend, an enchanting ginger cat with curled whiskers, and they play together delightfully. I wish you could see them.'

'Ginger cats! My favourite thing!' said Maxine.

Miss MacFarren was glad she had remembered this preference casually mentioned one tea-time when there had been a rendez-vous of cats in the garden.

'This one is the prettiest creature. It has a wonderful silky coat, nearly orange-coloured, and a tail like a fox's brush. I wish you could see them together,' she repeated, planting the suggestion boldly but with much the same quivering upheaval beneath the diaphragm that she had experienced when the Great Racing car had taken its first precipitous plunge. 'They look like Beauty and the Beast.'

'We ought to go round some evening,' said Maxine, lowering her eyes which had been fixed on her watchfully.

'No time like the present,' urged Captain Bankes, almost visibly recalling that his wife's absence from home was likely to be a rare event.

By a small but helpful coincidence, the sherry decanter was empty, and in a high-spirited manner, Miss MacFarren held it up for inspection. 'There's nothing more here! Shall we put on our coats and walk round? Seriously?'

'Now don't let's do a thing like that too seriously,' he admonished her. And thus in five minutes they were on their way to The Yorkshire Rose, and in twenty their friendship had advanced by such leaps and bounds that Miss MacFarren's double life was a joke they all shared, and Maxine was calling Captain Bankes by his Christian name, and he had assured her that, if she could only be photographed in colour with the ginger cat in her arms, it would make a magazine cover that would raise fan mail from the four corners of the globe.

'Even from Englishmen, though they're so frigid, poor fellows, it's miraculous to me how they manage to keep the race going.'

'With apologies to Mory's aunt,' said Maxine, 'you can take it from me they manage nicely.'

Mory's aunt accepted the apologies with an indulgent smile.

Mr. Penroyd was too busy, on a Saturday evening, to remain with them more than a moment or two, but, impressed by Maxine, and really on amiable terms with Miss MacFarren as she had described, he had invited them at once into his private sitting-room, where Butterfly was lying snugly on the hearthrug, had stirred the fire to a blaze and served them with an air of cheerful liberality seldom seen nowadays in an English publican. And, set free to some extent by the novelty of finding themselves together in this unlikely scene, they summoned up an atmosphere of such conviviality as leaves a lingering warmth behind.

Maxine went straight from The Yorkshire Rose to keep one of her numerous engagements, and Captain Bankes strolled home with Miss MacFarren, taking her arm each time they left the kerb with that solicitous politeness which was no doubt a matter of training and habit in him, but which always seemed like an expression of strongly personal regard—that politeness which, for half a year, had so effectively kept her hands tied.

'Maxine is a very nice girl, Miss MacFarren.' His half-repressed exuberance conveyed a sentiment that would not be denied utterance. 'An intelligent girl too. She has a sense of humour.'

'Yes, and a lovely face,' she rejoined a little breathlessly, for he walked with such long and loping steps that she had some ado to keep up with him.

'I'm only sorry she doesn't seem to get on with Tonia.' His tongue was loosened as much by the intimacy of the occasion as by the drinks he had taken. 'I guess it's Tonia's fault at that. She's liable to take peculiar prejudices. I hope it hasn't made you uncomfortable, Miss MacFarren, seeing Maxine's your guest, and you've always been very kind and tolerant with ours . . . though I have a sneaking idea they must have got on your nerves from time to time.' As she replied only with a not too dissident murmur, he continued in meditative vein a speech which was almost a soliloquy: 'As a matter of fact, they get on my nerves more than a little, some of those snickering young women. But they kept Tonia out of mischief while I was away, and thank the Lord they haven't been too much in evidence lately. That's the way it is with Tonia wherever we go. She takes up people with such enthusiasm, you'd think she couldn't live without them, then she suddenly gets sick of them and hey presto! they're gone and she's taking up a new batch.'

Miss MacFarren's opinion, reviewed in silence, was that Antonia's friendships were precarious, not so much because she was fickle as because, sooner or later, she was found out. The façade of joyous popularity that she had first presented revealed itself, at close quarters, as a smart front elevation with nothing but disordered and ramshackle rooms behind it. Of all the lively troupe who had invaded the house at the beginning, suggesting with their gaieties and endearments an eternal amity, not half a dozen were still on visiting terms. One after another they had fallen away, some positively alienated, like the owner of Jimjams, some merely wearied for the time being, like Froggie's mother or Miss Hall-Brown, who had grown remote since the exposure of Antonia's elaborate lies about the dog's death.

Another circle was in the process of formation, the womenfolk of Joss's new associates, and Antonia hardly appeared to notice the defection of her old friends in her pleasure at charming new ones. By now it was possible to guess that she might never have been able to call any friend 'old' if it were not for the nomad habits of life that had kept her relationships on a generally superficial level, and the reflected glow of Joss's popularity, which was no façade but a real structure.

Precluded from giving utterance to this view, Miss MacFarren remarked, by way of diversion, that Mrs. Jermyn, at any rate, had proved a friend in need by taking the two children.

'I don't know how long that can go on,' he muttered with a sigh in which the last of his festive spirits evaporated. 'When she finds they've just been dumped on her for an indefinite period, she isn't going to feel so good about it. I met Tom Jermyn in the city yesterday and I thought he was giving me a pretty broad hint. That's why I made Tonia at least go down and see them today.'

'It's an awkward situation, but I'm afraid Maxine must stay until she finds a flat, and after that—'

'Oh, please, Miss MacFarren,' he interrupted earnestly, 'don't get me all wrong! Tonia's had plenty of use out of the spare room, and now it's your turn. We wouldn't—I wouldn't make Maxine feel unwelcome for anything. My only complaint is that Tonia didn't have the sense to let me leave the children in the States.'

'Perhaps,' she suggested cunningly, 'she thought you'd go somewhere else where there'd be more room for you all.'

'Oh no, no!' His denial was measured but emphatic. 'I said to Tonia, "I like this house, I like the books, I like the whole outfit; if I have to be in Europe I want to stay right here. The only thing that's wrong is—we don't have our little family with us." So she had this brain-wave about making a nursery out of the top bedroom and all that, and she said she'd fix it with you so that, naturally, you got more money from us. . . .'

As his voice rumbled away into inaudible deeps of embarrassment, she tried to remember exactly how much she had promised Antonia to conceal in that brief conversation, so vague yet so decisive, when she had certainly pledged herself to discretion on an extensive scale, and she decided she might go as far as to answer:

'I wish you'd talked to me about it before you went to America.'

'Maybe I should have, but she thought it would be kind of tactless, and I left it to her. I never stop asking myself why she made such a hell of a muddle of it.'

'Have you stopped asking her?' she ventured rather wickedly.

He gave a melancholy laugh. 'Yes, because the answer doesn't make sense. She tells me she was crazy to see the children, but she isn't acting that way now she has the opportunity. The fact is, I suppose she's just plain scatterbrained.'

Antonia's conduct had never before inspired anything so near open and ill-humoured disapproval; she had evidently been carrying childishness beyond the bounds within which he found it attractive. Her attitude to Maxine, for instance, which had been petulant and ungracious in her presence and was probably much worse behind her back, showed her in an unprepossessing light, however excusable the jealous apprehension from which it sprang. That it was disturbingly in his mind, he made clear by reverting to the subject as they approached the house, lowering his voice as if she were already within earshot:

'I'm really sorry—no, honestly I am, Miss MacFarren—that there seems to be this little prejudice against your friend.'

'I don't think it worries Maxine.' She felt almost guilty as she remembered how much amusement Mrs. Bankes's hostility had actually afforded her.

'But they ought to get along so well together. They have a lot in common,' he added astonishingly.

'What makes you think that, Captain Bankes?'

'Well, they're both just kids really. That sophisticated talk Maxine hands out—it's a line she's picked up in the studios. I saw that directly, and I'll bet you did too. I've noticed that, in your quiet way, you're a very astute woman.'

Miss MacFarren was grateful for Maxine's dimples, her round face, her innocent eyes, but she hoped they would not work more havoc than was strictly requisite to dislodge the enemy.

As soon as they entered the house, Mrs. Bankes darted out from the sitting-room, wearing a fractious look which, in the last few days, had been seen oftener than her usual placid smile.

'Where have you been, Joss?' she demanded irritably, glancing from him to his companion with knitted brows.

'I've been out to have a drink, dear.' His candour was a trifle over-stressed, as though he were assuring himself that there was no cause for concealment.

'What? With Miss MacFarren?' Her scornful incredulity verged on insult.

He replied with deliberation: 'Yes, and her friend. . . . Well, what was it like in Oxford, dear? Did the children meet you there?'

Without making any answer, she retreated to the sitting-room and slammed the door in a gesture of such violence that the ornaments on the console table quivered.

'You must excuse her, Miss MacFarren,' he said quietly, with a little apologetic shrug. 'I told you she was just a kid.' But his face was angry as he opened the door and strode in after her.

Miss MacFarren was conscious of having substantially gained ground, and she adjured herself not to falter until victory was complete; but she was too ill at ease to settle down to the corned-beef sandwiches and the evening's letter-writing she had promised herself, and, after wandering about her study for ten minutes in a troubled frame of mind, she went out and took a seat for the second house of a music-hall performance at Victoria. There she was able to recapture a sort of cosy echo of the good humour generated at The Yorkshire Rose, and to escape into a world where the roving eyes of married men, the jealousy of wives, the allurements of beautiful young women with irresistible curves, were a pleasantly familiar joke at which the huge, respectable audience could laugh without a qualm.

15

MISS MACFARREN had never cared to commit herself so far as to appeal explicitly for Maxine's help in vanquishing Mrs. Bankes, feeling a natural distaste in the circumstances for plain words. She paid the penalty of specious delicacy by being unable to make any frank enquiry into those parts of the situation that were beyond her direct line of vision.

She knew that the little party at The Yorkshire Rose had duly paved the way for other meetings, but since they took place, as if accidentally at first, without her presence, she could only guess at the degree of their significance. On one occasion, Joss arrived home late because he had met Maxine, by the merest chance, he said, at the Savoy, where she had an appointment to dine with the Harrowbys, and he had stayed to have a drink with her there: on another he happened to run into her coming out of a house-agent's office where, in fact, she went almost every morning, and he had been able, in his own quaint term, to buy her lunch. Immediately after this, he contrived to take her over a flat which one of his colleagues desired to sub-let. It turned out to be unsuitable in every particular, but the excursion together still further increased their rapidly growing intimacy.

There is probably no married happiness so secure that it is quite proof against insidious undermining by a third party whose attack is favourably timed. Maxine had made her appearance just when Antonia's rash and inconsiderate behaviour towards her two children had upset her husband's normally equable temper. Moreover, those aspects of her perennial youthfulness which must have been of value to him during his years as a wandering reporter—the readiness for adventure, the willing acceptance of every different environment—had been obscured during a prolonged period of domesticity by other aspects less congenial, her improvidence, her restlessness and negligence. During each of his previous visits to London, he had been on holiday, but now he was hoping to settle down to a workaday life, and might expect the comfort of regular meals, quiet hours for reading, some care for his clothes, some sense of order in the day's procedure—amenities which his wife could never provide for more than a few days together.

And unlike Mrs. Manders, who had exhausted herself in covering up the defects of Antonia's housekeeping, the stony-hearted Pearson took a delight in letting them be seen and felt.

Antonia's weaknesses thus uppermost, her merits in eclipse, and Maxine's attractions disturbingly near at hand, Joss's attitude

grew, by perceptible stages, critical. His manner was still indulgent, still fatherly, but now a certain undercurrent of exasperation
suggested the parent who realizes that he has to deal with a problem child. He was in the mood when a long habit of affection may
begin to crumble.

'And she doesn't show any sign at all of growing up,' Miss
MacFarren almost wailed, having tea in the back parlour at Greenway's nearly a fortnight after her rather alarmingly successful little
machination. 'Maxine is dreadfully provocative, and she reacts in
such an unbelievably childish way, it has a sort of pathos, Harriet.'

'Don't weaken!' Harriet commanded, adamant in the same
degree as she had before been vulnerable. 'Don't weaken, or you
won't have an ornament left whole, my dear!'

Miss MacFarren could see she was thinking of her bon-bon box.

'I'm determined I shall get her out of the house by hook or by
crook. The trouble is, it's turning out to be mostly crook.'

'Elinor,' said Harriet sternly, 'you're too squeamish.'

'No, but it isn't nice, my dear, at my age, to have thrown two
people together who—well, who definitely ought not to be thrown
together.'

'Elinor'—the vigorous repetition of the name carried a strong
admonitory intention—'if you used to have one fault, one tiny fault,
my dear, it was that you were becoming—no, let me say you were in
danger of becoming smug. This Bankes situation has been a great
ordeal, but it's done you all the good in the world. It's humanized
you. It's broadened your mind. You're a far more adaptable woman
than you were this time last year.'

Miss MacFarren sat nodding over her tea-cup with a grave and
yet by no means displeased expression. She knew that Harriet's
words contained much truth, more than the speaker herself realized, for she had not cared to disclose quite the full extent of her
new broad-mindedness.

'Very well then,' Harriet went on as if the assent had been
spoken. 'Don't spoil it all by priggishness just when you're in sight
of the goal!'

'But *am* I in sight of the goal? I don't believe she's doing anything
about moving. She won't go house-hunting. She seems afraid to
leave the house in case anything should go on behind her back.'

'Surely her husband isn't there all day?'

'Not all day, but his hours are irregular, and he's liable to turn up at odd times. She's terrified in case he should happen to meet Maxine while's she's out.'

'Haven't you spoken to her? Haven't you told her she absolutely must be gone by April?'

'Yes, and she answers with lies, says she has friends who are out searching for flats all day long for her, and nonsense of that kind.' Automatically responding to Harriet's equally automatic gesture with the teapot, she passed her cup across the pearl-inlaid table and took it back refilled. 'She seems to have completely lost her head. So far from growing up, she's reached the very depths of silliness. It was positively embarrassing when Mark Harrowby came.'

'The film star? I must say you're going the pace!' Harriet's amusement was tinged with mild envy.

'He and his wife are great friends of Maxine's, so Mory brought him along one evening for a drink.'

'For a drink! You have the line of talk quite pat, I see.'

'Of course I took them all into the study, and it was really most pleasant. Did you know Mark Harrowby collected porcelain? He was charmed with the Chinese cats that Mory gave me. I liked him immensely.'

'Yes, but what happened with Mrs. Bankes?'

'Well, it came out in conversation that he'd met Captain Bankes a few evenings before, with Maxine at the Savoy—I told you about that little episode—and he'd only realized afterwards that it was Joss Bankes, the journalist, whom he'd been reading for years. So, thinking it would be nice for them to meet again, when I heard Captain Bankes come in, I went into the hall and asked him to have a drink with us—'

'These drinks, Elinor! What you must be spending on them!'

'I regard it as an investment. . . . Mrs. Bankes put her head out of the sitting-room door at once and heard me explaining that Mark Harrowby was with us, but I hardened my heart and pretended not to see her.'

'Poor creature! How maddening not to be invited to meet that luscious man when he was actually in the house!'

'Captain Bankes was in a rather awkward situation. He couldn't bring his wife, as she hadn't been asked, and it wasn't very easy for him to come without her, so he said he'd just "look in" on us. Would you believe, Harriet, he'd hardly been with us three minutes, when she sent Pearson with a message that she wanted to see him urgently!'

'I should have thought she'd have managed things better!' Harriet ate a biscuit with severe disapproval.

'My dear, that's not the worst. I'd only that instant handed him his drink, so he said, 'Tell Mrs. Bankes I'll be with her presently.' It sounds incredible, but in no time at all she came to the study door herself, in that utterly undignified way of hers, and called to him to come out. Naturally, I had to invite her to come *in*, but she refused as rudely as could be, and I think that irritated him because instead of going out, he stood where he was and asked her what was the matter.'

'That was naughty of him,' said Harriet, passing a plate of biscuits as if it had been a judicial rite.

'Thank you. It was obtuse. But then, Harriet, men are obtuse about these social nuances, and she was very annoying. Do you know, she was so fatuous that she hadn't even thought up a reasonable pretext. All she could say was that she'd like to have dinner out.'

'I'm afraid you *are* making me sorry for her,' Harriet acknowledged. 'She must be tormented with jealousy.'

'I told you it was pathetic. And men do seem to get so awfully cross when a woman makes her jealousy public. Captain Bankes said quite coldly—not in the least like his usual self—that it wasn't seven o'clock yet, and she said she was too hungry to wait. So he excused himself and left us, covered with confusion. As he went out, he caught Maxine's eye, and she gave him such a funny little smile— mocking and yet cosy, if you know what I mean.'

'She sounds like a dangerous young person, Elinor.'

'Oh, she is!' cried Miss MacFarren proudly.

'But at the moment, she's defeating your ends, since Mrs. Bankes is so frightened that she won't go out of the house. It's the 19th of March. She'll have to work fast if she's to find some other home and move into it by the 1st of April.'

'Yes, indeed, and I daren't give her any latitude about the date. Maxine has found a little service flat. At least, Mory has managed by all kinds of bribery to get one for her in that shockingly expensive building where he lives. He came in to tell us so last night. She'll be leaving at the beginning of the month.'

'Ah!' Harriet's frown showed that she was devoting the full energy of her intelligence to weighing the consequences of this change. 'And if once she's gone and Mrs. Bankes feels safe again, you'll be exactly where you were before.'

'Worse even, for she's bound to squeeze her unfortunate children in by some ruse or other when the spare room's empty. And Pearson will be leaving too the moment Dr. Wilmot returns,' she groaned, seeing all her troubles rolling back upon her in a grey tide. 'They've both promised to let Mrs. Bankes think they're staying on, but you see, that can only be kept up a short time longer.'

'You'll have to do something drastic. Set aside your scruples! If she's not an adult, I've seen her put up a very convincing imitation of one.'

'But what can I do? It would be wicked of me to encourage Maxine to go further than she's gone already.'

'Then be wicked for once! This situation requires emergency tactics. There's less than a fortnight left.'

'I might be breaking up the marriage.'

'What? You think this pet siren of yours is in love with Bankes?'

'It hardly seems likely—she's such a cool customer—but I'm pretty sure he's, at any rate, three-quarters in love with her. And he's a serious man; whatever he feels will be felt thoroughly.'

'It takes two to make an adultery,' said Harriet, tapping her snuff-box with an authoritative air. 'If she doesn't want him, the marriage is safe, because no man will break with a wife he's fond of for a woman who's unattainable.'

Miss MacFarren gave a delicate cough. 'I couldn't guarantee that Maxine would be unattainable,' she said diffidently. 'Not absolutely.'

'You mean that even if she's not in love with him, she might—'

'I haven't any idea.' Miss MacFarren averted her eyes. 'I only say I can't guarantee. She takes such a delight in driving Mrs. Bankes to distraction.'

'But to go as far as that! Surely—?'

'Maxine's moral standards are so different from ours.'

'You certainly have become broad-minded,' said Harriet with a remote smile.

'If you could see her!' Miss MacFarren stammered, conscious of reproof. 'There's something so disarming . . . even though she does give one shocks. And you tell me "Don't be squeamish!"'

'Agreed. But when it comes to breaking up happy marriages just for the fun of the thing, you really are playing with edged tools.'

'I know it.' Her sigh plumbed the gloomy depths of apprehension. 'I suppose I ought to speak to her and find out what she actually intends.'

'Now don't go to the other extreme and throw in your hand. There must be a happy medium between ruining the silly woman's life, and letting her ruin your home.'

Miss MacFarren slightly shook her head, and continued to shake it as if its inward perplexities had set it in motion.

'Have a pinch of snuff,' said Harriet. 'It'll clear your brain.'

'No thank you,' she replied flinching. 'Not today, Harriet.'

'This is just when you need it, my dear. It clarifies the thoughts as nothing else does. You've admitted it yourself.'

She thrust out her gold snuff-box with a kind of unreasonable determination which, in small matters as in big, was prone at sudden moments to take possession of her. Miss MacFarren yielded with the best grace she could summon, telling herself it was a judgment upon her for lying. On several previous occasions when Harriet had pressed her to take snuff, wanting the moral courage to go on refusing, she had accepted a small pinch and secretly dropped it on the carpet or down the side of her chair, pretending, to gratify Harriet, that her head was very much cleared. Today, with her friend's eyes fixed intently on her, she found herself unable to get rid of the obnoxious grains except by actually sniffing them, and the conversation ended in a violent bout of sneezing which she feared must have very effectually betrayed her former want of candour.

Outside her house when she returned, Mory's car was drawn up at the kerb, and she found him in her study with a tea-tray provided by Pearson and a fire just lighted, which he was coaxing with a thoughtfully manipulated poker. Lately he had made quite a habit of this casual visiting, attributed by her partly to the congenial presence of Maxine, partly to his being a little at a loose end in the first days of the break with Geraldine, and in some small degree to his growing appreciation of her own company since he had learned that she could get on with his friends. She would have given Maxine all the credit of his new attentiveness, but that, though interested and even inquisitive as to everything that concerned her, he was always detached, and if it turned out that only his aunt was at home, he showed no sign of discontent but sat down to gossip as happily as if he had come to see no one but herself.

Today, however, for the first time, he seemed put out when she told him that Maxine had a sequence of engagements and would not be in till late that night. The smile with which he had greeted her faded to a look of disappointment, and he said facetiously but with evident annoyance:

'Now confess she's out with Bankes, fulfilling your immoral instructions!'

'No, not at all!' Her vigorous denial soothed a sensitive conscience. 'As a matter of fact, she's dining this evening with Pio Martinez.'

'Pio? But she was out with him yesterday.'

'As to that—I don't know.' She rebuked herself for having, in self-exculpation, perhaps said more than was discreet.

'Yes, he dropped her here in his car just as I arrived. And good God! now I come to think of it, she turned up at the studio with him the other day and they spent hours together. What are they supposed to be up to? Isn't Bankes enough to keep her busy?'

She was surprised, both at his unwonted outburst of some emotion very near anger, and at Maxine's having been so much with a man whose name she had scarcely mentioned until this morning.

'It must have something to do with her work,' she suggested appeasingly.

Mory's ill humour was merely aggravated. 'Hell!' He banged a lump of coal with every appearance of personal animosity. 'If there was one bloody complication I didn't want . . . I'm sorry, darling, but you've taken the wind out of my sails. I came here feeling like fairy godfather.' He waved the poker gracefully from side to side. 'Stella Hawthorne's going to Hollywood. You know she was to have been the star in my next picture?'

'Oh, *do* say it's to be Maxine instead!' Excitement made her rise from the chair in which she had scarcely seated herself, and while she was standing, she took the opportunity of moving her blue china cat. 'Do, Mory! It would be so marvellous.'

'Well, it suddenly occurred to me—-why not? I've been seeing her sequences in *Cranford*. They come over nicely, although the camera work is uninspired. I want to use that face where it'll have some value . . . innocence, purity, simplicity, and what-not. In my film she'd be a young novice in a convent.'

'How that would suit her! Suit her face, I mean.'

'Of course, the characterization as written for Hawthorne will have to be revised. That's easy.'

'Maxine will be overjoyed. I don't believe anything in the world could please her so much.'

'Not if Pio's been cutting the ground from under my feet offering her the lead in that corney *Heart for Hire* he's going to direct for the Unicorn outfit. It's just a bigger and sillier version of her tart rôle in *Cranford*—that's Pio's weakness: he goes on and on casting to type, and in her case he's wrong about the type—but if he's got in first promising to build her up into a star . . .'

'I think she would have mentioned it, Mory, if anything so important had been going forward.'

'Nonsense, Aunt Ellie, if you'll pardon me! Maxine is capable of being very secretive in important matters. She has us both completely fogged at this moment as to whether she's leading your lodger, Bankes, up the garden path or straight into bed.'

'Mory! How can you talk so lightly of her?'

'I don't mean it lightly.' Meticulously, he traced the pattern on the carpet with the poker. 'I'm by way of being rather shocked now I come to look at the situation.'

'I wish you'd said so before. You gave me the impression that you were quite enjoying it.'

'Darling, human feelings aren't static, and you mustn't expect them to be.'

She stared at him with astonishment, trying to realize the implication of his words, while he continued assiduously to draw invisible lines with the poker.

'You sound as if you're becoming jealous of her.' She masked her daring with a breathless laugh.

'Jealous! Not in the least!' His calm and measured assurance just missed conviction. 'I'm interested in her future, and I think this Bankes affair, which is not particularly amusing to the spectators, is dragging on too long and that it's time it was brought to a conclusion.'

Miss MacFarren decided to change the baffling subject. Mory's recent behaviour, the trouble he had taken to find Maxine a flat, his new-born desire to advance her career, certainly indicated the development of some state of mind which was different from that in which he had lent himself so willingly to the hatching of 'Auntie's wicked plot'. And until she had weighed her own reaction to this new sentiment privately and at leisure, she shrank from probing it further.

'Talking of bringing things to conclusions,' she said, 'what about this interminable divorce business? Has it been postponed again?'

'Believe it or not, it comes off tomorrow. And I was going to tell you, Aunt Ellie, only we got into such a huddle about Maxie, there's been an ignominious collapse on the other side. Stevie Mace has withdrawn his claim for damages.'

'How wonderful! What splendid news you're bringing today!' Even in the joy of her relief, which was very real—for the thought of her brother's modest and hard-earned fortune being sliced away to reward the odious Mace for the infidelity of a notorious wife had been little less humiliating than the loss of his herbals—she had the presence of mind to remove the poker from Mory's hand: he had begun to practise golf strokes with it.

'My solicitor rang up and told me this afternoon. The relief was so glorious, I haven't quite realized it yet. Without the fascinating legal arguments about how much Geraldine was worth, the publicity will be practically innocuous. Take away Vernon Bradley's eloquence and all the dainty trimmings, and it's just one more undefended divorce. I shan't even have to appear in court.'

'What do you think can have caused such a change of front?' she enquired with a faint stirring of some gratifying prescience.

'I suppose his lawyers have found out that, after all, it wasn't quite an open-and-shut case. Or Stevie got a little chilly when he came to reckon up all the people who knew the facts of his domestic life.'

'Isn't that mysterious, though, after he'd taken it so far, and got this famous counsel and everything? I think someone must have befriended you.'

'Who? And how?' he asked with a sceptical smile. 'All my friends are having the time of their lives saying "I told you so." They're probably longing to see me get soaked.' He had risen and picked up his walking stick as he spoke. 'I must go, dear. Don't tell Maxie what I've been planning!'

'Then break it to her soon, Mory! She'll be so happy.'

'She may be committed to Pio by now. . . . By the way, Aunt Ellie, what's your financial position going to be like when these Bankeses leave?'

'Rather a problem,' she admitted. 'They haven't saved me as much as I expected—in the long run, nothing at all when you consider the wear and tear—but it has been something to count on having half the rent and rates paid.'

'Since I'm not going to be stung as badly as I expected, I'll be able to tide you over.'

She interrupted to thank him warmly, but without agreeing to accept his offer. 'You'll still be hard up, my dear boy, what with costs to meet and things you can't foresee.'

'Well, that's true. There were certain unanticipated expenses in parting with Geraldine. . . . I'm not exactly flush. But lately, Aunt Ellie, I've been engaged in a little graft that might help you out in a really big way. How would you like to come into the film business?'

'The film business!' She could only repeat the phrase in pure incredulity.

'Have you read *Murder in the Hothouse*?'

She nodded with something of solemnity, for the conversation had taken a very odd and unexpected turn.

'You know we're going to do it at Cornfields?'

'As a film?' She was lost in wonder as to what might!! follow. The novel in question was one of those detective stories in which the author uses the narrative as an ingenious means of displaying his knowledge of some highly specialized subject; in this case, the cultivation of stove-plants. It had been given her by a friend as likely to be 'up her street', but she found herself quite unable to anticipate Mory's explanation.

'I believe I can manoeuvre you in,' he said after watching her bewildered face with amusement, 'to be a sort of floral consultant. The murder's committed in a chain of green-houses. There's a lot of sequences at different times of the year with backgrounds of flowers and plants—rather beautiful it ought to be, all done in colour—and I've been selling Swanziger the idea that he ought to try an almost documentary style and have an expert adviser.'

'Wouldn't the author be best for that?'

'She lives in Cornwall. They'll be weeks taking the greenhouse scenes, and the expert ought to be available all the time.'

'You mean, like Sir William Waterbond?'

'Yes, it's just the same kind of job.'

'But I'm primarily a botanist, Mory. Don't you think it would be much more sensible if they got someone who actually runs green-houses in a practical way? One of the big commercial firms—?'

'Of course it would be more sensible, but it wouldn't put a shilling in your pocket. And besides, your name will have prestige with the people who know. Swanziger's quite capable of appreciating that. In fact, he places an almost excessive value on names. That's why Willie Waterbond draws a handsome salary at Cornfields for just sitting around.'

'I don't think I should like that, Mory,' she said apologetically. 'It would be enthralling if they'd really let me earn the money they were paying; but if they had me there to advise and then disregarded everything I said—'

'As they will, dear, unless it fits in with what the technicians want. But you'll simply have to get the Waterbond attitude. Remember, it's their money you're after.'

'It's a very, very interesting suggestion certainly,' she said, 'and I'm most obliged.' But though there was a lively sense of obligation in her tone, there was no certainty.

A few weeks ago, she might have felt the same thrill at the prospect of working in a film studio as almost any other member of the public, but eight hours at Cornfields had convinced her that one would need to love either money or motion pictures with a passion beyond her own comprehension to be able to endure, week after week, for a protracted period, the terrible *longueurs* of the studio day. To leave home early every morning and sit about till late afternoon, constrained to watch innumerable and interminable mechanical processes, on the mere off-chance of occasionally being allowed to prevent some error, and to know all the time that one's real work, the still-frustrated *History of Floriculture*, was lying unfinished in one's desk, would be a fate only a few degrees less gloomy than sharing a house with Mrs. Bankes.

Nevertheless, she was obliged to contemplate it, and to acknowledge that she was lucky to have such a chance. It was the only alternative to taking other strangers into her home after the Bankeses had gone, and this she was resolved never in any extremity to attempt again. Indeed, when in the light of her own vexations she considered all that must have been suffered in the past six years by that huge section of the public which had been deprived of privacy, deprived by bombing, by billeting, by conscription, by the housing shortage, and by the compulsory guardianship of other people's children, she marvelled at the stability of the human nervous system which had been strained so desperately far without breaking into sheer insanity.

16

THE NEXT MORNING Maxine, who had come in too late the night before to share the customary brew of whisky toddy, presented herself at the study door as early as ten o'clock, wearing her hat and holding her coat over her arm. Thanks to the intelligent ministrations of Pearson, Miss MacFarren no longer had to spend her whole morning at housework, and she was already busy co-ordinating notes from her card index: but Maxine's intrusions were so rare, and the charm of her morning appearance so refreshing that she felt rather glad than otherwise to be disturbed.

'Come in and sit down,' she said. 'You can't be going out at this hour.'

'For your sake, I am. Joss is running me to the Savoy in his new car.'

'Where does "my sake" come in?'

'My date isn't till eleven, but I'm going earlier because it'll madden Mrs. Bankes to see me leave the house with Joss. It's time to put some pressure on. She's begun to talk about moving.'

'Well, that is good news!' said Miss MacFarren. Then she dropped her voice; for Maxine, in coming into the room, had left the door open, and lately Mrs. Bankes had been driven by her anxiety to at least a strong semblance of listening and watching. 'Not that it's likely to get any further than talk if she never goes out and does anything about it. Still, it's something to know she's broached the subject.'

'Joss is in a low state of mind, torn between wanting to have the children with him and wanting to go on living here in the Home Beautiful. He only asked for the London job because he'd taken such a fancy to this set-up.'

'Yes, I know. He was very much misled. I do feel sorry for him about his children. He's such a fatherly character.'

'Fatherly! I'll say!' Maxine's dimples appeared and disappeared in an ingenuous-seeming smile. 'You should see him trying to teach little Maxie not to say naughty words! It seems I swear because I'm just a kid, and I wouldn't if I really understood what I was saying. Doesn't that bring the tears to your eyes?'

Miss MacFarren did, in fact, see a certain pathos in the innocence of Captain Bankes. She hesitated, on the verge of adjuring Maxine not to disillusion him too cruelly, to argue with herself that he ought, at the earliest possible: stage, to be disillusioned; and ended by asking with a stretch of courage:

'Is it entirely for my sake that you're beguiling this poor man?'

Maxine gave an expert wink which looked, however, like some little impudence learned, not very long before, in the nursery. 'Beguiling poor men is cosy work if you can get it, and I seem to get a lot of it one way and another. Beguiling rich men is what a girl really enjoys.' It was plain that she had no intention of giving a serious answer, and she went on at a more rapid pace than was customary to her: 'But I do try to do things for your sake, Mory's aunt. I've been working like a beaver for you the last few days. That's what I came to tell you. . . . The reprieve has been granted. The mortgage has been paid off. The villain has relented. Can you guess what I'm breaking to you?'

'No,' said Miss MacFarren, lying.

'Stevie Mace has stopped trying to cash in. There aren't going to be any damages or any touching speeches about the paradise he and Geraldine lived in before the old serpent Mory came along. It's going to be just a quiet, respectable divorce that any film director might get mixed up in.'

'Oh, Maxine, how in the world did you do it?' False surprise was quite lost in true gratitude.

'I got Pio to do it, and I'm not going to pretend it was easy. Pio isn't exactly addicted to Mory—not in a big way—and he wasn't falling over himself to do him a good turn. But I set to work on him gently, and made him feel there must be *esprit de corps* among Geraldine's ex-lovers. What's that classy word of yours?—I beguiled him.'

'I hope you didn't have to—to commit yourself—' Miss MacFarren began, trying, rather vainly even in her own ears, to sound at ease on this peculiar ground.

'I didn't have to commit anything. You don't know how non-committal I can be. But it takes more effort, trying to get something for nothing,' she added pensively.

'You succeeded at any rate.' Miss MacFarren felt a faint desire not to know any more about the price paid or left unpaid for Mory's rescue: there were things about Maxine that one couldn't understand and had better ignore.

'Yes. I took legal advice first—in the Cocktail Bar at the Ritz, from a very sweet barrister I've known for years. And then Pio wrote that mercenary bastard a letter. . . . Like to see it?'

She took from her bag a pencilled draft which Miss MacFarren read with the respectful curiosity of one who is allowed to handle a rare manuscript in a museum, for such a document had never come her way before:

DEAR STEVIE,

I am interested to hear your divorce is coming off at last, and I do hope all goes smoothly. If you will forgive me offering some advice, I think it is a mistake to ask for damages, because you might have to commit rather a lot of perjury to get them.

Lately MacFarren has become a friend of mine, and I know he would like to borrow the letters you wrote me at the time when you were being so very obliging about Geraldine. It is not often that a husband is as obliging as you were, and what a pity it is to think that, if those letters should be read out in court, your generosity would be completely misunderstood!

Think it over, Stevie. When the case comes up, I shall be there. Greetings,

P. M.

'Sinister, isn't it?' said Maxine with pride. 'We wrote it together. It's a bluff, because Pio wouldn't really have gone any further to help Mory. But it worked. Yesterday Stevie rang Pio up and said a whole rigmarole about only asking for damages on the advice of his solicitor, and if Pio didn't think it was a good idea, he'd wash it out at once; And he ended by asking for a job on the next picture as a consolation prize. Isn't he fantastic?'

'And you actually did this for me?' Miss MacFarren asked as searchingly as she dared.

'Well, I didn't do it so that Mory could afford to go out and buy himself another pet man-eating tiger. Though I dare say he will,' she suggested, with the touch of scorn that this topic always evoked in her.

She would have said more, but the sound of Captain Bankes's weighty footstep on the strip of parquet outside silenced her, and a moment later he tapped on the open door and, apologizing ceremoniously for his intrusion, informed Maxine that he was on his way to the garage.

'I wondered if you'd care to stroll around with me as it's such a grand morning; or shall I come back to pick you up?'

She paused, doubtless to decide which course would give the most annoyance to Mrs. Bankes, and before she had made up her mind, the telephone rang. Captain Bankes retreated to take the call, and Maxine, following him with her eyes, murmured a shade regretfully, 'You must admit he has a very pretty shape!'

Presently he reappeared, announcing that Miss MacFarren's nephew wanted to speak to Maxine. 'I might as well get the car while you're talking.' His flat tone revealed a sudden loss of cheerfulness. 'It's rather late after all.'

As the front door slammed, Miss MacFarren went back to her card index, but she could not help being aware of the gist of Maxine's conversation, since the telephone was in the hall only a few yards away. She was making an appointment to dine with Mory that evening, and it was evident from her responses that he had told her he had something of importance to discuss with her, and that Maxine supposed he was going to tell her what she already knew about the divorce suit. Miss MacFarren sat feeling strangely elated, as if some stroke of brilliant fortune had fallen to her own lot. Maxine, she never doubted for a moment, would be a film star, and she knew enough about film stars to be aware that their order is the most privileged and, in all practical senses of the word, the most exalted that exists below royalty and the commanders of great armies. To one who was almost maternally disposed to her, the prospect of stardom for Maxine was little less splendid than if, being born two or three generations earlier, she had seen her favourite niece captivate a duke.

And it added to her pleasure to find the means of this glorification in the hands of her own nephew. She was glad he had made the plan while still in ignorance of the immense service Maxine had been able to perform for him, a service that was equally or even more disinterested. Mory would have the actress he wanted for his film, but Maxine had expected nothing beyond the pleasure of obliging a friend. Of obliging two friends. She had not vanity enough to suppose that so much trouble had been taken solely, or even primarily, to gratify her.

That Maxine liked Mory personally and admired him professionally she was sure. That Mory was beginning to be jealous of Maxine she had since yesterday been well aware. Indeed, looking back, she could perceive that the detached amusement with which at first he had all but boasted of her accomplished coquetries had been over-emphatic, a mode of defending himself against an emotion he feared. The question now presented itself—was his fear well-based? Had his instinct been right when he had told her, months ago, to 'take care of her lodger' lest Maxine should be attracted by him? She had certainly entered with alarming zest into the tacit plot to drive

Mrs. Bankes from the house by making her feel afraid of losing her husband. Might not this readiness have been due to a predilection for Captain Bankes, whose handsome figure had always taken her eye and whose naïvete perhaps appealed to her more than Mory's sophistication?

Last August, when her ears had been so shocked by Maxine's uninhibited commentary at their first meeting, she would have thought it hard to find a more undesirable young woman for wife or sweetheart. But in those days she had been, as Harriet had soundly pointed out, in danger of becoming a prig. Now she could ask herself dispassionately, what right had Mory to aspire to a virtuous woman? Or, to do him justice, since he had never shown the slightest interest in any such object, what right had his relatives to aspire after virtuous womanhood on his behalf. He was raffish and cynical and Maxine was his female counterpart. It was lucky—that is, it would be lucky if she were to love him—that she matched him likewise in the fundamental warmth and good nature that lay beneath her superficial destructiveness. She had a talent worth cultivating, she was ambitious, she was beautiful. So far from deeming her undesirable, Miss MacFarren was now of the opinion that Mory would be fortunate if he could replace the worthless Geraldine by any successor half so meritorious.

This train of thought, with all its interesting implications, distracted her from the conference on the telephone, and when her mind wandered back, Maxine was explaining that Pio had given her an introduction to someone she described as 'Bamberger of A.P.A.' who was staying at the Savoy, where she had an appointment to meet him that morning. The news seemed to occasion a contemptuous protest, and Maxine was at pains to explain that she couldn't afford to turn up her nose at Bamberger, and that Joss was just about to run her to the Savoy, when an extraordinary interruption caused her to ring off abruptly.

'What do you mean by calling my husband by his Christian name?' said Mrs. Bankes's voice with an insensate anger that drew Miss MacFarren to her feet incontinently.

'Mory,' Maxine remarked with no change of tone, 'a little something has begun to happen at this end. See you tonight. Goodbye.'

She replaced the receiver just as Miss MacFarren hurried into the hall. Mrs. Bankes had spoken from the staircase and was descending the stairs. Her face, not yet made up, was pallid, her loosely pinned hair a mere bird's nest, and her appearance in a crumpled and slightly soiled dressing-gown altogether lacking its usual elegance. She had been crying and her eyes were swollen and red-rimmed. The sight of her distress, to which she had wholly, almost defiantly, abandoned herself, was painful to Miss MacFarren; but Maxine was able to reply with mocking coolness:

'Why do I call your husband by his Christian name? I think it must be because he calls me by mine.'

Mrs. Bankes turned where she stood, and grasped the stair rail with vehement hands while fresh tears started from her eyes.

'I want to know why you're throwing yourself at Joss?' she cried passionately. 'You're throwing yourself headlong at him. You know you are.'

'I do it to see how fast he can jump out of my way.' Maxine rejoined as if after a pause for reflection.

'What do you want with him?' Insult subsided wretchedly into abjectness. 'Why can't you leave him alone?'

'Do you think he'd like that much?' Maxine seemed by her manner to be considering an abstract problem.

'What do you want with him?' Mrs. Bankes's misery was heightened by her inarticulateness. She struggled in vain for words, and then repeated with a louder emphasis: 'What do you *want* with him?'

'Oh, I can imagine ways he might come in useful.' The long lashes fell modestly over the limpid eyes. 'Frankly, I've taken a fancy to him. I don't see what you've got to grumble about. He's put up with you for ten years.'

'Maxine!' Miss MacFarren pleaded, astonished and dismayed.

'Now you keep out of this, Mory's aunt!' she commanded good-humouredly. 'Tonia and I must have our quarrel in peace. Oh, I forgot you don't like Christian names, Mrs. Bankes. I'm so accustomed to hearing yours from Joss.'

Antonia, weeping copiously, wrung her hands, twisting the diamond ring she wore upon her wedding finger in a helpless agony. 'You're a beast!' she sobbed, scarcely attempting now to express herself like an adult. 'A beast! A beast, I tell you! I hate you! I loathe you! I wish you were dead!'

Pearson and Captain Bankes arrived at this point simultaneously, Pearson from the basement and Captain Bankes through the front door, both declaring their amazement on their faces.

'She's a beast—a beast!' Antonia screamed frantically. 'She's a loathsome, horrible slut!' And looking round for something to do violence to, she took Maxine's coat, which had been left lying over the chair by the telephone, and trampled it under her feet.

Everyone except Maxine stooped to retrieve it, Pearson, succeeding, muttered wrathfully: 'What a tantrum! And what language! My goodness! A nice way to go on!'

Antonia caught her husband by the arms and deliriously tried to shake him. 'Joss, she wants to take you away from me! Joss, listen! She wants to take you away!'

'Nonsense! Nonsense!' He put her hands away with a sufficiently firm gesture, but his face was so flushed and furrowed with embarrassment that Miss MacFarren tried, by a movement Maxine failed to observe, to suggest their withdrawal. 'Go on upstairs, Tonia, and get yourself under control. Please!'

'She wants to take you away. She said so.'

'Nonsense!'

'I swear before God she said so. I wish she was dead, and I wish I was dead too!'

'That's no way to talk,' he said lamely. 'I can't stay to listen anyway—I'm late for the office as it is. . . .'

'You're not going to the office. You're going out with her.'

'Oh, hell!' said Captain Bankes, and Miss MacFarren thought she had never seen a man in so pathetic a confusion of guilt and innocence, indignation and humility. 'Come along up, Tonia, and stop all this moaning!' He took her by the arm not without solicitude for she had worked herself up into a pitiable condition, and had mounted the first two or three steps with her when she shook him rudely off. 'Leave me alone!' she shouted. 'Get back to your trollop! Leave me alone, I tell you!'

As she darted up the stairs, he turned back with an angry shrug. 'A man can take just so many scenes . . . This is where I get off. . . . Let's go, Maxine!'

But Maxine had already slipped away.

'She's going by taxi, sir,' Pearson volunteered in a small discreet voice, and pretended to be busy with a duster.

'Hell!' Captain Bankes proclaimed again, as if it were an official ultimatum. 'Will someone kindly explain to me what happened?'

'It's not really for me to explain.' Miss MacFarren, who had been shocked by Maxine's wantonness and disappointed by the admission of her preference for Captain Bankes, was rather irritable. 'If you go at once, you'll probably catch up with her.'

'Thanks, Miss MacFarren, that's what I'd better do.'

Hastily, like a man in need of fresh air, he made for the door, leaving her standing with a sense of anti-climax. Sighing and frowning, she moved off towards her study, seeing no other prospect them to contemplate the melancholy scene in solitude over a cup of coffee; when Pearson, sidling up to her with a bird-like cautiousness, whispered dramatically: '*Now*, miss! Now's the time! If you don't get rid of her now you never will. You go and strike while the iron's hot!'

Miss MacFarren felt as if she were being enjoined to strike, not iron, but the trembling flesh of Antonia; yet she perceived, vaguely at first, then with a sudden clarity of focus, that am emergency had arisen which had brought her straight into the thick of a decisive battle. She braced herself, nodded at Pearson without catching her eye, and sturdily mounted the stairs. The thought of the pale and tear-stained figure whom she knew she would find lying on the bed filled her with compunction, but as she went she heartened herself with a kind of litany:

'Breakages. Mice. Cockroaches. Noise. Lies. Dirt. Missing rations. Scorched dressing-table. Half-starved love-birds. *Jimjams.*'

With this fatal name on her lips, she knocked purposefully on the door of the bedroom that had once been hers and would soon, she was grimly resolved, be hers again.

'If you come in, I'll kill myself!' cried Antonia.

Miss MacFarren went in. The bed on which Antonia was lying face downwards, as her mind's eye had predicted was tumbled as if it had been the scene of a struggle. Pillows and counterpane were on the floor (the splendid patchwork counterpane which the admiring owner had always folded every night with loving care, even when high explosives were raining on London). Antonia had doubled over the bolster, and was clutching it convulsively.

'Mrs. Bankes,' she said in a calm and kind voice, 'you must get up and dress and go out to look for some other place to live. For your own sake as much as mine. Do you hear?'

'I'll kill myself, I'll kill myself!' sobbed Antonia, thumping on the bolster.

'Sit up, Mrs. Bankes! I can't talk to you while you behave like that. Sit up, please, and then we can wash the tears off your face and get you ready to go out.'

She spoke by a natural and unthinking impulse as if she were really dealing with an hysterical child, and it gave her no surprise that Antonia, with an expression of grudging compliance, rose slowly to a sitting position.

'What do you want?' she asked sullenly. 'I'm not going to talk to you.'

'All the better, because I'm going to talk to you. Now listen! If you want to keep your husband, you've got to get him out of this house.'

'It's too late,' said Antonia lugubriously.

'Not yet, but it soon might be. However well he wants to behave, so long as you three are living under the same roof, he'll be under perpetual temptation. You'll be weeping and worried and bad-tempered, as you are now. Maxine will have you at a terrible disadvantage. . . .'

'You planned this!' Antonia broke in with a swift resentful glance of intuition.

Miss MacFarren would not lie, but she said evasively as she picked up the counterpane: 'Everything that has just happened was a complete surprise to me. How could I know you were going to make such a ridiculous scene?' Then, lest she should seem to be recriminating, she pressed on: 'The only way to avoid more scenes now that we've had this one is to get your husband away immediately.'

'He won't go,' said Antonia, sniffing dismally into a handker-chief.

'What? Have you asked him?'

'Yes. I wanted to go back to the Asturias, because it's been horrible here since *she* came, but he said he wouldn't move unless we could settle down and have the children with us.'

'He may feel differently since there's been this row.'

'Rows only make Joss obstinate.' Abstractedly she restored the pillows to their normal position. 'He might be more set on staying than ever now he knows *she* wants him.'

'It wasn't very wise of you to tell him that, was it?'

Antonia looked sheepish, and seeing that she had obviously gained some ascendancy, Miss MacFarren continued in the same candidly authoritative manner: 'If you had somewhere to go where the children could be with you, there surely couldn't be any argument. You must get out at once and find a house or flat.'

'How can I? There isn't such a thing to be had.'

'Not unfurnished—that's out of the question—but you want a furnished place, don't you? That might be easier; and I do believe, Mrs. Bankes, that if anyone in England can find one, you can.'

'Why do you say that?' Antonia enquired with sulky interest.

'You usually get what you want. You told me so yourself. And don't you remember saying you could be a whirlwind once you started? I know that was true. When you definitely want something, you have great energy and great charm too. Go out and charm a house agent!'

Antonia sat down heavily on the dressing-table stool, and gazed at herself in the mirror. 'How can I—looking like this?' she demanded tragically.

'You must bathe your face with cold water.' Miss MacFarren spoke in a matter-of-fact voice but inwardly she was troubled, as she surveyed Antonia's woebegone reflection, to realize how much her anxiety had aged her. Without the radiance of her smile, which brought so much animation to her eyes, her face seemed full of sad little shadows, accentuated by the droop of her head. If she were deserted by her husband, the years her happy and confident love had held at bay would descend upon her like a withering frost, and in a night the tenuous façade of her youth might be laid waste. The childish mind behind a middle-aged mask would retain no vestige of attraction: once Joss was gone, she would never get him back.

Miss MacFarren forgot her house and all her grievances. She remembered how Antonia had rushed into Joss's arms the day she had first seen them together, and with what a beautiful and enveloping gesture he had bent his head to kiss her. Not for Mory's sake, but strangely, preposterously, to defend the happiness of Mrs. Bankes, she would, if she could manage it, prevail upon Maxine to relinquish her conquest, implore her out of her generosity to leave the marriage intact.

'When you've bathed your face,' she went on collectedly, 'lie down for half an hour with pads of wet cotton-wool over your eyes. I shall stay with you and make a list of the likely house agents and their addresses. And first I'll ring up and order a car to fetch you in an hour, because you'd better do it in comfort. Keep the car all day and don't come back until you've found what you need.'

'It's impossible!' Antonia protested, but she was already at the wash-basin dashing cold water on her eyelids. 'No one will let furnished flats or houses to people with children. Mrs. Jermyn has been trying like a mad thing to get one for us, and she couldn't.'

Being antipathetic to Mrs. Jermyn, Miss MacFarren could not repress a smile at this sidelight on her life with the little Bankeses.

'Though perhaps it was silly of her,' Antonia added, after a thoughtful silence, 'to admit there were any children. I don't suppose she really need have mentioned them at all.' Miss MacFarren felt a qualm for the unknown landlord of whom nothing could as yet be foretold with certainty except that he would prove unfortunate; but she held her peace, rationalizing that the Bankes children must be fiendish indeed if they were more destructive than their mother. So far did the necessity of victory override the scruples of honour that she had no hesitation in murmuring speculatively when Antonia had duly subsided on to the bed with pads of witch hazel on her eyes:

'They say some of the house agents' clerks keep all the good things up their sleeve for clients who make it worth their while. And hall porters in these big blocks of flats—they sometimes accept presents. . . . It's very wrong, of course, very annoying for those who can't afford that way of doing things: but the housing shortage has come to such a pass, people are driven to extremities. And in your case, when so much is at stake—'

'You seem to think Joss is in love with that stupid girl!' Antonia exclaimed, half-raising herself in a sudden spasm of injured pride. 'Just because she's throwing herself at his head! Joss has never looked at anyone but me for nearly eleven years—not unless they forced themselves on him. Maxine Albert isn't even attractive. She has a baby face. She'll be disgustingly fat when she's forty.'

'Keep still, Mrs. Bankes!' was all Miss MacFarren chose to reply to this rather touching outburst. 'Relax for half an hour! You have a very hard day's work before you.'

*   *   *

Soon after Mrs. Bankes had set out on her mission, presenting an appearance which, though less jaunty than usual, was proof of an exceptional resilience, there was a telephone call from her husband.

'Is that you, Miss MacFarren?' He seemed glad that it was she who had answered; lately he had behaved more than ever as if some close sympathy existed between them, 'I just felt I'd better find out how things are going along in Harberton Square. They were in pretty poor shape when I left.'

'All quiet now on the Westminster front,' she responded pleasantly. She wondered whether she ought to tell him that his wife had gone out to look for other quarters, but decided that this news had better be kept till there was something definite in prospect.

'I still don't understand what happened,' he said. 'Maxine had vanished when I got out into the street. I'm mystified, Miss MacFarren—mystified and mortified. I realize I owe you an apology, and I certainly must be in bad with Maxine after the names Tonia called her: but I can't imagine how the situation arose.'

As she offered no assistance, he stumbled on, diffidently groping: 'I know it isn't easy right now to give me explanations over the 'phone, but if you could only put me wise on one point . . . did Maxine really say anything resembling . . . ? I mean, did she actually make any remark that could possibly be construed . . . that is, was there any foundation at all . . . ?'

His voice ran down on the words like a mechanism that slowly whirrs into silence.

She felt keenly for him, but could venture no more than: 'I think they both gave each other a great deal of provocation.'

'I guess you've good reason for being cagey,' he pleaded, 'but couldn't you—as a friend—couldn't you give me a notion at least whether there was any basis for what Tonia seemed to be saying?'

'She seemed to be saying anything that came into her head.'

'Do you mean there was *no* basis?'

If any trace of relief were audible in his inflection—the relief of a man who finds he has been making too much of his problem— it was easily overwhelmed by disappointment. Miss MacFarren was far from desirous at this stage of encouraging his sentiment for Maxine, but there was no point in suppressing the truth that Maxine herself was probably only too disposed to reveal, and she said guardedly, 'I believe there was some basis. Maxine spoke as if she were attracted by you. I'd much rather not talk about it, Captain Bankes.' She tried to move the conversation on to a lighter plane. 'You must feel quite Byronic with two beautiful women quarrelling over you.'

'Byronic! That's the last thing I want to be. I hate to hurt anyone, Miss MacFarren, least of all Tonia. But there comes a moment when patience may give out. . . . Look, I have to talk to Maxine. Do you know where I can get hold of her?'

'She'll be about at the same times as usual, I suppose.'

'No, I mean away from the house.'

'I can't help you.'

'Must I take that literally or figuratively?'

'Both, I'm afraid.'

'You're not the one who's afraid,' he returned gloomily.

'Well, Miss MacFarren, I understand how it is. I don't want to make you uncomfortable.' And muttering on a reproachful note that he would be 'seeing her', he rang off, leaving her strangely uncomfortable all the same.

But despite the agitations of the morning, she sat down to work between lunch and tea-time with greater concentration than she had been able to achieve for months. The certainty that a crisis had arisen of so drastic a nature that even Mrs. Bankes must take it seriously released some tension of her nerves which had long made both writing and drawing a painful effort. She accomplished several paragraphs with a facility which provided an inspiring fore- taste of freedom regained, and by the time Pearson came in with

258 | DORIS LANGLEY MOORE

the tea-tray, had succeeded in relegating all domestic affairs to the
shadowy background of her thoughts.

It was very much to Pearson's credit that she had been content
to dispose of the morning excitements with a few terse comments
immediately after Mrs. Bankes's departure: and had not shown any
tendency to hover about, harping on the topic. Miss MacFarren
was framing some remark subtly suggestive of gratitude when she
found herself saying instead, with a look of apprehension:

'Two cups?'

'I can take one away, miss, if you want to go on working. Miss
Albert's come in. She rang up first to see if the coast was clear.
I didn't disturb you seeing you were so nicely in the vein, as Dr.
Wilmot calls it, but I thought you might like her to have a cup of
tea with you.'

'Oh yes!' Miss MacFarren, in one swift though reluctant
movement of the mind, dammed up a luxurious flow of ideas on
night-scented flowers. 'By all means, do ask her to join me!'

'She seems to be packing. I only hope Mrs. Bankes's insults
haven't driven her away.'

'I hope not indeed,' said Miss MacFarren, but inwardly she
acknowledged that many future troubles might be averted if
Maxine at this point ceased to be an inmate of the house. Sincerely
as she would be missed, useful as was the part she had undoubtedly
played, her presence now would be fraught with dangers enough to
outweigh its advantages. And as she poured out the tea and sliced
the cake, she wondered how she could put it to Maxine that she
would esteem it a favour if the fancy she had so explicitly taken to
Captain Bankes could be curbed. It was not an easy boon to ask.
Maxine was likely to be resentful of interference, and after all, she
had been given encouragement. Two attractive people had deliberately been thrown together. The moral guilt devolved upon herself,
Elinor MacFarren, that decadent character who might have done
better to remain a prig.

Maxine entered on tiptoe with her finger to her lips, and an
elaborate pretence of terror lest she should be overheard. 'I crept
in,' she whispered, 'while the girl bride was out of the way, to drop
a few things into a bag. I don't think I ought to sleep here tonight,
do you?'

'It's a shame that you should be put to this inconvenience,' said Miss MacFarren with a fair assumption of concern. 'I'm extremely sorry you were involved in that unexpected scene.'

'The scene was just what we needed, and it wasn't as unexpected as you think.' Dropping on to the hearthrug, she dabbled her spoon in her tea with a look of contentment. 'But I don't think I could face poor Yankee-Bankee for a day or two. I'm conscience-stricken about him after my goings-on this morning.'

'You were certainly blunt with Mrs. Bankes, but he will be flattered, no doubt—'

'That's what I'm afraid of. She's such a moron—shrieking that I was going to take him away from her!'

'You practically said so, you know.'

'Of course I said so. And it worked, didn't it? It frightened her almost into a fever. But hell! I can't go on keeping it up, not even to please you, Mory's aunt. You see, I honestly like the man.'

Miss MacFarren turned on her a face of such bewilderment that she burst into a laugh. 'Too much heart—that's my trouble. Stringing someone along is no fun to me. It's this damn better nature of mine.'

'Then you don't want Captain Bankes?'

'My God, what would I do with him? He'd never stop bringing me up the way I ought to go. Life with Father—that's what it would be. It's all right for child-wifie, but I'm getting to be a big girl now.'

'Strange,' said Miss MacFarren, abashed. 'I believed what you were saying.'

'Then I must be a better actress than Mr. Bloody Bamberger thinks. Do you know that mass producer of tripe kept me hanging round for an hour and then gave me a lecture on the mistake of wanting to be in pictures? And all the while his wife, if you please, Hedwig Kettner, who was an extra when he met her, was strolling round their suite at the Savoy dripping with emeralds, trying to decide which of fourteen fur coats she'd wear to go to lunch with a field-marshal. Christ, those dreary warnings successful people always give you when they think you're trying to break in on their racket!'

'That phase is over for you, I'm sure,' said Miss MacFarren with a cheerfulness that was both real and apparent.

'Do you feel it in your bones? I wish Master Mory did too.'

Miss MacFarren, keeping Mory's secret with praise-wor self-control, dared to enquire: 'Why him in particular?'

'I've always admired his style. I'd like to work with him,' Max rejoined simply.

There was one secret of Mory's which Miss MacFarren did now feel obliged to keep—which, on the contrary, it had beco almost a duty to reveal—and she said eagerly: 'Mory admires y too, and not only for your work.'

'What makes you think so?' The question was uttered with Maxine's characteristic languor of diction, but she paused to he the reply with her cup halfway to her lips.

'He said so—well, he all but said so. . . .'

'All but!' She put down her cup unfinished and lit a cigaret 'I'm not sure that it's a compliment to be admired by Geraldin boy friend.'

'You're always very severe on him about Geraldine.'

'Severe! Who wouldn't be, seeing him led round the town o chain by that she-wolf?'

Miss MacFarren perceived, with some surprise at her forn density, that Maxine's disgust at Mory's folly had not been wi out its content of a personal bitterness that closely resembl wounded *amour propre*.

She surrendered to the matchmaking impulse which gives rewarding a sense of power. 'Geraldine is done with now. If he h known you first, she never would have had any influence.'

'Why?' Maxine demanded challengingly.

He told me you had an irresistible appeal for men, some fasc ation no one could contend against.' She was aware that she w lending a somewhat romantic colour to Mory's frivolous expr sions of months before, but she had engaged herself now to ca her point, and was mastered by her own persuasiveness. 'I ask him why he hadn't fallen in love with you himself, and he said would have done, only he was involved with that woman before saw you.'

'You old procuress!' cried Maxine, her face lighting with a b liant and affectionate smile. 'Beguiling poor men indeed! Wl about beguiling poor girls and trying to entrap them for your nephew, who's quite able, let me tell you, to do his own seducing.'

'My intentions are honourable.'

'What about his? Mory never had an honourable intention in his life.'

'Oh, Maxine! And I brought him up!'

'Well, you haven't exactly got the Galahad touch. Personally I don't miss it.'

'I shall miss *you*!' Miss MacFarren heard herself declaring involuntarily. Suddenly she realized in full force the variety of ways in which Maxine's advent had been a blessing, how entertaining, how obliging, how altogether comforting, she had proved. She was stung with self-reproach for having so readily accepted, even secretly wished for, her proposed departure, and she added penitently:

'I do hope, when you talk of going to sleep somewhere else, that you have a place to go to.'

'I dare say I shall find a bed.'

'That sounds so forlorn, my dear. Why not change your mind and stay here after all?'

'No, it would only mean a showdown with Joss, which I'd hate. I'll be elusive for the next few days. But don't admit I've gone. We must never let up playing bogy-bogy with the Beautiful Zany till she's finally out of the house.'

'I shall owe it entirely to you,' said Miss MacFarren. 'Won't you let me at least try and get you a room in some hotel?'

'No thanks, duckie. I'm having dinner with Mory. He'll find me a bed.'

'Mory will?' Miss MacFarren repeated faintly.

'Yes, you know that's just the sort of way he likes to make himself useful.'

Miss MacFarren coughed with nervous emphasis. 'I don't think you should quite rely on Mory.'

'What do you bet?'

'My dear, I shouldn't like to feel that I was responsible for—for anything I shouldn't like to be responsible for. . . .'

'Aha, you're afraid your salesmanship was too good!' Maxine laughed with lively amusement. 'You think I can't wait to get my fascinating hands on Master Mory. As a matter of fact, it is going

to be rather delicious seeing him in all this new light you've bee[n]
shedding. Who can resist being called irresistible? Mory's aun[t]
with your gifts as a saleswoman, I can't think how you ever kept o[ut]
of Mrs. Warren's profession.'

Miss MacFarren stared into the fire with a dazed look. Wha[t]
ever course one took with Maxine, whether one allowed her to go [or]
pressed her to remain, it was liable to lead to consequences whic[h]
she felt had simply better not be dwelt upon. And all the tim[e]
presenting these facets from which one averted one's eyes, th[e]
rakish personality had some special warmth about it that made [it]
seem quite an endearment when she called one an old procures[s.]
Nevertheless, Mory's aunt hoped the impeachment, however so[ft]
was and would remain unmerited.

17

ANTONIA ARRIVED, conveniently, after Maxine had gone and whi[le]
Captain Bankes was still absent. Her return had been awaited wit[h]
curiosity but without anxiety. Miss MacFarren had the stron[g]
est faith in her capacity for getting what she wanted, and at lor[g]
last she had been compelled to want, with the full energy of h[er]
powerful ego, another roof. Her prospects of success were great[er]
than those of a normally responsible adult, for she could plea[d]
coax, worry, weep, offer untenable promises with as little restrai[n]
as an over-petted child. Harriet had exhorted her friend to mak[e]
Antonia grow up, but though there had been moments in whic[h]
Miss MacFarren had longed to achieve this miracle, close conta[ct]
had persuaded her that to remain immature was, for a case s[o]
incorrigible, a mode of self-preservation. The methods of a chi[ld]
had served her well, and it was too late for her to attempt with ar[y]
skill to be a woman.

She walked into the study precipitately without knockin[g]
and though her springy step flagged a little, she was wearing a[n]
engaging, even a cheerful, smile. Her whole demeanour suggeste[d]
the consciousness of having earned applause.

'I'm dead!' she exclaimed. 'Stone dead! I've never been so tire[d]
since I was born.' She flung herself as gracefully and familiarly in[to]

an armchair as if she had always been on the best of terms with its usual occupant. Indeed, her manner could not have been freer from any sign of grievance or more oblivious to the strained relations of the past weeks.

'What sort of day did you have?' Miss MacFarren asked solicitously. 'A difficult one, I'm sure.'

'Oh, I've walked through thousands of horrible-looking rooms that Joss wouldn't live in if you gave him a million pounds. Revolting furniture and dingy, beastly colours, and wallpaper peeling off the walls—I knew Joss would never put up with that sort of thing after living in this house!'

Miss MacFarren's head was bowed under coals of fire as she said at random: 'People haven't been able to have anything done up for years.'

'I went to three agents and saw all the furnished houses they could show me. Most of them still had people living in them who weren't going to move out for weeks, so that was no good anyway. The only one we could have got into right away was nothing but a Chamber of Horrors. If I make Joss move when he doesn't want to, it'll have to be a place he can like, don't you agree?'

Miss MacFarren nodded encouragingly, waiting for the happy ending which she was sure was indicated by so complacent a manner.

'At last, when I was nearly in despair, I noticed a board up outside a sort of mansion building saying *Flat to Let*, so I stopped the car—that car was a divine idea, Miss MacFarren—and I went in and spoke to the porter about it. And you can imagine how cross I was when he told me I'd have to apply to the agents, Something and Something miles away, and get an order to view. And then I remembered what you'd said about giving hall-porters presents and I took out a pound and asked him ever so sweetly, "Do let me look over it now! It'll save such a lot of trouble and I'm so weary!" So he melted and showed me over, and it was three dark little poky rooms. The porter told me himself they used to be servants' quarters for one of the big flats.'

'Oh!' Miss MacFarren responded blankly. She had expected quite another conclusion.

'But that's not the end. I asked him almost on my knees if he knew of anywhere else, and as I'd practically turned myself inside out to charm him—following your advice—he melted a little more and told me there was a most beautiful flat to be let furnished for a gentleman who was abroad, but nothing could be done till he'd had all his personal things moved into storage; and it was going to be twenty guineas a week.'

'Twenty guineas!' Her voice rose steeply in consternation. The Bankeses' weekly share of her own expenses was scarcely half this sum, and it would be a hollow victory for Antonia to have secured a flat if it turned out to cost more than her husband could afford.

'Oh, but wait till you hear of my plan! I handed him another pound—the last I had—and he took me to see the flat, and it was absolutely wonderful—lovely big rooms, and a view of the park, and a heavenly pair of those Minton oyster dishes that revolve. The furniture was a bit old-fashioned and stodgy, but it was awfully good quality, and one can do so much with flowers and one's own odds and ends.'

Miss MacFarren had suffered too poignantly from odds and ends to utter a verbal acquiescence, but she nodded again.

'So I said to the porter, "We must, *must* have this flat, and if we get it, I'll give you twenty pounds." I'll have to sell a ring or something,' she dropped her voice to say in hasty parenthesis. 'Then he promised not to breathe a syllable about it to anyone else—nobody knows about it yet, you see, because the owner only sent word about letting it this morning—and he gave me the address of the solicitors who are dealing with it, and I dived straight into the car and rushed off like a mad thing to their office right down in the city, and I got there just before five. At first they were rather annoyed with me for coming without an appointment, and Mr. Dorridge didn't want to see me. (Isn't that a funny name, Dorridge? It rhymes with porridge!) But I begged so hard, his secretary or clerk or whatever-it-is went and talked him round. And he did see me, and I spoke in an American accent because after all I'm an American citizen.'

Miss MacFarren looked so astounded that she elucidated with a giggle which showed how successfully the adventures of the afternoon had divorced her mind from the morning's miseries: 'People like to let flats to Americans; they're supposed to be rich. I told him about Joss being over here as London correspondent, and how we didn't want to live in a hotel, and all the whole rigmarole, you know—'

This time Miss MacFarren's nod was accompanied by a barely stifled sigh. 'The whole rigmarole' was painfully clear in her remembrance . . . the quiet couple . . . the domesticated woman so fond of lovely things, so responsively eager to enter into all the conditions. She could picture the solicitor's gratification at his client's luck in finding such a tenant.

'So he asked for references,' Antonia went on, 'and I gave him the ones I gave you, and then he said: "It's usual to have a landlord's reference, but I don't suppose you can supply that as you're not residents?" And I didn't like to mention you, Miss MacFarren, because I know I sometimes make you nervy'—she spoke with a delicate sympathy, as if this nerviness were a mysterious ailment— 'so I said, wouldn't it be good enough to have a letter from the American Embassy, because Joss has friends there: and he seemed quite pleased with that. And then I came to the difficult part, about getting in the week after next, and I suggested that, if the owner couldn't get his things fetched at once, he might leave them for the time being and we'd be madly careful of them, and perhaps he could have them taken away later. And he said if the references were in order, he'd send a cable and see what could be arranged. You could tell he'd made up his mind to help us, so I feel absolutely all right about it.'

Miss MacFarren tried to thrust the fate of the owner's valuables aside as no affair of hers, though the thought preyed on her mind: 'If she has treated my things so badly when I am on the spot to complain, what will she do with this poor man's possessions in his absence?' The most pressing consideration, however, was whether the rent would not prove beyond Captain Bankes's means, and she said gravely:

'But twenty guineas a week, Mrs. Bankes!'

'I told you I had a glorious plan about that. You see, Joss's mother is arriving in May, and if she comes to stay with us, she can pay half the expenses, and she'll be able to look after the children. She'll love that.'

'Will she?' Miss MacFarren feebly rejoined.

'Oh yes, she practically brought them up, you know. She adores doing everything for them. And ten guineas a week will be less than she'd pay in a good hotel.'

'Hotels provide service and regular meals,' her native sense of the value of money, combined with her painful experience of Antonia's housekeeping, obliged her to point out.

'Mamma Bankes will be so glad to be with Joss, things like that won't worry her a bit.' Antonia had never spoken more airily. 'Besides, she's such a good housekeeper, and a good cook too, she'll probably prefer to do it all herself. It'll be wonderful for her having Joss *and* the children to look after at one fell swoop. I never interfere with her, you know. I let her do everything her own way. That's why we almost never quarrel.'

Miss MacFarren retracted her thoughts from the burdens to be laid upon the shoulders of Mrs. Bankes's mother-in-law. It was not for her to concern herself with the ordeals of victims she had never seen.

'Captain Bankes may object to such a high rent all the same,' she said, not so much to discourage Antonia as to reassure herself, to be convinced that the prospect of release was not too good to be true.

'He expects to pay more, lots more, when we have the children with us,' Antonia argued sagely. 'And it's such a lovely big flat. When Mamma Bankes has gone home, we can let off a room to visiting Americans and charge masses of money for it.'

'There may be something in the agreement against that.'

'But Dr. Wilmot's going to be abroad, so he'll never know anything about it.'

'Dr. Wilmot!' Miss MacFarren had the sensation of growing pale. 'Where is this flat?'

'King Charles Mansions . . . Oh, good heavens, what am I thinking of? The man's waiting outside to be paid—the man with the hired car. Could you let me have the money for him? I spent my last two pounds on the hall-porter. Seven hours at twelve-and-six an hour. But it was worth it, don't you think? Ought I to give him a tip?' Miss MacFarren, with a stupefaction so complete that it produced no external reaction of any kind, went to the lobby to fetch her bag and handed over five pound notes in the manner of an automaton.

As she returned alone to her study, Pearson tapped on the door, causing her to start as guiltily as if Antonia had already used a sheaf of Dr. Wilmot's French prints to light the fire.

'You haven't read the Doctor's news, miss.' She presented a letter on a salver, with a look of carefully non-committal expectation.

'Did it come by the afternoon post?'

'Yes, and one for me too, miss. Air-mail, you see. I won't say you could knock me down with a feather, because Dr. Wilmot's a very impulsive gentleman at times, but I'll put it this way—I'm surprised.' A very slight sniff indicated that the surprise was not altogether to her liking.

'Don't go, Pearson!' she commanded, partly in response to an evident desire to see what she made of the letter, and partly because she was sensible that the maid's presence would enable her to avoid immediately resuming the discussion with Antonia which had reached, as far as she was concerned, so fatal an impasse. And with a hand that fairly trembled from the shock of her dashed hopes, she spread out the page decorated with Dr. Wilmot's shapely handwriting:

My Dear Miss MacFarren,

By a side wind blown from this Conference I have been offered the Desherbes Professorship at the Sorbonne, and seeing that my own university seems only too pleased to get Dr. Alphonse Lunet in exchange, I have accepted and shall start in the summer term; which leaves me no time to return to England first. As you'd know if you were enlightened enough to read the *British Journal of Semantics*, the appointment only lasts a year, and no doubt I shall be appearing in London from time to time, but I can't afford to keep my flat unoccupied and have asked my solicitors to let it for me (at a rent which will compensate me in advance for all the damage the tenant is certain to leave).

This letter is to ask you whether you would allow Pearson to go and pack up my clothes and chief treasures, of which I am sending her a list, so that they can be dealt with according to instructions. If she should need any help with the botanical items, yours would be most gratefully appreciated. You are the only rival I could completely trust on such a mission.

As to Pearson herself, there can be of course no question of her permanently leaving my service after twenty-two years, and I have written to tell her so. But I see little prospect of having her with me in Paris. She seems happy with you and will be happier when you are no longer encumbered. I have therefore urged her to remain for the time being if you can keep her. If not, I have named a colleague who will be delighted to hear from her.

I look forward to seeing you on my first visit to London, and hope you will give me the pleasure of dining with me. Las Palmas has proved an unexpectedly fruitful field, and if it were possible for you to feel envy—which I know to be foreign to your nature—I should say you would envy the acquisitions I have picked up here for less than a song. It grieves me, for example, to think of the high price you paid for Mrs. Champney's *Floral Repository*. I found on a book-stall here a charming copy inscribed by the author, which I bought, by a little dexterous bargaining, for the equivalent of fifteen shillings. If I remember rightly you paid as many guineas at Hodgson's *without* the inscription. And am I wrong in imagining that your copy was weak at the joints?

Yours with cordial greetings,

ALOYSIUS WILMOT.

She put down the letter and pushed it indignantly away from her. Then her exasperation at the gloating taunt—so tasteless and so typical—dissolved in the welcome hope of being able to stave off for a year her dreaded parting from the most congenial of servants. Glimmering through oppressive shadows, that ray of comfort made itself felt.

'Oh, Pearson,' she said, 'I do so very much want you to stay!'

Pearson looked pleased only for a fleeting instant. Then her face assumed its buttoned-up expression. 'I don't say but what I'd stay for your sake, miss. The Doctor's got a right to do what he thinks fit, I suppose, though Paris at his age seems to be going what I'd call a bit too far. But since he intends to let the flat to strangers, and there's no stopping him once he's made his mind up, I'd just as soon be here as anywhere else. The question is this—has that Mrs. Bankes found somewhere else to go or not? If not, I'm afraid I must make other arrangements. She's more than I can bear and that's a fact.'

Miss MacFarren could have groaned aloud to contemplate the cruelty of her dilemma. She had only to hold her peace for a few days. Captain Bankes's references would be in perfect order, and the solicitor would certainly be prevailed upon to speed up the formalities for the sake of candidates so desirable, particularly as Dr. Wilmot's own maid would be available to remove his more private belongings. It would be easy to stop Antonia from describing her future abode in front of Pearson, with whom she was by no means on conversational terms. Under favouring conditions months might pass before the Doctor realized his tenants' identity. The name of Bankes would convey no warning, for it had probably never been fixed in his mind. For him Antonia had been an entirely off-stage character referred to as 'that woman'; Joss had never been discussed at all. The rent he was asking would, on his own show-ing, cover all the damage that even the Bankes ménage was likely to inflict. Besides, most of the furniture was nondescript or even ugly, and he himself had no affection for it.

She had but to keep quiet and her home in a week or two would be her own again. If on the other hand she did as honour demanded, she would lose a servant of pre-1914 quality: Mrs. Bankes would perhaps have to be worked up all over again to make such another effort as she had made today, and there was no guarantee that it would produce any acceptable results: complications might ensue between Joss and Maxine, between Joss and Mory, indeed between any two people out of several who were, one way and another, affected. She herself was nearly at the end of her tether, and a small annoyance might now precipitate the scene she had striven so hard to avert—the scene in which Joss would learn, with astonishment equalled only by his unbounded embarrassment, that she had been trying to get rid of them for months. She had always tremendously wanted to part from him on agreeable terms, and here, in a situa-tion growing daily more precarious, might be her last chance.

And Dr. Wilmot was a sneering rival who never missed an opportunity of pointing out the defects in her treasures. It would serve him right if his rosewood dining-table were scratched. . . .

She held her breath, brought to her senses by the shock of finding that her mind was capable of framing so base a thought. To harbour it for a moment would be to admit total demoralization. And he had said he trusted her! She acted instantly:

'Pearson, an appalling thing has happened. Mrs. Bankes has practically taken the flat at King Charles Mansions.'

'The Doctor's flat? Never!' cried Pearson as eloquently as the words could be uttered.

'It's the strangest, most unfortunate thing that could be imagined. It must be stopped immediately, of course. . . . I'm trying to make up my mind what step I ought to take.'

'Well, this time you *could* knock me down with a feather!' Pearson looked as if she rather wished someone would try the feat so that she might enjoy the relaxation of dropping gently to the floor. 'However in the world did she get to hear the flat was going?'

Walking up and down a narrow strip of carpet, clasping and unclasping her usually reposeful hands, Miss MacFarren told Antonia's story, relieved to have launched for better or for worse upon the course compatible with integrity, and grateful for the listener's quick recognition of the issues.

'My goodness me! You are between the devil and the deep sea and no mistake,' Pearson finally summed up after responding with a series of commiserative noises. 'It's a real sacrifice for you when you could shunt her quietly off on Dr. Wilmot and him not a penny the wiser. But mind you, I think the Doctor will appreciate what you're doing. He's selfish in little things but in big ones you'll always find him a gentleman.'

Even in her agitation Miss MacFarren paused to weigh sceptically the position of collecting in the Doctor's scheme of affairs. No such thoughts, however, appeared on her face as she enquired: 'Do you think I ought to cable him at Las Palmas or would it be better to write to his solicitors?'

'He'll be in Paris by now, miss. He was flying there, according to the letter I had from him. Flying to Paris at his age!' She pretended scorn but obviously felt pride.

'What next, I wonder?'

'If he's given you his address, I can write him at once. That would be far better than cabling.'

'Yes, I've got his letter here, miss, with all the lists and directions about what he wants done with his things.' Diving into her apron pocket, she produced a pair of glasses and an envelope with several enclosures. 'A nice job it's going to be too, packing up all that stuff! I dare say he thinks it'll take two or three hours, but it's two or three days more likely. Oh, there's a bit that concerns you, miss. I was going to tell you.' She cleared her throat and, peering through her glasses, read slowly, in a detached and official manner:

> 'To go into store, all the books in the lower half of the big bookcase, except those which Miss MacFarren might like to keep on her own shelves—particularly, the herbals in vellum cases; she will know which. No one is to handle these but her.'

Miss MacFarren, being overwrought, found her eyes filling with tears, and it was with difficulty that she copied the Doctor's Paris address from the page held out to her. The tendency to literal-mindedness which had perhaps been the basis of her skill as a botanical artist was deflected by a kindness so unlooked for coming at such a moment, and she was inclined to see the herbals as a symbol. Everything had gone wrong since she had parted with them; everything would go right when they were restored.

In the fullness of her heart, her letter to Dr. Wilmot was lengthened by a paragraph that an hour before had been undreamed of:

> 'I am so glad to know you will not be abroad a year without visiting England. Why not let Pearson bring some of your clothes here, and use this house as your *pied-à-terre*? When the Bankeses have gone—and go they must and shall however it is to be managed!—the room I am now occupying could easily be prepared for your visits. To make it more homely for you, I could keep your portfolios of prints here if you were disposed to entrust them to me. They would thus be more accessible to you and would receive from me the care they will never get in a warehouse. Do please, dear Dr.

Wilmot, take this suggestion seriously. It would give me great pleasure to house the owner as well as the herbals.'

Pure gratitude and friendliness had dictated this offer, but it produced an effect that might have been planned by self-interest. On hearing that so very eligible an invitation had been extended (for Miss MacFarren deemed it tactful to keep the maid informed of everything that related to a master she looked on as her personal property), Pearson decided that she would not, after all, make the 'other arrangements' she had threatened. She would wait, she said, and see how things worked out.

Miss MacFarren called her back as she was leaving the house to take the letter to the post, and wrote across the flap of the envelope: 'My copy of the *Floral Repository* is the one that belonged to Charles Darwin. It is not at all weak at the joints.' Gratitude was all very well, but there was nothing estimable in lying down to be trampled on.

*   *   *

It had come as an agreeable surprise that she had been able to write her substantial letter at leisure without any interruption from Mrs. Bankes, who might have been expected to continue at the earliest moment her unfinished conversation. Captain Bankes, she decided, must have come home during her talk with Pearson, and his wife had probably not lost an instant in laying the great project of removal before him. She could not but feel treacherous to both when she considered how she had been occupied. Poor Antonia, glorying in her achievement, which was really remarkable in its way, of having found and as good as secured an excellent flat within seven hours! Troublesome as she was, there was something genuinely disarming in her unguardedness, her total freedom from bitterness, her unquestioning confidence that those she dealt with would be ready to forgive and forget offences. These were the qualities in which she was childlike rather than childish, the lovable aspects of her character—lovable, that is, to one who could begin by liking her.

But it was useless to sit regretting that one had been obliged to frustrate her when the question was still unsolved, what was the next move? Days would be lost—possibly as much as a week—if she waited till Dr. Wilmot acted from Paris and his solicitors informed the applicants that the flat was not available. In what terms could she break it to Antonia at once that her search, which she supposed triumphantly ended, must begin again tomorrow? Could she confess that she had written a warning to Dr. Wilmot? And what could be said to Captain Bankes, who by now would have been told all about the beautiful apartment where his mother and his children would be united?

For the second time that evening, she started at the sound of someone knocking for admission. Maxine never knocked, Pearson tapped discreetly, Antonia beat a light facetious tattoo; only Captain Bankes had knuckles strong enough for a loud double rap like a postman. She braced herself to call 'Come in!'

He closed the door behind him quietly and carefully, with a gravity of aspect that increased the tension of her nerves.

'Miss MacFarren, I trust I'm not disturbing you?'

'Not in the least. Won't you sit down, Captain Bankes?'

'I guess I'd rather move about, if it doesn't bother you.' He walked to the french window and stood in silhouette against the evening light, his shoulders and long limbs forming an almost too assertively masculine pattern among the feminine graces of her draped curtains.

'Have you had dinner, Miss MacFarren?' he asked considerately.

'No, Pearson will be bringing me a tray.'

'I won't take up too much of your time then.' He gazed out into the little garden. 'My, you've made it pretty here. I shall be sorry to go. I liked this house.'

Unequal to an answer, she was silent.

'For you, it'll be a relief. . . . I can understand that. I blame myself a lot.'

'Oh, no,' she protested earnestly, 'no, you have only behaved like a man. . . . Men are obtuse in some things. I've often said so. But'—despite herself her words and voice were emotional—'I've always been very fond of you, Captain Bankes.'

He turned his face towards her, and though she could not see his eyes, she knew their kindly, their affectionate regard.

'I realized from the start, Miss MacFarren, it was a privilege to know you.'

She was amused at her own discomfiture. How could she tell him after such an interchange that she had already thwarted his wife's plan? And yet it would be wrong to leave him under a misapprehension. Gripping the arms of her chair, she began: 'I hope you won't think I've been officious. A situation has arisen that really is, for me, a moral problem—'

'For me too,' he broke in with unusual vehemence. 'You don't suppose, for goodness' sake, I drifted into this without any kind of a struggle?' He pulled himself up, weighed his words conscientiously, and resumed: 'Well, that's not quite accurate either. The fact is I was taking the count before I knew what had hit me. Miss MacFarren, that girl's lethal. She knocked me stone cold.'

She could not help smiling to see how absurdly they had been talking at cross-purposes. There was nothing for it but to let him say his say, as in any case he was bent on doing.

'I didn't want to start up any trouble for you. I didn't want to start up trouble for myself if it comes to that. I'm a happily married man, Miss MacFarren,' he insisted as if she were contradicting him. 'At least, I was until this tornado struck me. Now I've got a kind of hunch it isn't ever going to be the same again. No, not ever any more,' he added with full dramatic solemnity. 'It's a funny thing, I always knew deep down inside me this house had a sort of destiny for me. Hell, I'm talking in clichés!' He moved away from the window to the work-table and, picking up a box of water colours, examined it minutely. 'That's because I've been acting in clichés all day . . . doing the square thing, fighting the good fight, setting my house in order. Do you know, sacrifice makes a living cliché out of a man. That's what I've become. That's what I shall be for a long, long time.'

'What have you decided to do?' she asked, bewildered. The affair of Dr. Wilmot's flat had so filled her mind that she had lost the thread of Captain Bankes's personal difficulties.

'I have decided,' he drawled with frankly elaborate casualness, holding one of the paintbrushes up to the light, 'to leave for the States with my wife and family next Tuesday.'

Her heart leapt so that she found it hard to speak steadily.

'Captain Bankes, what an announcement! How can you, when you've only just taken the appointment in London?'

'It's all fixed.'

'You can't mean it!' She knew he did mean it, and her face flushed from the effort of concealing her joy.

'Of course, you must have a month's rent and all that in lieu of notice,' he dropped in rapidly and without expression, averting his thoughts, it seemed, from the offensively prosaic words.

'There's no need for that at all.' She was wondering if it could be possible that he had not yet been told how Antonia had spent the day. 'But how have you been able to arrange such a drastic step?'

'That was the easiest part of the business.' He took up a position opposite her armchair, leaning against the mantelpiece, and she found herself disloyally astonished that Maxine, who had so appreciated his beautiful physique, could have preferred Mory.

'My editor had a fifty-dollar bet with me I wouldn't hold down a routine job three months. My cable this afternoon must have handed him a rich laugh. I've lasted three weeks.'

'Surely you've not resigned from your post?' she cried dismally.

'No, no! I haven't lost my mind. Not absolutely.' He shook his head with a wan smile. 'May I smoke?'

His wide brow, strong cheekbones, and high-bridged nose glowed in the flickering light of his match, and she smiled too, reminded of the camp fire, the pipe of peace, all the adventure book panoply that had given him so picturesque and so irrational a charm for her.

'I imagine American journalism may be one of the few subjects you don't know a thing about, Miss MacFarren.' He blew a cloud of smoke in so attentive and interested a fashion that it might have been his first cigarette. 'Briefly, I wrote a feature which was syndicated by the *Washington Recorder*.'

'Yes, of course. A very famous feature, I know that much.'

'I used to go here, there, and everywhere covering assignments generally of a rather tough type; every kind of commotion, civil and uncivil; anything sensational from a prize fight to an armed riot. Well, when a man gets to be thirty-five, he's liable to grow tired of stepping in and out of specially chartered planes and being wakened up in the night and whipped off to the scene of some unseemly event. He hankers for a quiet life. So, as you're only too well aware, I elected to be London correspondent. My editor was not exactly over-joyed, but I talked him into it. A few days ago he cabled that readers were getting grouchy about my sedate London letter. They consider my turn for describing the aberrations of nature, human and other-wise, is wasted in trying to forecast how Britons will react to the proposed nationalization of this or that, and whether Londoners will go back to wearing evening dress at Covent Garden, and what draws the longest queues of women to the shops. My public, which has quite a vivid way of expressing itself, wants me to remain in my natural element of murder and rapine. I cabled back "Let them gripe!" knowing I was doing my job efficiently here, and that, given time, they'd get used to the change. But today, after I spoke to you on the 'phone about Maxine, I went away and had lunch by myself and thought it all over pro and con, and in short, the whole thing's tied up. I'm getting back into my old harness.'

'I think, if Maxine affects you as you say, you've made a wise decision,' she responded, after a pretence of pausing for reflection.

'It isn't what I feel about her that clinched the deal,' he said, stroking one of the blue china cats with frowning tenderness, 'though that's not irrelevant. It's what she feels about me.'

'Yes of course,' she agreed, remembering a little apologetically Maxine's *cri de coeur*. 'My God, what would I do with him?'

'Being in love with her I might have put up some kind of fight against it. I only had to get my second wind. But if she's in love with me, there's nothing for it but to take to flight.'

'In love with you!' She glanced up at him, doubting her ears.

'It sounds kind of conceited, just stated baldly that way, but I'm only going by what you told me.' His gentle reproach was not without anxiety lest he should have blundered. 'I didn't believe it from Tonia. Even when she said it in front of Maxine, I could hardly credit it. But when I had *your* word for it, I knew it was time to beat it. A man has to realize when he's licked.'

Miss MacFarren's brain reeled. She had completely forgotten the phrase she had used in answering his question on the tele-phone—had all but forgotten that she had talked to him at all since the morning's scene—but now it was recalled to her that she had certainly, in her own delusion, said something deluding.

Was it worth while to set him right? Since, despite the intensification of his problems, he must be pleased and flattered to believe his feelings reciprocated, since his plans for departure were definitely made and it could not but disappoint him to find they had been made on a false premise, would it not be kinder and more sensible to leave him to his error? Maxine had gone: she had spoken of 'a few days' but it was unlikely that she would sleep under that roof again while Mrs. Bankes did so. No further temptations would be offered to Captain Bankes. He could leave the country in the heartening, the almost happy conviction, that he had honourably, self-sacrificingly turned his back on an alluring woman who had desired him. To enlighten him at this stage would be cruel, pointless, and inexpedient.

'Yes, I think,' she repeated firmly, 'you're very wise to go, when so much is at stake. Does your wife know—?'

'Oh no, no! It's just the fear of hurting her that I'm running away from.'

'I mean, does she know you've arranged to leave England?'

'That, yes. I naturally told her the minute I entered the house.' He sucked in his cheeks with a look of intimate self-communion. 'I was determined not to go back to where I left off this morning, so I came in primed to create a diversion. Not that it's Tonia's disposition to let anything rankle. I've never known anyone whose temper blew over so quickly as a general rule, but this time—maybe I felt a twinge of guilt, and I took it more seriously.'

Miss MacFarren had it on the tip of her tongue that he too was exceptionally forgiving, bearing so little grudge for the outburst which had sent him out in high anger, but she suppressed the comment, telling herself that it must be easy for a man to pardon the jealousy that sprang from an uncontrolled affection for himself. Instead she asked curiously:

'How did she take it?'

'At first she just wouldn't take it. She'd been hatching a gorgeous plot of her own for spiriting me away to some big apartment full of oyster dishes.' He laughed, indulgently understanding yet with a feint trace of irritation. 'But when she realized we'd be flying, and in less than a week, all other ideas fell to the ground with a resounding crash. You see, she's never done the trans-atlantic crossing by air before. Tonia loves new experiences. She's at her best when there's plenty of change and excitement.'

'I know.'

'She'll quickly forget this little episode here—if you can call it an episode,' he said sombrely. 'But I shan't forget, not in a long while.' He dropped his cigarette into the fire with a conclusive gesture. 'Now that you can trust me not to make any complications, please will you let me see Maxine?'

'What! Do you think I've concealed her?' She spoke with easy pleasantry but avoided his eye.

'I feel pretty sure you've smuggled her out of the house because the situation was getting out of hand. It isn't out of hand any more. Where can I see her?'

Miss MacFarren slowly shook her head, appealing to her conscience to be lenient with her. 'She smuggled herself out, Captain Bankes. I dare say she felt she couldn't trust herself to see you after all the revelations of this morning.'

'Did she tell you so?'

'Yes.'

'I have to see her, Miss MacFarren. I have to explain myself just once.'

'Don't build good resolutions with one hand and destroy them with the other. In any case, I don't as yet know where she's gone.'

'Is that true?'

'Yes,' she said again. Her lowered eyes fell on her watch and she saw that this was the hour for Maxine to keep her appointment with Mory.

'When you hear where she is—because of course you will hear— will you ask her if she'll let me say goodbye?'

'If you wish to make things more difficult for yourself.'

'Maybe I do too. Maybe I've a kind of cussedness that wants to make things more difficult for both of us.'

'That's not like you.'

'I can't stop myself being human—though God knows I'm having a good try.' He stared into the haughty eyes of the Chinese cat. 'I'm going to miss that silly little face of hers so much, and the only consolation I ask is to hear there's something she might miss about me.'

There was no alternative now but to throw oneself on Maxine's mercy not to disillusion him. If she was a good enough actress to play a nun in Mory's next picture, she could take in her stride one sentimental scene with Captain Bankes. It must be asked of her as a last kindness. A strange kindness indeed for Elinor MacFarren to require! Celibate ladies in their fifties really shouldn't be mixed up in this sort of thing. Smug or cured of smugness, they were liable to blunder.

Yet, looking back, she couldn't see how she could have acted differently. And everything had worked out for the best. Everything except, perhaps, the fundamental happiness of Captain Bankes's marriage; but he was such a very kind man, his wife would probably never be allowed to know the difference.

Such a very kind man and so splendidly built, exactly like the Argyll and Sutherland Highlander with whom she had exchanged those heart-warming kisses thirty years ago. What had Mrs. Bankes said?—that she had 'a thing' about him. It was absurdly untrue of course. She had been spared the misery of hankering after young men. Her life had been full: her work and her family had sufficed her. Not only was her regard for Captain Bankes no more than friendly, but the circumstances in which she had known him were so distasteful that she was glad he was going away. But she was glad too that she had told him she was fond of him.

18

EVEN AMONG the moors, the hills, the sea spaces of the Hebrides, Miss MacFarren had never experienced so wonderful a sense of freedom as she found in her own house when from the sitting-room window, she had waved the final goodbye to Mrs. Bankes—Mrs. Bankes who had actually blown kisses as the car that was conducting her to the airport blessedly made its way from Harberton Square.

She had turned from the front door with a feeling of relief so boundless that it seemed to cry out for physical expression. If she had been younger and less solid, she would have danced, would have run from room to room shouting and singing. As it was, she set out in silence and at an even pace, but with a step that seemed wonderfully light and elastic, to inspect her domain, her castle, her kingdom, the territory over which she had waged and won the battle that would be historic in the annals of fifty years.

She surveyed a battlefield not without grievous scars, and the sight of some of them, even in this day of triumph, brought deep frowns to her brow. The satin-topped chess table embroidered by her grandmother was stained with coffee: it was doubtful if the most expert treatment would restore it. There were cigarette burns along the edge of the carved mantelpiece. The cushions, from frequent use as bed-pillows, were now so shabby that they would need new covers, and such brocade could never be procured again. The inkstain on the hall carpet had defied all the efforts of the Spik-span service. There would be much cleaning, much renovating to be done, many replacements to be made before the feckless shade of Mrs. Bankes would cease to haunt the scene she had so disastrously dominated.

But still, when every injury had been assessed even to the chipped crockery and the damaged linen, the joy of being sole mistress of her own realm after seven months in durance remained one of the most exhilarating sensations of her life.

Upstairs and down she wandered, throwing open drawers and cupboards in the rooms that had belonged to Mrs. Bankes for the mere pleasure of proving to herself that she could now do as she liked there; unable to apply herself to any useful task, yet pleasingly conscious of the energy with which very soon she would devote her whole being to the business of rehabilitation, and above all to the completion of her great work—which could be lovingly embraced now rather than wrestled with—*The History of Floriculture*.

On her desk lay an encouraging document, a letter from the New Aldine Press proposing definite and highly acceptable terms for the American edition of her last book, and offering, which was unforeseen, a contract for the new one. With her income thus to be augmented from the source the most thoroughly comforting to her self-respect, she had been able to decline, with all possible gratitude, Mory's proffered attempt to get her into the film business. If money ran out before the advance from the New York publishers arrived, she would accept his offer to lend her what was necessary to keep the house going; for she felt on reflection that he owed her something.

Directly or indirectly, she had been responsible both for Maxine's exertions in checking the mercenary designs of Geraldine's husband, and for creating an atmosphere, through some elements she herself could scarcely define—though she knew that the presence of Joss Bankes had formed a vital part of it—propitious to the realization of their attachment. Now they were obviously going to be lovers: she liked to think they might even get married. Maxine would after all be a much more interesting wife for Mory than the nice ordinary girl whom, in her smug days, she had hoped he would choose.

For all the tribulations she had been through, everything in the end had worked out in the most wonderful way. There was the invaluable Pearson already hard at work removing the traces of the Bankes visitation, her presence the outcome of a phase in the struggle. And there were the herbals waiting to be put back on her shelves tomorrow: it was unlikely that she would ever have become sufficiently intimate with Dr. Wilmot for so handsome an offer to be made if it had not been for the various small events, the result of her domestic difficulties, which had brought her into a closer contact with him than had once seemed conceivable. Of course, he had only lent her the herbals for his year abroad, but much might happen in that time. In this superb flow of high spirits, a year was a long and pleasant vista at the end of which all sorts of favourable turns lay unforeseen.

She stood in cheerful reverie at the door of her bedroom, not the top room, which would now become a *pied-à-terre* for Dr. Wilmot, but her old bedroom, in which, as soon as Pearson had turned it out, she was going to be reinstated. No whisky bottle had ever lurked in her wardrobe there, and she hoped that none was ever likely to . . . though, in her resolution to eschew every trace of priggishness, she would not deny the value of that midnight solace when Mrs. Bankes and her chorus of girl friends had raised a barrier of thorns between herself and sleep.

From tomorrow she would be able to resume her old routine, and yet she believed her horizons would be wider than they had been before. They would stretch at least to the Red Indians on the one side, and the vocabulary of Maxine Albert on the other.

'Can I give you any help?' she asked, in the comfortable knowledge that Pearson, who always preferred to work single-handed, would reject the offer.

'No thank you, miss. She's left a lot of clearing up to be done, but it might have been worse.'

'It was beautifully spring-cleaned by the Spikspan firm just before you came,' said Miss MacFarren, with an inward motion of recognition to Harriet, 'so the dirt won't be deep-seated.'

'No, but look at all this rubbish!' Pearson indicated a pile of crumpled wrapping papers, dog-eared magazines, and discarded items of the feminine toilet, from a worn-out powder-puff to a broken scent-bottle. 'Why couldn't she clear it out herself, I'd like to know? She was supposed to leave the place as she found it, wasn't she?'

'I think we must be grateful that she got off at all. There was a stage when I was afraid she never would. And then, what a blessing that we managed to get rid of all the other—I was going to say junk, but I dare say that's putting it rather harshly.'

She was referring to the fruits of Mrs. Bankes's numerous shopping excursions, which, under the stress of preparations for so hurried a departure, had become a mere nuisance to their owner. Her husband having declined emphatically to cope with the problem of their packing and transport, she had, half-magnanimous, half-imploring, offered them to Miss MacFarren as compensation for breakages and other damage; most of which had been concealed from Captain Bankes not less assiduously and far more successfully than from his landlady. Since there were few of these ill-assorted objects that were not themselves broken or damaged, the proposal had proved extremely disconcerting.

But in a moment of happy resourcefulness, it had occurred to her to suggest that Mrs. Bankes should bestow these treasures as keepsakes on her friends and acquaintances, leaving only the extra bed in the spare room, the chandelier that had never been unpacked from its crate, the gilt grottoes, and one or two other large pieces which Miss MacFarren might in some measure recompense herself by selling.

Mrs. Bankes, who delighted in giving presents, had entered into this idea with eagerness, and at a farewell party on their last night there had been a grand distribution of prizes. Mollified by the knowledge that she was going for good, several of her first batch of friends, who had fallen away weeks or months ago, had returned to bid her goodbye; and Miss MacFarren, who was one of the guests, saw Mrs. Reece receive the slightly battered St. Francis in his shrine, and Froggie the Georgian glove box which had lost its hinges, while Miss Hall-Brown was awarded the foxed Boucher prints in their somewhat unsightly frames and the Bohemian decanter, for which as yet no stopper had been found.

Mrs. Jermyn had not been able to attend, being fully occupied in getting the Bankes children ready for their impending journey—those mystified little girls of whom it could only be hoped that they loved change and excitement as much as their mother—and it was agreed that when Joss drove down to Oxford early next morning to fetch them, he was to take their kind hostess the two love-birds in the cage.

Miss MacFarren had spent much of the evening rather morbidly wondering who was to get the oil-painting of the wedding group, and when, by the time the guests thinned down to a handful, it had not been assigned, she was in considerable fear lest it should be left on her hands. She was asking herself whether the frame could be made to serve any purpose if the canvas was removed, when Mrs. Bankes had approached with a glowing smile and, pointing to the picture, whispered:

'I couldn't give away that celestial object to anyone who knows Penny, seeing it was a present from her, but Joss refuses to take it to America, and so I wonder if you'd be very, very kind and see that Mrs. Greenway gets it.'

'Harriet!' Miss MacFarren had at first recoiled palpably on her friend's behalf.

'Yes, I invited her to the party, but you see she hasn't turned up. I believe I must have made her cross somehow or other—but all the same I should like her to have a keepsake. She was always so nice to me. Of course, I know it's not a beautiful antique like she goes in for, but it's divine in its way, don't you think?'

After the initial shock, Miss MacFarren had derived a certain pleasure, not quite devoid of malice, from the idea of Harriet as the recipient of this parting gift, and she had undertaken graciously to deliver it.

'Now,' she said to Pearson, 'we'll be able to get those crates taken away that have been cluttering up the basement passage. And talking of the basement, we must get in a pestologist, or whatever they're called, to deal with the mice and the black beetles.'

'They're not so bad now, miss. I've been putting down traps and beetle powder every night.'

'I know you've worked wonders, Pearson, but we might as well be on the safe side. I don't think I want *any* relics of Mrs. Bankes, least of all those.'

'Talking of relics—though it's not the same sort of thing by a long way, I admit—I suppose you've noticed the birds are still there?'

'Yes, isn't it tiresome? Captain Bankes must have forgotten to take them. I do hope Mrs. Jermyn's husband will fetch them.'

'No, miss, I ought to have told you, but we've been in such a bustle. The lady rang up first thing this morning—the minute I came downstairs it was, and asked me to give Captain Bankes a message that she really couldn't do with the birds. She said there was too many cats in the house, and they've already got such a lot of pets to look after. When Mrs. Bankes heard, she said you could take them back to the pet shop or do anything you liked with them.'

Miss MacFarren descended once more to the sitting-room with that lowering of the spiritual temperature which she always experienced when confronted by the futile lives of these lonely and alienated creatures.

'You can get quite a price for them at the pet shop,' said Pearson, following her, 'and the cage could be sold too, I expect. It would pay for that five pounds you lent her the day she hired the car. I'll bet you never got a penny of that back.'

'I couldn't in fairness expect it, the way things turned out.'

'You're too soft, miss. But they're asking six guineas each for budgies in the pet shop, so you'll get a few pounds for them.'

'No, Pearson, I don't think I'd like to sell them. One doesn't know who'd get them or how they'd be treated. I always think people who *want* to keep birds in little cages must be very stupid.'

'They take a lot of looking after,' Pearson agreed dispassionately.

'Do you know what I'm going to do with them? I'm going to set them free.'

'Oh, you can't do that, miss! They'd only die.'

'Everyone says they'd only die, but how can anyone be sure since nobody ever lets a bird out of a cage? For all we know, these budgerigars will fly away and live happily ever after.'

'I don't think they could, miss. Not when they've been used to having all their food brought to them—every mortal thing done for them as you might say.'

Miss MacFarren took up the cage and went from the sitting-room to her study. 'Very well, Pearson, suppose they die! Isn't it better to die in freedom them to live for years a dreary, aimless life of having everything done for them?'

Pearson shook her head with her thinnest smile. 'I'm sure I don't know what they'd say to that, miss. If you'll excuse me, there's the front-door bell.'

The sunlight was pouring into the little garden and her next-door neighbour's apple tree was in blossom. Perhaps if she had looked out on a grey sky and leafless branches, Miss MacFarren's impulse would have languished, but with this lively encouragement from nature, she set the cage on her stone table and unclosed the wire door. At first, she was afraid the birds were going to insist on remaining in captivity, so little did they seem disposed to leave the cage; but in a space of minutes, they began, with delicate movements of enquiry and amazement, to investigate, and then the braver suddenly emerged. It fluttered up to the tree on astounded wings, and instantly its partner followed. They lingered quivering among the blossoms, two green jewels more brilliant than any leaf or flower she had ever painted.

'So you've let them go, miss?' said Pearson's voice, politely reproachful. 'I don't know anyone but Dr. Wilmot who would have done such a thing.'

'Whatever happens to them, if they've had anything like the same pleasure coming out of their house as I've had getting into mine, it'll be worth it.'

'Getting into yours? You've been in it all along!'

'In it, but not at home. I've understood during the last few years, what with the war and Mrs. Bankes, why people were once so proud to say, "An Englishman's house is his castle."'

'There can't be many saying that today,' Pearson remarked grimly, 'not unless they're locked up in Bedlam. . . . Aren't you going to look at your flowers?'

Miss MacFarren's eyes had been so busy trying to keep sight of the birds darting and hopping in a transport, she hoped and believed, of delight, that she had not observed the large florist's box which Pearson had laid beside the empty cage. She opened it now and saw a choice assortment of spring flowers. A slight revulsion overcame her in case they should be a last gesture from Mrs. Bankes, but the note was in Joss's hand, and it said only:

'I was very fond of you too.'

The birds had vanished once and for all, and she was a little disturbed to see they had flown off in different directions. Still, it had been a beautiful and rewarding experience to release them, a festive experience, like drinking champagne; and she was sure they would never want to return to their cage. But she would leave it there with the door open just in case they were fools enough to come back.

She picked up the florist's box and went into the study. 'Pearson,' she commanded, 'I shall want some vases. And would you bring me the two cats out of the hall—the ones that smile. I must have those on my mantelpiece today.'

She set the frowning and implacable blue gods on one side, and made way for the radiant gods in flowered jackets.

THE END

FURROWED MIDDLEBROW